*My dearest,*

*The kiss you s... ... ... ...* all but vanished for the many times I've held it to my lips. You wish a thousand kisses from me? You hold them in your hands now. This paper is bound with kisses, so fine their weaving that you cannot tell where one might begin and another ends. So if you kiss one, then you shall have another, and another, and another.*

*Does your heart flutter when you hold this letter? Does your throat dry and your tongue glance out to wet your lips as you anticipate my kiss? Can you feel my presence in every word on this page with a palpable longing that burns ... deep ... and lingering?*

*I hold my left hand to my breast as I write. My breaths rise and fall, not quickly, but in heavy anticipation of your touch. I wish it were your hand resting on my bosom, just dipping over the lace of my chemise. I can feel your caress if I close my eyes. You trace the contours of my body with your fingers, as if they were brushes stroking across a canvas.*

*I need your touch. Please send it to me. Quickly!*

"So! You going to read it to everyone?"

Fanning Josephine's letter before his face, Matthieu tore himself from the dizzying images to look his regiment mate in the eye—the only hint of white on his face. No one had come close to a pond or stream or even a bowl of rainwater in the last two weeks. Everyone was filthy, stinking, and in a foul mood.

But not him!

"I don't think I can," Matthieu said as he folded the letter. "It ... reveals ... some personal things ..."

# <u>BOOK YOUR PLACE ON OUR WEBSITE</u><br>AND MAKE THE<br><u>READING CONNECTION!</u>

We've created a customized website just for our very special readers, where you can get the inside scoop on everything that's going on with Zebra, Pinnacle and Kensington books.

When you come online, you'll have the exciting opportunity to:

- View covers of upcoming books
- Read sample chapters
- Learn about our future publishing schedule (listed by publication month *and author*)
- Find out when your favorite authors will be visiting a city near you
- Search for and order backlist books from our online catalog
- Check out author bios and background information
- Send e-mail to your favorite authors
- Meet the Kensington staff online
- Join us in weekly chats with authors, readers and other guests
- Get writing guidelines
- AND MUCH MORE!

**Visit our website at<br>http://www.zebrabooks.com**

# HERE IS MY HEART

## Michele Hauf

Zebra Books
Kensington Publishing Corp.

http://www.zebrabooks.com

ZEBRA BOOKS are published by

Kensington Publishing Corp.
850 Third Avenue
New York, NY 10022

Copyright © 1999 by Michele Hauf

All rights reserved. No part of this book may be reproduced
in any form or by any means without the prior written consent
of the Publisher, excepting brief quotes used in reviews.

If you purchased this book without a cover you should be aware
that this book is stolen property. It was reported as "unsold
and destroyed" to the Publisher and neither the Author nor the
Publisher has received any payment for this "stripped book."

Zebra, the Z logo and Splendor Reg. U.S. Pat. & TM Off.

First Printing: March, 1999
10  9  8  7  6  5  4  3  2  1

Printed in the United States of America

*For Jeff,*
*who holds my heart.*
*Forever.*

# Part One

When you have received a letter you first of all sit
  down;
cutting open the envelope is done slowly and resolutely,
as though diffidently raising the lid of an enchanted
  chest.

> —*Karel Capek (1890-1938),*
> *Czech journalist and writer*

# Prologue

*Mademoiselle Lalique,*

*I have only just met you, but I feel as though I have known you all my life. I trace the lines in my palm and see the curve of your smiling face. Wind blows past my ear and I hear your whispers, soft and sure. I study my reflection in the muddy puddles formed by the boots of marching soldiers. And I see you. In my heartbeat thrums the rhythm of your presence, solid, steady, and graceful.*

*Oh, that you might feel the same.*

*I miss you more than a windmill misses the wind. As the battle fires rage and I am but a beast focused for the charge, I sometimes do not even know who I am. The finer graces lose hold. Survival becomes a dark cloak of armor screwed in many sections to my body. I am unable to free myself of this pull to bloody warfare. Am I really capable of such destruction?*

*There are times I believe I cannot be the same man who marched from a snow-glittered Paris months ago. Other times, I manage to grasp a tiny ray of hope in my*

cold, unwashed hands. That shard of lightness and beauty
is you, Helene. A mere crinkle of your letter, tucked
against my heart, can calm the madness that war brews
in sane men.

I cannot offer witty repartee, nor verses extolling perfect communion between a man and a woman. I am but
a simple man, with simple desires and dreams. I desire
freedom from war. And I dream of you.

> Desperately,
> Chevalier Julien Delaroche

# Chapter 1

One letter. That was all it had taken for Josephine Lalique to fall in love with the Chevalier Delaroche. So she had come to the decision to ignore the unfortunate fact that the letter, as all the others to follow, was addressed not to her, but to her sister, Helene.

Now, as their friends Olympe and Constance lazed close by, Josephine dipped her toes into the cool waters of the pond just behind the cozy chateau she called home, and casually asked, "Is that another letter from Chevalier Delaroche?" The elusive gel-touch of a giant carp slithered beneath her arch.

Constance dragged a finger through the pond. Olympe, deathly afraid of any pool of liquid larger than a wine goblet, snuggled next to Helene on the moss-covered log hidden beneath the umbrellic vines of the massive willow that also shaded half the pond.

"Yes, another lovelorn soldier has succumbed to my long-distance seductions." Helene Lalique fanned her exquisitely

12 *Michele Hauf*

pale countenance with a folded missive. "I think that brings the count to somewhere around six or seven."

"High time you weeded out the undesirables," Constance said as she stood and joined the two women in the grass near Olympe's gray satin skirts.

"I intend to do just that," Helene said with a lazy yawn.

"You've so many to correspond with, Helene, it makes me envious." Olympe laid her head on Helene's blue-skirted lap and fingered the bottom of the letter. "Read it to us."

"Please do," Constance echoed. Her coiled rust curls danced across her cheeks as she rested her head against the log and settled into a comfortable position. "You know your letters always make the afternoons so interesting."

"Yes," Josephine called as she chased the path of a fat bullfrog, her fingers dredging through the gentle currents swooshed by his legs. Water droplets splashed in the pond as she raised her wet fingers to cup her chin in thoughtful anticipation. "I do so love to hear what the chevalier has to say. His words . . . they are . . . so much from the heart." Suddenly she snatched at water and weeds and slimy flesh. "Ah!" She proudly displayed her catch, drizzles of crystal water trailing down her arm to the sleeve of her holland chemise billowed at her elbow. "A prince to kiss!"

"About all you'll be kissing if you insist upon childish games," Helene admonished from behind the missive she was poised to read.

Josephine gave her unseeing sister a sneer and retained her prize, all slime and gangly legs and nervously pumping heart. "Ever curious," she singsonged, knowing her fascination with nature and its inhabitants repulsed Helene and her friends. She had her father, Pascal Lalique—self-proclaimed Professor of Oddities and Spectaculars—to thank for her limitless curiosity. Plopping into a cross-legged position next to Olympe in the grass, Josephine then helped her prince-in-training settle to a carefully guarded perch upon the sway of her skirts between her folded legs.

Helene snapped the letter in preparation to read, bringing all to attention. "As for Chevalier Delaroche ... I've become much too bored with Julien's ramblings about my lovely complexion and the smell of my hair. And if I must hear one more time how my words are an antidote to the horrors of battle! But if it will engage the three of you ..."

"Oh yes!" Olympe cheered. "Don't be a pinchfist, Helene. You know we live vicariously through your love letters."

"Speak for yourself," Constance purred as she plucked at the festoon of fuchsia ribbons bordering her low décolletage.

The woman chose to wear her bodices scandalously low, and as for the tight lacing, well, Josephine was quite surprised Constance could even breathe with her bosom in her nose and her ribs corralled to a slender column. Constance never went anywhere without Olympe, for her fainting spells were notorious. "Is that because men are always obliged to catch you before you swoon in the mud or across the table into their ale?" Josephine wondered aloud.

Olympe stifled a giggle while Helene nudged Josephine in the hip with her slippered toe. "Ouch!"

"You can only dream of having a man catch you in his arms," Constance retorted. She paused for her usual rest between sentences, for her lung capacity would allow no more than a short speech. "And when he touches your slimy frog fingers ..." Pause. "... he will drop you in the mud with a splash!"

Josephine turned her shoulder to Constance and studied her prince. Constance had a tendency to speak above her station. A trait borrowed from Helene, no doubt. Besides, Josephine could have any man she wished. Whenever she wished. And she needn't swoon to do it either. "The chevalier waits our audience," she said, hoping to listen to a more intriguing topic than her lack of a lover.

"Yes, please!" Olympe shrieked and tugged Helene's skirts. "Enough with frogs, I want to hear something romantic."

"And desperately pining," Constance yearned, as she drew

an absent finger across her well-bound décolletage. "He wants you, Helene. And we want to hear him. Don't keep us in suspense."

Helene gave a satisfied nod and began to read. Almost. "Oh no."

Greatly impatient to have her sister begin, Josephine snapped, "What?"

"The man has taken to calling me *precious*. How very dreadful."

And what is so dreadful about that? Josephine thought. Her sister had so many suitors the woman had forgotten the meaning of appreciation. Of gratitude. Of just plain being . . . wanted.

"So it begins 'My precious Helene.' " With a roll of her obsidian eyes beneath her wide straw hat brim, Helene sighed.

"Oh, don't do that," Constance said with an impatient wave of her hand. "Just read and save the comments for after."

A bored sigh, another roll of her eyes, and Helene began again in a tone of what Josephine could only term suppressed exasperation.

*It is April the seventeenth and I find our regiment has been granted a blessed day of reprieve from enemy fire. Time enough to eat a crust of bread, drink a shared tankard of wine, and finally . . . to sit beneath a willow behind our makeshift barracks. It is not so grand as the willow behind your home, Helene; many of the lower branches have been stripped to weave as shields, or the thicker, dry branches have been used for firewood. But just knowing that you may at this very moment be sitting beneath its long spindly vines, languishing in the shade, sets my heart racing.*

"Now I don't recall Julien ever being in our backyard," Helene said.

"Continue," Olympe pleaded. "We shall dissect his words later."

"Oh, very well."

The frog leapt from Josephine's lap, leaving behind an ornament of muddy toe prints on her mint and cream striped skirt. One spring landed him on Constance's lap, the next leap granted the startled frog the sanctity of the high grasses behind the log. Constance's shriek could have woken the dead, as could the death grip she latched on Helene's arm.

Slamming the letter onto her lap, Helene admonished her sister, "Bother! Can you try for just one moment to be a lady?"

Shrinking from her sister's words, Josephine offered a silent nod. It wouldn't do to argue with any of the three, all of whom put fashion and the ability to charm above all else. But what was the fun of acting the lady and swooning for men and fussing over your appearance for hours on end, when it prevented one from really enjoying life?

"Are you quite all right?" Olympe implored Constance.

"Yes, please continue, Helene," Constance said on a heavy exhalation. "If I must endure wild animals scampering across my body, then you'd best make this a quick read."

Facing the pond, and away from the threesome behind her, Josephine silently mocked Constance's sharpness. Such a pity her prince did not scamper across the woman's twin peaks. That would have really riled her!

> *For you see, Helene, at this very moment one of the long silvery leaves from this battle-ravaged willow has just brushed across my cheek. By luck or fortune, it still retains an innocent softness. The sensation calls forth the memory of a kiss you once gave me. Do you remember, my precious Helene? You brushed your lips across my cheek, soft and gentle, like a velvet-fleshed willow leaf.*

Oh, what Josephine wouldn't give to be kissed in such a way.

> *Memories of you always touch the darkest places of my heart with a ray of warmth. I have come to think of you*

*as Helene, my Hope. While it becomes more difficult as
each day passes to find the optimism that had once always
held me buoyant, be glad in knowing that your memory
is what helps me endure this daily hell.*

*Please write, Helene, my Hope. And please . . . I wish
to touch something that has been caressed by your lips.*

*Until we touch again,*
*Chevalier Julien Delaroche*

Josephine's sigh whispered as softly as the amber tail of
the pond carp swishing through the clear waters. " 'To touch
something caressed by your lips.' Oh, such longing in his
voice."

The sudden outburst of laughter startled Josephine out of her
reverie. "What?" She always became lost in the chevalier's
words. She turned and shuffled to her knees, imploring the
giggling faces to enlighten her. "The man writes from his
heart."

"A man's heart does not reveal itself in pen and ink," Helene
opined.

"More like in musket and sword," Olympe said.

"Yes," Helene agreed. "And not especially the sword he
wears along his hip."

Another collection of giggles echoed throughout the quiet
garden cove. And a snort. Constance actually snorted!

They were wrong. All of them. The man's soul graced every
single word he placed on paper. He voiced passion in ways
most men could not begin to conceive. And Josephine longed
to know him more thoroughly than as just simple lines on
paper.

And there Helene sat laughing at his soul-wrenched words.

"My dear sister." She looked to Helene, who suppressed
another giggle behind the letter. "How can you be so cruel to
the man by continuing to write him when he is only another
feather upon your hat?"

"I don't plan to continue, dear bleeding heart of mine. I've absolutely gone beyond boredom with his letters."

"Boredom!" Josephine stood and splayed her hands before her. "Of all the soldiers you have writing you—I dare not count, for I may run out of fingers and toes—Chevalier Delaroche is by far the most decent and true-hearted of the lot. He demands nothing save your promised affections. He pines for you, Helene. A willow leaf across his cheek? Such heavenly words! While the others merely list the ways they shall satisfy their lusts when they return, or report how they do it by themselves in the dark of night after the battle fires have died."

"I must say I've learned a lot from Monsieur du Bois," Constance said matter-of-factly. "How the man can make it so . . . erect . . . over and over!"

"Yes, well he is exactly your sort, isn't he?" Josephine snapped at the giggling coquette.

"At least I have a sort," Constance defended proudly.

"That is enough, the two of you!" Helene laughed. "We all know your sort, Constance, and wouldn't we just love a moment in your skirts?"

Josephine turned with a huff and slammed her arms to her chest. Helene was as pure as she was; she knew her sister only teased. "You cannot give him up. Not Chevalier Delaroche."

"The man has become far too attached for my comfort."

"Oh!"

"Josephine," Helene said. "Never have I seen you so passionate about . . . well . . . about anything! It's as if you are Father and have just come up with another silly invention."

"Father's inventions are not silly," she pouted. Helene never took more than a moment to look over the creations of which Pascal Lalique was so proud. Time could not be afforded to delve deeper than the surface waters, to really discover what lay beneath. The same was true with the men who wrote her.

"Why, I believe the girl is in love," Constance taunted, drawing a plucked pond reed beneath her chin.

"Just so," Olympe added with a playful tug to Josephine's skirts.

"I think not," Josephine was quick to retort. She turned and paced the soft grasses in her bare feet, her shoes abandoned near a tumble of smooth rocks at the pond's edge. "I only feel for a man whose heart will surely be broken when he returns to a woman who uses him as fodder for her silly games. You flash these letters about as if they are trophies."

"But they are," Helene slyly cooed as she trailed the chevalier's letter across her crimson lips. "Souvenirs to tack upon my trousseau, battle prizes to tuck beneath my pillow. A woman cannot be expected to take seriously any of these men's words. Come now, Josephine, you know I've only spent two evenings with him."

"You're such a tease, Helene."

Her sister smiled in satisfaction as she lazily fanned her face.

"A heartless tease," Josephine snapped.

"How can you speak as his champion when you've never met the man yourself?"

"I know him through his words. He's written three times now, and each missive reveals more and more of his soul. Can you not see? Words reveal the inner self, Helene. And it is from those pages that he has drawn you a map of his heart."

"You read far too much from simple scribblings on parchment," Olympe warned with her usual carefree gaiety. "Helene's suitors know as well as she that their liaisons will go no farther than flat paper and sanded ink."

Helene arched a dark brow. "Unless I wish it."

More heartless giggles. And yet another snort. They would never understand. Josephine felt sure that Julien Delaroche did not know the unwritten rules of her sister's game of empty words and paper hearts. He really cared for her. Could Helene not see?

"So you choose to sever all communication with him?" Josephine blurted out. "Is that it?"

"It is what I always do." Helene refolded the parchment

and prepared to toss it in the basket at her feet which contained
half a dozen more of the same.

"Perhaps Josephine would like the letter to press between
her pillow and linens as she dreams?" Constance gave a sly
bat of her lashes from over Helene's shoulders.

Oh, wouldn't she!

Josephine spun and faced the trio. Hard as it was not to
plead, she stiffened her jaw and remained impassive. Much as
she'd like to keep the Chevalier's words beneath her pillow,
she'd endured too much teasing this afternoon to further humili-
ate herself.

"Oh yes!" Helene jumped to her feet and danced over to
Josephine. She waved the letter between two fingers, eyeing
her with a teasing look. "You wish it, don't you, Josephine?"

She shook her head no and turned to the side, which allowed
the wind to dance a rogue strand of her hair across her lips.
Helene skipped around and bent to catch her downward gaze.
"Come now, sister. You've no suitors of your own. Save that
silly Matthieu Bouchet who likes to climb trees and chase
butterflies with you. At least you'll have words on paper to
keep you company at night."

"Oh, leave me!" Josephine closed her eyes and tried to shut
out her sister's taunts. Of course she hadn't any suitors. As
soon as a man got a look at Helene's milk-white skin and her
wide dark gaze set beneath coy, fluttering lashes, he became
infatuated.

She felt the sharp square of folded paper dig into her breast
and opened her eyes to see Helene pushing it into her décolletage. "I bequeath Julien Delaroche to you. May his words of
undying love serve you more justly than they have served
myself."

In an eruption of hearty laughter, Helene signaled the others
that the afternoon had come to a close. Gathering up shoes and
unhooking skirts from their waists, they started for the back of
the Lalique house, leaving Josephine standing at the edge of
the great willow falls.

"Coming, dear bleeding heart?" Helene called.

Ripping the letter from her bodice, she huffed back, "No!"

More giggles. And finally only the sound of rippling willow leaves and a single chirp from an overflying robin.

Josephine sighed. The parchment, crisp in her hands, pleaded for investigation. Great care had been taken to insure the paper remained as clean as possible. Quite a task, Josephine felt sure, amidst the din and destruction of battle. And then to travel numerous leagues in a post carrier's pouch before finally reaching Paris. An ink smudge on the back of the letter bore a few precious whorls from his thumb. She ran the tip of her nail along the curled evidence of his presence. His touch.

And oh . . . his words.

*Until we touch again.*

Pressing the letter to her breast, Josephine closed her eyes. "They may laugh, but you've a soul as bright and wide as the sun. Your words are the costume of your heart, woven of fine and luxurious fabric.

"You've no idea that the woman on whom you waste your words takes great delight in the mastery of her male prizes. You poor man. These letters are perhaps your only light in a dismal life. I cannot even imagine the horrors you must endure daily. And yet, you write with such freedom, such . . . passion. War has not touched your soul, Chevalier Delaroche. *Merci à Dieu.*"

As she stepped forward beneath the willow, spring-fresh leaves brushed over her loosely bound hair and caressed her face with soft kisses. Josephine closed her eyes and tilted her head back. The tip of one leaf traced the length of her nose. She moved so it tickled across her cheek. Soft and sweetly fragrant, tracing gently over her flesh, stirring her sense of touch to stunning awareness. Almost like a finger gliding a curious trail towards her lips.

*When you kissed me once, so soft, so gently . . .*

Never had Josephine kissed a man on the lips. Ah, but she had once kissed a man. On the cheek if she remembered correctly. It might have been a few summers ago. Matthieu Bouchet—a friend since she could recall back to infant skirts. She'd brushed his cheek in a moment of play. Thinking herself quite the brazen at the time, she'd since come to learn that desire and imagination can stir up far greater passions.

Her next kiss, she vowed, would be passionate and reckless and that of her dreams.

The memory reminded Josephine that Matthieu, too, was at war. In the same regiment as Julien. Not a place for a man such as he. A *fantaisiste,* he belonged with paintbrush in hand and splatters of color mixed through his wavy dark hair, creating the whimsical images that always made her smile. A man of the arts; not the art of war. She whispered a silent prayer for his safety.

The letter crunched in her grasp. Julien Delaroche was a man fit for the rigors of war. Though it was hard to believe such enduring and passionate prose coming from a muscled chevalier, Helene had once described him as beautiful and valiant, a warrior in rogue's clothing. Sharp blond hair set upon a brutely square face. Hard as stone his eyes, yet hot as fire his touch.

The very thought of a man's touch being as hot as fire . . . Well, she just couldn't fathom it! Josephine turned to the pond and caught her wavering reflection looking up at her. "Someday I shall know. But for now," she brushed the letter across her lips. "I can dream."

Julien's final pleas for affection had been dropped into her care. Without so much as a by-your-leave from Helene, he had been discarded.

She pressed the folds of paper between her fingers, being careful not to mar the thumbprint with her own frog-slimed digits. He deserved a reply of some sort. But which would be more painful, a letter stating that Helene was no longer inter-ested, or . . . to continue the charade?

The thought of corresponding with the very man who had won her heart with simple lines scrawled on paper heated

Josephine's blood to a simmer. She felt her cheeks flush with anticipation.

"Oh, Chevalier . . ." She pressed the letter to her heart. "Dare I?"

# Chapter 2

*Dear Chevalier Delaroche,*

"Oh, not so formal." Josephine erased the cold salutation from her mind. She daren't touch pen to paper until she'd come up with the perfect greeting. And when he already termed her sister *my precious Helene,* and *Helene, my Hope,* she had better conjure something a little more intimate.

"Julien, my love," she drawled. She caught her forehead in her palm with a dull *smack.* "Oh please, you cannot be so forward. Something halfway between just friends and . . . wanting to know you more." *So much more.*

But how to put her mood to paper? She must speak to him using the same emotion he siphoned from his ink bottle and traced upon paper. Words that tickled her heart with desire. Words that would prove to him her interest.

"Should I really do this?"

*If you don't at least try, you shall never know if this might have been the one man for you.*

She did so long to know what it was like to have a man's interest.

"Yes, I must!"

Back to the task at hand. Josephine had snuck a single sheet of writing paper from Helene's stationery box just after her sister went downstairs to break her fast. Now with Helene gone to market with Marie Claire, Josephine had at least an hour to compose a letter. But she would get nowhere unless she devised the correct greeting.

To use the word love would be absolutely scandalous. But a simple *dear Chevalier* would be an affront to him. Josephine tried to recall how a month ago, Helene had addressed her first declaration of undying love to Chevalier Delaroche. A giggling declaration. How her sister could be so cruel to so many men at one time was beyond Josephine. And the fact that Helene had not been caught in her deceptions never ceased to amaze.

Josephine studied the letter that lay on the rosewood desk beneath her right hand. Such careful words. Small and cramped, much like the tracks an insect might make should it dip its toes in ink and scamper across the page. Even the cross-outs she loved. The act of divining their meaning was truly a joy not to be rushed, an extension of the satisfaction she received in reading the entire thing. One could not hurry the consumption of passion.

*Recollections of you always touch the darkest places of my heart with a ray of warmth . . . Be glad in knowing that your memory is what helps me endure this daily hell . . . Until we touch again . . .*

"He does want more," she whispered, as she silently scanned his words, her lips moving softly. "This is no casual flirt. He is in love with my sister. Oh, I cannot do this!"

She turned away from the desk. She hadn't a clue how to address the chevalier's obvious desire. When it came to matters of love and passion, Josephine was quite unskilled. Oh, the fact that man desired woman, and in turn woman desired man, was very obvious to her. But what it was that stirred the desire, then took it one step farther to commitment between two people, confused her.

For as much as Helene was always trying to get her to improve her appearance so she might attract a man, Josephine felt that just wasn't what was needed. She hadn't the time or the inclination to be constantly guarding her posture or lowering her eyes coyly. Helene made it seem as if love depended on physical appearance. Why couldn't she just be herself?

With a heavy sigh, Josephine hooked a stray dart of hair over her ear and pressed a hand to the letter. At least she needn't worry of turning away this man with her lack of social graces. He would only know her on paper. Would never know she'd rather gambol through a room instead of glide, or that her skin was not of fresh morning cream like Helene's, for all the time she spent in the sun had given her a warm glow.

For a moment she doubted what she was about to do. Surely a man so kind as he deserved an honest explanation. But to know that Helene only toyed with his affections?

"No, it would crush him." Josephine turned back to the letter. The words, *Until we touch again,* flashed like a searching beacon. *Notice me, remember me, never forget me.*

"Forget you? Impossible. Besides . . . I cannot bear to never read your words again, Julien." To speak his Christian name felt a little scandalous, daring. As if she had just laid claim to him.

"It matters not that I have never laid eyes upon you or shared a spoken word. I know your soul. I know your heart. And you have mine."

Dipping a freshly shaven quill into her sister's borrowed inkpot, she drew it up and held it still over the small glass rim. One, two, three drops of midnight liquid fell into the tiny receptacle. One, two, three beats of her heart.

"Forgive me for my selfish desires," she said to the blank paper, and then touched the quill to the heavy parchment.

"My . . . dearest . . . Julien . . ."

*A fortnight later . . .*

With daybreak came a restive calm and an anticipatory hull of nervousness that cloaked one and all like a black beetle's shell. Battle flames had lit the evening sky well past midnight. Until silence finally settled with the first rays of light.

A few hours' rest. A bit of stale bread and cured beef to break his fast. Chevalier Julien Delaroche waited for cadet Bouchet to relieve him of watch duty. He'd found a generous oak with a rotted-out trunk to squat against. The tree rose on a hill, so he had a good view of the trampled meadows of heather that surrounded their entrenchment.

A move to retrieve his musket crinkled the ribbon-tied paper that rested between his leather doublet and lawn shirt.

She'd written again.

An earth-bound angel, Helene Lalique. Her face was delicate and fine, rather like the dolls he'd only glimpsed through the windows of elegant Paris shops. And while she'd practiced discretion in her return of his advances—a batting lash here, a touch of his hand there—he hadn't been the least surprised she'd let him kiss her on their second encounter. Though he'd only the pleasure of calling on her twice before his regiment had marched to battle, twice was more than enough to have ignited his desire.

Demon fire, where was Bouchet? He wanted him here. Now!

The sound of rustling underbrush and a musket clattering along an ill-repaired wooden fence told Julien that Bouchet neared. The pup wasn't cut out for battle. Why Bouchet had joined the ranks was beyond him. He belonged at home with his paints, as he so often grumbled. It had been a surprise to Julien to discover that the man was actually older than he by a few months. He'd thought him a few years younger, with his naive approach to war.

Much as he would prefer to associate with the upper ranks— as aide de camp, he did quite often—than to waste his time on a green cadet, the advantages of befriending the wayward

artisan far outweighed the disadvantages. For it was only
Bouchet who could lift his tormented soul out of the dregs.

"Bouchet, how many times have I told you, hold your musket
while clearing an obstacle. And practice stealth, man. You're
a walking alarm! I'll have to find you a new lookout, for surely
the enemy has spied us both by now."

"Then we shall do just that!"

Never had Julien seen a man who could smile while literal
walls of fire burned around him and enemy shot constantly
whizzed past his ears. It was an easy curve, his smile, perma-
nently engraved upon his visage. And such funny blue eyes
that seemed to hold the same glee.

Insufferable that a man could be so cheerful at a time like
this.

"You have the oddest way, you know that, Bouchet? Always
so . . ."

"Positive?"

"Yes. Positive! Why is that? No man can be so eternally
optimistic and blind to the misfortunes of war. It's as if you've
never been touched by tragedy. You've never known a dark
moment in your life, have you, Bouchet?"

"Perhaps it is because of how I choose to view life," he
offered with a resolute sigh.

I know better, Julien thought.

"I've been through some hard times—"

Yes.

"Doubtful." Julien crossed his ankles and slammed his arms
across his chest. "Name one."

"My father was murdered . . . years ago."

Exactly. Julien knew that much about Bouchet's past. "So
was mine."

Matthieu turned and held his gaze for a long moment. He
would not speak. Julien wasn't about to elaborate, for elabora-
tion would only stir up painful memories.

"My life is not my past," Bouchet finally said, "but a future

of my own making.'' He turned away to stomp out a patch of
tall grass in which to sit.

Julien pushed the man's musket ahead, saving him from a
hang-up in the grass just as he settled beside him. ''One of
these days, Bouchet, you're going to blast your ass off. What
will you do then, Monsieur Happiness, when you have to return
home with a wide black hole in the back of your breeches?''

''Ha, ha! And to even think of relieving myself,'' Matthieu
said on a chuckle as he situated his musket between his legs
and leant against the tree beside Julien. ''The post come through
this morning?''

''Ah yes!'' He'd almost forgotten, having lost himself in the
hilarious image of blowing off his hindquarters. Ah, but the
nursing he would need from a fine wench!

Pulling the folded post from his shirt, Julien stuffed it in
Matthieu's hand. He shared all his posts; Bouchet hadn't a
woman back home. He did mention the Lalique sister quite
frequently, but he'd never once written her, so Julien wasn't
sure what to think of their relationship. ''But a fortnight for
her reply. She's smitten, I know it.''

As usual Matthieu went into his peculiar ritual whenever he
held a lady's post in his hands. That odd tracing of the seal; a
fleur-de-lis pressed into deep blue wax. The strange balancing
of the paper upon his palm. His eyes closed as he drew the
paper beneath his nose.

''You're going to breathe the words right off the paper,
man!''

''Hyacinth,'' Bouchet said in a strange, dreamy tone. ''I do
love that scent. Not quite as appealing as the fresh clean perfume
of a woman's bare flesh, but a near second, I do believe. Of
course, gardenia, now that is a delicious aroma.''

''Why a woman even bothers with scent is a mystery to
me.'' Julien heeled the ground with his spur, impatience making
him tense. ''I'd much prefer the essence of beef or pheasant
coating her words than some silly flowers.''

"Yes, I see that you do," Matthieu said with a glance at the bread crust Julien held.

"Enough already!" Julien shoved the final chunk of dry bread in his mouth and demanded through sputtering crumbs, "Read it."

"Patience." Bouchet scanned the horizon, a wavy scatter of his hair blocking his vision as he did so. "Aren't we supposed to be watching for the enemy? The sun has risen."

"The enemy watches us after your clamber through the forest. As long as we remain still, they will not move. But if we change position the fire will begin anew, and you shall never have a moment to read Mademoiselle Lalique's words."

"Your logic stuns me."

"As it should. Now. Read."

"Very well."

So the two leant back against the billowing shade of the oak tree, Matthieu's legs crossed casually, Julien hanging eagerly upon every word the man spoke.

*My dearest Julien,*
   *As—*

"Did you hear that!" Julien could barely contain his excitement. "She used the word dearest!"

"Of course I heard that. I spoke the word myself." Matthieu pushed a hand back through his hair, then drew a narrow finger along the sentence he'd just read. "Dearest is quite a step up from her previous 'soldier Julien.' "

"I am making headway with Helene, I know it. Continue." Julien tapped the paper impatiently.

*My dearest Julien,*
   *As I read your letter . . . No, no, no, I do not read your letter, I devour it like a fish starved for water. Your words arrive on flat paper, but when the paper is unfolded they spring to life and breathe a passion so deep I can almost*

*feel it. They twine into a spiral that traces round my
heart. I am that fish, caught in a whirlpool stirred by
your words.*

*So, as I* devour *your letter—*


"Did you see how she made the word devour kind of squiggly
and dark?"

"Of course I did!" Delaroche slapped his knee. "Enough
of your remarks!"

"Very well, I just thought the emphasis was a nice touch."

"Bouchet."


*I stand beneath the very willow tree you mention. I, too,
feel the soft caress of the leaves as they flutter over my
cheek and trace along my lips, and can only imagine the
same caresses administered by your touch.*

*A single leaf, long and silver, tickles my forehead as
if I mustn't ignore it. So I've plucked it and traced it
over my lips to imbue it with my whisper. And what do
I whisper? My dearest Julien . . . My dear, dear sweet
Julien.*

*Is that the sort of touch you desire?*

*Be brave, Julien. Write again.*

> *Yours in thought and touch,*
> *Helene Lalique*


*PS—I need your words to ensure my survival. Please do
not starve this little fish!*


"She's coming around," Matthieu observed as he fingered
the edges of the paper.

Julien chuffed out a laugh. "What do you mean, coming
around? She was mine before I left Paris. On our second meeting
she could not refuse my kiss! Playful little scamp."

"Yes, but it seems the tone of her voice has taken on a

more passionate edge. This starving for your words. Hmm . . . Helene? A little fish?''

The man could be obnoxious in his analytical approach to everything. If it wasn't the precise measurement of powder before loading his musket amidst a din of battle whistles and bloodshed, it was carefully rationing his food into tiny portions, and brushing the dirt from his hose each morning and worrying the hems of his breeches until they were just so. Not your average soldier.

"Analyze all you wish, *mon ami.*" Julien slapped a wide palm across Matthieu's knee. "The woman is enthralled. She pines for my letters. She will starve without me."

"Without another *letter,* you mean."

"She loves me."

"She hasn't said as much."

"It would be foolish to reveal such emotion in a mere letter. She is wise," Julien mused. "But when she is in my arms, she will submit willingly. I know." He cocked a brow and hitched a thumb at the brim of his hat.

Ah, the power simple words could have over the female species. She would swoon into his arms when finally he returned to her doorstep. By the eternal, he had fallen in love upon first sight of Helene Lalique leaving the patisserie with a basket dangling from one arm, a single soft dark curl dancing across her forehead, and her toying gaze as she'd suddenly discovered his interest.

He'd kissed her that night beneath the moonlit sky at the edge of her father's estate, but a stone's toss from the Porte de St. Jacques. Pity her father was eccentric and spent the majority of his time at court hawking bizarre inventions to the king and pontificating. Or so Delaroche had heard. He wasn't sure what pontificating was, himself. But it couldn't be good, whatever it was. The two sisters were oftentimes left alone for weeks, with only the house servants as their chaperones. Julien had never met Josephine Lalique, though he could only imagine she must be quite pretty as well, with a sister so divine.

Thoughts of the younger sister reminded him of something.
*Bouchet knew the sisters.* Hmm, this could be an advantage.
How, he could not yet be sure. But surely it would help him
steer his way into Helene's heart. And then there was that *other*
matter. The one concerning . . . revenge.

"Where's the leaf?"

"Huh?"

"The leaf?" Matthieu reiterated. "Did she send it along
with her whisper?"

"Er, um . . . yes. I . . . might have misplaced it." Delaroche
scanned the ground. So that was what that wilted thing was!
Hm, must be underfoot somewhere.

"Do you plan to write again?"

Matthieu's voice brought Julien out of his study of the
ground. The chevalier toed the heavy leather satchel that
Bouchet hoarded with the utmost care. "You've more paper
in that fancy little writing box of yours?"

"Always." The man's eagerness to assist made Delaroche
wonder. Did the man get some sort of vicarious thrill out of
his love letters?

Surely not. It was just Bouchet's manner to be, well . . .
different.

# Chapter 3

The shed behind the Lalique home was always blessedly cool, and the glass roof provided excellent light for Professor Lalique's studies. Father's latest brilliant idea had been to breed ladybugs for the Queen's aphid-infested roses in the formal gardens at the Louvre. He and Josephine had gathered a few dozen beetles last fall and they'd thrived through the winter. The project had developed into an interesting excursion into the habits of the colorful little creatures.

"I've two letters today!" Helene announced to Josephine as she strolled across the stone floor, her skirts clutched tight to her hips to avoid the constant carpet of dust that never did seem to take to a broom. Or rather, it could be that a broom hadn't taken to the dust lately.

More letters, always more letters, but no word from the chevalier, Josephine thought as she made notations in her notebook regarding the birth of three new families of ladybugs. It had been weeks since she'd mailed off her post to the chevalier. Of course, her letter might not have even made it into Julien's hands. Post carriers were often shot by accident, or there were other problems. Poor health, overworked traveling beasts, the all-too-common sidetrack stop at a warm inn and the loss of all posts, left behind beneath a whore's bed to be later discovered and read with sticky fingers and crude laughter.

"Why so glum? Cheer up, sister. You'll attract suitors some day. You've just to learn to be more . . . well . . . ladylike."

Josephine fluttered her fingers dismissively over her head. "So you say. What is wrong with adventure and curiosity?"

"Isn't it curiosity that killed some wretched little beast?"

"A cat, Helene."

"Of course." Helene patted her palms up under the generous bloom of curls that showered either side on her head. "Men much prefer a cooing lovebird to a scratching, hissing she-cat. La! What are those disgusting black bugs?"

Josephine cracked a smile. "Ladybugs."

"How can that be? They're not cute or orange like the others. Where are their spots?"

"The ladybug begins its life as a small black beetle before developing wings and its hard bright shell."

Helene shuffled back against the wall. "Oh, I cannot bear to look!"

Josephine sighed and brushed Helene's dramatics aside. "As you've said, I haven't much experience around men. I haven't a notion what to say or how to stand. And whatever should I do with my hands?"

How had her sister ever come to be so comfortable in the company of men? Men commanded your attention in the way they looked at you, the way they spoke, the way they moved. Some dressed in elegant silks and laces and pranced about with the finest airs and speech, while others swaggered through the streets in dirtied boots, a sword cutting the air by their side, causing every woman's head to turn in their wake.

But the idea that any man should even speak to her, *let alone send her passionate letters,* made Josephine's heart flip and flop like a shore-driven carp.

"What of Matthieu?" Helene said, a nervous twinge biting

into her words. She daren't approach the ladybugs' aquarium, Josephine knew.

"Matthieu Bouchet?"

"Yes, the one who calls you bunny rabbit or lizard—"

"Ladybug," Josephine offered.

"I knew it was some sort of beast. What is it with you and these . . . horrific creatures?"

Josephine rolled her eyes. Helene and her intimate knowledge of the animal kingdom. Animals were either beasts or ornaments; the latter including peacocks, ostriches, and minks, which provided much of Helene's wardrobe. "These *creatures* are only horrific because they've not yet developed the fashion sense you require, dear Helene. Pity the poor man of plain dress and manners."

"Speaking of Matthieu . . ."

Shouldn't she have seen that one coming?

"He's been lollygagging about your ankles since you were but five or six. A quiet man, but not altogether unattractive. His face is young and rather pretty. Though far from a cavalier, he does have potential. It shall be a pity if he returns scarred or maimed."

"Matthieu would blush to hear you say such things." Vanity wasn't a word in his vocabulary. Josephine knew Matthieu Bouchet like a brother, for a brother he had been to her since childhood. There weren't too many days she had missed speaking to him or sharing some secret.

If he only knew of her latest secret. That she had fallen in love with a man whom she'd never even met.

"What about Matthieu?" Josephine wondered.

Helene plucked the letters out of the basket dangling from the crook of her elbow and, as usual, smelled them before choosing which one to open. Not that she expected them to be perfumed; sometimes the post went through the most horrendous of substances before arriving in one's hands. "You are very comfortable around Monsieur Bouchet. Why is it that you cannot do the same around other men?"

"Matthieu is different. I don't think of him as a man."

Helene looked up from her perusal of the letters, her dark eyes now wider than Josephine thought possible.

"What I mean is . . . While other men could be construed as possible suitors, he's more like a brother to me."

"A shame," Helene said as she unfolded the first letter. "I should like to imagine how it would feel to kiss him. Which I could only do with information provided by you. That is, if he should ever kiss you. Gentle men such as he might not offer the excitement of a real man, but they are tender and sweet. Things that are nice when kissing."

"I've kissed Matthieu," Josephine defended proudly.

The letter slipped from Helen's fingers as she rose and broached Josephine's side in less than a breath. "Do tell! You sneak! You've kissed Matthieu and you never told me?"

Now quite flustered that she would be forced to divulge details, Josephine shifted on her heels. If she opened the punched tin aquarium cover—just a sliver—Helene would run screaming, forgetting her question . . .

"Spill!" Helene squealed. "Or I shall tell the others. And you know how Constance can be when someone has a secret."

The woman became a literal parasite. And those breasts, how they heaved in expectation!

"Very well," Josephine succumbed. Though it would have been delicious sport to see Helene run. "If you promise not to tell. It was just a simple kiss. Not even on the lips."

"Oh." Her sister's posture deflated and the delight left her eyes.

"I kissed his cheek."

"So it was not he who kissed you?"

"No."

"Oh." Even more deflation.

"You see," Josephine stood and smoothed her hands down her skirts. "Perhaps you don't see. You have all the world's men pining for you, Helene. They compose poems for you, and fight ruffians in your honor. I—I am just too ill at ease around a man.''

The swish of Helene's skirts dusted the quiet as she stood and embraced Josephine from behind. ''There is a fine and handsome man out there. Somewhere. He just hasn't found you yet.''

''There are days I fear he's stumbled and lost his direction.''

''Silly ladybug. Eww.'' Aware of the aquarium's contents again, Helene backed away from the table. ''Some journeys are much longer and fraught with danger. He will come to you, Josephine. You must have patience. In the meantime, you've my love affairs to share.'' Helene bent over her basket and plucked up the letters. ''Now come. Let's skip to the pond and we'll see who has written me today.''

A twinge of guilt held Josephine in place in the center of the sun-showered shed, the tiny skitter of ladybug wings against the glass holding court. What would Helene say should she learn the truth? That she hadn't just shared her love affairs, Josephine had stepped in and taken charge of one.

Oh, foolish girl!

The actuality of what she had done hit hard. As frivolous as Helene was with her affections, Josephine should have never taken it upon herself to continue correspondence with the chevalier. It was Helene's reputation she toyed with, and her sister's trust.

Josephine prayed the post carrier would stop for the night in one of those rowdy inns, and by morning a nameless whore would have her silly words instead of Julien Delaroche.


''Josephine?''

At the nervous whisper, Josephine set down the curl of crimson moiré she had been coaxing into a shimmery petaled rose. Thursdays always found her in the back of Madame Lamarck's Dress Emporium, designing ornamental flowers and decorations for Madame's creations. She scampered to the door that separated the workroom from the elegant salon that displayed deliciously elaborate goods, but she saw no one through the crack in the doorway. Madame Lamarck's voice echoed from near the display window, where she discussed the resurgent fashion in hinged iron corsets with Her Grace, the Duchess Rochambeau.

An ostrich feather, of its own volition, tickled Josephine's cheek. And then it sneezed the tiniest of suppressed sneezes.

"Who's there?"

"Me, Mademoiselle Josephine."

The voice came from amidst a froth of pink ostrich feathers. "Simon?"

"I've your sister's posts."

Grabbing the boa of feathers, Josephine pulled what felt like an arm into the back room of the shop, knowing a body must follow. She stripped off the feathers and found, beneath a wide-brimmed felt hat, pale eyes darting about the lavish display of fine fabrics and laces waiting to become gowns. Madame Lamarck had expressly forbidden the less-than-sanitary thing from entering her shop after he'd accidentally smeared her Chinese silk with dirt.

"How did you get past Madame Lamarck?"

"I followed a lady's skirts and hid for a moment before the two started cooing over a piece of shiny fabric. My eyes nearly fell out of my head, do you know, when a man holds a sneeze inside like that."

"A man, eh?" she mocked the wide-eyed urchin, no more than thirteen. He bristled his shoulders and thrust out his chest. If she were alone, Josephine would have laughed, but she had best whisper to avoid Madame discovering her illicit visitor. "And just how do you plan to get out of here?"

"I'll leave that to you, Mademoiselle," he offered with a proud grin.

"Oh, will you?"

He patted the dirt-encrusted front of his vest. "You want to see your sister's letters?"

Impertinent ragbag. By rights she should drag him out into the salon by his crusty little ear and leave him to Madame's fury. But not until she got what she wanted from him. Josephine could not imagine losing even one of Helene's posts before she had looked over the handwriting.

"Oh, very well. I'm finished here anyway. Perhaps I can walk you out behind cover of my skirts."

"Or under them," he offered enthusiastically.

"I think not." Snatching the small pile of letters he clutched in hands that most likely hadn't seen water in months, Josephine perused the handwriting. Most of Helene's amours came from different regiments. Though she did hear from one other officer in Julien and Matthieu's corp, the 26th Foot. Josephine was surprised none of the men had not discovered their shared correspondent. She'd heard soldiers often sat around the fire sharing love letters sent them. Not much else in their dreary lives, at least it added a bit of hope—

Horrors! Her heart started a swiftly ticking pace. If Chevalier Delaroche had read her letter to anyone else!

No. Pressing a hand to her thundering chest, Josephine shook her head. She still felt quite certain that Julien had never received her foolishly written prose. It had become lost in the post. *Please, it must have.*

An inexplicable surge of knowing hit her like an arrow to the heart, as *his* handwriting appeared. *Mademoiselle Helene Lalique, Faubourg St. Jacques, Paris.* The M in Mademoiselle flowed like a song traced in the snow. So smooth and perfect, but delicate, as if a heavy breath could bend one of the graceful curves into a sharp vee. He took a certain amount of pride in writing his letters, she sensed that.

"That it?" Simon prompted.

"Hmm? Oh, it is." Josephine returned the other letters to the boy's ragged satchel. "You must be more careful with them, Simon. You see here?" She flipped Julien's letter over to reveal a slash of dirt.

''Sow's breath, Mademoiselle! I don't have to do this for you. For as little as you pay me—''

''Another sou per delivery,'' she hastened to cut off his tirade, with a finger to her lips to remind him that he stood on restricted ground.

''Not enough.''

''Not enough? But—''

''How's about you throw in one of those there ribbons?''

Josephine turned to the pile of satin roses she'd stitched this afternoon. Madame Lamarck had taken her under her wing when Josephine was only six, after noticing Pascal's lack of parental skills on a much-needed shopping trip for new dresses. Although Josephine did not need to earn money, she enjoyed helping Madame.

''For my lady friend,'' Simon offered with a shy glance up from beneath a slash of dirty bangs.

''Very well, you may choose, but be quick about it. I must get you out of here before the Duchess leaves.''

A boy drooling before a baker's window could not have been more eager. Grimy fingers danced like wounded spider legs above the collection of faux flowers. In his endeavors to seek out the perfect rose, Simon succeeded in dirtying a half dozen of Josephine's creations.

''Oh dear, Madame Lamarck will be irate. They smell like— like muck!''

''Josephine!''

''Coming, Madame!''

''I've a dinner invitation this evening,'' echoed through the doorway. ''Do hurry, so I can lock up.''

Grabbing the soiled roses, Josephine stuffed them into Simon's hands, picked up Julien's letter, and carefully slid it between her stays and chemise and spread her skirts wide. ''Duck and waddle,'' she instructed the boy. ''And no sneez-ing!''

* * *

By the time she reached water's edge, Josephine had loosened her bodice ribbons. Such a retreat from the world demanded comfort. She hiked up her generous petticoats and tucked a few ends inside her waistband. She always wore petticoats with plain stomachers, as opposed to Helene's extravagant toilette. To even begin to worry about mussing her skirts or tangling her hair would not do. Much as Helene lamented that a bit of rouge might enhance her horridly sun-browned complexion, Josephine was quite comfortable with her clothes and her skin.

And if Father only knew that Helene had been submitting to monthly blood-lettings to make her countenance paler!

In the distance a slash of whitewashed pine darted through the air, followed by another slash, and yet another. Matthieu's family had lived but a quarter league outside the Porte St. Jacques just beyond that white windmill. An entirely different country and class, as Helene so often pointed out about the Bouchets' farmlands, and, inadvertently, Matthieu. Certainly not Paris, she'd explain in that condescending tone of hers. Though Helene would never admit she herself lived outside the walls—only near the wall. With such a remark, one never need articulate *which* side.

A turquoise dragonfly skimmed the glassy pond surface. Allowing her body to fall into a tumble, Josephine rolled across the grass until her head found the log as a pillow. The paper crinkled. Her smile, liquid as the pond, slipped unbidden across her face. No more dillydallying. The time had come. Slipping her thumb down between her breasts, she plied up the folded post. A quick sniff—a trait picked up from Helene—revealed a hint of leather. Most likely the parcel used to carry the post from his hands to hers.

*His hands to hers.*

A fidgety pleasure spread through her being. She held something from Julien Delaroche! It hadn't been perused and laughingly picked to shreds by Helene and her band of henclucks. This letter had come directly to *her*.

Well, as direct as it could having been intercepted so expertly this afternoon. Of course, the words were addressed to Helene, perhaps even the thoughts were inspired by Helene, but they were in reply to *her* words.

And that made some difference.

Didn't it?

No wax seal secured the paper. Pulling one end from the envelope of folds, Josephine carefully spread open the entire letter. Her heart raced as each precise movement disclosed his insect scrawls. An entire page of words! So much more than he had ever written before.

Surely, this must mean something.

Before the thought to read even crossed her mind, Josephine took a few moments to admire the craftsmanship of the post. Each crease was sharp, as if smoothed exactly by his finger. Such time he had placed in the mere creation of folds! And the paper was amazingly clean, the thick fibers visible and rough beneath her fingertip. How a soldier could store paper and keep it so spotless was beyond her. Only a prized possession would be so thoughtfully cared for.

And the words, black and small and sharply scrawled. A tense hand might have disclosed such ink to paper, but Josephine ventured to imagine that perhaps it was a sweet anxiety over the creation of his heart's voice that held his words in such close and exact design. The metallic smell of ink lingered. A few grains of fine sand skittered across the paper as her touch released them from the dried ink.


*My precious Helene,*


A grimace and a tongue thrust at the horrid salutation was all Josephine could muster. She must remember not to read the opening line of any future posts.

*A letter from you is like clean cool water to a desert-parched animal. Refreshing. Satisfying. Sustaining. Did you receive my touch? It is forever embedded in the fibers of the letter you now hold in your lovely hands. I pressed my hand to these words, imbuing them with my desire to touch you.*

*I remember your soft skin, smooth against my cheek as you unleashed a whisper across my ear. 'Tis a precious memory I stir up often. Your letters are as sweet as your touch. I fancy were I to gather them into pastry papers and sell them as confections, they would command a king's ransom. An immediate sell-out!*

*The candle flame is dying in a pool of wax. We must conserve tapers, for supplies are low as well as spirits. Four months of endless fighting and marching and trenching has begun to wear upon my very soul. But the thought of yet another post by your hand causes my spirits to soar above the clouds. Your words heal the darkness within my heart, Helene, my Hope.*

*Write again. Please. I must request a kiss from you, though. Another to add to my collection and to rekindle the magic of your touch.*

*Awaiting your kiss,*
*Julien*

Josephine pressed the missive to her breast. "Your words make me lose all rational thought. Oh, Julien, I wish it were to me your sentiments were addressed. My sister does not love you as I do."

"Speaking to the trees, are we?"

Startled upright, Josephine clutched the letter, wrinkling the paper against her palm. "Helene, you frightened me!"

"Oh sister." Helene sat next to Josephine, her embroidered skirts ploofing across the long grasses. She held her fingers spread and stiff and the strong scent of Marie Claire's rosemary manicure oil filled the air. "Don't tell me you are still carrying

Julien's letter with you? How many times have you read that
ragged piece of soldier's drivel?''

''It was in my pocket when I put my skirt on this morning,''
Josephine said as she crushed the paper and stuffed it into her
pocket. Hide all evidence! ''I must have forgotten it there when
you had last given it to me.''

''But you wear the same skirt every day, much to my horror.
You needn't make up stories, Josephine. It is well and fine that
you have your desires. But the chevalier is far out of your
league.''

''Whatever do you mean?'' Josephine pushed up and sat on
top of the log, pressing one hand safely over the post beneath
her skirt. Vexation, she'd crushed his words! ''Are you
implying that I am beneath Chevalier Delaroche?'' She used
her sudden anger to overcome her nervous surprise at Helene
finding her with the contraband letter. ''He was good enough
for you.''

''I imply no such thing. You are beneath no man, Josephine,
and I wish you never to forget it.'' She tapped the air with her
fingers, blowing them gently to speed the drying of the clear
lacquer. ''I simply mean that most soldiers are after only one
thing, and that is a carnal reward upon their return from a
campaign well done. You cannot possibly think they would
otherwise afford the time to write letters? It is their loins that
sincerely mourn the absence of a woman, and not their hearts.''

''How do you know? Monsieur Bouchet serves in the same
regiment as Chevalier Delaroche. You can't possibly tell me
*he* is sending out false love letters in hopes of reaping his—''

''Matthieu Bouchet is of a different ilk,'' Helene said. ''He
is kind and sweet, but a most odd little man. I fear the only
way he might find himself in a compromising position is if a
hurricane should blow an unsuspecting young woman into his
arms.''

''But he kissed me!''

''On the cheek. Though I thought it was *you* who delivered
the chaste little morsel?''

Josephine sighed. Of course Helene was right about Matthieu. She was always right. Matthieu was much too busy with his sketches and paints to turn an eye towards a beautiful woman. And what did Josephine care?

"I would not spend a moment's thought on Monsieur Bouchet's amorous liaisons," she said.

"But you do for Julien's?"

The paper crinkled inside Josephine's pocket. Yes, yes, and yes, she thought a great deal of the exquisite spinner of passionate prose. "Not at all. I shouldn't wish to associate with such a cad. I'm quite surprised you allowed your name to be associated with his."

"Well, he is a superb kisser."

A superb kisser? Oh, what she wouldn't give to discover that truth herself.

Helene stood and smoothed her fingers across her skirts. A sigh and a kick at the log Josephine sat on, and she turned to leave. "You will find that flirting with danger is just as exciting as the actual act."

"The actual act?" Josephine thrust a haughty nose into the air at her sister's back. "As if you would know. Hmmph."

But then again . . . Josephine's experiments into passion had recently become quite exciting.

Superb, eh?

She prayed the day would come when she would be privy to the Chevalier's kisses.

# Chapter 4

"Another post!" Julien declared victoriously. He untied the dainty pink ribbon from the folded letter, forgetting its presence as quickly as it was trampled by one of his boot heels. "I'll be damned if the woman hasn't written me immediately. She must finally realize how much I need to hear from her." He sat down on the fraying wool blanket occupied by Matthieu Bouchet.

Setting his spotless musket aside, Matthieu pushed bothersome locks from his eyes and offered a brief laugh. "You need to *hear* from her, or you *need* her?"

"I need her," Julien sang out, which prompted *here heres* from the few men who occupied the makeshift barracks set up inside an abandoned flour mill. "And I need to hear from her. You don't think these few precious words help to pass the time?"

"Until the time comes that you may pass upon her."

"You think I'm just securing my interests for leave?"

"Of course you are," Edmond Cuvier called from his game of cards. He played a ragged ace of spades on top of a dirt-smeared king. "The same reason we all write to our women. To ensure a hearty welcome home, a warm embrace, and a hot bed."

Amid male grunts of approval, Julien turned to Matthieu. "If that be so, than what of you, my scholarly friend? Have you no ladylove with whom to correspond and ensure a passionate greeting when you finally return home?"

"You're changing the subject, Delaroche."

"Indeed."

Bouchet flung out a hopeful splay of hand. "I may. But I've no intention of stringing her along with hollow words of devotion in hopes she will greet me with open arms. This heart requires much more than the satisfaction of carnal lusts."

Julien chuffed out a laugh. "The heart is not the organ that needs the attention we are talking about, Bouchet. What is her name?"

"She is merely a friend."

"Not so from the tone of your voice, man. Nor the revealing spark in your eyes. Is it that she does not return said devotion?"

Matthieu shrugged and reached for the folded letter in Julien's hand. "We've never broached the subject, but I feel sure she deems me more a brother than prospective suitor."

Julien snatched the post from his friend's fingers before he could secure a grip. "Tell. Or you won't be reading Mademoiselle Lalique's post tonight."

Catching his fingers up in his hair, Matthieu laughed as he rested his chin upon his bent knee. "In which case you will never read the damned post either."

Julien gave it a moment's thought. The man was right. The whole barracks knew he was right, though they held their tongues for fear of retaliation. Julien had seen to it from the very first day in drills and practice that all knew he possessed the pride and strength to hold his own. He was quick with sword and musket, and equally as skilled when left with only his hands.

Clenching his fist, Delaroche squeezed until two knuckles *popped*. It irritated him beyond all hell that Bouchet had let such a remark slip. The cramped and stinking barracks had gone silent with anticipation of his response. He could have bit through the tension and chewed it like a piece of year-old jerky. Damn his own pride.

"Well then," Julien unfolded the crisp paper, practicing casual indifference, as ever. "I guess we shall read."

A *whoosh* of released breaths, followed by snapping cards and shuffling boots, broke the heavy fog of silence. Julien spread the paper flat, while Matthieu—whose articulate voice was once again being borrowed to recite words—looked over his shoulder and read aloud. It was an unspoken courtesy that a man share an occasional post with all, and besides, Julien's letters received the most interest. Far more interesting than Edmond's posts, whose wife listed the sundry tasks of her day, or Gaspard's, whose amour could not construct an understandable sentence to save her life.

My dearest Julien,
   I pore over your every word with the fine perception of an entomologist's microscope.

Matthieu paused. Julien gripped the air in frustration. "What? Go on!"

"I wasn't aware that Helene had an interest in entomology. How peculiar."

Yes, yes, Matthieu knew the Lalique family. It had to be the sister whom Matthieu was so tight-lipped regarding his affections. Mentally filing that information away, Julien returned with a snapping, "No matter! Finish the letter without interruption or I shall see that it is you who marches first in the advance on the Spaniards tomorrow."

"And what would you do without me when I'm dead?" Matthieu challenged.

Again the entire room hung on Delaroche's response.

Julien thought about it. If Matthieu were to perish, that would mean . . . The devil! A smug little painter he was! What had gotten into Bouchet's craw that he felt the need to challenge him on every little thing today?

Julien released a heavy breath and gestured impatiently. "Go on." And then he added, "If you please." Best to keep the man in good spirits. For the moment.

"Yes," called Gaspard as he shuffled the sodden pile of playing cards. "Read us the good parts and leave the discussion for later."

"What's an enta—enta—" Edmond stumbled to place the word on his tongue. "That thing she mentioned?"

"A scientist who studies bugs," Matthieu offered.

"Your woman is writing about bugs, Delaroche? Ha!" Edmond slapped his powder-stained knee and stirred up a ruckus of matched laughter and guffaws.

"Perhaps I should proceed?" Bouchet yelled above the din of hilarity.

Julien did not even bother to reply. He merely crossed his arms firmly across his chest, jutted out his chin, and eyed Edmond, who skittered back to his cards and lowered his head.

*By the time you receive this post you may have grown*
*stiff and somber in your waiting—*

"Stiff for sure!" Jean-Jacques burst out, making a lewd pumping gesture against his groin.

Julien transferred his gaze from Edmond to Jean-Jacques. The man's jaw snapped shut and he ceased his pumping motions. Total silence. Mice don't squeal when trapped in the cat's gaze.

"Shall I finish?" Matthieu wondered.

"Please do." Julien's single command had a deadening effect. Jean-Jacques swallowed and slithered to his bunk.

"In reward for your simple request (and valiant waiting)," Matthieu took up in grand flourish . . .

*I send upon this very paper—a kiss. Born of my heart
and given life by my lips. Press your mouth to the letter.
Do you feel it?*

Cards hung in midair, waiting to be played. Julien's hand
shook. Matthieu reached over his shoulder to take the letter
from his cohort's hand. Gaspard hung his head and exposed
his cards to all, but none were the wiser, so caught up were
they in Matthieu's soft recitation.

*And then another kiss. Not too long, mind you, but you
may linger just long enough so that this paper kiss may
not be construed as . . . chaste.*

''Blessed Mary,'' Gaspard whimpered.
''Shh,'' echoed about the wooden shack.

*For in studying your words, written with ink drawn from
your very soul, I have come to a level of passion that goes
beyond a simple polite exchange of letters. And so, Julien,
my sweet, press this letter to your lips again and again.
And again. I've chosen a fine and thick piece of paper so
you may not fear to tear it in your repeated endeavors. (I
should know, I lingered a bit myself to ensure the kiss would
stay until you folded the paper open.)*
*Paper can not begin to replace the touch of your lips
to mine. Black ink is but a shadow of the vivid red blood
that simmers at the thought of your touch, Julien. But
they must both do for the moment. I have never until now
known my own capacity for loneliness. I feel as though
a piece of me were missing. Might that piece be you,
Julien?*
*I linger in anticipation of your words.*

*Yours exclusively,*
*Helene Lalique*

Julien tried to rip the letter from Matthieu's hand, but Bouchet held firm. "There's a smudge on the H here."

"Probably from her sweaty fingers. She had to have been panting after writing this! Let me have it. What are you looking at?"

The room, frozen in a captivated lull, broke from the ice at Julien's sharp tone and reluctantly turned back to cards and cleaning of weapons. A quiet buzz of conversation started now that the letter had been read.

"It looks as though the H was written over another letter," Matthieu said as he relinquished the paper.

Julien stood and folded the letter, not following the original folds which made it a thick bundle to stuff inside his waistband. "You are too damned analytical, you know that, Bouchet? How do you ever expect to find a woman of your own if you insist on picking apart every bit of life and love?"

Matthieu could only offer a shrug. He picked up his musket and examined the shiny fire pan. "I like to see beyond the surface. 'Tis not such a bad thing." He blew on the pan and stuffed a wedge of his shirt inside to polish further. "You might try seeing things with more than just your breeches on occasion. A woman is not an object to be toyed with. If you wish her respect, you must earn it. And to earn it you must know her inside and out."

"Artists!" Julien tromped out of the barracks, the post falling from his waistband and to the floor of the shack as he did.

Matthieu eyed the crumpled post. If Helene only knew the object of her exposed feelings treated them with such disregard. Julien did not love her as he claimed. How could he?

Gaspard dashed to retrieve the forgotten letter, his triumphant shout alerting the others to his find. Then the sandy-bearded old man pressed the clean paper against his dirt-crusted mouth and closed his eyes.

A passionate sigh echoed through the ranks.

*    *    *

For some odd reason the flare of cannon fire was always a rather interesting sight. Ornamental almost. Like those Chinese sparklers Paris shot off in celebration of King Louis's birthday. Protected by a wall of deeply trenched dirt Julien reached behind himself. A powder horn was slapped into his palm.

*"Merci,"* he said to Matthieu as he bit off the carved bone cap and tapped another round into his musket barrel. A wad and bullet followed; Bouchet then handed him his ramrod.

"I don't think you should write her anymore."

"What?" Jamming harder than necessary with the thin steel rod, Julien received a raised brow from Bouchet. Julien replaced the rod beneath the musket barrel and took aim. The fizz of golden sparks showered over his arms and dusted Matthieu's breeches. The pound of gunfire echoed in a nightmare tune matched by dozens of other surrounding musket charges.

Dropping the cock on his own musket, Matthieu took aim and fired. "It's not right you continue this charade with Helene Lalique. You do not love her."

"What the hell makes you think I don't?" Julien slammed down his musket, knowing it hit Matthieu on the leg, and reached for his pistol and the powder horn.

"You mean you do?"

"Of course." He tapped the horn over the fire pan and succeeded in showering powder all over his knee, as well as piling too much in the steel pan. "I love Helene," he insisted as he slapped the powder from his breeches.

"But you said you'd only had the two encounters before you were called to serve." Matthieu turned his back to the dirt wall and rested his head against the hastily shoveled barricade. Musket fire had begun to settle to a few shots every minute. It was early morning. Both sides were exhausted.

The hiss of a musketball soared over their heads. Firing quickly, Julien held his arm straight until he knew that his bullet had hit its mark. He always waited until the sparks had ceased to burn across his wrist. He ducked next to Matthieu. "As hard as you may find it to believe, coming from a man such as me, I have fallen in love with her. And being away from her only makes me desire her all the more."

"Absence makes—"

"I know, I know," Julien hissed, "makes the heart grow firmer."

"I believe that's fonder. You're thinking with your loins again, Delaroche."

"As you most likely never do. But you were right when you said a man should know a woman inside and out. I want more than just ..." Oh hell, this was going to hurt! "More than her ... body." Yes, very painful. "I want ..." Must he say this? "I want her respect!" Ouch! But he had to admit, it was getting easier. Of course he loved Helene! But he couldn't have Bouchet suspect his other intentions. "I want her love, and her desire as well."

"Well, that changes things." Matthieu clamped a firm hand across Julien's back. "Forgive me for my doubts, Chevalier. Write her again. And perhaps your next post should reveal some of what you just told me. The way to win a woman's heart is to expose your own."

"Bouchet."

"Yes?"

"You've just too damned many ... how shall I put it— words of wisdom. Where do you get all this information?"

Matthieu thumped a fist against his chest. "Right here, my friend."


"Mademoiselle Josephine!"

Simon stood beneath a wooden apothecary sign, fanning his grimy, gaunt face with a single clean letter. Josephine dashed to him, dodging a meandering blind man who groped the walls for direction, and nearly groped her in the process.

"Only the one?" she asked, trying to grab it from his hands as he raised it playfully above his head.

"Indeed, only the one." With that, he displayed it before his face so the script was readable. "But is it the right one?"

Impatient with his games, yet not willing to appear too desperate, Josephine feigned disinterest. An impossible feat once she'd caught a glimpse of the tightly cramped scrawls. She knew his handwriting as she knew her own heart. Were a hundred different men to write a single word upon paper, she would immediately know Julien's hand.

"Perhaps I don't care a wit," she forced out, and turned away from Simon, crossing her arms over her breasts. He couldn't possibly realize how hard her spine fought against that action.

"Oh, so I can be on to the Lalique house then? A good thing, I've my chores at home before the night comes."

Josephine hooked an arm through his, jerking him to a stumbling halt. Her dress suffered the consequence. The inside of her left sleeve sucked up the dirt from Simon's body like a leech taking blood.

"Oh! Now look what you've made me do. Give me that." She ripped the post from his hands. "Now be off with you, ruffian. Don't you know a gentleman never soils a lady?"

"Unless the lady wishes a good soiling."

Josephine turned to catch his glinting smirk and nearly smacked him for his nasty mouth. But he threw up a protective barrier of filth-ridden hands. "I plead lunacy, Mademoiselle."

"Good day, Simon."

"Not without my pay."

"Very well, you've more than earned your keep." She slipped a length of violet moiré ribbon from her skirt pocket. "I do appreciate your help, Simon. You will hold your tongue?"

"I shall bind it with ribbons fair," he singsonged, and demonstrated by pulling the shiny purple strand across his mouth.

"You roll that and tuck it away in your purse or your lady friend will never be able to remove the dirt stains."

"Yes, Mademoiselle. I'll be off now."

"Merci," she called and skipped down the Grande Rue de St. Jacques.


"I need your assistance, Josephine!"

"A moment!" she called down from her chambers. Bother, that the world should clamber at her door when she was in most dire need of a few moment's silence to read the prize she'd tucked in her stays.

Helene's insistent call echoed up from below. Marie Claire was woefully unskilled in any task that required a needle. Josephine did all Helene's mending, sewed her hats, and attached ribbon bouquets to her dresses. She did her hair on occasion, too, when Marie Claire's palsy-ridden joints acted up. Josephine could spend hours running her fingers lazily through Helene's hair—soft and luxurious as a fox's fall coat— as the two sat beneath the ivy canopy in the gardens.

As for her own hair . . . A glance to her looking glass found a half-dozen locks that had pulled loose from her chignon. As dark as a bear's winter cave, their father would say of the color. Hers was soft and shiny like Helene's, but it just didn't take well to direction. It chose its own design more often than not. Perfectly fine, as far as Josephine was concerned.

Licking her palm and pasting back a few of the fine strands, Josephine turned to go downstairs. Something crinkled within her stays.

She'd nearly forgotten.

She slipped the folded paper out and held it in shaking hands. "Oh, how can I continue with this charade? The chevalier would be devastated to learn I've involved him in such deceit. But . . ."

A hint of gunpowder imbued the fibers of the paper. She ran a finger along one thick fold, tracing its grace, the bend marks where perhaps it had been stuffed into a baldric or doublet, or traveling parcel. And his lovely script. Tiny insect tracks meandering across the page, teasing her to enter the folds and discover the nest of secrets it guarded.

"I have never felt so deeply about a man before," she whispered.

It was as though her heart beat to a new rhythm when she held his words in her hand. As if her soul screamed out in triumph. Sensations became much more acute. Everything; sights, sounds, tastes, smells, took on a new vibrancy whenever she read Julien's words. It was as if he spoke directly to her, stood but a hand's width away from her and whispered so that no other could hear.

She had always done the right thing. Always. And as much as she knew that reading this letter and writing back would be the wrong thing, her heart argued that perhaps it wasn't as dishonorable as it seemed.

"I am giving him hope. Perhaps making his long days go a little more quickly. I wonder if he rereads my posts, as I do his."

"Josephine!"

"Coming, Helene!"

She squeezed the post in her hand. For a brief moment a twinge enveloped her heart with wire, barbed and tight. "No. I am only doing this to serve my own desperate needs. Am I jealous of my own sister to do such a thing? Oh! I mustn't continue. This is so wrong!"

She crossed her room and tossed the post into the empty hearth. A rose-festooned pewter tinderbox sat on the vanity to her right, beneath the mauve fringe of her beaded lampshade. "I'll burn it tonight. Forgive me, Julien, but I must abort all correspondence now, else I fear I may never end it. I don't wish to hurt you. As much as it hurts me . . ."

Bravely, she forced her chin up to counterbalance her sinking heart. Helene waited below.

# Chapter 5

It was for Josephine, Helene Lalique's younger sister, that Bouchet held a torch. This information proved most worthy of consideration as Julien settled into the darkness of night, watching for the bright orange fire of enemy approach. While the Spaniards had already shown their reluctance to continue the battle, Commander Marechal always posted a dozen men during the night. Half the regiment slept lightly, gaining much needed rest, while the other half silently trenched their way closer to enemy lines. The shifts worked in four-hour rotation while the moon was high. The schedule was hell on a man's mind—nay, his very soul—but Delaroche had learned to endure.

He had endured much. Life had not chosen to gift him with an easy run of his place on this earth. But since joining the King's army, he'd been able to lose memories of the harder times in the mindless marching and drilling and endless nights of scanning the blackened sky with the fear of meeting the enemy face-to-face.

It was fear that pushed him. Fear of death made him super-sensitive to sounds and movement. Fear of mockery made him quick on the draw, always ready to defend his name and actions. Fear of the past kept the memories roped and bound. And a fear of insanity kept that *name* from his thoughts.

He hadn't thought the name for years. Hadn't allowed its haunting tone to intrude upon his daily life. Until Bouchet had been transferred from the 16th Foot to his regiment just last year. Now hadn't that been the sword in his gut? Matthieu Bouchet fighting alongside Julien Delaroche. Damn!

He hated the man. And every day he looked upon his stupidly naive grin, that name rebirthed in his mind. *Isabelle*.

Ah, but for all outward appearances he was a friend. Until the time was right.

And with his sneaking suspicion regarding Bouchet's feelings for the younger sister, Julien was now armed with deadly ammunition.

Soon Matthieu Bouchet would know what it was like to be haunted by a name. The name Julien . . . Well . . . he'd leave it at that for now.

*Might I be so bold as to offer you my heart?*

She whispered the final line of his post over and over again. Her pulse raced. Her fingers trembled. The paper shook as if an elder leaf tossed to and fro on a bluster of wind.

The letter had gone unburned and forgotten yesterday, thanks to the large tear in Helene's skirts and Marie Claire's sudden fever. Josephine, along with Cook, had sat with the maid far into the night, until finally the fever broke and she settled to rest. Exhausted and heavy with sleep, Josephine had literally snored a path back to her own chambers.

Now this morning, finding that Marie Claire had recovered enough to drag herself down for a bite to eat, Josephine broke her fast on tart green-apple jam smeared over hearth-warm baguettes. She thanked Cook with a hug, slipped her fingers around a goblet of wine, and dashed out to the pond, determination quickening her strides. She hadn't the heart to burn the letter this morning, reasoning that anything Julien had spent precious time to write, should be honored by at least being read once.

But she could not read it once. Nor twice. This was perhaps the sixth or seventh time she'd read the short, yet telling epistle.

*Helene, my one constant in this world,*

*A kiss can speak so many ways of promises and desires and dreams. The kiss you sent me spoke of all these things. And more. I fear you have committed a crime against my person, Helene. Can you guess your fateful sin?*

*Dare I dream that your correspondence goes far beyond that of kindness and compassion for a soldier who simply needs companionship at a time of tragic solitude and disaster? I write to you for more reasons than to secure a welcome embrace when I arrive home. You do know that, don't you, Helene? I write to you because if I do not, this lifeline strung between the two of us shall be severed with a blow of silence as deadly as enemy steel. Promise me one thing, Helene. You do not play with my affections. Cease to write if you ever have such a notion.*

*I pray I shall hear from you again.*

*And now, that crime. I hereby charge Helene Lalique with the crime of theft. A lovely woman who has burrowed into my soul and placed her touch upon my heart. She has stolen this heavy organ that beats to a rhythm in her name.*

*I may not even be the man you imagine me to be. I may not be brave as a knight, nor as witty as a King's prized jester. My pleasures are simple, my aspirations few, yet solid. A simple promise and vow is all I can offer you. Here is my heart, clever thief. It is yours.*

*Julien*

"Here is my heart? Oh, *mon dieu.*"

Josephine fanned her face with the letter. A feared swoon did not come, for her thoughts were too busy with dreams, fantasies, and imagining to shut down in a sudden faint.

"He has offered his heart to me," she said incredulously. And then, "Dear no, it is Helene to whom he has offered his heart. Oh, this has gone much too far. This man, this dear sweet man, has fallen in love with me. But he thinks it is Helene. And as much as this should disturb me, it does not, because I love him, too. And I've never once looked upon his face!"

She continued her fanning. "Great Goddess of Irony, you must have had a heavy hand in my life lately. What am I to do?"

She reached for her goblet of raspberry wine, but found she'd finished the entire thing while greedily reading through Julien's letter, so excited she had been. A few crumbles of bread sat in the cradle of her skirts, but she no longer had the stomach to eat. Eat? When the most desirable man in the world had just offered her his heart?

"But how do I know he is desirable to look at?"

She didn't. But it also did not matter. For she desired his heart and soul, two things plainly painted out in glorious colors with his written word. It mattered not if he had a scar down one cheek, or a limp, or even if he were an ogre!

"Oh no," she interrupted her thoughts. "Not an ogre. I must draw the line somewhere."

She smiled at her fanciful imagination. Ah, to dance in the arms of her faceless rogue. Surely the man cut a dashing figure, for he had attracted Helene. And Helene was known to speak only to the most lovely and elegant of men. She would never bat a lash for anyone less than handsome.

"I wonder what he looks like."

Was he tall and statuesque, charming to a fault, or short, brooding and silently intriguing? Helene had once mentioned his delicious blond hair. A single lovelock he'd worn over his right shoulder, braided through with narrow red ribbon. He has a fine-shaped head, Helene had once remarked, more as a justification that she did see something in the man beyond the passion that he had once so obviously stirred in her. And a jaw carved of hard angles and tension, but a quick and cavalier smile.

Smiling to herself, Josephine closed her eyes and began to ruminate on the fine shape of her mystery man's jaw. Hard and tense. Hmm . . . a stern and regal man. Perfect for a soldier. And a cavalier smile. That thought segued into grander designs upon his person. He stood tall and broad, sword in hand and steely regard in his eyes. Hmm, make those steely *blue* eyes. Yes, much like the sky just before a summer rain . . .

But at first sight of her, a liquid desire waters through his summer-rain eyes, and with but a blink, he summons her to his side.

"You are my one true love, Josephine," he says as he sweeps her into a dipping embrace.

Twining her arms around his neck, Josephine waits, lips pursed, eyes closed for his touch. Which comes with all the fire and surprise of the delightful unknown. He brands her with his kiss, making her his own, and he her champion.

"I offer you my heart," he whispers in a deadly seductive voice that shivers up her spine like cool ice on a hot summer's eve.

"And I accept it," she answers quickly, for a swoon dances through her body, leaving a fine dusting of shiver bumps in its wake.

"Oh!" Startled out of her daydream, Josephine jumped at the press of hands over her eyes. "Who is it? Helene?" She touched the warm, broad hands that covered her sight. A man's hands.

Horrors! A man had snuck up behind her in her reverie and now offered no sound. Fright scurried up her spine. She knew no man who was such a fond acquaintance to do such a thing.

"You must tell me who you are or I shall scream," she warned, now trying to straighten herself, perhaps hook a leg beneath the other in preparation to rise and run. The hands pressed gently over her eyes, but they did not waver.

"Guess," came a gruff, obviously altered voice.

She gripped her skirts in both hands, crinkling the letter. Only the fresh meadow grasses filled her nostrils, no hint of her aggressor's origins. "You frighten me, monsieur."

"I vow, you've no fear of me. But you must guess."

Guess her attacker? Did he plan to ravage her? To violate her? No. Wouldn't he have started with the ravaging by now? Bother! "Is it Simon?"

No answer.

No. Simon's hands would be much smaller and not as wide. And she would have smelled him before he had a chance to get close enough to touch her.

"You must tell, or I shall scream as promised. I fear your actions, monsieur, for there are no men in my life dear enough to play such games."

The hands slipped away. Josephine spun round and did scream.

"Matthieu!"

He caught her hug in a twirling spin and his laughter bubbled into duet with hers. Giddy with joy, Josephine nearly toppled the two over. She kissed his cheek with unabashed confidence and spread her fingers through his hair.

"Oh, Matthieu, it is you! You silly man, frightening me so."

"I didn't mean to frighten you, ladybug." Their spin settled to a stop and he set her on the ground but did not release her. Quirking a dark brow, he wondered, "But who is Simon? And why do you not consider me dear enough to play so?"

"Simon . . . delivers the mail. I'm so sorry, Matthieu. Of course you are dear to me. I cannot believe it is really you! This must mean the fighting has ended?"

"For a time." He set his long musket against the mossy log and tossed his head back, scattering long waves of earth-brown hair across his shoulders with reckless disregard. "We've driven the Spaniards back to St. Amand. But that merely grants us leave. Commander Marechal is sure they will advance again. Not for weeks. I hope. But I don't wish to discuss war right now. Look at you!'' He reached out and pulled her into his embrace. Running a hand down the side of her face, he tucked a loose strand of her hair behind her ear. ''Still the most beautiful woman in the entire country, I dare say.''

''And still you've never been farther than fifty leagues from Paris, so your knowledge of such does not apply,'' she said with an admonishing tap to his nose.

''You look good yourself.'' She studied his eyes as they danced back and forth between hers. Always bright and inquisitive, they were a fascinating mixture of indigo and gold; ''the gold from me and the blue a gift from the heavens,'' as his mother Isabelle had once said to her. There curved traces of dark circles beneath his eyes though. And Josephine now noticed he seemed a bit gaunt. Weary to the bone. ''You are a trifle thinner than last I saw you.''

''Military rations do not hold a candle to a king's feast, ladybug.''

Five summers ago, she'd posed for one of his sketches, and he had drawn her sitting upon a jeweled ladybug, the beetle mid-flight. He had a knack for creating fantastical images and most of the people he sketched sported wings or antennae or some sort of insect legs. Angels, bejeweled insects, winged mice, swimming horses, and wildly colored landscapes lived in his head. Josephine wore the title of ladybug with pride.

''How long have you been back? From your dress I'd say you've just climbed out of the trenches.''

''Indeed.''

''Have you spoken to Helene?''

''I said a few words to your sister when I arrived, but she was much too preoccupied with choosing a proper mask, for I believe she was on her way out. And I've not even been to the homestead yet to check on the renters. Which reminds me, I shall have to see to letting an apartment in town for the time we've been granted leave. And I must retrieve my things. Cook has taken care of them for me?''

''Actually, Richelieu keeps them in his chambers. He didn't think it right for a woman to hold a young man's things for him.''

''Good. I shall speak to him before I leave. But I could think of nowhere else I'd rather go than here, Josephine. I marked a course for your front door as soon as our regiment set foot in Paris. That is, as soon as I could bathe. Wouldn't want to subject you to a soldier's, er ... perfume.''

''Matthieu ... I'm—'' She wasn't sure how to feel. This man was like a missing piece pressed into place. The brother she had never had. Her emotions scurried from excitement to dancing-on-clouds joy, to a sudden sadness at not having written him. How cruel of her to have ignored his needs when she was at home safe from war, embroiling herself in a lascivious correspondence with an unknown soldier.

''It's been six months,'' he took up her hand. Tender warmth traced over her knuckles. He had long, strong fingers, perfect for holding a paintbrush or caressing a woman's jaw. ''I missed you, Josephine. You must know you were in my thoughts every day.''

''I missed you, too.'' She hugged him, pressing her cheek against his shoulder for he stood a head taller than she. He smelled like the earth at her feet, and just an acrid hint of musket powder. Familiar and right, his scent. Just like the feeling she got standing near him.

Julien's letter forgotten in the crevice between the log and the rumpled grasses, Josephine walked with Matthieu to the edge of the pond, where the two settled onto the grassy bank and held hands.

Matthieu's presence set her confidence free. She always felt comfortable and relaxed with him. They were soulmates; they'd decided that a few years back. It might have been the time she'd fallen out of the beech tree, Josephine recalled. She'd bruised only her ego, but the afternoon had been spent laughing about each other's mistakes and mishaps. Destined to be friends for life. Mirrors of one another's joys, pains, and desires at times. And at other times so complementary in their differences that after a brief spat over right from wrong they would be laughing in one another's arms.

A true friend. She loved him dearly.

"Why did you not write to me?" Josephine said suddenly as she dipped a toe into the cool pond waters. "Forgive me, you must have been terribly busy. If anyone should have written, it should have been me. Oh, Matthieu, are you all right?" She pressed his head against her shoulder and smoothed a reassuring hand over the carefree waves of his hair. "Tell me that war has not hardened you. Tell me your heart is still as true and fantastical as always."

"It is true that war is an ugly mar upon any man's soul," he said as he played with a portion of her skirts. "But even now as I sit by your side, I can feel the darkness recede, with the promise of complete recovery."

"I'm pleased to hear you say that. I worried for you, Matthieu."

"I worried myself, at first. But our regiment was peopled with many good men, stout fighters. The Chevalier Delaroche took me under his wing—so to speak. I learned much from him, and after a month's time I felt quite confident lurking in the trenches and charging enemies under the rain of amber fire."

"Julien Delaroche? Oh . . ."

Josephine's hand slipped from Matthieu's head. A sudden wave of humming dizziness overtook her, but she snapped her body around, quickly defeating the oncoming swoon. She spied the letter on the ground. How quickly she had forgotten Julien with Matthieu's presence!

"Are you quite well, ladybug? Josephine?"

"Hmm? Oh, certainly." She scrambled over to the log and quickly snagged the letter, turning to tuck it in her bodice so

Matthieu would not see. "So you know the chevalier? You say he was kind to you?"

"Most kind." Matthieu kicked his boot toe against the wide rock they'd been sitting on to remove the sand from his spurs. They clacked dully.

"The chevalier has returned to Paris also?" This realization really did make her want to swoon. Josephine quickly sat on the log. She tucked her shaking fingers beneath her thighs and pasted a smile to her face, though she felt sure Matthieu would see through her anxiety.

"Yes," he said, his brows narrowing and his speech slowing in confusion. "He marched by my side on the way home. Ah! I understand your curiosity now. I imagine you have heard much about Julien from Helene's letters?"

"Oh? Of course! You could put it that way. Perhaps . . . Though, you shouldn't mention it to Helene, she doesn't like me to speak of her amours."

"Trust that I will not." He knelt before her, his gaze studying her carefully. Her heart had climbed in a leap of fear, and now pumped somewhere in the vicinity of her throat. Gently, he touched two fingers to her forehead. Josephine smiled, knowing what was to come. She closed her eyes. He then traced a curve over her lips. Matthieu's unspoken way of saying, yes, I am your friend, and I do care.

But enough about friendship and caring—Julien Delaroche was in town! This can not be happening. She'd not prepared!

"You do not look well." Matthieu's warm hand to her forehead nearly toppled her over, so weak she felt. He caught her by the upper arm as she swayed, the slide of his hand across her satin bodice producing a delicious sing. "Josephine? What is it?"

"Nothing for you to worry about, Matthieu. I think perhaps . . ." She could not believe she had to gasp for a breath! Helene had tightened her stays to the extreme this morning. "I just need to lie down. I . . . stayed up far too late last eve—

Marie Claire was ill—and I rose very early this morning. I fear
the lack of sleep may have caught me unawares just now."

"You must lie down. I'll carry you back to the house."

"No!" She slipped her arm from his tender touches. She
couldn't bear the thought of Helene questioning her upon seeing
Matthieu toting her into the house. Nor could she bear his
touches when she'd promised herself to another man's attentions. Much as she did desire Matthieu's company . . . "I can
walk. I'm so sorry, Matthieu, I've gone and spoiled your home-
coming."

He hefted up his musket and slung the leather strap over his
shoulder. A glint of sun glanced off the shiny metal parts.
"Nonsense, I'll return on the morrow."

"Oh, would you?" That would give her time to make a plan.
To ensure that Chevalier Delaroche . . . well . . . what did she
need to do? Oh! Right now she must give Matthieu her attention.
It was only fair. She had missed him so. If only she hadn't this
new disaster to worry about!

"That would be acceptable?" he asked as they walked slowly
to the house, he supporting her with an arm around her waist.
"If I returned tomorrow?"

"I should die if you did not return, Matthieu." Stalks of
scattered heather snapped under her slippers. "I feel perfectly
horrible for not writing you."

"I wouldn't have had the time to answer," he offered in a
barely perceptible whisper.

"I want to spend the entire day with you to make up for
time lost. I feel so foolish that this has come over me. A
vaporish woman is such a sight."

"I've never known you to be vaporish." Matthieu pulled
her close, an intimate closeness the two were accustomed to.
"Now Helene . . ." he teased.

His knowledge of her sister's ways made Josephine giggle.

As they entered the garden, Matthieu bent before Cook's
cross and crossed himself, forehead to chest, left to right shoulder, as he always did.

They landed the back door, just a one-story climb to her bedroom; Josephine was thankful for that small mercy. The shade of the grapevine-laced pergola provided respite from her sudden fever.

"As it is, I've overstayed my unannounced welcome. You go lie down and rest your pretty head, so that we may spend the entire day tomorrow talking and strolling the streets of Paris. We'll go to Sabatier's and eat cream cakes until our stomachs burst and we've both cream mustaches."

She smiled at the memory of the good times they had shared. "It is good to have you home, Matthieu."

"It is good to be home. And to see my ladybug." He pressed a long kiss to her knuckles, almost possessive in his lingering attention. And then he bowed grandly, sweeping his felt hat across the cobbled path. "Until the morrow, my lady. You've given this gentleman a fine welcome home."

"Don't forget your things. Richelieu is most likely in his chambers."

"Of course. *Au revoir,* ladybug."

Josephine watched as he strolled into her house, quite familiar with its layout, and took an immediate right to where the servants' quarters lay. And then sank to her knees.

"All hell shall break loose if Chevalier Delaroche comes to call on Helene. I must stop that from happening. But how?"

# Chapter 6

Josephine fitfully paced the floor of her room from bedstead to vanity, and back again. 'Twas a good thing she'd foregone the idea of an Aubusson rug in favor of cool wooden boards on quiet fall mornings, or it would be worn to threads by now.

She'd dismissed the idea of running away, for she hadn't a clue where to go. Most assuredly Richelieu would see her no farther than the Louvre as Father had instructed. And she much feared taking off on her own, leaving the comforting boundaries of her Paris. She thought for only a moment about going to Madame Lamarck for advice; a much-needed replacement for the mother Josephine had never known. No she didn't feel right discussing such a dilemma with her.

It seemed there was only one conclusion to be drawn; and this plan could only work if she hurried. Time was of the essence. Every moment she hesitated the hourglass sands sifted more swiftly.

Dashing to her writing desk Josephine discovered but one piece of paper. Enough for her plan. The ink had dried in the silver pan. Cook would be outraged at the waste. Cursing her carelessness, Josephine poured a few dribbles of dark ink from the bottle over the crusted black flakes.

Her hands shook so terribly she had to stop three times and shake her fingers out before the salutation was even complete.

Simon usually arrived by high noon; he was due within the hour. If she hurried, the boy could have a letter in Julien's hands by mid-afternoon with the excuse that he was just getting ready to post it to the military route, but after hearing the 26th Foot had arrived in Paris, he had decided to deliver it personally.

She dated the letter four days earlier. It must look as though Helene had written another letter without knowledge of his return. The contents of the letter would explain Helene's growing disinterest and ask that Julien no longer correspond with her. Deepest regrets, et cetera, but it would be best for both of them, for she had found someone new. Josephine had listened enough times as Helene composed her ''dear Jacques'' letters for numerous others.

This was the most vile and wicked act Josephine had ever committed against her sister. But it was necessary to protect her own hide. If her plan was successful, Julien Delaroche would never grace their front door, nor would she need fear Helene's discovery of her secret betrayal.

Neither Julien nor Helene would be the wiser.

But Josephine would now suffer dearly for her actions. She would never again be privy to Julien's heartfelt words.

The man she loved was being ripped from her heart. By her very own hand.

Sanding the quickly scrawled words, Josephine sat back and drew in a deep breath. She must look upon this experience as simply the source of great and passionate memories. Her first love. Her only love. One that she would always hold in her heart.

''Josephine?''

''Helene!''

Helene stood in their chamber doorway, spinning a lace-frilled velvet mask; from her hooded cape and gloves, it was apparent she was readying for a walk.

"Why I believe I frightened you right out of your skin, sister. La! What is it? What secret missives are you composing?"

Her jaw dropped, heavy as a rock. Josephine snapped her mouth shut. "Secret missives? Why, sister, how coy you are this morning. No, really, I'm just practicing my letters."

"You? Of all people, Josephine, you've the loveliest hand-writing I've yet seen. Let me see that."

Standing to form a blockade between her sister's approaching figure and her evil deed, Josephine also formed a cage around the desk with either arm thrust backwards.

"Just letters," she forced out, though she could barely suppress the nervousness in her tone.

But Helene did not seem to notice. She gave a flip of her mask, hooking it expertly over her shoulder. "Very well. If it is a secret, you know I shall wrench it from you sooner or later." Deviousness sparked in the look she cocked at Josephine. "A secret amour? Perhaps Monsieur Bouchet?"

"Matthieu? Oh no—"

"Come now, Josephine, you're absolutely ashen. The color has run from your face and puddles at your feet. I've interrupted a passionate epistle to the consummately droll Matthieu Bouchet. 'Tis fine and well you've finally taken notice of the attraction between the two of you. Though . . . he was looking rather disheartened after you sent him away just now."

"Sent him—no, I—Attraction?" Josephine barely muttered.

Helene's laughter followed her to the door. "You see? It is as they say, you never notice love for it blocks your vision, and not until it is right in front of your face do you finally cry out. Oh! Marie Claire, you surprised me. What are you doing lurking out there?"

"Forgive me, milady, I wasn't lurking. You've a gentleman caller below."

"Monsieur Michelet? We plan to spend the afternoon at the

Tuileries, studying the new sculptures,'' Helene directed back at Josephine.

"No, milady. It is not Monsieur Michelet."

"Then who, Marie Claire, spit it out!"

"He said his name was Julien Delaroche. A chevalier, I believe."

The crow quill in Josephine's hand split neatly in two.

"Julien?" Helene's expression exploded to surprise. "Hmm, so he's returned from campaign. Whatever reason does he have to call on me? Oh dear, I do hope he did not take my lack of correspondence in some encouraging way. Is the man daft?"

Helene seemed to be waiting for a positive response from Josephine. But Josephine could not move to think, let alone speak!

"Bother and biscuits. Tell him I'll be right down," Helene said to the maid.

Biscuits? Damnation and a thousand evil curses! The hard hollow cylinder of the quill dug into Josephine's palm. If Helene did not leave soon, she would see blood drip from the steel nib instead of ink.

"What could this mean?" Helene implored Josephine, a befuddlement of twisted lips and concerned brows falling over her countenance.

A fine time for her older sister to start begging advice from her!

"Perhaps . . ." Josephine swallowed, struggling to maintain composure. Her wrists were beginning to shake behind her as she still held her awkward position. " 'Tis not a social visit?"

"Then what?" Helene tapped the soft tip of the mask against her crimson-stained lips.

"Why are you asking me? Go to him! The answer is below, not up here."

"Well. You certainly are testy this fine day. Very well. I'll just go find out for myself." A hurrumph preceded Helene's exit.

Josephine pricked her ears to listen as her sister's wide russet skirts flicked in and out of the ornate iron railing that bordered the stairs to the main foyer. Swish, swush, swish. Dashing to her chamber door, she clung to the frame, her bottom lip clenched between her teeth. The angle of the ceiling cut off her view of most of the foyer below. Impossible to see anything more than . . . a pair of boots!

Scuffling inside her room, Josephine pressed her back to the open door. "Horrors! I will be discovered. Fool, fool, fool!" she dared in a whispered hiss. "Chevalier Delaroche cannot have come here for anything but a rendezvous with the lover to whom he thinks he has been writing. Oh dear, how did I create such a mess?"

A thousand dozen of those damned burned biscuits! She knew exactly how she had brewed up such a disaster. She'd been listening to her heart, blocking out reason. But it was her heart that now pushed her further out on the balcony, where she stuck her nose between the curled rococo iron to get a better glimpse of Julien Delaroche.

From her viewpoint Josephine could trace the ornamental brocade set in lighter peach tones against the deep rust fabric of her sister's skirts. Hyacinth lingered in the air. Helene used entirely too much perfume. And standing before her sister . . .

The chevalier's felt hat shaded his face, save his chin, which sported a blond pointed goatee. Stiff and squared as a statue his shoulders were, yet a graceful arm, clothed in slashed blue wool, waved through the air as he spoke words Josephine could not hear. She traced her eyes over his blue soldier's tunic, freshly washed, for there were no telltale signs of dirt. His boots were clean, lapping just below his knees and capped with wide white lace. Quite the dandy. He had not come here upon arriving in Paris. Obviously he'd wanted to neaten himself up . . . for some reason. Oh damn!

Helene stuffed her fists to her hips.

A warning twinge pulled Josephine upright. She scrambled inside her room, carefully closing the door behind her.

"Josephine!"

The call of a beast enraged. Helene knew. Julien had told her of the series of letters he had received from Helene's presumptive hand.

Josephine dashed to her writing desk and began to tear up the letter she had intended to send Julien. *We must write no more,* was torn into shreds and *I shall always love you,* reduced to irreparable shards. *I shall always treasure the gift of your heart,* obliterated to single torn letters and broken promises.

"What is the meaning of this!"

Before her sister could stuff the evidence into her bodice Helene whipped Josephine around by the arm and let out a scream at sight of the torn paper.

"So you really did write to him!"

The flames in her sister's eyes were more those of shock and outrage than a fiery hatred. One small reason to be thankful. And now was as good a time as any to start counting small blessings. Josephine let the paper shreds slip from her trembling hands. They flaked across her skirts like heavy December snow.

"What d-did he say?" she managed.

"He?" Helene hissed in a voice she saved only for when she was angered by Marie Claire's ignorance of the current hair fashions. "He knows nothing. Yet. Of course *I* know all. Or do I? He holds in his hands a stack of correspondence. From *me!* I cannot believe you would do such a thing!"

"But you said he knows nothing?" Josephine managed with a meek cringe.

"I told him I had to speak to you for a moment. The man stands down there unaware of what has been taking place. You really wrote to him? How could you?"

"I—"

"You forged my name!" Helene continued her diatribe, not backing away, nor allowing Josephine respite from her snapping forefinger. "I had thought you'd only press it beneath your pillow and conjure lascivious dreams. But he holds a handful of letters. How many times did you write him? And what did you say? Should I be aware of an engagement I've agreed to?"

"No, Helene, it was nothing like that!" She landed in the writing chair with a swishy pouf of skirts, for Helene leaned closer and closer. The clack of silver against glass made her dash around and catch the inkpot before it fell to the floor. Snatched from Josephine's fingers, Helene slammed the glass well on her desk, then snapped upright. She stood there, hands on hips, waiting for Josephine's confession.

"Forgive me. I know you trusted me when you gave me that first letter."

"Fool that I was!" Helene splayed her hands over her head in exasperation.

"I could not help myself. I—I love him, Helene." Slippery tears skidded down Josephine's cheek.

Helene bent before her, reaching a finely manicured hand to tilt Josephine's head up by the chin. "Love? You don't even know Julien Delaroche. You've yet to meet him."

"I know his heart!" Josephine bravely defended through sniffles.

"His heart? Again with your silly romantic prattle!"

"His words speak of a kind and gentle soul." Another sniffle. "It matters not that I've never met him, I know his inner self. His heart, Helene. I know his heart through his words."

"Words!" Helene's abrupt spin stirred the scattered paper shreds into a billowing tornado. "Words are worth no more than the paper they are written on. You foolish girl! Now tell me. Just what are we going to do about the man who waits below? The man whose heart you've toyed with, and deceived and betrayed in the worst possible ways?"

Deceived? Betrayed? She needn't use such harsh words! Josephine almost wished Helene would wind up and punch her instead of this verbal tirade. The pain would be much easier to bear than the knowledge that she had hurt this man so cruelly.

And all to satisfy her own desires.

"But I love him," she whispered. Tears overtook her in shaking waves. She could no longer reason, no longer judge the situation correctly. She had only acted from her heart. Was it such a crime to love one as eloquent as Julien Delaroche?

She would tell him her entire crime, and win his love. Yes! "I will confess."

"Damned right you will."

Helene gripped her arm. The stairs slipped under Josephine's skirts in three large steps. As they gained the front entrance, Josephine snapped her head to study the floor and the sudden appearance of dark suede boots. The tip of a leather-sheathed sword skirted near his left ankle. How could she possibly look at this man, knowing what she must confess?

"Chevalier Delaroche, I'd like you to meet my sister, Josephine."

"Ah, yes, the sweet younger of the two. I do recall your mentioning her on occasion. And Monsieur Bouchet also mentioned your beauty. Often. *Bon jour,* Mademoiselle Lalique."

Her eyes still fixed to the motion of his sword, Josephine did manage an abbreviated curtsey. And then she checked her behavior. As much as the situation dripped with a heavy syrup of tension, she must think of her future chances with this man.

She looked up to offer a *bon jour,* but lost her voice in the depth of his wide green eyes. Green, not blue as she had imagined. But that was perfectly well and fine. A smile sparkled within the mossy depths, matching the straight line of his lips that just barely curved up on the right side. A cavalier smile, as Helene had said, painted upon a regal, sharp-edged jaw. Now that she had imagined with perfect clarity.

"Chevalier," she sighed longingly.

Helene's sudden cough masked the sound of her foot connecting with Josephine's ankle. Much as it should have hurt, Josephine didn't cry out. Pain did not exist when swimming in the luxurious ocean of Julien Delaroche's eyes.

A muscle pulsed in his jaw. A triangle of dark blond beard skirted his lower lip. Lips that were plump and moist, parted slightly as if to speak. Or maybe kiss . . .

Looking over Josephine's shoulder, Julien cast her sister an expectant smirk. "So Helene, we may speak alone?"

"No, Chevalier. I believe you must hear what my sister has to say. She's a confession to make regarding your amours."

"My amours?" He darted a look to Josephine.

This conversation was superfluous. Josephine needed only to be wrapped in the arms of this strong soldier and have him speak his words of love to her. But another kick to her ankle jarred her out of her daydreams. "Huh?"

"Your confession," Helene hissed at her right ear. "Chevalier Delaroche waits. Go on, Josephine. You've dug this hole you stand in, 'tis high time you climbed out."

"I could use a bit of rope," she said on a weak breath. It was obvious Helene had no intention of helping. At least she stood behind her, to catch her should she faint.

"Is this necessary?" Julien cocked a hand on his hip and took to tapping the floor with his boot toe, each beat punctuated by a clink of spurs. "I don't see what it is your sister can possibly know about my—"

"I wrote the letters!" Josephine clapped both hands over her mouth. She tried to step back, but Helene would not budge.

"You wrote . . ." Julien struggled to voice the next words. "The . . . the letters?" He opened his mouth. No sound. His jaw clamped shut. Julien smoothed a palm across his forehead, a gesture that removed his felt hat and smoothed out his hair at the same time.

Ah, such style.

"*My* letters? The ones—" He looked to Helene. Again, the wordless open mouth.

"I had no idea she corresponded with you," Helene said. "And I'm more shocked to find she signed my name to them."

"But—" He took a step back, turned at the waist, and searched the wall where the iron candelabra waited for tapers to light the evening. Again, he pushed his hand back through his hair, setting the narrow red ribbon tied at the end of a braided lovelock across his shoulder. He blew out a breath and spun round. "I don't understand. Is this some sport you are having with me?"

Both sisters shook their heads.

"Why?"

"Forgive me, Chevalier, but I acted from my heart, blindly forgoing good sense." Resigned that all must be told if she were to save face in this situation, Josephine blurted out, "Helene gave me your letter after she decided she no longer wished to write you."

"What?"

"Bother," Helene muttered. "You needn't have mentioned that."

"But Helene," he started.

" 'Tis true." Josephine took a bit of sweet vengeance in that confession. But no more. "You see, she knew that I adored your letters. I must admit, I have come to care quite deeply for the man who has written such sweet missives. I could not bear the idea of you at war, waiting a kind word from Helene, knowing that you might never hear from her again. I simply had to write."

"And then you wrote back," she continued, now lost in her own excitement. "So revealing your letters are, Chevalier—"

"No!" Julien held up his hands. "I don't want to hear another word."

He turned and stomped to the door, stopped and pressed his hands to his hips. Josephine checked Helene for her reaction, but her sister merely shrugged as the two watched him silently ruminate on all he had learned. A heavy sigh. A fist pounded into the opposite palm.

He is taking this very well, Josephine thought. His sword still remains sheathed. No fists have been raised . . .

Yet.

At the sound of steel sliding across leather, Josephine froze. Julien worked his sword in and out of its sheath, up and down, as he thought. After a long moment he spun to face the two sisters.

"It was not you who wrote me?" he asked Helene, the disappointment obvious in his faltering voice.

"Twice, I must confess. The rest were from Josephine."

"And you do not . . . love me?"

"Hardly."

Her sister's quick retort cut the soldier's shoulders down like a battering ram to a castle wall. Josephine couldn't help wishing Helene had been kinder in her words. Though by all means, Julien mustn't be allowed to harbor lingering hope for a woman who had no interest in him.

"This has been a most vile and deceitful trick," he said, his clenched teeth giving his words a hiss.

"No, I did not mean—"

"Silence!" Julien cut off Josephine. "You have toyed with my affections, little girl!"

Little girl?

"If I were a cad, I'd whip you for your betrayals, but as it is I am a man of honor. I'll not expend another breath in this household. An *adieu* is far too good for the both of you."

He turned and marched out, slamming the door behind him.

"And good riddance to you!" Helene called after him.

So that was it? He'd just heard Josephine confess deep feelings for him, yet he'd not even taken a moment to consider her words before leaving in a flurry of hatred. Gone.

No. This isn't the way it was supposed to happen!

"No, Julien!" Material ripped as Josephine stepped forward. She turned and saw a scrap of her mint satin under Helen's shoe. "I must go after him! I must get through to him, make him understand that I truly do love him."

"You've done more than enough already." Helene gripped Josephine's arm and pulled her into a hug to keep her from struggling away. "I understand your feelings for this man. His words seduced a naive young girl, but—"

"No, Helene!" Josephine pulled from her sister's grasp and raced for the stairs. "You will never understand!"

# Chapter 7

"You're a fool if you believe you can win his heart."

Framed in the doorway of Josephine's bedchamber, Helene stood, arms crossed over her jeweled stays as she watched Marie Claire pull a scarlet skirt over Josephine's petticoats.

"But you won't stop me?" Josephine held her arms wide as the maid pinned the matching scarlet stomacher to her bodice. Black threads criss-crossed in a lattice screen over the blazing red, like a trellis set against a hot summer sunset.

"I've far too much to worry about myself."

True, Helene had three potential suitors dangling on her chain, with no decision of which to drop and which to continue stringing along. Within a two-hour period this very morning, all had come to call on her, one from Julien's regiment and two others from a mounted regiment that had marched before Julien's corps. Such decisions to be made. And all because Helene's fickleness had finally come to haunt her.

"So you wish to win over the chevalier." Helene sauntered in and twirled her forefinger around a loose curl that dangled near Josephine's ear. "Yet here you stand, dressing in your finest damask and spending an inordinate amount of time on your hair. And for who?''

How smug she sounded. Ah, but Josephine could not go back on a promise to a friend. Much as she had other matters to worry about at the moment.

"Matthieu and I are friends, Helene. It's been half a year. I just want to look nice for him.''

"Bouchet? La! Much as I disapprove of your pursuit of a man you do not even know—if you do wish to win him, shouldn't you be concentrating your efforts on Chevalier Delaroche? He is the man you've fallen head over heels for, isn't he?''

Yes, of course. And much as she'd thought to run after him following his hasty retreat yesterday, to look over the encounter in today's new light served her far better than a gut reaction to the chevalier's foul words. It wouldn't do to approach him so soon. A day to gather his wits and think on what he had learned would serve him as well as it had served Josephine.

Besides, she was always true to her word. Even though her *words* had only served to embroil her in trouble lately. She would not disappoint Matthieu.

"I promised Matthieu we'd spend the day together. And I do need to allow the chevalier time to think. Perhaps if the man considers what I said to him last night . . .''

"Oh. So you want him to stew in his anger?''

"Oh no, but—''

"That is exactly what he will do.'' Helene leaned over the vanity and checked the star mouche on her cheek, giving it a little wiggle with a twist of her lips. "It is Julien who should be seeing you in this fine dress. Unless . . .''

"Unless what?'' Josephine stretched out an imploring arm, ripping the pins from her right sleeve.

"Mademoiselle!''

"Sorry, Marie Claire. What are you implying, Helene?''

"Only that perhaps it is really Monsieur Bouchet you wish to attract with your temptress's skirts.'' She spun over and tickled her nails across Josephine's powdered bosom. "A whole day of looking upon this décolletage shall have the man swooning at your slippers."

"Oh!" Josephine spun around and bent before the pewter-framed looking glass. The scarlet damask *was* rather low in the front. When she leaned forward the rosy shadows of her nipples just peeked above the black lace of her chemise. "Oh dear. Perhaps I should wear the gray velvet? With the lace fichu?"

"Nonsense." Helene hugged her from behind and looked over Josephine's shoulder into the mirror. She tugged the renegade curl back behind Josephine's ear. "You look beautiful, sister. Friend or not, any man deserves such a sight after six months of war. Not so much rouge though." She smoothed her palm over Josephine's cheek. "You mustn't distract from your eyes. You can touch or ensnare a man with your eyes. You can even wound a man with a simple look."

Touch? Ensnare? Wound? Josephine raised her brows and widened her gaze at the mirror. Personally, she thought she looked rather forlorn with such an expression.

"Remember, any longer than a few seconds' glance and you've promised a man more than you may be willing to give. Don't waste your looks on Monsieur Bouchet, save them for the one you love. If Julien is the one you really love . . . ?"

"Of course he is." Josephine's reflection pouted at the two of them. "But I always look at Matthieu. He is my friend. You cannot expect me to spend an entire day with him without ever meeting his eyes."

She tried a wide-eyed stare, wrinkled her nose, then fluttered her lashes in an awkward attempt at what should have been seduction. More like call-the-surgeon-I-feel-vaporish.

"For no more than a few seconds," Helene reminded. "That is not so difficult." Mist of hyacinth lingered in Helene's wake as she strolled with romantic grace across the floor. Pausing dramatically near the window, she drawled, "Why, I've heard men boast of their winning a lady's approving eye. That lingering gaze, a promise of affection. Hoard that sought-after prize well, Josephine. You will know when the time comes whose eyes you wish to linger upon. Who you wish to grant your silent promise of yes.''

"Yes?" Josephine whispered. Her reflection batted one eye and cocked an awkward grimace.

Helene slipped away, along with Marie Claire, leaving Josephine staring at her image.

"Yes," she said to her wondering visage. And then she lowered her tone and dripped out more slowly, "Yes, Julien."

Sabatier's cream-filled puffs were heaven on earth. Josephine sucked the luscious filling from inside the light brown pastry, savoring the smooth vanilla flavor. Matthieu's puff lay untouched on the flattened paper cone lying near her skirts and abandoned mask. He sat sketching in his ever-present drawing folio with his back to one of the numerous stone vases that lined a small pond but five feet from her maple tree. The delicate sprinkle of water spitting from the fountain behind her seduced Josephine into a blissful reverie.

They always slipped over to the Fontaine de Médicis after visiting Sabatiers on the boulevard Saint Michel. The grotto boasted beautifully lush maple trees and hornbeam lining either side of the pond, their branches and leaves forming a canopy that allowed sunlight to filter through, creating a serene hideaway. Farther away, where stone tables and chairs held their ground, multiplumed and laced cavaliers waxed poetic, and women swooned behind velvet masks.

Plunging a finger deep inside her pastry, Josephine mined a delicious wodge of cream and licked it clean. Sugar had a most delightful effect on her mood. The city could fall around her and she would not care were someone to lay another Sabatier puff in her palm.

Matthieu held such a whimsical air since arriving at her house this morning. He seemed ready to sprout wings, just as the subjects of his drawings often did. He possessed unfathomable *joie de vivre*. Perhaps it was his positivity that saw him through the campaign. It had seen him through so much more, Josephine knew.

Crossed at the ankle, his scuffed leather boots—normally worn unrolled to the thigh to prevent soiling his breeches and hose from the Paris muck—now puddled beneath his knees, the wide leather cuffs great waves of soft rust-tinted hide. Plain tan breeches dipped into his bucket-topped boots. No lacy frills or colorful ribbons here. He'd discarded his heavy wool cape, beneath which he wore a pristine holland shirt. The lace sewn around the modest cuffs had been taken from his mother's wedding gown. He always wore the shirt when visiting her at the convent. He'd once mentioned how she liked to trail her fingers along the lace, lost in what could only be delicious memories of her departed husband, as they would sit in companionable silence together.

The wind pulled fine strands of his wavy walnut hair across his face, but he gave it no mind. Matthieu looked up from his sketching and matched Josephine's curious gaze.

*Do not spare a friend more than a few seconds' glance.* She snapped her eyes to the half-eaten pastry in her hand. Curse Helene for giving her such a lecture, today of all days. When she only wanted to relax with Matthieu and abandon her worries in the calm waters of the vase-bordered pond.

"Your pastry sits untouched, Matthieu. You've always loved Sabatier's treats. Set your drawing aside and join me. I feel overindulgent stuffing my face with sweet treats, and you there recording every gluttonous bite with charcoal and paper."

He gave a relaxed chuckle. "I am leaving the pastry out of this portrait. Much as I do enjoy that smudge of cream on your cheek . . ."

Josephine swiped her fist across her cheek. "Oh, Matthieu, how could you sit there without saying anything?"

"I just did!"

He thrust up his leather folio to avoid her vengeance, but

the last morsel of her pastry hit him on the jaw just as he pulled down his shield. He popped it in his mouth. "Not bad. But you sucked out all the cream!"

She stuck out her tongue at him.

He caught her mischievous flirt with a raise of his brow, then resumed his concentration, charcoal pencil dashing across paper. When captured by his muse, his star-sprinkled azure eyes glittered, his concentration fiercely sharp. Though he was never so lost that he could not hold a conversation.

She licked the last trace of cream from her finger, lingering on the tip as she eyed his bowed head. While they had resumed their friendship with relative ease after a six-month absence—both slipping into relaxed comfort around the other—he seemed guarded. Almost reluctant to discuss anything other than frivolities such as the food or the quiet warmth of the day.

"So do tell all, Matthieu. You've been gone since winter. I've not shared an intimate secret with you for ages, it seems. And for all I've heard of war, I should think you've a heavy heart."

He gave a little smile and a shrug of his shoulders.

She would not press him. It would come out sooner or later.

"War would not be of interest to you, ladybug. I slept in stinking quarters, sometimes on the ground. I ate a rat's rations, sometimes the rat, and I developed an aversion to the sound of enemy fire."

"You mean to say you could tell the difference between enemy fire and that of your comrades?"

He nodded. "Enemy shot whistles through the devil's teeth. You always expect it, yet never get used to the shrill of its bite. Friendly fire is often the scream that saves a man's hide."

Even the soft rustle of overhead leaves seemed to still as the two exchanged silent stares. She'd not expected him to be quite so blunt. Matthieu Bouchet had returned with some scars that were invisible to the naked eye.

"I am thankful to be alive and in one piece. I wish to forget everything beyond that. That is why I brought my supplies with me today. I can think of no better way to reenter the world and start anew, than to study the loveliest face in Paris for the entire afternoon.''

As much as she was not susceptible to flattery, Josephine felt a hot flush ride up her neck and suffuse her cheeks. She looked away, through the dozens of thin-trunked birch that dotted the grounds around the fountain. Matthieu had always been forthright with her, dropping comments about her appearance without so much as a second thought. But today, for some reason she could not explain, his words actually touched her. Deep inside. In a different sort of way. Almost . . . intimately.

Ah! She'd been thinking too much with her heart lately. That she would react to him—to any man—in such a way was no surprise.

She looked back to Matthieu. A smile always sparkled in his eyes. Even when he was sad it seemed that deliciously easy smile would not retreat. He had been watching her the entire time. ''What are you looking at?'' she could not help but snap.

''A beautiful woman. Made all the more lovely by the rosy blush that paints her cheeks.''

''Matthieu!'' She lifted his pastry, preparing to fling it at him.

''All right, all right, I surrender. Put the cream-filled mortar down, fair lady. You've never bristled so at my compliments.''

''You've never said them in such a manner before.''

''Meaning?''

''Well, you know. As if . . .'' As if he thought she was the pastry and he anticipated tasting her. ''It's just different from your usual manner. You're different today, Matthieu. Quieter. Perhaps a little secretive.''

''Perhaps tired,'' he quickly interjected.

Of course he would be. But there was more to it than his feeble excuse of exhaustion. What exactly, she could not determine. ''Are you almost finished? I want to see.''

''Not yet. Just a few more touches to your dress. I rather

like that bodice, how it allows the crimson underdress to peek through the black, like a temptress peeking through her webs.''

Temptress? ''Um ...'' Josephine stumbled to speak. Yet another comment that, this time, burned the blush down to her bosom. ''Er, it's um ... Richelieu cut-work.''

''The cardinal has taken to dictating fashion as well as the king, eh?'' He gave his signature chuckle, two short *ha-ha's!* ''Incredible. Or maybe it's your houseman? Has old Richelieu taken to dressmaking as well as his other sundry tasks?''

''Silly! Actually it is the cardinal I speak of. The style has been popular for quite some time now.''

''Well, as you may have noticed, I am not much for fashion. Though, I do have buttons on my breeches.'' He shifted to proudly display the row of tiny silver buttons that skated down the side of his leg.

''Yes, and now you need them on your cape, your sleeves, your coat, your hat.''

''Ha, ha! Next you'll be tying ribbons around my cuffs and in my hair.''

''A lovelock would look sweet in your hair, Matthieu.''

Without looking up, he said, ''I've no lady to tie such a ribbon in my hair.''

''Perhaps so, you being away so long. But I think it not long before there are dozens of colored ribbons streaming from your hair.''

''You flatter with the most ridiculous notions,'' he said in a more serious tone. ''There is but one I should wish to wear with pride.''

''From whom?'' Josephine leaned forward, eager to discover the name of Matthieu's beloved. He'd never mentioned such before. Perhaps that was his secret!

''No, don't move! I've just got the ruffles around your décolletage to finish.''

Changing the subject, eh? Well, she wasn't about to let him— Wait. Er ... Her ... décolletage? Dropping her gaze to the area he focused on, Josephine felt another healthy blush fall over her. She drew in a heavy breath, and then, suddenly, realized her actions lifted her breasts high in two enticing mounds. She blew out quickly.

"Keep still," he said, his gaze intent on her bosom as his charcoal stick moved of its own volition across the sketchpad propped against his bent knee.

Keep still? Easy for him to say. It wasn't as if *he* were sitting there, a portrait study for her. Why, she felt virtually naked knowing he scrutinized her so closely. Rather like a study for one of Madame Lamarck's drawings! Josephine knew of the two sketch pads hidden above Madame's desk between sample books of fabric. One contained female nudes, the other, men. She'd not yet been able to do more than peek in the book of men. Though her attempts had been, and would continue to be, diligent.

And what if Matthieu were to model for one of those? Then he would know the meaning of discomfort. Josephine could not help but giggle to imagine Matthieu stretched out on a fancy chaise, naked to the world as she sat sternly before him, sketching his most secret of male parts. Wouldn't that be an interesting afternoon between friends!

"What has got you in such a chuckle?" He laid the drawing vellum and folio on the thick padding of moss next to him and leaned his head back against the stone railing.

"Are you finished?"

"No, not until you tell me what has tickled your fancy so."

"I, well . . ." No, she could never reveal her lascivious thoughts. His male part rigid and proud, exposed only to her? Where had that thought even birthed? She'd never before thought of Matthieu in such a way. Why, it was utterly ridiculous even to assume he had such a . . . part. Of course he did. But he was . . . oh dear, he was just a friend!

Bother. Now she was beyond all hope of ever regaining her normal coloring.

"Tell," he coaxed and leaned on all fours to crawl over to her. "You've got a secret and I am the one to hear it. Come now, ladybug. What is it that puts the smile on your face and the pink in your cheeks?''

He toyed with the hem of her crimson skirts. She toed his hand away, but he would not stop. Instead he turned to lie on his side next to her. His fingers walked up her leg, intent on coaxing the information from her.

"Matthieu." She pressed his face away, but he snapped at her. Actually nipped her fingers with his teeth!

"Mmm," he drawled. "Vanilla cream. I do love the sweet taste of Josephine."

"Matthieu?"

"Huh? Oh. Er, um . . . yes. What were we talking about?" He caught his forehead in his palm with a smack, shook his wavy locks, then snapped back up with a new thought. "Oh yes, your blushes. Come now, Josephine, tell."

What had he just been thinking that he'd suddenly snapped out of? How odd for Matthieu to act that way. Sweet taste of Josephine? Though . . . she did rather like the sound of that. To imagine . . . a man actually *tasting* her. Drawing his tongue over her flesh . . .

"Josephine?"

"Hmm?" Now *she* was being caught unawares! "What was the question?"

"Your blushes?"

She clamped a hand over his, stopping his fingers mid-thigh. Had he intentions of going higher? What a rogue Matthieu had become since she'd last seen him! "I was just thinking of the drawings Madame Lamarck keeps above her desk. She is working on a series of fashion plates. Though she claims to have the most horrendous time with fabric and drapery, she is a marvel with the human figure."

"I enjoy drawing clothing." Matthieu absently trailed a finger down her skirts, which in reality trailed all down her leg, though Josephine couldn't be sure he realized what he was doing. Or did he? "The soft draping, the change of shadows and light in the same color of fabric as it travels over the body's curves.''

''Perhaps you and Madame Lamarck should work together,'' Josephine said, too intent on the tingling sensations Matthieu's actions worked on her leg to pay much attention. He couldn't realize what he was doing. Never had Matthieu's attentions broached such . . . intimacy.

''And what parts of the drawings doesn't she have difficulty with?''

''Oh, I'm not sure, I've never really had a chance to look closely. Certainly not the fabric,'' Josephine said on a lingering sigh.

''Really? So you've had a chance to peek?''

She straightened at his choked remark. What had she just said? A dozen wench's warts! ''Matthieu, no, I did not mean—''

''Of course you did.'' He rose on his elbows, hearty chuckles punctuating his words. ''You mean to tell me you spend your time browsing through pictures of nude people?''

''I just told you I hadn't the time—''

''But you are aware of such drawings?''

''Well, of course, I've stumbled upon them. Oh Matthieu!''

''Ha, ha! Josephine, you have changed much since I've last seen you.''

And he hadn't?

''They've been no more than glances, really,'' she managed. ''And *less* than a glance through the men's sketches.''

''Of course. Certainly *less* than a glance at the men. Did you see anything to your liking?''

''Matthieu!''

This time she really did want to throw something at him. But he grabbed the pastry before she had a chance.

''Oh!'' She gave him a gentle punch to his shoulder and he mocked a suffering wince and fell to his back, gripping his wound. ''Serves you justly.''

"Me?" he managed through a healthy bite of pastry. "You are the one who spends all her time looking at naked men."

He rolled away before she could deliver another punch. With a grand display he succeeded in shoving the remaining half of pastry into his mouth, and then granted her a child's triumphant grin.

It was good to have Matthieu back. Strange. But definitely good.

# Chapter 8

It was well past six bells before the twosome decided to call it a day. Matthieu had refused to show Josephine his sketch, claiming he wanted it to be a surprise. Actually he planned to take it home and add a color wash. Perhaps something might come of the simple sketch and he could show it to Madame Lamarck. Much as the idea of designing dresses and hats for court had no appeal whatsoever, if he was paid for such a sketch, that would be a different story.

Leaving the walls of Paris, they walked the Grand Rue de Saint Jacques to the Lalique home, their fingers loosely twined, their arms swinging opposite their steps. They were in no hurry. Time stopped when they were together. At least that is how Matthieu felt.

Josephine did not fully realize the depth of his admiration for her. She could not, for he daren't tell her. They'd been friends for so long, the idea of stepping across the line of friendship to—something more—was, well, nerve-wracking if not utterly frightening.

What he'd almost done earlier! When he'd nipped her hand

and then made that foolish declaration about her tasting sweet. Fool! But only as foolish as one struck by love can be. For aren't those in love mere fools?

She was oddly quiet now as the iron filigree gates that surrounded her home came into view. "Tell me your thoughts," he prompted, wanting to listen to her sweet words instead of his own inner voice.

She pulled her hand from his and crossed her arms over her chest. So elegant and luscious she looked in the deep red damask. Had she dressed for him today? The wide neckline curved just slightly off her shoulders, revealing more of her than he'd ever seen. Every rise of her bosom matched his tromping heartbeats. And when she took a deep breath her breasts rose and fell and exposed the delicious color of her—

"I wish to tell you something," she started on a nervous beat. "But I don't know how. Oh, Matthieu, you know me so well. I've a secret. And I so wish to share it, but I don't know how or where to start."

They stopped near an oak tree and she leaned against the trunk. Matthieu sensed something heavy weighed upon her; she just needed to know she could trust him enough to reveal it. They had been apart too long if she could not just blurt out her thoughts as she usually did.

"Ladybug?" He touched her chin and brought her dancing gaze up to meet his. Odd, how she'd been avoiding his eyes all day. As if by looking directly at him she might go up in smoke! Perhaps they needed more than a day to revive their bond of friendship. To be sure, it wasn't easy after so long a time, to act as if no more than a day had passed. "You know you can tell me anything. I will keep your confidence."

"I know that, Matthieu. You are a trustworthy man." She squeezed his hand and slipped both of hers into his. The texture of her fingers felt like newborn skin compared to his own rough palm. Then she immediately pulled away and walked a few paces into the center of the road.

If he was so trustworthy, than why did she balk? What had

happened to his precious ladybug in the six months he'd been away? He could kick himself for not writing her. Though he hadn't the time or energy when at battle, heaven knows he did do some writing. But not a day had passed that he hadn't thought of her sweet smile. She had been his inspiration for . . . certain tasks he no longer wished to associate himself with.

The click of carriage wheels echoed a street away. Josephine turned to see the gilded six-horse swipe quickly across the end of the street. Matthieu caught the thick column of hair that fell from her upsweep as she turned. He hadn't touched such softness in ages. Though he'd imagined this very moment over and over . . . when finally he touched her intimately.

"I'm in love, Matthieu," she blurted out.

He faltered, slipping his hand down her neck and resting it on her shoulder. In love? A smile tickled the corner of his mouth. How he had wanted to hear such words from her. No wonder it was difficult for her to speak to him. She must have been fretting over how to say such a thing all day. "That's wonderful, Josephine—"

"No, it's perfectly horrible!"

She stepped away and buried her face in her hands, her back to him.

"Horrible? Oh no, Josephine. This is an exquisite announcement."

"You think so?" She looked up from her hands. Another jerk of her head and the entire nest of hair would tumble from the jeweled clip and over her shoulders. Or a perfectly placed touch from him.

But Matthieu stayed himself. This moment was too perfect to go changing the stage directions on a whim. She returned to his arms and gifted him with a generous hug. Finally it was reality, to stand in Josephine Lalique's sun-and vanilla cream-scented arms and know her warmth and kindness in the most physical sense.

But he mustn't seem too eager.

"You must tell me who it is who has stolen your heart, ladybug."

She seemed ready to burst from joy as she pulled back from him and spun in a grand circle. "I love the Chevalier Julien Delaroche!" she announced to the world. An invisible musketball pierced Matthieu's heart.

Julien?

Cold blood of betrayal flowed down to his gut. An army of scrambling frogs clogged in his throat.

Delaroche?

He tried to swallow, to speak, but he felt sure a bullet-scarred bullfrog would escape.

"But my heart beats in vain!" Josephine continued, totally unaware of Matthieu's sudden state as she paced back and forth before him, dusting her vivid skirts over the raised oak roots. "I am in love with a man who abhors me. Can you believe it? He hates me! He loves Helene, but she loves the entire 26th regiment, and the 27th as well. While I love him. But he thinks me a despicable wench. Now do you see? I've such a horrible predicament. I don't wish to burden you with my troubles, but you insisted."

"Yes . . . I suppose I . . . uh . . . did." He turned away so she would not see his struggle to remain stone-faced.

Julien Delaroche? Josephine was in love with Julien Delaroche? Impossible. Hadn't Helene written all those letters? How had the sisters . . . How had Josephine become enamored of a man she had never met? This was too strange. Too horrible, as Josephine had just said.

"Julien, er . . . Delaroche never once mentioned you," he managed. A fierce kick sent a spray of dirt-dusted pebbles scattering across a stretch of trimmed grass.

"What?" Josephine raced to him and gripped him by the shirtfront. Her eyes darted to his, insistent on answers. "But of course, you mentioned yesterday he took you under his wing. Why did I not realize before . . . Oh, Matthieu, how well do you know him?"

"Well enough." He started to walk towards the gates to her home, but Josephine wouldn't budge. She stood in front of him, unmoving. He could either push her out of the way or face her questions with as much pride and dignity as he could muster. Much as he preferred pushing this whole conversation over a cliff, he could not treat a woman so.

"Well?" she insisted with a hopeful tone.

"You might say we looked after one another. But Josephine, help me understand this sudden amour, when I know personally that Delaroche spent the entire time answering love letters from your sister!"

"I know." Great tendrils of soft angel hair fell from over her ear and swept across her neck when she bowed her head. How Matthieu wanted to touch her. To just lose himself in the softness of her being.

But even more, he wanted to get to the bottom of this incredible story.

"Of course you know. Helene must have shared her correspondence with you." He began to pace before her, speaking his thoughts as they entered his mind like a ricocheting bullet. "She must have read them all to you. That can be the only way. You and Julien? No, no. But you just said as much. So you fell in love with the letters or the man?"

"The man, oh definitely the man," she swooned, in a manner he would much rather not see directed at Julien Delaroche.

"I don't understand." Matthieu pressed a finger to his aching brow. "I don't think I want to."

"That is the whole horrible part of this," she said, once again blocking him from walking on and just ending this entire day for good. "Julien thought he was writing to Helene, but all the time it was I who returned his missives."

"You?"

She lowered her head with a nod. "I dared not sign my own name, and I did not want Helene to abandon Julien without word as she had planned. I just couldn't allow such a sweet,

kind, and caring man to suffer that sort of treatment. And once
I wrote, I found I could not resist continuing.''

Sweet? Kind? Caring?

Julien Delaroche?

When the devil is blind!

So it had been Josephine returning the letters the whole time?
*Mon Dieu,* what this meant!

What *did* it mean exactly?

And more importantly, what must he do about it? What
would the chevalier do when he discovered he'd not been
corresponding with Helene? Josephine actually *loved* Julien
Delaroche? The very same man who trampled said love letters beneath his boots as quickly as he learned their contents?
Matthieu was still not convinced that Julien hadn't pursued
Helene only to secure a warm bed on his return. Thinking of
which . . .

"Did the chevalier call on Helene last eve?"

"Horrors!" Josephine threw a hand over her forehead, a
dramatic display most likely learned from Helene.

"I assume that to be an affirmative?"

"He did come," she said as Matthieu gripped her around
the waist and escorted her up the walk to her house. "But
Helene forced me to reveal my deceptions. Right then, without
so much as a second to think. He hates me, Matthieu. The man
I adore hates me! I am simply a wretch without him. Oh!"

How could she have become so enamored of the chevalier
through a simple correspondence?

"Forgive me." She adjusted her skirts, unaware that the
black lace that bordered her neckline was bent forward to reveal
a slip of rosy breast.

Matthieu bit his lip.

"I should be going in," she said. "Richelieu will come
scouting for me if I do not make an appearance for supper."

"Of course."

She kissed his brow, much too quickly to even allow him to
feel the heat of her mouth. "Thank you for listening, Matthieu.

You've always been such a dear friend to me.'' She begged his pardon and promised they would have him over for a meal very soon, but right now she must go lie down.

*Such a dear friend.*

As the door closed in his face, Matthieu swallowed the defiant shout that struggled for release. Friend? Such a cold word suddenly. A word they'd both embraced over the years. But now, it just wouldn't do.

And in review . . .

The woman Julien Delaroche lusts for does not return the feeling.

The man Josephine adores hates her.

And the woman Matthieu loves thinks him a dear friend.

What to do? Should he storm the door this very moment, sweep her into his arms and tell her the truth?

Sounded easy enough. Romantic and chivalrous. All the things that women pined for.

*How she had pined over the chevalier. She'd nearly swooned at the thought of him despising her.*

''*Mon dieu,* but Josephine really does love that bastard Delaroche.'' Matthieu turned from the house and walked towards the street, not aware his feet were actually moving, so tormented were his thoughts. ''What would this do to her? If I revealed . . .''

He paused at the iron gates and turned back to the house. Inside Cook most likely had a tasty meal on the table, and Richelieu was sneaking an extra portion from the pot before the meal was served to the sisters. Comfortable and happy, the Lalique girls. Josephine had never known a bleak day in her life. Matthieu had seen to it. He would walk the world for her happiness, and if he died trying, at least he would know he had given his all.

He must continue to do whatever was necessary to ensure Josephine's happiness.

But . . . could he stand back and allow her to love Julien Delaroche?

# Chapter 9

With a grunt and a wince Julien tossed the mildewed feather pillow he had slapped over his head across the room. His skull ached. Something had crawled inside his mouth last night . . . and died. Even the hairs on his chin seemed to pierce through his jaw like tiny devil's pitchforks. Yet for all the pain, his ears seemed to have gained sensitivity. He could hear everything. Amplified a thousandfold. And in a head that still spun from his decadent dance with spirits last eve, that did not bode well.

"I've got to get out of here. Away!" he said with a crack to his dry voice. He stumbled to the window and pushed open the panes. "At least were I in the trenches I'd not wake to this terrible aching head. Battle mortars whizzing through the air are like music in comparison. It has been far too long since I have imbibed—oh, ouch—and now I must suffer."

Not for long. He jammed his feet into his boots and pulled them high to his thighs, not bothering that the fine venetian lace was now smudged from his crawl on the ground last night. For what choice had he but to drown out Helene's mocking declaration of indifference with ale?

Hooking sword belt and cape in one arm, he descended to the streets. A ragamuffin dashed across his path causing Delaroche to stumble back against the door to the inn. The tinny clang of copper pots jangling upon their ropes punched at his tormented brain as a hawker wheeled his heavily laden cart down the street. Indescribable street muck flew up from the center gutter as horses and people and carts all made way. And everywhere the stench of rotting fish.

Cast the entire mess into the Seine!

Julien had almost forgotten the serenity offered by a long campaign march, or long hours spent camped in a meadow or forest while they waited the enemy's next move. Who would have thought he'd once thrived on the hustle and grime of the city, couldn't imagine a quiet country estate or worse yet, a family, serene and idyllic, on one of those country estates.

But today . . .

"Much as I could never admit it before, today I desire the peace of the country. The solace of just one night's rest. Oh, this horrible ache!"

Ah, but the only country escape he knew of belonged to Helene Lalique. Not a woman topping his list this day. For where the fickle Helene Lalique resided, he would most assuredly run into the conniving deceitful sister.

*She didn't want to correspond with you.*

Helene had actually ceased writing him. Him!

And her sister, Josephine, cared for him? Incomprehensible! Those damned letters! What had it been about those letters that had wrangled him the wrong woman?

He would love only one woman, and that woman couldn't care whether he breathed his last breath or moved an ocean away. Spoiled, capricious Helene Lalique. How could he have been so blind as to not see what was happening?

How had Josephine come to feel so amorously towards him? From nothing but the written word? And why hadn't Matthieu noticed? He had read every post Julien had received. Bouchet knew both Helene and Josephine. Surely if anyone would have noticed the change in handwriting . . .

Just what was that naive musket-shining pup up to? He had to have known about the switch. Did Bouchet have his own plans for revenge? As far as Julien knew, Matthieu wasn't the wiser to his true identity. A chevalier? Ha! Though the title had served him well thus far.

And now . . . hmm . . .

Julien paused in the center of the street, oblivious to the commotion on all sides as a most devious thought popped into his head. Perhaps he could put to use this strange liaison with the younger Lalique sister. Bouchet cared for her. Yet, she had offered her heart on paper to him. *Him.*

Smoothing a finger along his jaw, Julien allowed the evil notion to trace a smile onto his face. ''Yes, this could prove most amusing.''


Vermilion. The perfect color. As if plucked from her lips and ground to an emulsion worthy of a painter's brush. Exquisite.

Matthieu swirled his paint-heavy brush through a pan of water he'd carried up from the city well. A few final strokes across the page, and the dress he'd sketched this afternoon would be complete. He'd only done washes a few times, but was quite pleased with his work today. The paint was lucid enough to allow the charcoal lines to show, but held enough color to give the flat picture depth, and yes, even life.

Just a dash of brown in the circles of her eyes and a bit of cerulean on the crown of the mushroom. As an afterthought he'd sketched a princely frog offering the fair Josephine a bejeweled ladybug on a mushroom tray. Dangling from one of Josephine's fingers was a heart bound in twine. His heart.

Matthieu slapped his brush down on the desk.

She loved Julien Delaroche. Impossible to fathom, knowing Josephine's desires had never run toward the gallant. Or maybe he had just never noticed. Matthieu had always thought her more of a cerebral woman. Soldiers did not interest her. Why, the one time Matthieu had playfully challenged her to a duel, she had won! (Of course, he *had* been the one to teach her fencing.) She didn't need a man to boast and show off in order to win her; she could protect herself very well. Brawn did not impress her.

Or so he'd thought.

"Was I so wrong?"

A skitter of red paint dashed the inside of the glass as Matthieu dropped his brush inside. He slammed his fists across his chest, finding his mood had soured.

They were just too damned close. Matthieu could not pin down the day his feelings had snuck up on him.

Might it have been just last year? The summer of Helene's discontent. She'd cleaned out her armoire, tossing dresses and frivolous shoes and gloves and petticoats Josephine's way. How bored she had become with everything! All the while, Matthieu and Josephine had watched with shared laughter. That summer, Matthieu visited the Laliques daily. He'd sketched the pond and Josephine sitting with a frog on her shoulder. Maybe it was that kiss she'd pressed to the reptile's warty visage that had won Matthieu over, heart and soul and spirit.

It could have been much earlier than that. It might have been the year he'd signed on as a cadet in the guards and had proudly marched over to the Laliques' to display his newly issued musket. Helene had giggled behind a cupped palm. Josephine had sighed and hugged him proudly. "I suppose you'll become cocky now," she'd said. "Testing your steel against all who even dare look at you crooked. A soldier. Ha!"

But her teasing jests had stopped there. Later that afternoon she'd coaxed him out behind the Professor's shed and begged him to show her how to shoot . . .

"Ram this? Down there?" She stood in bare pink cotton holding the long steel ramrod as delicately as one would a violin bow and peered down the shaft of his long musket.

"Yes. You must ram a wad in first, than the bullet, than more wadding. Here, I'll do it for you."

"No!"

She'd done a fair job of it and could even hold the heavy musket long enough to fire. Golden sparks showered over her arms, and she jumped with a triumphant hoot. "I did it!"

"Most skillful," Matthieu cheered and clapped twice. "What were you aiming for?"

"Aiming?" She gave a shrug of her shoulders, a sweet toss of her messily pinned locks. "Nothing."

"Well then, you were right on. Ha, ha!"

She let the musket fall and turned to wrap her arms about his shoulders. The sudden intensity of her gaze clued Matthieu that the lightness of the moment had just taken a heavy turn. He couldn't gauge her intentions, couldn't even begin—

She kissed him! Long and deep and with the surprising skill of one who has kissed many times before. Slipping his hands around her narrow waist, Matthieu pulled Josephine close to his body. Her eyes were closed. His would not close.

She was actually kissing him. *Him!*

Wait.

"Oh hell, that's not the way it was!" Matthieu thudded his palm against his forehead, jarring his memories out of their strange twist. That particular kiss had never occurred. Though he had wished it at the time, the actual kiss had merely been a simple peck on the cheek.

Hell, it wasn't that summer he had realized his feelings went beyond friendship for Josephine. It had been a few summers before that. Yes. His sixteenth, her fifteenth. The summer her girlish pudge had transformed into womanly curves. The summer her voice had developed a hush when she spoke quietly to him of things she admired, things she desired, things she dreamed about. The summer his life had taken a dreadful turn. A summer Josephine had fittingly titled, That Dreaded Summer. For beyond all the happiness and joy that had seemed to abound in their lives that one particular summer, an event of profound impact had slashed over it all and forever changed the both of them.

Ah, but Matthieu did not want to ruminate on that particular time right now. He'd since learned to ignore the hauntings of his past, how to sort out the good memories from the bad by raising the good ones high and taking the bad ones and disposing of them in the method he wished to dispose of all evil things. Wouldn't it be wonderful if the world truly were flat as had once been thought; for then Matthieu could escort all the evil people to the edge and push them over.

"No!" he corrected his thoughts with a curt bark. "Don't waste your time on the things you cannot change."

Instead? Instead he must focus on the hope that perhaps there was one thing he could change.

She'd gone about her pursuit of love in the wrong manner. Well, that was putting things lightly. She'd fired an all-out attack on Julien Delaroche's heart. Her words had been masked for fear of losing the one thing she had never had before.

And now that the mask had been ripped away, Julien hated her.

Josephine couldn't give up without a fight. She was not about to back down when so much was at stake. This man had stolen her heart! He owned a piece of her soul. Did he not realize that?

She had to make it known. Perhaps if Julien realized the impact of his words upon her heart, then he could learn to love her. She was not so very different from Helene, his original object of love. Well, a little different. In dress and manners and style and grace and voice, and . . . Oh, damn it all!

So she was quite different from Helene. But so much better for her differences, Josephine thought. And Julien would come to learn that.

But how to go about righting her wrongs? She needed influence. Some way in which to acquaint him with her charms

without her actually being present. Someone ... must speak
to him. Encourage his interest in her.

"But of course!"

Why did she not think of this before? There was a man who
had gained Julien's trust and respect. A man who proclaimed
himself friend and confidant to the very man she desired.

# Chapter 10

Lamarck's Dress Emporium was closed. A sign on the door stated Madame Lamarck would be absent for the remainder of the week while she served her clients at Fountenay.

Disappointed, Matthieu marched down the long west gallery of the Palais de Justice and out into the bright sun. Josephine hadn't mentioned as much. But why would she? She no longer had reason to confide in him. She could now tell Julien Delaroche everything. He was the man she loved.

Not that her feelings were returned.

But Josephine had just the sort of ambition that would see Julien's head and heart turned. The chevalier—fickle as he was—would be madly in love in no time. She had a sort of gift when it came to charming herself into people's lives. How could one not adore her?

"Matthieu!"

An artist's dream in billowing lavender silk and long dark ringlets, Josephine came daintily rushing towards him, her skirts lifted to reveal her slippers and clocked hose. He'd been privy to the sight of those slender limbs many a time sitting beneath a slash of afternoon shade or scampering across the pond. Josephine was impervious to embarrassment around him. He liked that she felt so comfortable in his presence.

But he wished he might make her blush more often. As she had yesterday. His attentions had definitely touched her in a way she'd never felt before. He needed that response more often. Actually, the need was more like a craving. As deep and relentless as the ever-present lust that churned in his loins.

Matthieu's arms thrust out of their own volition and caught the falling arms and limbs of Mademoiselle Lalique as she tripped over what could have only been her own two feet. She plunged into his embrace, her cheek kissing his and her breasts hugging his chest.

"Ha ha! My flutter-winged ladybugs, you were meant to soar through the skies, not to be grounded."

"You've become conditioned to catch me before I even know myself I'm to fall."

She blew a stray ringlet from her face. She did not push out of his embrace, which Matthieu didn't mind at all. Until a flash of Julien Delaroche's vainglorious visage invaded his thoughts.

"You're in quite a hurry. And where is Richelieu?"

"I sent him home. The day is too beautiful to travel in a cramped and stuffy carriage. Besides, he couldn't argue when I told him I planned to see you."

He offered her a hand as she sat on a stone bench which bordered the formal gardens behind them. She fussed with the torn hem of her skirts for a moment, then with a dismissive wave of her hand left the silk. "I need to speak to you, Matthieu. It is urgent. And it is of the utmost importance."

"Really." He sat next to her, her skirts cushioning his leg. "Then I am listening. Your needs and desires are paramount to me. What is it that has got you breathless and wide-eyed?"

She turned and spread her fingers through his right hand, pulling them up to her breast where she held him breathlessly captive. He could feel the timorous beat of her heart. Her breasts rose and fell with the hurry she'd taken in getting here. An ache of longing fired in his chest.

Did she not see? Had she become so accustomed to their casual relationship that she could never even think he'd pine for her? Desire her? Want her?

Matthieu made to pull away, but she held firm.

She was making this as difficult as possible; and yet she was completely unaware of his inner torture.

"Listen, please," she said. "I've a favor to ask of you. Believe me, I would never dream to ask such a thing if it did not mean more than the world to me. You are the only one I can turn to. I need your help."

She needed him. Oh yes!

"I cannot imagine what might trouble such a carefree, sweet soul as you." Oh, he could. But did he have to actually think of that bastard?

"I've told you already. I am in love."

Matthieu dragged his gaze along the ground. A leathery green oak leaf fluttered at his boot heel, trapped by the scuffed black leather. Inside, the ache began to burn, painfully.

"And Julien does not return my love," she continued.

Every mention of that man's name rammed the crucifying nail deeper into Matthieu's heart. But the conviction with which Josephine spoke would not allow him to voice his feelings. Not yet. She truly believed in the love she held for this man. It would not be right for him to reveal his own desires and wound her even more. For wouldn't she take that as an act of jealousy? She thought him a *dear friend*.

Gad, how he had come to hate those words!

"What is it you wish of me?"

"Oh Matthieu." She smoothed both her fine hands over his cheeks, bracketing his face into a frame that displayed only her pleading eyes and quivering lips to his view. Just a kiss? A sweet little peck? "You must speak to him for me. You must tell him of me."

"No." He pushed out of her greedy hold and stood.

"Please." He hadn't noticed the simple black ribbon and gold cross dangling from her neck. So pure and so unaware of the dangers she had stepped into. Or perhaps it was only his own misgivings against Delaroche that made him want to believe Josephine might be in danger. She could be perfectly safe for all he knew. He prayed.

"I am mad for his attentions. Surely if the man were to learn about me—if someone who knew me could speak to him. Explain that my actions were purely out of love—"

He wanted to cover his ears with his hands, to run from these horrifying confessions that dripped from the mouth of the woman he adored.

"I love him," came her pleas. "I wish only that he can forgive my deception—"

"I do not believe any word from me can change that man's mind. No amount of conniving and convincing can induce a man to fall in love. And can you really say you want him on such terms?"

On her feet and before him, Josephine grasped his arms in an intimate embrace he'd much rather avoid. Always she smelled of a summer garden overgrown with wild roses and gardenia. The scent lingered on his tongue like a sweet teasingly touched to the tip, then hastily snatched away.

"Of course I do not want you to connive," she said. "Do you not think that if the man gets to know me he might begin to . . . well . . . like me?"

Like? What man would not like a woman such as she? Fine and soft and ethereal in her actions. Even her frequent stumbles were perfectly divine, especially when she landed in his arms. Of course Julien would come to like her after he had forgotten his shallow affections for Helene and looked past the silly correspondence with—

*No. It had not been silly. Never.*

"I should think it virtually impossible for any man not to like you, Josephine." He hated himself for speaking the words. But they were so true. Matthieu held his jaw firm and continued,

"Besides being most pleasing to behold, you are smart and witty and infinitely charming."

"So you believe Chevalier Delaroche might have a change of heart?"

"I did not say that. I did not say either that I would speak to him."

He turned and paced a few feet away. A gentleman's rapier swung at his side; he had forgone the heavy battle sword for this morning's potential business meeting. Standing tall he crossed his arms over his chest and closed his eyes. *No, do not ask such a thing of me. I cannot.*

"You are right," she said from behind him. "It was cruel of me to ask you to speak to the chevalier. This is a problem I have created. Only I can see it solved. Can you forgive my indiscretion, Matthieu?"

The delicate fall of her hand to his shoulder was like a crisp new snowflake to a garden stone. Softness upon cold hard nothing. How unfeeling he was! In all the years he had known her, Matthieu had never denied Josephine anything she had asked. Never had he refused to run an errand, to help her with the sundry experiments her father was always conducting, to escort her to and from the Palais du Justice on a cold winter's day when Richelieu refused to leave the warmth of his chambers. To guard and protect her secrets, and to comfort her when Helene, in her coldness and vanity, would overlook her younger sister's feelings.

Josephine was his sweet ladybug, sitting upon his palm, ever confident of safety and protection in his shadow.

To deny her anything would be like crushing her delicate wings.

"I must return home," she said, her hand slipping from his shoulder. "Cook wishes you to come for supper. She's preparing pheasant and stuffed squash."

"With the dark sugar and raisins?" he muttered as she slowly turned and began to walk.

"Of course," she said on a defeated sigh. "I shall see you this evening?"

"Of course," he said to himself as she walked on, not even waiting for his reply.


Women most definitely had the upper hand when it came to battle maneuvers. Their wide skirts granted them the power to command your attention, like it or not. And so Matthieu was quite helpless to flee when Helene's swishy patina skirts trapped him in a corner between Cook's experimental rose grafts and a lithe marble sculpture of a nameless nymph before he could step outside to the verandah.

"Helene." He had the distinct feeling he was being held down by enemy colors, her darting eyes gauging which of his organs to stab first with her weapon. "Tasty meal. Cook always outdoes herself."

"I could not help notice your dismay over the pheasant this evening, Matthieu," she said in a floaty yet narrow voice. Her gaze held him like a street cat eyed a refuse-fattened rat.

"My—my dismay? The pheasant was excellent."

"My sister's presence just across the table seemed to discomfit you. You've never been so fretful at table before. I could see it in your lingering gazes, your guarded smiles. You care for my sister, don't you, Matthieu?"

His name dripped from her lips like a long forgotten sweet, melted upon a hot stone. Sticky and distasteful. "Of course not."

"Oh, that's all my eye!"

Yes, yes, and his eye, too.

"You know that I do, Helene. We have been friends since childhood."

She pressed closer, which succeeded in cementing his legs to the wall with an overabundance of silk and white fluffy stuff. What a success his regiment would see to send Helene across enemy lines and set her loose with her all-knowing gaze and deadly skirts.

"You know what I mean, Matthieu. You love my sister, I know that you do."

Words refused to register on his tongue. Love? How could she even say—Well . . . no! He just . . . cared for Josephine beyond the normal means. Yes, that was it. As a sister. A sister whom he often thought of touching and kissing and . . .

"As I suspected," Helene said with a triumphant smile. "Why do you not tell Josephine?"

"What ever you deem to suspect is far from the truth," he managed to say in a soft, defeated voice. "Besides, it matters not what I think of your sister. She loves another."

Damn, it hurt to say such words!

"Oh, Matthieu. Sweet, naive Matthieu." The touch of Helene's finger to his chin was the most surprising thing. She'd always been one to avoid him, treat him as if he were a gauche leper. "You wear your heart on your sleeve. All the world knows you are enamored of my sister."

Well . . .

"You must confess your feelings to Josephine. This is madness, her foolish obsession with Julien Delaroche. The stupid blind fool. She would not know love if it jumped out of the pond and landed in her lap."

"I beg to differ." He straightened, but Helene only leaned closer. How quickly he forgot he was under enemy gun. "She was quite passionate in her letters—"

"You read the letters she sent to Julien?"

"Of course—Oh." Damn. Should he have revealed that information? "Well, of course Julien shared them with the entire regiment. It is a man's unspoken duty to do so in order to keep morale high."

"I see." She stepped back a pace. Still her skirts barred his escape. Cunning, she was. Reading his thoughts with her piercing eyes. Gauging his possible move, and adjusting her hips to swish her skirts into the best possible barrier. "But as I told Josephine, words are nothing more than lines shaped into readable form. They mean nothing. They hold no emotion.''

"Oh, but they do, Mademoiselle. I must beg a differing opinion there. A man can bare his soul with pen and ink. Words capture the heart and expose the soul's dreams, its very desires. Much as a drawing or a . . . an—an invention! Like your father's works. His inventions are created from the soul. I believe Josephine truly does love—''

"You speak as a man who knows intimately the power of such words.''

Matthieu swallowed. He'd talked himself into an inescapable corner. Judging from the delicately raised brow and slightly open lips, Helene suspected far more than his probable love for her sister. And she was closing in on him again.

"I was privy to all the letters from Josephine to Chevalier Delaroche,'' he admitted. "Though we all believed them to have come from your hand.''

"That cocky chevalier holds no interest for me.''

"Then you should not worry about your sister's interest in him.'' Fool to defend that man so!

"Do you not believe him a rake? Chevalier Delaroche could never return the love my sister proclaims. He is simply not the sort. While I may have only met him on the two occasions, it was more than enough for me to learn that Julien is not an *homme de coeur*. He is a rogue, a cavalier, by no means the proper match for our Josephine.''

"Perhaps Josephine needs to discover that for herself.''

As he spoke the words, Matthieu was torn between the evil desire to let Josephine learn what a lout Julien could be, and the right thing to do, which was to protect her from ever being hurt, by agreeing with Helene and stopping Josephine's silly affections.

But her heart was set. She had but one course. To pursue the man she loved. And neither he nor Helene could stand in her way. Perhaps . . . they mustn't. For maybe Josephine saw beyond what the two of them knew and would win a prize of kindness and charity in one Julien Delaroche.

"Please give my request some consideration, Monsieur Bouchet. If you care a morsel for my sister, you will not allow her to continue this fruitless venture."

"I shall." He breathed a heavy sigh as Helene stepped back, her storm of skirts receding to allow him escape. "If you will swear to keep this conversation behind lock and key?"

Delicate laughter segued to a biting twist. "Why must you torture yourself so?"

"To reveal my feelings to your sister would be the cruelest act of all. I do not wish to torment Josephine any more than she already is. I would truly do anything to ensure her happiness. And if happiness means allowing her to pursue the chevalier, then I must abide by her wishes. Promise you'll not tell?"

Helene let out a heavy sigh, along with a dramatic tilt of her perfectly coifed head. "I will not. But I do not wish my sister hurt by Chevalier Delaroche. Certainly she might be allowed this . . . ridiculous infatuation. But if he should develop feelings for her . . ."

"He will treat her well," Matthieu forced out. For he had come to reason that if he could not be the man in her life, than he must ensure Josephine not be hurt.

"Here she comes. Josephine, I've occupied your dashing young soldier for more time than is proper." Helene bussed Matthieu's cheek with a chaste kiss. "I leave him to you now. She is all yours, Matthieu. Handle her with the utmost care."

Josephine quirked a brow at her sister's dramatic exit.

His heart racing and his throat threatening to swell and close, Matthieu gripped Josephine's hand and spoke before he could lose the courage to speak at all. "I'll do it," he said. "I shall speak to Chevalier Delaroche for you."

Her smile, as splendid as the morning sun, offered little salve for Matthieu's breaking heart. And it was her hug that crushed the remains to a pile of bloody ash.

# Chapter 11

"Bouchet! Just the man I've been searching for."

Matthieu looked up from his sketch of the rope swinging from the gallows at the Place de Grieve to find Delaroche lumbering across the square towards him. What did Josephine see in this oversized oxen, whose idea of grace was expressed in the cut of his sword through his enemy's throat?

"Searching, eh? And what is it about me that inspires such diligence?"

"I've come to hear you confess your deception."

The man snapped his arm straight. Matthieu felt a point of steel pricking his neck. He touched the edge of the blade and carefully steered it away. Delaroche allowed it, but stood ready.

"Deception?" Resolutely, Matthieu set his drawing aside and pushed his hands back through his hair. The day was hot; perspiration ran down his scalp. "I'm not sure what you are speaking about. Perhaps if you enlightened me?"

"I shall lighten your body of those damned traitorous hands if you do not explain to me why you didn't reveal the Lalique sisters' switch. You must have known that the younger had taken on the task of writing those letters—''

"I did not. I swear to you, chevalier. Believe me, I wish I had." How he wished he had noticed! For then things would have been different. Very different.

"You cannot tell me the two sisters write with the identical style."

"I can't say I've seen an example of Helene's writing, nor have I ever paid much attention to Josephine's letters," Matthieu said, but he thought regretfully of that one time he'd been surprised at "Helene's" reference to entomology.

"I swear to you I would have said something had I guessed. It was certainly a misguided attempt to your affections."

"Misguided? Ha! The girl knew exactly what she was doing. Stabbing me with a poison pen!"

"Josephine claims she loves you." It hurt to say the words, and so he could give them no more power than a lackluster tone.

Delaroche bristled and swiped his swordless hand through the air. "Love? The woman hadn't even met me!" He pressed a fist to his brow, squinting. The man did rather have a hard time when it came to thinking.

A grunt from Delaroche told Matthieu that the man was indeed lost in intense thought. Prisoner to his own feeble mind and its struggles to make something of the situation. Pity the woman who won his heart and ever asked him to have an idea.

Ah, Josephine . . .

*How can you be so blind?*

"So, I take it from your . . . consternation . . . you've given up on Helene as well?"

"Well now, Bouchet, that's where the oddest notions enter into the picture. You see, I've been thinking."

"I know that," Matthieu muttered. "I heard the cogs grinding."

"What was that?"

"Nothing. You still desire the woman who spurned you?"

"Helene? Never. He who grovels over sour sweets is not worth his steel."

"If you say so."

Delaroche hiked a leg up on the tree stump Matthieu had perched on and laid one arm across his knee. A single row of gold buttons skimmed the side of his breeches and a thin mauve ribbon used to secure his hose nudged its way over his folded boot top. "Actually, I've given this intriguing scenario a great deal of thought."

"And?"

"I need a favor of you, Bouchet."

Another favor. This would be the second within a half day's time. He hadn't even wanted to agree to the first. "Which is?"

"I need you to help me endear myself to Josephine Lalique."

"Josephine," he whispered. A sacred prayer of sorts. But no God listened to his anxiety-laden thoughts. "You can't possibly mean—"

Julien delivered a hearty slap to Matthieu's back, which set him off balance. "I've had a change of heart, Bouchet. I realize this sweet girl wrote to me for a reason. And I''—he thrust his thumbs towards his chest, a proud peacock displaying his colors—"am that reason. She adores me, and I must not disappoint."

Delaroche's ego was blinding. Matthieu would have laughed but this was a serious announcement. This was not the way things were supposed to go. Delaroche was supposed to wash his hands of both Lalique sisters and march off into the sunset, leaving Matthieu to return to Josephine's arms, claiming he'd done his best to endear her to him, but with no luck.

Why had he been embroiled in such a fiasco? And his sweet ladybug; she had no idea of the torments he would endure for her happiness.

"Why do you ask my help? You say she adores you. Go to her." He shoved his sketch pad under his arm and started to walk away, no longer in the mood for conversation.

"But I cannot!" Julien matched Matthieu's hasty steps. Spi-

rals of greasy smoke steered Matthieu away from a sausage
vendor's cart. His stomach was nothing but queasy. "I was
very cruel to her. I've committed a grave error against her
affections. I cannot simply waltz up to her and ask forgiveness
as if nothing were amiss."

"Yes, you can."

"You think?"

Matthieu stopped. As much as he hated to admit it ... "I
know."

Delaroche, smoothing a finger along his jaw, considered
Matthieu's words. Hell, he was thinking again.

"No, I must do this correctly. I need a mediator, someone
who can smooth the troubled waters between us. An introduction if you will. Just a few simple words of apology passed on
to her from you. I should think that would ease my entrance
into her heart."

His entrance into her heart! Matthieu resumed walking, double speed. Julien had to break into a jog, his sword clinking
against his hip and his boot spurs matching rhythm.

"What is your hurry, man?"

Matthieu blew the long white puff of ostrich feather that
fluttered from Delaroche's felt hat out of his eyes. "I've an
engagement I just remembered."

"I'll not detain you." Julien stopped, wrenching Matthieu
to an abrupt halt by gripping his arm. "I beg of you, Bouchet,
I am but a clod when it comes to women and anything beyond
bedding them. I've no idea how to stand face-to-face with
Mademoiselle Lalique and confess my growing interest in her."

*But you would whisk her from her feet and throw her flat to
your bed if given an opportunity,* Matthieu thought.

Josephine wanted Julien. And now Julien had for indetermi-
nate reasons decided that he wanted her as well. Had Helene
suddenly fallen from his image of the world? He'd been so
seemingly enamored of her.

"Just what is it that has changed your mind?" Matthieu
asked. "Why this sudden switch from one sister to the other?

You hadn't a word for Josephine while we were on campaign. You had angry and foul words for her just the other night. I can't help but wonder if you're up to something, Delaroche. Tell me. You know I am more than a brother to Josephine. I'll not allow any man to approach her with ill intentions."

"As well you should not. The woman is very lucky to have a protector such as you."

"And protect her I will," Matthieu said as he brushed his right hand over the silver hilt of his sword.

Julien's eyes glinted. "Your feeble cheese-toaster is but a twig when matched to my own." As proof, he gripped the hilt of his own sword.

"Is that a threat?"

"Take it as you wish."

Matthieu drew his sword, the tip connecting to the slash of lace skirting Delaroche's doublet collar. The two held tense court, toe to toe, glare to glare. Matthieu knew well and good it was a threat. But he'd protect Josephine with his life. "Your sudden attentions to Mademoiselle Lalique are strangely out of character, Delaroche. Why Josephine? When only a day ago you left her in a torrent of hateful words."

"I was a fool. Had I only taken a moment to think and not blown up upon first discovering what she had done, perhaps she and I would be arm and arm at this moment."

Julien stepped back. Matthieu did not yield his position. One wrong syllable and the man would be twisting his tongue around his rapier instead of words. "Go ahead, convince me of your sincerity."

"Of course you are aware of my affections for Helene."

"If you must call them affections."

"If you must question my sudden attraction to the lovely Josephine, then perhaps you should also question her attraction to a man she had never seen before."

"Meaning?"

"Sometimes love comes quickly, Bouchet. I believe the saying is, love at first sight. Or in my case, love after finally allowing the steam to settle and appreciating the woman for the generous heart she has. She wrote those wonderful letters—''

''Trampled like day-old refuse beneath your boots.''

''It was just the one I misplaced.''

Damn this all to hell! Matthieu snapped his sword away and turned from Delaroche's simpering expression. Why was the obvious difference between him and Delaroche so *un*obvious to Josephine?

''She is a lovely woman,'' Delaroche called over Matthieu's shoulder. ''Fine of feature and delicate of face.''

He knew that.

''So graceful and elegant in her movements . . .''

Graceful?

''She's an oxen on wheels,'' Matthieu chuckled as he resumed his walking. The man knew nothing about the woman he intended to pursue. And he'd not help him either.

*Please, Matthieu. You must help me. I love Julien.*

But he had made a promise to Josephine. The devil take him!

''An oxen?'' Julien followed but was stopped short as Matthieu paused and swung round. He almost kissed the man in the face he came so close, but both veered backward.

''Very well,'' Matthieu said. ''I'll do it. But—''

''Yes?''

''I cannot speak to her today.'' *Or tomorrow, or ever.* ''I've . . . things to do.''

''But you must! I cannot wait.''

Too damned eager, the man. Definitely up to something. But what?

''Perhaps . . .'' Matthieu again cursed himself for agreeing to be the bridge between the woman he loved and the man he was quickly coming to hate. ''You should write her?''

''Write?'' Julien smoothed two fingers along his mustache, thinking.

Another long silence.

"No. No, that is what got me into this mess in the first place."

"*Mess?* How can you call the introduction to a woman you now claim to desire a mess?" Matthieu narrowed his gaze. If Delaroche was up to something—and Matthieu felt sure he was—he intended to keep close tabs on this man and his actions.

"But another letter?"

"It is what endeared her to you in the first place."

"Yes, yes, you are right. But I should wish to deliver it this evening. I'll need your expert advice."

Of course he would.

And so it began. Again.

"Give me an hour. I shall meet you at the Louvre in the cadet hall." Matthieu did sat not even wait for a reply. He desperately needed some distance from Julien Delaroche and this whole *mess* in which he was now deeply embroiled.

A fine supper to fill his stomach this evening. Cook's gravy biscuits simmered in his gut, and it felt good. Matthieu had almost forgotten what real food should taste like after half a year of military fare. Dried jerky and stolen goat's milk were not culinary delights.

Walking behind Josephine, her pale mint skirts skimming the vibrant grasses behind the Lalique house, Matthieu felt somehow—set apart—from the realm from whence she'd come. Long dark ringlets danced in adulation across her narrow shoulders and down her back, kissing her elbows with every step she took. Her slender waist, regal in its design, beckoned sculptors to study the luscious curves to forever preserve them in stone.

"You're very quiet this evening, Matthieu," she called back as she stepped carefully down the moss-embroidered stone path that led to the Professor's shed. She was a queen upon a royal carpet, all the trees and foliage holding court around her.

And he, her lowly servant, destined to please her until death. No matter what pain it caused him.

She passed the Celtic stone cross that Cook had settled in the back of the garden over a decade ago. Matthieu paused, fell to one knee, and crossed himself. The thought of passing a cross and not acknowledging the good Lord was unthinkable.

''Have you had a chance to speak to Chevalier Delaroche?''

Matthieu stood and brushed a scrunched elm leaf from his knee. So hopeful she was, like a small child waiting a grand revelation. Please, can I have a treat today, Monsieur Baker? I've been so very good.

To think of treats, of pleasures beyond indulgence, set Matthieu's heart pounding. He stood and followed her into the sun-dusted solitude of the shed. The treat of Josephine's mouth, pursed in expectant silence. A delicious fruit cleaved open with one's thumbs to reveal the thick and succulent flesh within. Ah, to suck out the juice of her desire and cure it into the wine that would make him a drunk and happy man forever.

Leaning over the glass aquariums that held scads of spotted ladybugs, Josephine peered down and scanned the colonies. ''Hmm, Matthieu?''

''I have,'' he finally said. It pained him to know what must come. ''And I bring word from him.''

''Oh!'' She forgot her minuscule subjects and rushed around the lab table. Her skirts dusted up scattered leaves and twigs as she snuggled next to him and slipped an arm through his. ''Why didn't you tell me before, silly one? You made me suffer all through supper without so much as a clue that you had spoken to him. What does he say? Can he ever forgive me?''

Matthieu slipped a hand inside his shirt and reached down to his waist, where he secured the folded letter. Each fold precise, perfect. As Julien Delaroche's letters demanded. ''You'll have to discover for yourself.''

Her silent cry amazed him. Too shocked to speak, Josephine spread her fingers wide as her jaw fell slack.

"It'll not hurt you." He snapped the letter with a finger. "Go on, I know he does not use poison in his ink."

"For me," she breathed as she carefully took the paper between two fingers. So delicate, her actions, as if she held a decaying parchment instead of the thick clean paper. "I could not have expected—What did he write? Perhaps it is a command never to come near him again?"

Matthieu shrugged and paced past her. He could only wish it were so. The scrape of a wooden stool across the floor stones alerted him that she had sat. He did not bother to turn around; instead he bent to study the hoards of vermilion beetles that crawled the sides of the aquarium.

"What if it is not? What if he has forgiven me? Oh, Matthieu—"

"Read it, damn it!" He stood and paced to the shed door, slamming his hand against the rotted pine jam. "Read it and then you shall know."

"Very well."

Matthieu stood perfectly still, listening as the faint cacophony of crisp ladybug wings flitted and banged against the thick glass. That sound was replaced by the careful and precise unfolding of the letter. So slow. It was as if she were prolonging every moment, stretching each second to its ultimate end for means of—divining pleasure?—or perhaps she was just so nervous.

He recognized the crinkling sound of her palm pressing flat to the opened missive upon her skirts. She cleared her throat.

No.

"My sweet Josephine."

No, not out loud. *Please no.*

*You may regard my sudden change of heart with a mea-sure of reluctance. Hear me out, for I promise to chase away all negative sentiments formed between the two of us.*

Pressing his lids tightly closed, Matthieu strained to remain still, to allow her this time to read without interruption. But to hear those words. To know . . .

*Apologies are showered upon you with heartfelt regret. If only an apology wasn't necessary. If only I had not spoken such hateful words to you on the night of my return. If only . . .*

*Ah, but who would have known that it was you I wrote to over the course of many months? Josephine Lalique, of the sprite-dancing smile and warm tender eyes. While I cannot simply act as though Helene was not my first love, I've come to learn that true passion is born of the heart and soul. Yes, the soul, Josephine. And your soul has spoken to me with tearful eyes and a brave beating fist. Notice me, I care for you! you shouted valiantly at my face.*

*And now I have noticed you, sweet Josephine.*

*I ask only that we can begin anew. If you can promise to overlook my indiscretions, I will promise to forget that other sister's name . . . What was her name? I can do that for you, Josephine.*

*Anything, I would do absolutely anything, to see the smile on your face. Please tell me you can do as much for me.*

> *Humble and apologetic,*
> *Chevalier Julien Delaroche*

"Oh, *mon dieu.*"

The sound of paper sliding down silk and landing upon the wood floor would live forever in Matthieu's memory. The sound of complete and total surrender to the promises written upon that paper. Why, she might at this very moment be in a swoon.

He did not want to look at her. Did not want to see the look a woman's face possesses when she is dreaming of the man she loves.

A man other than himself.

*Anything, I would do absolutely anything, to see the smile on your face.*

He could not bear another second of this charade. "Good eve, Mademoiselle. I can see you're no longer in need of my services." He stepped outside and strode towards the house, completely forgoing his usual attention to Cook's cross.

# Chapter 12

*Julien, my dear,*

*It is done. I have forgotten all that should be forgotten. I cannot even call to mind that which I should no longer know. You see how giddy your words have made me? I stumble through my letters like a silly young girl. But to know that you are willing to give me a chance to prove my love to you is enough to replace the foolish smirk with a grand and delicious smile. I wish you could see my smile right now, Julien. Because it is only for you.*

"And it goes on and on." Matthieu hastened through the remaining paragraph, promises of more smiles and such devotion that it made him want to . . . punch something!

Delaroche snatched the letter and pressed it flat before him on the trestle table. Around them the slosh of the Seine kissing the stone walls splattered and crashed. A sea kestrel keeled overhead. Matthieu had just been unfortunate enough to stumble across the chevalier enroute to the Palais du Justice.

"I am truly amazed that these silly scribblings really do

work,'' Julien said as he analyzed the flowing black script, tracing a thick forefinger under each word. "So that is all it takes? A few paper promises?"

"Apparently so." Matthieu stood and snapped his felt hat against his thigh, than placed it on his head, pulling the brim low over his brow. "I'll be off then."

"Yes," Delaroche muttered, his attention burning a hole through the fragrant piece of paper. "No, wait, Bouchet."

Matthieu paused just outside the door. The bright sunlight beamed down on him, making his view inside the tavern an impossibility. Coached by a little voice sitting on his left shoulder, he worked the sudden halt to a quick pace. *Just pretend I didn't even hear,* he agreed with the voice. *I've had enough of matchmaking.*

It was always a pleasure to step inside Madame Lamarck's shop. Sitting in a corner chair while one of the seamstresses summoned her mistress, Matthieu marveled over the stacks of exquisite fabrics carefully lining the wall behind the lengthy marble counter. A rainbow showered from ceiling to floor, shot through with streaks of gold and silver threading. Fabrics for which he hadn't a proper name danced and shifted from muted shades to delicious tints with a slight movement of his head. And the smells—of new thread and long bolts of cloth, saffron dyes and the brew of vanilla-spiced chocolate Madame always made available to her customers.

To his left stood a headless iron beauty whose skirts of shimmery gold made Matthieu wonder just how many meals he could eat for the price of that dress. Surely more than a year's worth. Must be a piece Madame had designed for court. Louis XIII demanded elegance and luxury beyond what Matthieu could understand. He was perfectly happy with his plain unslashed doublet, ribbonless breeches, and thin lace rimming his sleeves. Perhaps a thick velvet ribbon for his hair on occasion, but he'd certainly forgo the temptation to strap an elaborately embroidered baldric across his chest, as was the fashion rage.

"Ah, *chérie*, it is so good to see you."

A familiar in Madame Lamarck's shop since a very young age when his mother would bring him along, Matthieu stood to receive the woman in his arms. She pressed kisses to each of his cheeks and squeezed his free hand in both of hers.

"You are dashing as ever," she cooed. Flirtatious copper lashes fluttered as she scanned him from blushing smile to toes. The flirtation felt good, and Matthieu did not look nervously away as he usually did.

"Josephine tells me you wish to see me about something? Come," she said as she pulled him towards the crimson portières.

He recognized Josephine's worktable for the scatter of unwound ribbon and flowers in all states of completion. It was good of Madame to allow Josephine the opportunity to put her boundless energy to such creative ends. Matthieu also liked that over the years Madame Lamarck had become a sort of surrogate mother for Josephine, and was always there for her when she needed a gentle shoulder to rest her head upon.

"You've something to show me?" Madame perused the folio Matthieu held under his arm.

"Oh yes." He held out the folio. "If I may be so bold, I spoke to Mademoiselle Lalique the other day—"

"She is looking rather lovely lately, isn't she?"

"Huh? Oh, well certainly. Josephine is always a fresh flower amongst a sea of insignificant grasses. But she mentioned—"

"A fine catch for a man such as yourself."

The insinuating pitch of her final words irritated Matthieu. Why did everyone he spoke to presume that he and Josephine should be together? He could have her if he wished.

He could. Really.

But *she* did not wish it. And so he must respect her desires.

Besides, if she could fall for Delaroche's sudden *change of heart*, perhaps Josephine really had changed since he'd last seen her. Perhaps she wasn't even the woman he thought he cared so much for.

"As I said, Madame Lamarck, Josephine mentioned your desire to hire an artist skilled in cloth and drapery."

"But of course. And you have brought me some sketches? Let me see."

He opened his leather valise, which held the one picture of Josephine and a few other sketches of people he'd done on the sly while sitting in the Place de Grieve. Not much of a portfolio, he knew, but he did rather like the one of a small boy whom he'd gifted with dragonfly wings. It had seemed appropriate to give the ragged urchin the means to fly away to any dream he should desire.

"Ah! Such whimsy!" Madame said as she tapped the glittering antennae that Matthieu had given a haggard washerwoman. He'd purposely drawn her shoes floating above the ground, lifting her up and away from her dreary work. "You have an interesting way of expressing the common man. Aha," she nodded as she looked over the wash of vivid reds that brought life to the sketch of his ladybug. "So it is just as I suspected."

"Madame?"

She laid the portrait on Josephine's table and clutched Matthieu's hand. "You *are* in love with her."

"No."

"Oh yes." She would not allow him to pull free. Instead she sidled closer, her woman's knowing gaze dancing across his face in triumphant delight. "Your skills are excellent, Monsieur Bouchet. You've captured the very soul of our precious Josephine. Can you not see it with your own eyes?"

He studied the portrait, fitfully aware of Madame Lamarck's gaze fixed to his face as he tried to keep his expression neutral. "You see things that are not there. It is simply watered down paint and charcoal set to flat paper."

She cooed softly as she took his hand and placed it upon the drawing. "Do you feel it? The paper pulses with her heartbeat, sighs with her breath. Monsieur Bouchet, you cannot tell me you do not love this woman. Michelangelo could not have snared her soul and reenvisioned it the way you have. Look into her eyes . . .''

True, he'd worked near to an hour mixing colors and adding water to get just the right shade of toasted chocolate that danced in her eyes. And the sparkle that always resided there. It had been a difficult task, but one well worth the labor. As for the frog and the rope-bound heart . . .

''You mustn't tell her,'' he found himself saying as he drew a finger along the curved dark lines that were Josephine's hair.

''Why not?''

''She loves another.''

''Ah, that Chevalier Delaroche, is it?'' Madame Lamarck made a noise that resembled a spit, but Matthieu could not be sure. ''He is no good for her. You know that.''

''I do. But how can you, Madame Lamarck? Are you acquainted with the chevalier?''

''I do not need to be acquainted with anyone who would keep you from sweeping our sweet Josephine into your arms, away from the dangers of this rake who wishes only to claim yet another notch upon his musket.''

''I will not destroy her dreams.'' Matthieu straightened and matched Madame Lamarck's gaze. ''She loves him. It matters not what you or I think of the man. In Josephine's heart he is the one who can stir the passion.''

''And what of your heart?''

Matthieu laid his hand over the delicate fingers Madame Lamarck set upon his chest. Much as it hurt to say it—''I am comforted to know that I have done all I can to ensure Josephine's happiness.''

''Sacrifice is not always the courageous road,'' she offered.

''It is the only path available at this time.''

''Ha, ha! The man does not know how deeply in love he really is. Why do you deny it, Monsieur Bouchet? Are you afraid of something?''

"I deny nothing." He'd revealed too much. Now he was uncomfortable under this prying female eye.

"You deny your heart, and you deny Josephine your heart."

"Ridiculous. I really do need to be going now, Madame Lamarck. If you'll excuse me?"

"Oh no." She picked up the portrait. "You are now my employee, Monsieur Bouchet."

A delighted thrill replaced the shuddering thud inside his heart. Employee? As in one who would receive wages for his work?

"But can you work quickly?"

He shrugged. "What is it you request?"

"I go to court again this weekend. I want to bring along some of your sketches to show the queen."

"Madame Lamarck!" Such an honor she offered him.

"Can you do it? If I have you sketch a few of my dresses and then suggest changes and additions, will you do it?"

"Of course. I can begin immediately."

"And I should wish you to create some fantastical designs also. The King plans a ball for midsummer's eve. My child, you must be the one to design the costumes!"

"Madame Lamarck. Matthieu!"

"Ah, Josephine."

Matthieu caught Madame's secretive wink as she went to Josephine and pushed her towards him. As usual a messy scatter of stray hairs danced over her lashes. With a quick breath from her lips, they floated upward to rearrange themselves upon her head.

He could have done much better with a smooth of his hand.

"I've a most important assignment for you today," Madame Lamarck said to Josephine as she walked her over to Matthieu and positioned her directly in front of him. "I've just hired Monsieur Bouchet to do some sketches for me."

"Oh, Matthieu!"

Always so genuinely thrilled for his happiness. If only he could be as excited over hers.

"You will model dresses for him today. Will you change into the saffron open-skirt?"

"Of course!" Josephine bustled past the two of them into a draped room and Matthieu heard the sound of rustling fabric.

Today? Right now? Josephine, his model?

"I don't know, Madame," he started.

"Of course you do." With a thimble-capped finger, she tilted his chin up. "You shall have a half-dozen sketches ready by this weekend?"

"That will be no problem but—"

"You do not like my choice of model?" she pouted, a vainglorious glint dancing in her green eyes. "Josephine is the only one who will do. Especially after seeing your drawing of her. The Queen shall fall in love with her face, and then naturally she will fall in love with the dress."

"Of course." Matthieu conceded with a nod.

"Abandon your denial," Madame singsonged *a mezzo voce,* so only Matthieu could hear as she began to stroll back up to the shop. "You know you are in love."

To touch a woman without her even being aware of that touch gave Matthieu a sentient thrill. Though they'd exchanged pleasantries for the first hour of their time together, alone in the back of Madame Lamarck's Dress Emporium, Josephine had slowly begun to shut off due to her lack of movement. To close her eyes and become a somnambulant mannequin poised before him.

Still he touched her with an intangible caress.

And she so unaware.

The dark tip of his charcoal skated the smooth surface of the paper, designing itself into voluptuous curves and delicate arches, heady rises and lingering falls. He studied now her lips, his eyes holding court upon those two perfect mounds. His touch, soft and lingering, its weight unnoticeable as she still held her eyes closed.

The lips. The most intimate part of a woman's body, yet revealed every day without a worry or embarrassed glance. Displayed to the world, the exquisite central receiver of passion and giver of desire.

Josephine wore but a sheer wash of crimson across her lips, enough to entice his heart to a rapid pace. And to imagine the heat generated by the press of their lips. Chastely at first. Barely touching, testing, drawing in the flavors of one another before fully tasting. To devour her mouth with his own. Lay claim to her most revealing feature, the one that expressed joy and sadness, giggled and exclaimed, pouted and quivered. Ah, to feel her tiny pout quivering into an accepting, wanting, pining instrument of joy.

The tip of Matthieu's charcoal snapped. A miniature cone of black circled around its tip upon the ribbonned bodice of his drawing. "Damn."

"A problem?" she asked sweetly, her eyes flashing wide as if she'd no more than blinked.

"No, no, I've another." He scrounged through his box of pencils and knives and brushes and paints. "You are not tiring?"

She offered her vivid smile. "It is very peaceful just to stand here and clear my mind."

Matthieu's heart melted. *Abandon your denial.*

"You don't mind my silence?"

"Not at all. But if you wish, you may sit. I've completed the dress. I've only a few final touches."

"Perhaps I shall." She settled upon the waist-high stool that stood before her table. "Might I close my eyes again?"

"Please."

With a few careful strokes the black splotch from the broken lead was removed. Matthieu then dashed a few shadows beneath her chin. His pencil worked of its own volition as it danced over the entire drawing, adding darkness here, creating volume there with a few subtle strokes to shadow. Finally there was just the one portion he'd saved for last. Well, more like avoided.

The slow rise and fall of her décolletage threatened to disrupt the calm observance of his model. Press on, he urged inwardly. Just a few more moments of this blissful torture and you may look away. Until she reappears with yet another dress. Madame Lamarck certainly was a wicked conniver. She'd known exactly what result her efforts would have when pairing the two of them.

But Josephine remained unaware of his torment, so enamored was she of Julien Delaroche. Why, she probably thought of him at this very moment.

A long sigh pulled her bosom high within the low neckline of the blue silk.

Yes, she thought of her lover.

And Matthieu could only dream of her. He pressed pencil to paper, steeling himself against studying his model for any longer than necessary. The plan worked well.

For about ten seconds.

How luscious a feeling it must be for a man to rest his hand, palm wide, upon that bosom. To divine with every breath that stirred through her body the heat of her flesh, the comforting cushions upon which he could rest his head. How they must smell, those delicious mounds of heaven. For a dot of fragrance placed between them must be brewed to a heady mist of mead there in that secret and delectable of places. How divine to strip away the stiff stomacher embroidered over with curling ribbons and sparkling silver threads. To reveal the heavy fruits of woman and cup his hand beneath them. Suckle them until he grew dizzy and full from their magic . . .

"Yes, never stop."

He looked up from his attentions to her naked breasts, finding that single act painstakingly difficult. Her pale countenance blossomed with a delicious blush, her inquiring brown eyes heavy-lidded with passion. "I wouldn't dream of it," he whispered and pressed his lips to her breast. Her body rose to meet his touch, pleading, wanting, knowing exactly what it must have.

Lost in her sweet essence, a slave to each subtle movement of her body, Matthieu suckled langorously. A melody of her dulcet whimpers played against the percussion of his pounding heart. He moved up to kiss her cherry lips, to feast upon her mouth in a possessive need to milk her whimpers to a grand symphony.

"Matthieu, I want you . . . now . . . please . . ."

"Yes, my love, now."

"Matthieu. Matthieu?"

Ah, such music to his ears. His name slipping over her lips. And he slipping his tongue over her body . . .

"Matthieu?"

Matthieu let out a sigh and opened his eyes to find a wide grin spreading across his subject's face. She was clothed. Not a hint of nipple or—

"Oh. Oh God . . ." What he had just been thinking! "Sorry, I started to . . . drift . . . a bit there." He stood and turned away from the goddess of temptation. "I believe we've both been sitting far too long. You may change and stretch your limbs. I believe I shall step out for a moment."

"Are you well?"

"Certainly," he said without turning back. Her suppressed giggle made him wonder if she had just been privy to his secret thoughts. Please no. "I just need to quench . . . my thirst."

He was duly aware that Josephine followed him out into the shop as he exited, but did not dare turn back to see if she watched him from the window.

To turn around at this moment would reveal his own . . . burgeoning desires.

From over Josephine's shoulder, Madame Lamarck giggled.

"What is so funny?"

"You are pursuing the wrong man," she sang out, giving the final word two dancing syllables.

"Nonsense." Josephine turned and marched towards the heavy crimson damask, determined to cut all conversation regarding Matthieu Bouchet short. "I just worry for him. He seemed a trifle ... scattered ... in there. I'm not sure he's feeling well.''

"Oh, he feels," Madame Lamarck said on a breathy note. "And it would do you well to start noticing."

Allowing the curtains to fall closed behind her, Josephine stopped and touched the sketch Matthieu had tossed upon her worktable. "I notice Matthieu," she defended quietly. "He is a dear, sweet man. A friend. I love him. But it is not the kind of love everyone insists we share. He does not feel that way about me."

*Oh, he feels.*

Yes, of course he did. But what *were* his true feelings towards her? Did they go beyond friendship, as his looks so often hinted?

"No," Josephine said with new wonder. "He couldn't possibly. Could he?"

# Chapter 13

Julien looked down at the frothy pride of flowers in his fist. Meant for Josephine Lalique, in the interest of winning her affections. Change of heart had come quick enough. What woman wasn't worth the effort when her affections were also sought by someone else? Especially Bouchet. Anger rippled through Julien's veins until he found he had to relax his clenching fingers before he snapped the bouquet in two. For to finally stand against Matthieu Bouchet, to bring the man down, would reap great satisfaction in his heart.

"You will know my name, Bouchet. It will haunt you as the name Isabelle haunts me."

Drops of cold river water trickled over his wrist. He shook the bouquet.

But wouldn't these flowers serve him much better in the hands of Helene Lalique? For as horrid as he felt knowing that Helene had only been toying with his affections, he still could not begin to despise her as he knew he should. He'd not wrestled a bevy of women to his bed as he would have most men believe, but it was more than a handful, carefully chosen, and mostly from titled families. He was choosy, damn it. Yet Helene Lalique's kisses had been the first and only that had ever worked like fire through his veins. Like a crossbow flaming brightly, shot through his heart and traveling his entire body. The passion he had experienced from a few simple kisses granted by those luscious, full lips!

The sound of familiar laughter heading his way made Julien snap to attention. He made haste as he paid a frazzle-haired hawker for the bouquet of red ranunculus. Then he dashed behind a tower of double barrels, emptied of ale, that waited a cooper to come and haul them away.

"You cannot speak the truth!"

"Oh, but I do."

Constance Fleury, daughter of a local cure, Olympe . . . something or other, and Helene Lalique.

"I've narrowed my choices down to Monsieur Michelet and the Chevalier de Baron," came Helene's voice, crisp and clean as a morning rain.

From his position, Julien caught a glimpse of Helene walking by. The side of her doll's face revealed a small black patch at the corner of her lips that wriggled with every spoken word. In her gloved hand—oh, those soft, delicate fingers!—she held a cloved orange on a ribboned stick.

"You must choose before the fête this Friday," Constance said in a jubilant gush. "You've always an assortment of suitors to pick from."

"Yes, of course I must, and I shall. I won't be having my younger sister attend such an event in my absence. Can you imagine if I should have to hear secondhand the night's events—and from Josephine!"

"She is going with Matthieu?" Olympe asked.

The muscle in Julien's jaw tensed. Bouchet? Why would they assume—

"No. It's simply scandalous!" Helene lowered her voice and raised the orange to her lips. "She's accepted an invitation from the Chevalier Delaroche. Can you believe such a thing? The Chevalier has changed his colors regarding my sister far too quickly, if you ask me."

"Oh!"

Fine woman to be speaking of scandal, Julien thought as he let his shoulders fall back against the wall behind him, no longer interested in the chattering of three hens.

He would give Helene Lalique a scandal. He would show her exactly what it was she was missing at the party this Friday. And Josephine Lalique would help him do it.


"Mademoiselle Lalique!"

Josephine spun around, a tightly wound roll of violet moiré in hand, to find Julien Delaroche smiling widely at her. She looked around him, over his broad shoulders. The marketplace buzzed with a dozen different bodies, none interested in either of them. So that must mean . . .

He wanted to speak to her. Right now. This very instant.

Clearing her throat, and sensing her heating flesh, Josephine raised a hand to her neck, though she knew by now her cheeks were most likely flushed with color. It was still a little hard to fathom that he actually wanted to be with her. After receiving the invitation to the ball she'd swooned. For real!

"Chevalier Delaroche, what a pleasant surprise."

"I've been waiting for you," he said, a boyish smile creeping across his face. Such a fine square jaw only served to set off his smile even more, with its contrast of hard angles and soft curve. The brim of his wide felt hat could not disguise the delight dancing in his steely eyes.

Her summation of his attributes was suddenly blocked by a froth of vivid ranunculus blossoms, each a lacy circle of tightly meshed petals. "For me?" Now she was really set off kilter.

"I didn't want to come into the shop . . . disturb your work. You know." He fidgeted with the hilt of his sword, appearing almost as nervous as she. But that couldn't be possible from a man of such words. Could it? "Well, I'm not much for standing about in a dress shop, if you must know the truth."

"Really? I should think it a most interesting place for a man.

So many women, all with eager eyes, and in the mood to bring something home.''

He smoothed a finger along his chin, captured by her teasing tone. "I've never thought of it that way. Perhaps I should have come in!''

"It is a good thing you did not today. The Widow Sardou was the only customer when I left. I fear she's a wandering eye when it comes to a fine young gentleman such as you. If given the chance, she might hook a claw into your sword belt without your being aware.''

"Mademoiselle,'' he said as he shifted his embroidered and ribboned baldric regally, "I assure you when a female lays a hand on me I am most aware, be she young or old. But at this very moment there is just one particular woman who commands my attention.''

The touch of Julien's fingertip to her cheek made Josephine reach up quickly. But he would not allow her to push him away, and as quickly as she had moved, she resigned herself to let him do as he wished. She pulled her hand back.

"I like a woman who shows her modesty with a healthy burst of color,'' he said in a softer voice. "'Tis far more appealing than those women who do not color at even the bawdiest remark.''

Josephine started to walk slowly, and Julien matched her steps. The Petit Pont was just ahead; she'd chosen to walk to work this day instead of riding, for the sun was deliciously bright. And Richelieu had been more than compliant, yawning as he was, when she'd told him. "I should think a soldier would be used to bawdy women.''

As he walked beside her, his hand brushed casually across hers, not moving to purposely touch or join hands, but making contact every few swings. Just to entice.

"I'm not sure I approve of your having knowledge of that sort,'' he said, "but I must admit, like most soldiers, I've known one or two in my lifetime.''

"And they do not blush?''

"Not in the obvious places! Er, not that I'm the sort who knows. I've heard tell, you understand. You don't mind if I see you home?" he wondered, as they strolled beneath a sheltering canopy of elm leaves.

"To be escorted by the handsomest of soldiers? Of course not, Chevalier Delaroche. You must know a secret about me: I absolutely devour attention. I enjoy being fawned over."

"Than fawn I shall." He dashed in front of her, her gate now in view. Clutching her hand, he pulled her to the trunk of the oak that stood guard before the property. Too thrilled by this man's sudden attentions, Josephine allowed him to position her against the tree, his body not quite touching hers, but close enough for her to dream. He took her hand in his. Leather filled her senses, rich and male. The soft press of his lips to the back of her hand uncapped her anticipation and let it flow freely through her veins.

"You once mailed me a kiss," he said as he absently fingered the ruffled skirts of the flowers she held, her hand still resting on the curve of his fingers. "Perhaps it was a thousand? Yes. I must admit they were sweet, though not as fulfilling as I imagine the genuine thing to be. Will you now allow me to determine which of the two is preferable?"

Her heart pounded like two wild jackrabbits running circles in a meadow, her throat felt swollen with the thunder of the rabbit's feet, and her extremities tingled, threatening to become numb and topple her in a quivering mass upon the ground.

And he wanted her to concentrate on putting her lips together to form a kiss?

Of its own volition, her voice whispered, "Yes." And her eyelids fell shut. Not because she willed them, but because she hadn't the control to actually issue commands to her body parts at the moment.

Josephine waited as she sensed the heat of his hand press to the tree trunk near her head. Here it comes, she thought, a kiss. A true and genuine, on-the-lips kiss!

And she waited.

She knew he stepped closer by the sound of his boots scuffing across the raised tree root. But she dared not open her eyes for fear of spoiling the moment.

Instead, she waited.

The tension of knowing how close his body was to hers threatened to make her grip his arms and pull him close. But ... she waited.

Just a peek. Lifting one eyelid, Josephine saw two closed eyelids fringed in golden lashes, one hawklike nose, and two puckered lips moving steadily, yet slowly, closer. She snapped her eye shut.

Contact. His hot lips to hers. Gentle, but immediately firm. They were one. She was being kissed by a man, on the lips. Finally. Her heart thudded. Her fingertips tingled. And her body moved to meld against Julien. This was far better than she had ever imagined. Until ... what was he doing now? He thrust his tongue over her bottom lip!

Josephine jerked back at the weird touch of moistness to her lips, pulling Julien from his trance and forcing him straight.

He cleared his throat and plastered on a big smile. "Far sweeter than on paper," he cooed. "Er, perhaps I should be on my way?"

A question, but weak enough to be a plea for one more try.

"Yes, I believe so," she offered, lost in concern over what had just happened. The kiss had been so nice. Until he'd forced his tongue in her mouth. Well, it hadn't really been force. She'd just been so ... caught up.

"Might I see you tomorrow?"

"Of course!"

He smiled at her eagerness, traced the rim of his hat with a deft finger, and bid her *au revoir.*

Josephine released her breath and the coiled ribbon she'd clutched to a crumpled oval during the kiss. The flower stems bent over her hand, some obviously broken, the others just crushed.

What was it that had just occurred? A kiss? It felt too odd to be a kiss. She knew it was, but, she'd never expected, well . . . his tongue.

She skimmed the pad of her forefinger over her lips, wiping a trace of moist—well—spit—away. Is that how kisses were supposed to be? Uncomfortable and wet? Of course, first kisses were most likely always awkward and strained.

No. She would not allow herself to even think such a thing. A kiss from Julien Delaroche was a long awaited gift. The man she loved! His kisses were divine—as it had started—and nothing but. Warm and commanding. That was it. He held command of her heart with his every touch, and his kisses only proved it.

Out of sorts, and still not sure what it was she'd just been a part of, Josephine pushed open the gate to the yard and meandered into the house.

The Place de Grieve was not so ominous during the early morning hours that found hawkers just uncovering their wares and sleepy-eyed whores shuffling back to the sanctity of their darkened bordellos, like nocturnal creatures fleeing the blazing light of day.

Having secured an apartment on the left bank and broken his fast on his landlady's delicious sourdough and soft cheese, Matthieu now strolled easily through the crushing bustle, avoiding collisions with footmen and rat killers wielding noose-ended poles, with an occasional deft skip and a darting eye trained on the gutters.

He smoothed a hand over his wrist, and the soft narrow lace that skirted his cuff made him smile. From mother's wedding dress; she'd insisted on using it when sewing him a new shirt for his sixteenth birthday. She thought it high time she put to use the laces and fabric, instead of leaving it to the moths. And with the lace in plain sight on Matthieu's shirt, she said her memories of an exquisite day, the beginning of a blissful marriage, would live on forever.

Acrid fumes blasted Matthieu's senses, knocking him out of his happy thoughts with a swift kick to the brain. Fresh slaughter and week-old remains tainted the air and brought his the bile to his throat. He quickened his pace, dodging into a narrow alley that led away from the odor. By the time he stepped onto a new street the smell had receded and he could see the elegant spire of Sainte Geneviève but a stone's throw away.

Great wooden doors muffled the city sounds as they were closed behind him and a haze of mote-scattered sunlight shone down over Matthieu's shoulders. The sister who had greeted him disappeared swiftly and without a sound, leaving him alone to contemplate—the sudden tinkle of girlish laughter?

When he looked up, bright sunlight blinded his vision. A step backward brought into view the iron railing that circled a granite staircase and the retreating white skirts of a half-dozen young women.

Novices, Matthieu thought with a smile. Young and sweet and curious as newborn kittens to discover the world beyond these sacred walls of stone.

Mother Angelica appeared like a spectre through the wall and directed Matthieu to follow her out into the courtyard that was boxed in by the walls of the convent. The loud click of his heels echoing like battle fire made him self-conscious. Every step he took attracted the eager eyes of wimpled feminine heads overhead. He couldn't help but smile to himself at their curiosity.

Ever curious. Josephine's motto.

But this time her curiosity had taken her too far! Into the hands of an insipid soldier and out of *his* grasp.

"Matthieu!"

The image of Josephine swooning in Delaroche's arms was shattered by the sound of his mother's voice. Catching the tiny woman in his embrace, Matthieu lifted her from the ground as he hugged her tightly and pressed a kiss to her forehead. She was but a child in his arms, so petite and elegantly frail. He'd once thanked the Lord he'd gotten his height and stature from his father's side of the family. But his heart was definitely that of Isabelle Bouchet's.

"Oh!" she whispered with a gasp into his ear. "Set me down, Matthieu. You'll squeeze the breath right out of me!"

"Forgive me," he said as he lowered her to the plush lawn, quite surprised himself that his emotions had blinded him to his actions. "It has been so long, Mother. You look fine. Your cheeks are like the apples on this tree, and your smile the sun!"

"It is you that brings the smile to my face, son. Oh, come!" She gripped his hand and pulled him to the stone bench that circled the base of the huge apple tree that served the nuns cider and muffins well through the winter. Matthieu could never help but wonder just how his mother, always animated to the point of gaiety, endured the silence and strict conventions of the convent. She was a precious bloom. Certainly the convent protected her from lost petals or damage, but wouldn't the city produce a brighter blossom?

"The fighting is over?" she asked as she pulled him next to her on the bench and clutched both of his hands in her lap. She did not wear a habit, but had yet to leave her widow's weeds behind. Her long wavy hair, near to her waist, was neatly braided and coiled into an interesting veil that just kissed her shoulders.

"For the time. The Spaniards have retreated to St. Amand. But it is certain this respite will not go on forever."

"Oh, my son, I am so fretful when you are away."

"You mustn't worry, Mother. Thanks to Papa his son can shoot and handle a sword as well as the next man."

"But what of the enemy you cannot see? And when you are felled, how long before your mother is told to come and claim your bones?"

"Mama! Don't speak so!"

"Oh, I'm so sorry, Matthieu. Ah!" She waved a frail hand before her face. "What has become of me? I speak of horrors that will never come. My son is here by my side and that is all that matters."

She kissed his hand and clasped it to her lips. Though shrouded by the stone walls of Sainte Geneviève, still her eyes sparkled like champagne held up to the sun.

"Have you an apartment? Are the renters well?"

"Yes and yes, mother. I went to the farm yesterday afternoon. Monsieur Corbiau and his family have increased the acreage by a third by buying up Monsieur Roche's lands after his death. I'm thinking to let them buy our land outright."

"It would be a good thing."

The grip of her hand felt warm and solid. Comforting. This was the first time he'd ever mentioned selling the land left to him after his father's death. For some reason he'd always felt comfort in knowing he owned it. Like he had a home somewhere. A place he belonged. But to see Antoine Corbiau's pride as he'd walked Matthieu along the border of his property and pointed out the new crop of potatoes they'd had great luck in sowing, Matthieu knew that to give the gift of land ownership to this man would be far more honorable than to cling to a past he could not change.

"You'll always have a home right here," his mother said now as she laid his palm over her breast. "In my heart, Matthieu."

Yes, home needn't be a tangible thing that one could stand on or hold in one's hand. It was right here, holding him in her arms. Laying his head on his mother's fragile shoulder, Matthieu gently circled her waist, leaving his other hand on her heart. He closed his eyes, pressed a kiss to her hair, and whispered, "I love you, Mother."

No one disturbed them. Content to sit in silence, with only the pulse of his mother's heart steady beneath his palm, Matthieu closed his eyes. Thinking about his childhood home always stirred memories of that summer. His sixteenth. A summer of new discoveries and devastating changes . . .


Professor Lalique always had a new invention or interesting design. His last one, he called Hind-Sight: spectacles outfitted with tiny mirrors on either side, so one could see behind as well as in front. Quite the rage at court, especially amongst the king's circle. But the rich new clothing that his invention had bought him could not disguise his oddness.

"Papa, what is it you've got there?"

Josephine skipped across the well-swept floorboards in the cool sanctuary of her father's garden shed, Matthieu as always at her side. Pascal Lalique looked up from the item before him on the table, his spectacles almost slipping from the end of his nose. "Come see."

Helene, who'd been following Josephine and Matthieu from the pond at her own leisurely pace, now joined them with a sigh of exhaustion.

"Oh, Helene, come see what Papa has done! Fabulous!"

"Rather a fascinating thing, isn't it?" Pascal echoed Josephine's excitement.

At first sight of the bullfrog, pinned back-down to the table, its legs spread wide and its jaw pinned through with a long shiny needle, Helene screamed. Matthieu laughed and Josephine prodded the cut-open stomach with the tip of her finger.

"Don't touch it!" Helene shrieked and fell to the floor in a pouf of skirts—much to Matthieu's delight.

"Dear." Pascal Lalique looked over his eldest, lying on the floor. "She is rather fragile, isn't she? Hmm. Least she's safe on the floor." He snaked his spectacles up his nose with a few expert wiggles. "Matthieu, come over here and take a look at this."

Still panting from his jaunt across the meadow, Matthieu stepped over Helene with no more regard than Josephine or Pascal offered her, and examined the specimen more closely. "It's still alive!" he proclaimed with a glance to Josephine, who added her own excited nod.

"Do you see, he's carefully pulled back the skin to reveal the organs, but the heart still beats," she said.

Horror was quickly replaced by a teenage boy's fascination for how things worked. Not to mention that he mustn't allow

Josephine to best him with her own macabre fascination over all things slimy and small. He adored Josephine for her curiosity, and credited her for inducing his own interest in nature, which then inspired his drawings. "Monsieur Lalique, what prompted you to do such a thing?"

"Not sure." Pascal turned and shuffled through the scatter of items on the shelf behind him. His fingers played over a bent garden trowel, an empty beaker, the maid's mob cap. "Though now that you're here, Matthieu, I've an inspiration."

Both Josephine and Matthieu looked to the professor with hopeful eyes.

"Perhaps you could sketch this frog." Pascal handed Matthieu a few sheets of dusty paper. "I think it would be most helpful in your studies."

"Oh yes." Josephine skipped to her father's side and helped him rummage for a broken stick of charcoal. "You've sketched an entire pond of frogs, now you must study how they work."

"You've time?" Pascal asked as he laid the paper before Matthieu on the table.

"Yes, Papa and I finished early with the chores today. He and Mama have plans for an afternoon stroll. He said this with a wink," Matthieu added smartly. "I don't think he would mind if I lingered here for a while."

"Excellent. Josephine, hand me that lancet."

"Whatever for?"

"I find it rather cruel to leave this poor beast's heart beating while Matthieu whiles away the afternoon in its study. I think the kindest thing to do would be to end its struggle, don't you?"

Professor Lalique inserted the lancet into the frog's neck, explaining carefully to his eager students as he severed the carotid artery. Just then, Helene shuffled on the floor and pulled herself up by the edge of the table. A spurt of blood struck Josephine's nose. She giggled as Matthieu wiped at it.

Helene landed with a much softer splat this time.

"Dear. Not again." Pascal bent over his inert daughter. "I suppose I must attend to your sister then."

Josephine and Matthieu both giggled.

Pascal lifted Helene, his sleeves rolled up to expose flexing muscles. "Will you be joining us for supper this evening, Matthieu?"

"If I may?"

"You know you are always welcome. Well, you two have a time of it then." He checked Helene in his arms. "Do we have some smelling salts in the pantry?"

"Leave her to Marie Claire, Papa," Josephine reassured, though her concentration remained on the bullfrog's deflating heart as the blood quickly streamed from the slit in its neck. "Just toss her on her bed. She'll come around."

Pascal chuckled as he left the two of them to their studies . . .


The delicate tracing of his mother's fingertips over the lace encircling his wrist pulled Matthieu to the present. She could spend hours lingering on the lace, he knew. And twined deeply in her own memories. He supposed he had inherited that tendency from her. For once again, he found himself fighting the past when around Isabelle.

Always the need to broach the past, to learn the secret to that dreaded summer, snuck up on him unawares. *He so wanted to know!* "There was no love more perfect than yours and Papa's," he murmured.

"Your memories are selective," Isabelle said.

"As they should be." Horrifying remembrance. His father dying in a pool of blood, his killer retreating on horseback. While Isabelle remained silent, the horror in her eyes screaming louder than his father's death cries.

"And what of you?" Isabelle shifted on the bench and Matthieu sat up straight, releasing the horrid memories. "You've been to the Laliques'?"

"Of course."

"Oh! How could I possibly think otherwise," she teased in that motherly, I-know-you-well voice. "You always did like their cuisine better than mine!"

"Mama, now don't start—"

"Silly young man. I know it's not the food that keeps you a virtual stepchild there. How does the lovely Josephine fare? *Mon dieu,* I believe it's been well over three years since I've laid eyes on the young filly. I wager she's grown into a fine young woman. Matthieu? Your cheeks color so deliciously when I speak of her."

"Mother!"

"Oh!" she said with a glorious peal. "You love the girl."

Why did the conversation have to take this turn? On his feet, Matthieu paced beneath the heavy umbrella of green apple baubles, while his mother sat with a triumphant smile on her tiny doll face.

"Oh hell!" He spun around. "I do love her, Mother. I do, I do! Much as I try to deny it, I love her for all the world."

"But why would you deny such a thing?"

He waved her off with a careless gesture. "It is impossible."

The bells for prayer or devotions or some other ritual began to ring from within the massive spire. Matthieu did not want to interrupt his mother's schedule—Isabelle followed the nun's patterns, though she was free to leave whenever she wished— but more than that, this was the perfect excuse to drop the topic of discussion.

"Matthieu?"

"I must go. But I promise I'll return this week."

Prepared to march away without another hug or kiss, Matthieu was stopped by a jerk on his sleeve. Isabelle's tiny hand gripped his arm. "Tell her."

"You think I should?"

She nodded.

"I will." He drew in a heavy breath of apple-sweet air. And then with its release he forced out all his apprehensions regarding Josephine Lalique. "I must. It is what is right."

# Chapter 14

Lingering under the stone arch that opened to the gardens, Josephine's thoughts wandered over yesterday's odd encounter with the chevalier. She *did* love Julien. But why was it his kiss did not ignite her into a burning blaze of desire? That was what a man's kisses were supposed to do. Weren't they? The meager spark she had felt had been quickly doused by his tongue!

Marie Claire placed a plumed hat of Josephine's design on top of Helene's curls. A squeal of delight echoed from the foyer, for Helene was intent on an afternoon stroll with one of her suitors.

"Josephine? Are you listening to me?"

Had Helene said something to her?

"What's got you hovering in the shadows this morning?" Helene crossed the wide fieldstone floor, adjusting the lace ruffles at her elbows and poufing out her sleeves as she neared Josephine. "What is it, sister? You look as though the world has stopped moving. Is it Julien? Did he say something to you? You looked all giddy when you came in last evening."

Giddy? Try confused, perplexed, and utterly aghast at the notion of having a man's tongue sloshing about in her mouth.

"It is nothing." Oh! What were older sisters for if you could not confide your deepest desires and worries to them? "It is what he did."

"Marie Claire! Call the guard. I'll have the man in chains before his evening meal. Why did you not tell me?"

"Leave us, Marie Claire. It wasn't like that," Josephine hissed through a clenched jaw. The maid lingered, concern furrowing her brow, but Josephine waved her away, waiting until the curious maid disappeared, though she knew she was just around the corner. Embarrassed to even admit it, Josephine squeezed through her teeth, "It was his kiss."

"Mmm, so you are no longer a virgin of the flesh, eh?"

"It was just . . . so different," Josephine said as she searched for some way to explain what she could not understand herself. "Not as I expected."

"And what did you expect?"

"I do not know. What *should* I expect, Helene? Tell me what a kiss should be like. Please, it was just so . . ."

Helene nudged her pale countenance forward, waiting her grand explanation.

"Awkward," Josephine finally said. "Just plain awkward."

"Naturally."

"And well . . . distasteful. I think."

"Oh." Helene's shoulders wilted to match the dangle of the violet plume in her hat. "Well then, there is only one thing you can do."

"Which is?"

"Do not see Chevalier Delaroche any more. You cannot."

"But—"

"If the man's kisses do not ignite the tiniest bit of passion here," she pressed a hand to Josephine's breast, the smooth kid gloves feeling cool against her skin, "that will not change."

So why did Helene seem relieved to be making such an announcement? It was almost as if she did not approve. Why was everyone so intent on turning her head from the chevalier?

"It must take time," Josephine said, following as Helene retreated for the front door. "We are both new to each other."

"A man like that should know how to kiss a woman," Helene replied over her shoulder.

"But he kissed you!"

Her sister paused at the door, one gloved hand resting on the brass door handle. She tilted her head in thought.

"You raved of his kisses!" Josephine continued.

Still in thought, Helene held up one hand, palm out for silence. "I only raved because Constance would have taken too great a pleasure in mocking me had I not."

Josephine's jaw fell.

"So now you know."

"But you—Every man you speak about—" Josephine was stunned. Helene the beautiful had lied about Julien's kisses? And only to best Constance? "I shall never understand this game you must play with men!" she declared. "Must I do it also? I don't like it, Helene. It is not right. What is wrong with honesty?"

"Oh?" Helene directed her sullen gaze towards Josephine. "Such as the honesty you displayed in writing to the chevalier and signing my name to the missives?"

Defeated by the truth.

"I never did beg your forgiveness, Helene. It was most unthinking of me to use your name so carelessly. I am so sorry."

On a heavy sigh, Helene gave an understanding nod, her way of accepting Josephine's apology without all the fanfare and bother that might start a tear trailing down her perfectly rouged cheeks.

"As for the chevalier and his kisses," she added as she pulled the door open and set a trail of sun across the stone floor, "I knew he was not worth the paper his words were written on."

"He is worth it," Josephine said to the closing door. "He must be, for else I would not have fallen so hard." A sigh fell heavily from her lips. "But that kiss ... Ah, it is me, surely. I just need a little more experience."

*　*　*

"Josephine, what a surprise."

"Well, it shouldn't be," she said as she entered the tiny cubicle Matthieu called home. He'd let a room on the Boulevard Saint Michel, a quiet neighborhood that saw more artists and musicians scrambling around the Place Maubert than noisy hawkers and drunkards. The taverns were few, but the enlightening conversations and enriching seminars many. She tossed her plain straw hat on the chair without a care and walked over to see what he was doing. "Can't a friend call on you?"

"Yes, but I usually come to you." Matthieu dropped his brush in the cloudy waterwell and turned to Josephine. "What is it?"

She forced a smile and waved him off as she plopped onto his understuffed mattress, his one luxury that had depleted half his remaining soldier's earnings. Though by all means, he did appreciate a good night's sleep.

"It must be something. You look as though you've woken to find the flowers in your garden all plucked from the stems. Is it something with your studies? Has your father's experiment gone awry?"

"If only it were that simple," she said on a preoccupied sigh. Her darting gaze took in all corners of his meagerly furnished room, not judging, just accounting. "Perhaps I shouldn't have come here."

She didn't move from the bed. She wanted to talk. But for some odd reason, the words did not fly from her lips as they usually did. Must be something about Delaroche. Josephine had become so different since her confession of love for the man. And it was not the lovesick reverie that Matthieu had come to recognize from others. Her temperament was more anxious, almost tentative.

"It's about Julien?" he said, forcing his voice to remain genial. He turned back to his sketch—a design for Madame Lamarck featuring paste jewels and quilting—and lifted his

brush. Perhaps if he feigned disinterest she would find it easier
to spill her troubles. She certainly had developed a crippled
tongue since his return.

"I don't know." Another sigh. Ah, the sweet whisper of her
breath. "Perhaps . . ."

How trying. The only other time she'd been so evasive with
him—besides the night she had revealed her love for the chevalier—was when he'd left with his regiment. She hadn't wanted
to bid him *au revoir*. She must have thought not saying goodbye
meant he would never leave.

"It might just be me . . ."

Matthieu paused, brush loaded with sapphire, waiting for her
to continue.

"Helene thinks it is a sign."

A sign? What could she possibly—

"But I have to believe that most first kisses are awkward."

First kisses? A watery drop of blue splat upon the toes of
the sketch. Matthieu raced for a rag, but knocked the glass
waterwell off the desk.

"Oh!" Josephine dashed to catch the falling receptacle.
Murky water rained over her skirts and splattered her arms and
face.

"Curse me as a clumsy oaf, let me help you with that."
Matthieu dabbed at her face and shoulders with the rag. She'd
been stormed from face to skirt hem with a horrid mixture of
every color in the rainbow. If he had tried, he could not have
been more thorough. "I'm sorry, it is all my fault. I wasn't
paying attention."

"Matthieu," she grabbed his hand as he fretted over her
poufy sleeves, "relax. It's just water."

"Mixed with paint," he noted sharply. "It'll ruin your dress.
This fine silk. Damn!"

"I don't care." She gripped both his hands tight, so he had
no choice but to stop. "I shall have Marie Claire make an
attempt at removing the stains, but if not, I will not worry. This

is an old dress. Marie Claire has been eyeing it for pillows in the study.''

"It's the one you wore the day I left for my first campaign."

Her wide eyes blinked. Consternation settled on her brow. "You remember such a thing?"

He would never forget. "Well, you've only the few dresses that are your favorites. The lavender, the mint green, the sky blue whose hem you tore when we were picking daisies. The crimson you wore the other day must be a new addition since my departure, because I have never seen that one before."

"Why, Matthieu, I'm quite taken aback. You've better knowledge of my wardrobe than I."

Knowing that he'd exposed his careful observation of her, Matthieu turned away and went about cleaning up his drawing table. "A painter's eye, that is all." With a bit of creativity he could coax the blue droplet into a fashionable ruffle at the hem. Madame Lamarck would rave over his endless cache of ideas.

But he felt horrible about Josephine's dress. The dyes used in the sapphire paint would never be coaxed out of the fibers of her dress. He was such a cad! He listened as she settled back onto his bed and wiped the rag over her skirts. The dress was beyond salvage. Marie Claire would throw a fit. Pillows? Not unless they were minuscule. He would replace it. Yes, he must.

Now what had she been talking about? Ah yes, that damned first kiss. From the ever-so-charming Julien Delaroche, presumably. Best not to return to that topic if at all possible.

"Now, I was saying about my argument with Helene," Josephine began.

Matthieu caught his forehead in his palm.

"Oh, Matthieu, you don't mind that I tell you about this? I do need someone to talk to. And you being a man, well, I thought you might be able to enlighten me."

"Mind?" He squeezed his fingers against his forehead. Friendship had begun to demand incredible sacrifice lately. "How could I possibly mind when it concerns you? So . . . Chevalier Delaroche's kisses are . . . awkward?"

He relaxed a little. Awkward, eh? Ha, ha!

"Yes."

Good. Matthieu dropped his hand to his thigh and turned to
Josephine. So Delaroche was not as cavalier with the ladies as
he claimed to be. Perhaps he did want to hear more about this
first kiss. *All* about it.

"Awkward," he repeated. "As in clumsy? Cumbersome?
Unpleasant?"

The sweet shrug of her shoulders made her bosom rise in
two enticing mounds framed by stained lace. Matthieu averted
his eyes to the wall behind her.

"Yes." She clasped her hands in her lap, but could not keep
from nervously working them. Then she jumped to her feet
and paced before Matthieu. "Actually . . . well . . . it started
out quite nicely. Rather masterful."

Matthieu rolled his eyes. "Masterful."

"But then it became . . . well . . . soggy!"

He dropped his jaw and let out a ribald burst of laughter.

"Matthieu, it is not the least bit humorous!"

Her tiny fists beat the air. Josephine's rare ventures into
anger were always a delight to behold. Delicate tension carved
her features into a marble study of dismay and confusion. And
then he realized how cruel it was to laugh at her obvious cry
for understanding.

"Forgive me." He stood and pulled her into a gentle
embrace. "I should not have laughed." Though admittedly it
was damn hard not to smile still. He rested his chin on top of
her head and trailed lazy strokes up her back. "So you've not
found Delaroche's kisses to be at all to your liking?"

"I didn't say that. It's just I'm confused as to why I don't
feel . . . passion."

The desire with which she said the word surprised Matthieu.
So she knew of passion. And she did not have it. When she
had already confessed love. That was odd.

"Tell me, Matthieu." She looked up at him, and he released
her to lean against the wall just behind. "Shouldn't a man's

kiss—whether it be the first or the twentieth—stir some passion in a woman's soul? Yet those were the only two assessments I could conjure at the very moment Julien's tongue touched mine: awkward and soggy. I just thought it would be . . . so much more."

While it drove him insane to even discuss Julien and Josephine in the same breath as the subject of kissing, Matthieu couldn't resist answering her innocent query. The state she was in, the fragile worry, the abandoned inhibitions . . . His loins tightened at the realization of their close proximity.

"While I can only speak for myself, I think every kiss a woman receives should be exquisite and priceless." He touched her chin, carefully brushing away a spot of splattered paint-water. Now he noticed the aura of gardenia that surrounded her like a garden enclosed in a small greenhouse, heavy with aroma, eager to lure a wanderer inside to become lost in the heady scent.

"You make it sound like a gift," she said.

He had to shake himself out of his reverie. A gift? "Is it not? The most intimate act a man and woman can share? Should it not be a gift of the heart, a concentrated act of the inner soul?"

"I've always thought that. But the first one—"

"May be experimental," he offered, leaning closer to her. Soft skirts slipped over his thin breeches, awakening his every nerve ending to the delicious thrill of sensation. "But never awkward. There may be . . ." He checked his hand, which ached to run his fingers through her hair. *Control.* " . . . apprehension. For certainly, being a first kiss . . ." He studied the minute shards of amber that spotted the deep brown of her irises. ". . . it must be something he has . . . pined for."

"I imagine," she whispered, her own gaze captured by his.

"Now is his chance to kiss the lips . . ." He brushed his thumb over the plump flesh of her bottom lip, smooth, full, and achingly teasing. "The mouth he has venerated in his dreams."

"Venerated?" came her weak voice.

Her top lip was as exquisite as the lower. A fitting match to his imagination, which lay only a few feet away on flat paper.

"But it must be properly timed . . ." He leaned closer. Her hot breath whispered across his own lips. Tempting, luring him to the edge. "The man will perhaps lean in, bringing their bodies to but a whisper's distance. And then he will inhale."

"Inhale?" she gasped.

"Draw in the essence of her scent." He closed his eyes. "Catch a faint trail of the garden flowers she picked upon rising. The perfume of their petals imbuing their oils upon her cheeks, the tip of her nose. Mm, gardenia, that is what she held before her lips this morning."

"I did." Her eyelids fell softly shut.

"It is all about anticipation," he whispered. "Knowing what is soon to come, yet prolonging the act for the enjoyment of every sense. The smell of her flesh, her hair, even the remnants of morning chocolate lingering on her breath. The texture of her lips, the silky slide of her skirts across his ankle. The sound of her timorous breathing, the sight of her rising—Oh, *mon dieu.*"

Matthieu stumbled back and away from Josephine, who still stood with eyes closed and heart beating in frantic expectation against her paint-stained bodice.

What he had almost done!

"Forgive me."

She shook her head, rising from the mists of her own enchanted spell. "Oh . . ."

"I don't know what came over me." Two long strides forced him to the door, which he pulled open. "Perhaps you should—"

"Yes. Oh yes! I should." Her skirts kissed his ankles as she scrambled past him. She patted her hair, her bodice, her skirts, as she passed before him. "I don't know what has become of the time. But I do thank you for this little . . ." She flashed a brief but searching glance up at him. "Time. Good day, Matthieu."

# Chapter 15

They had been *so close*. Their lips but a finger's width apart. Every fiber in his being had stirred with want, with need, with desire for Josephine Lalique. If only he had kissed her. Maybe then she would know.

After purchasing a lemon ice near the Seine, Matthieu ambled over to the Louvre to see if any of his fellow soldiers were about. He reasoned now that it had been wise to stop as he had. Until she got over this girlish infatuation she had, Matthieu was resigned to wait in the shadows. She would see that Julien could never love her exclusively. Then perhaps her eyes would be opened to the devotion Matthieu could promise her forever.

As he entered the drilling grounds where soldiers practiced with muskets and foils, Matthieu kicked his toes in the dry dirt, stirring up a cloud befitting his mood.

"Bouchet!"

He offered a nod and a wave to those who recognized and called to him.

Dodging the swing of the circling wooden quintain, he bumped into another soldier. But instead of acknowledging

Matthieu's distracted *excusez-moi,* the man issued a challenge. Matthieu swung around. Julien Delaroche stood in breeches and open shirt, his sword *en garde* a grand smile decorating his face.

"Delaroche," Matthieu said. Instantly his grip found the hilt of his rapier.

"Chin up, man! Come! You're obviously here to test your steel. Match it against mine. I've not had a good challenge in days!"

Oh, hadn't he?

"What of the challenge that beckons your heart?" Matthieu slipped his sword from its sheath and drew the blade swiftly through his gloved fingers. He assumed *en garde.* He hadn't had a good challenge either. And he wasn't about to forego this one.

"Ah, you speak of Mademoiselle Lalique?"

"Is there already someone else who occupies your thoughts?"

Upon noticing the twitch in his opponent's elbow, Matthieu leapt forward to engage swords. The sing of steel worked to sharpen his senses.

"That can hardly be considered a challenge," Julien said as his sword danced across Matthieu's and the two passed each other, stirring up billows of dust. "The girl is already in love, she has confessed herself. What need I do but scoop her into my arms and carry her away?"

A swift flick of his wrist delivered a sharp blow to the hilt of Julien's blade, setting off what Matthieu knew to be a jaw-grinding twinge through his system. "If you harm her I shall see you hanged!"

"Bouchet, good man, settle your steel." Delaroche offered a cavalier flash of his white teeth. "I've no intention of harming Mademoiselle Lalique."

"See that I can trust those words."

"How can you accuse me of such a thing? I would never harm a woman."

"Perhaps not physically."

This time Delaroche matched Matthieu's parrying lunge with a swift riposte and the two came face to face, their blades intimate.

"I don't understand you, Bouchet." The man's jaw pulsed, but he did not move to disengage. "Are you saying I am not a gentleman? Those are serious dueling words. You'd best check yourself."

Much as he wanted to slash his blade in fury across the man's throat, Matthieu held back his anger. "All I am saying is that if you intend to court her, then do it with no plans to treat her like yesterday's greasy meal as soon as she has served your pleasures."

A wicked arc curled Delaroche's lips, and Matthieu sensed his suspicions might be truer than he thought. "You would not treat her so!" he exclaimed.

The clatter of steel overtook the courtyard as the two men embroiled themselves in the fight. Cadets stopped their drilling and boisterous roughhousing to watch as Matthieu pressed Julien across the practice yard, his sword acting for his heart, something he knew Julien Delaroche could never possess. Never.

Suddenly, Julien lunged forward and was able to fling Matthieu against the stone visage of the Louvre. The contact sent a bone-jarring shiver down his spine. Delaroche pinned his body against Matthieu's, his hand coming up to secure Matthieu's sword hand over his head. "What I do with my women is my own business."

A jerk of his shoulder and a knee to Delaroche's gut landed the chevalier flat on his back, with Matthieu right on top of him. "She is only yours because of me," Matthieu said.

"And I thank you for your cooperation." Julien coughed on the dust that steamed around them. His face grew crimson with rage and the embarrassment of lying pinned beneath a cadet. "But your assistance is no longer needed. Mademoiselle Lalique has agreed to accompany me to Treville's ball tomorrow evening. So you see, I'm treating her well enough."

"If you hurt her—"

"Then you shall be there to nurse her back to health. A fair exchange, if you ask me. I get what I want, and you get . . . whatever it is *you* want." He quirked a brow.

"Shut up." Stepping up from his opponent, Matthieu shoved his rapier back in the sheath. He'd not allow the man the satisfaction of knowing his heart.

"You do care for her, don't you!" Delaroche's laughing announcement pounded from ear to ear as Matthieu marched off towards the Pont Neuf.

To turn and resume the fight now would only answer the man's mocking declaration.

Still lying on the ground, Julien Delaroche rolled to his side and followed Bouchet's dusty trail as he retreated like a wounded fox towards the safety of the river. Damn, but it felt good to know he'd struck the man where it hurt the most. Right in the heart.


He had become this . . . this *thing* . . . that was consumed with Josephine!

"Consumed!" Matthieu chastised himself as he swaggered down the street, by-passing the Smokeless Dragon with a forced determination. Spirits would only force him lower than he had already come. "I can think of nothing but her. Eat, sleep, dream nothing but her. And now I am drawing steel in her name. Fool!"

Aware that he still gripped his sword hilt with a knuckle-busting hold, Matthieu quickly sheathed the weapon. His pace quickened, anger fueling his strides.

Not another thought must be wasted on her *or* the dandy she pursued. He would have no more of it! Rounding the corner of an apothecary shop, Matthieu punched a gloved fist into the stone wall. The pain did not even register.

"Damn it!" He ducked into an alleyway and kicked the wall, his frustration overtaking his own sense of direction. "She

has no interest in me whatsoever, so why should I care?'' he
declared to the narrow slash of sky above him. ''Consumed?
Bah!''

No, he didn't need this trouble. Didn't need the love of a
woman who would have that ramscuttle Delaroche. ''I don't
care what becomes of her. She can marry that scurvy bastard
for all I care!''

''You do love her.''

''What?'' Matthieu spun round, scanning the dank alley. A
pile of broken keg shafts and dirty rags lay heaped but three
strides away. But the stench! ''Who said that?''

''I did. And I said you love her.''

Matthieu looked up. Was *He* talking to him? Ha, ha! Nothing
would surprise Matthieu lately. He spoke to the air above him.
''I do not love Mademoiselle Lalique.''

''Do.''

''Don't!'' With that, Matthieu exited the narrow passage and
headed for home.

The street vagrant buried beneath a shield of tattered cloaks
muttered, ''He does, poor bastard.''

''I cannot believe Madame Lamarck would not reveal who
purchased this divine creation for you.''

Josephine followed her sister's reflection in the floor-length
mirror as she circled round her, studying every inch of the
shimmery cream satin gown.

''She said it was from an admirer.'' Infectious delight coated
Josephine's words as she smoothed her hands across the ribboned stomacher. ''Julien, I assume.''

''Hard to believe,'' Helene remarked flatly. She lifted the
elegant lace that dripped from Josephine's elbows. Hundreds
of precious pink stones had been sewn into the elaborate lace
at the sleeves, around the narrow neckline lace, and on the first
layer of petticoats.

''Madame Lamarck has surely outdone herself this time.''

Josephine could barely contain her excitement as she stood in this exquisite creation that looked is if it belonged on an angel and sparkled with the vibrancy of a star-dusted heaven. The underskirts were of muted rose, spotted with more of the pink stones. Every step she took swished and sparkled.

"I can't imagine the man going to such expense." Helene let the lace drop from her fingers. "But if you wish to believe."

"Who else could it possibly be?"

Her sister pressed a gloved finger to her lips, her lashes narrowing over her dark eyes as she thought. "I cannot say until I've had more time to think on it."

"Perhaps you just don't wish to believe that the chevalier can have feelings for me so quickly after you dismissed him from your bouquet of soldiers?"

"I did not say that. Though I stand by my assessment that he is a cad. Josephine, what would Father say about this?"

"Father is not home."

"He is but an overnight messenger away."

"You would not tell him!"

Helene's dark brow quirked. "Why are you so worried? If the chevalier is a good man than Father will have no objections."

"Oh, Helene, I do not run to Father regarding the many dozens of men you string along, nor do I tell him of your amorous games."

"Very well! My escort will be here soon," she said with a dismissal of the topic. "Are you soon finished, Marie Claire? I need final adjustments to my hair. When will Julien arrive for you, Josephine?"

"I believe soon."

"Mademoiselle Lalique, there is a gentleman below for you." Cook popped her head in and the two girls gave her an inquiring look. "Oh, Josephine."

"Julien?"

"No, Monsieur Bouchet."

"Oh dear." Josephine touched her lips, suddenly recalling yesterday's almost-kiss. "What could *he* be here for?"

Helene's jaw snapped shut and was replaced with a secretive smile. "You bruise Monsieur Bouchet with your cold indifference to him. Perhaps he's simply come to call. Did you tell him you had an engagement with Julien this evening?"

"I believe so. I don't recall. Oh bother, Helene, I don't know what to think about Matthieu anymore. He almost kissed me yesterday!"

"La! And you are only just now telling me? My, but you've become such a brazen since taking possession of that silly letter! How did it happen? Did an act of God blow the man into your arms?"

"Helene."

"No, no, forgive me. I shouldn't speak so of the poor man. Of course I've seen this coming for a long time. But what shall you do about the chevalier?"

"What do you mean? I've a ball to attend this evening, on his arm." A fluff to her left sleeve poufed the generous satin to a shimmery pillow. "Whatever do you expect I should do? It was just a fluke."

"Odd as he may be, I must hand it to Monsieur Bouchet for always and exclusively seeing to your best interests."

"But it wasn't even a tangible kiss. Only . . . well, it did startle me. In a way I wish it really had happened. Oh, Helene, what will I say to him? And what if Julien comes when he is here? I don't want to alienate Matthieu, but I cannot allow him to sabotage my chances with Julien."

"Pity he cannot . . ." Helene muttered.

"What?"

"Open your eyes, Josephine. In your pursuit of pleasure you trod upon the one person who offers you pure devotion. Matthieu Bouchet loves you."

"As a friend!" Josephine snapped and stamped her foot against the floor.

"You've been spending far too much time lounging under the sun," Helene said as she gave a final touch of the thick white powder puff to Josephine's throat. "The harsh rays have burned your eyes blind. *Friends* do not attempt to kiss one another in a way that should cause you such perplexity.''

Not willing to justify that remark with a response, Josephine snatched her silk throw from the bed and marched downstairs. ''Matthieu!''

He greeted her with a chaste kiss to either cheek. Had he so quickly forgotten what almost happened yesterday, to tease her so today? Oh, why was this visit even happening? And why did she even care about how Matthieu made her feel?

''Forgive my interruption. Marie Claire has informed me you are on your way out. I simply could not let a day pass without coming to offer my apologies.''

''Your apologies?'' So she had been correct to think that it had been a foolish mistake. Matthieu had no intention of kissing her, only he'd gotten carried away in his description of how a kiss should be. Unfortunate as that fact was, it was also just that. A fact. Matthieu was a friend. Nothing more. ''Speak no more of it, Matthieu. It's already been forgotten. It was a foolish thing to do.''

''Yes, of course. I should never have allowed my fantasies to carry me away—''

''Your fantasies?''

''Oh, I suppose I shouldn't have put it quite that way.''

I suppose not! Had he really fantasized about kissing her? Oh dear. Did friends have fantasies about one another? How to swallow this information with Julien due at her door so soon?

He managed an awkward smile, as if trying to hide his own embarrassment, then he suddenly noticed the rest of her. ''Josephine, this dress!''

''It was delivered this afternoon,'' she said, flouncing the cream lace at her elbows. She cared not if Helene did not like where it had come from, it had been given to her by the man she loved. ''From Julien. Madame Lamarck delivered it personally.''

''And she said it was from Julien?''

"An admirer. She was not allowed to reveal who. But who else?" She placed her hands on her hips and turned from side to side, thankful that the awkward moment had been trampled by something as mundane as fashion. "What is your opinion, Matthieu? How do I look?"

Catching an adoring sigh in his throat, Matthieu looked over the dress. Madame Lamarck had outdone herself and then some. There was no way the wages he had put forth had paid for such an elaborate piece as this! He surely owed Madame Lamarck many more months' wages.

"Matthieu? I asked what you think?"

"Ah . . . there . . . are simply no words to describe what I see." For if he began he would surely expose his longings. And hadn't his roaming mouth gotten him into enough trouble with Josephine lately?

"Oh. Well." She pulled her silk wrap to her stomach. "I'm quite sure the chevalier will have more than a few words. He is a master of words, you know."

Matthieu inclined his head and could only offer a weak snarl.

"You mustn't be jealous, Matthieu. You are a master of charcoals and paints. The fact that you cannot put your thoughts into words is nothing to be ashamed of." Her skirts swirled into a kaleidoscope of gold and rose and sparkling gemstones as she turned to the stairs.

Nothing to be ashamed of, eh? He couldn't let her get by with having the last word. Not when his pride was at stake. "Wait!"

She paused.

"Very well." Matthieu strode around her, appearing to take in her dress, while really he was fuming with rage. *The chevalier is a master of words.* What isn't he a master of? Besides the common graces and acting like a human! "If you wish a word of approval than so be it. I find your appearance this evening . . . well . . . most . . . delicious!"

There. He'd said it.

Crimson painted lips fell slack. She touched her throat. "Oh."

The urge to rush a kiss upon those honey-sweet lips raged in Matthieu's gut. But he'd already foiled that opportunity with all the grace of a stumbling lout.

"Delicious," she tried the word, a wide smile growing upon her face. "Really?"

"That is my choice of words. Do with it as you will. From now on I shall hold my silence so as not to upset you further. I shouldn't wish you looking strained for Delaroche."

The icy tone of his voice induced Josephine to recall Helene's words. *Matthieu Bouchet loves you.* No. He had never given her reason to believe he cared for her beyond friendship. Save yesterday. He had almost kissed her. And she had almost wanted him to. No, not almost. She *had* wanted Matthieu to kiss her.

Surely he would have said something to her if he did have feelings. Well, of course he did not. His touches were always too brief, too chaste, almost quick to the point of being wary.

But that almost-kiss . . . It had been the single most romantic moment of her entire life. If only he had . . . *Mon dieu,* what did she feel towards Matthieu? Did she have romantic inclinations towards this man?

"Your silence pleads me to inquire why. What is it you and Helene were arguing over just now?"

"Huh?" No, now was no time to start rethinking her relationship with Matthieu, when the man she really loved would be here at any moment!

"She disapproves of Julien. She is jealous, that is all. That he could have feelings for me and not her is beyond her comprehension."

"It is beyond mine also."

Josephine pressed both hands to her hips. It was time once and for all to get things clear. To all. Including her own mutinous conscience that suddenly could speak only of kissing Matthieu. "You question my heart?"

He offered a shrug. "I, like your sister, find it hard to believe that Julien Delaroche can so quickly give up on Helene and fall in love with you in much the same breath.''

''You will never understand,'' she hissed, finding her patience threatening to flee.

He sighed and took up both her hands in his. So gentle. Caressing. As tender as when he touched her lips yesterday. Why was it so hard to erase their encounter from her memory?

''Then make me understand,'' he said softly.

The husky tone startled and enticed. A wanting stirred within. But not as desperate as the wanting to finally have the one man she loved in her arms. A man who showered her with words of devotion and an elegant dress fit for a queen. She was the queen of Julien Delaroche's heart.

''Very well. I will make you understand the love I hold for Julien; then perhaps you will understand why he can love me so quickly.

''It is simple, really. For three months I corresponded with a man who had an immense ability to place his very heart and soul upon paper. It mattered not that I had never laid eyes upon him, or heard the timbre of his voice in conversation. For in his words, in the little black scribbles that formed letters and sounds, ran his very blood.

''Don't you see, Matthieu? I love the man who wrote those letters. He gave me his soul and promised me his heart. And though he may seem rough and irregular on the outside and completely lacking in social graces, I know that if it was his hand those words were fashioned of, than it is his heart to which I must be true.''

''You're serious?''

The stunned look on Matthieu's face did nothing but infuriate Josephine. She could not explain it more thoroughly than that!

''Dead serious.''

''You love the man who wrote the letters?''

''If you could read them, you would understand.'' She stepped away, slipping her hands from the warmth of his grasp—a strangely hard warmth to give up. "I do thank you for all you've done, Matthieu."

"But of course," came his stilted words.

There was nothing more she could offer. As much as she hated walking away from a man she cherished and trusted more than any other, the man who strode up the front path at this very moment was the one her heart belonged to. Josephine dashed outside, closing the door behind her so the chevalier would not spy Matthieu standing inside.

Matthieu cracked open the door and watched as Josephine's shiny satin skirts swayed and swished along the path to her gates and into Delaroche's arms. The skirts *he* had paid for, swishing around Delaroche's legs. Skirts befitting a princess of some fairytale land, whose knight must battle evil dragons to win her heart.

She did not even look back. Not once.

But now he did not need that reassurance.

She loved the man who wrote the letters. He'd put his heart and soul onto paper. And that was why she loved. She loved . . .

She loved!

A delicious smile overtook Matthieu's face. He could barely contain the simmering desire to leap high and kick his heels together like some folktale leprechaun in possession of his stolen treasure. For his treasure—a prize he'd cherished for years—had finally been granted him. And it shone with a brilliance to far surpass that of a king's ransom or a queen's tiara.

She loved the man who wrote the letters. *The man who wrote the letters!*

"Ah, Matthieu." Helene sauntered down the staircase, her wide skirts hissing. "I see my sister leaves you standing in the dust of her skirts. Forgive her, she is love-struck."

"Yes," he mused. "Love-struck. Struck by cupid's arrow.

Straight to the heart.'' His heart. Her heart. Together. *Love struck.* ''She is, isn't she?''

''And does that not bother you?''

''Huh? No,'' he absently offered. ''Of course not. Why should it?''

''Matthieu, did you hear me?'' Helene drew a worried glance over him. ''I just said Josephine was lovestruck. Over Julien Delaroche!'' Shaking her hands made the silly feather in her hat do a dance before her eyes, so while she tried to look serious, the constant blowing of the damned thing out of her face only succeeded in making her look ridiculous. ''The Chevalier,'' she reiterated. ''Not. You!''

''Perhaps,'' Matthieu offered.

''Hmmph.'' Helene snapped her fists into her black mink muff. ''I've always thought you a bit strange on occasion, Matthieu Bouchet. And this is one of them!''

He smiled at her. ''As you wish, Mademoiselle. I must be going.'' Matthieu slowly stepped back, and out the door.

Tonight was proving to be a very good night indeed.

# Chapter 16

Treville put on a spectacular soiree, Julien thought, with a bit of the king's assistance, of course. The occasional ball always served to lift Julien's spirits and heighten his awareness of the female species. He scanned the crowded Salles des Fêtes of Paris's city hall, allowing his gaze to linger on the feast of exposed décolletage, the chatter of pursing red lips, and the stolen winks from more than a few of the delicious beauties who attended the festivities.

Josephine had wandered off, saying she wanted to see if she might discover if her father attended tonight. Just what Julien needed. To meet the father. He heartily prayed the queer old card had taken the evening off. He needn't the hindrance of trying to impress the man. Especially when Josephine would serve him no more than the means for a long awaited revenge. No, Julien wanted to avoid the father at all costs.

But he did hope Josephine would hurry back to his side. He'd already spied Helene on some fop's arm. Best to avoid her until she could see exactly the sort of amorous attentions she'd given up. Julien had every intention of introducing Josephine to each and every one of his regiment mates and letting them all see just how devoted the young thing was to him.

As an added bonus, word was sure to get back to Bouchet. "Wine, Monsieur?"

Julien accepted the goblet offered by a royal blue liveried servant, but tapped the boy on the shoulder before he left. "That's *chevalier.*"

"Forgive me, Chevalier." A deep bow and the blushing young man disappeared.

Shrugging his shoulders to adjust the weight of his heavy doublet, Julien sneered at the callow servant before gulping his drink down in two swallows. His wig slipped while his head was back, but he caught it before it could go too far askew. Damned rug! Such short notice, the wigmaker had complained, so he'd had to settle for this heavy thing of black sausage curls and violet ribbons. Quite the cavalier, the wigmaker had remarked. And it doesn't look a bit loose.

A cavalier indeed! Plus these damned shoes pinched like he had a gaggle of geese pecking at his toes. And it had been a while since he'd worn silk hose. Such a wretched time he'd had trying to get the clocks straight! Ah well, Josephine had drawn in a breath and remarked on how dashing he looked. Good thing he'd gone with the white powder on his cheeks and the black spade mouche near his lip. It seemed to attract her interest. In fact, when she was around, she couldn't take her eyes from his face. Probably dreaming about how she wished the evening to end.

Well, he wasn't the man to disappoint.

"Julien! Forgive me, I've been away from you for so long." Looking every bit a gilded doll in the fine gold satin, Josephine received his hand and didn't even mind when he circled her slender waist with a firm hold. "I stumbled across one of Father's friends. The courtiers are staying in the upper rooms tonight. He expects Father to be here this evening. In fact, he's quite sure Father had plans to attend with the Duchess Champenois."

"The Duchess Champenois?" Quite a catch for the old bugger. "I understand she's heiress to quite a large sum. I had no idea your father kept such illustrious company."

"Neither did I. I've never heard him mention the Duchess. Though as for the company he keeps, he does have the King's ear."

Yes, he'd forgotten that part. Best to amuse the daughter as well as he could muster. Until of course, they were a good distance away from the father.

"Let's dance, Julien. They've begun a minuet in the ballroom. Can we please, before the night draws too long?"

"Certainly. But first, I wish to introduce you to a few people, some men from my regiment. Commander Marechal and Commander Treville, Captain of the King's Grand Musketeers."

"Of course." Her smooth alabaster shoulders wilted with his announcement. Damn it to hell, she could endure a few introductions if she expected him to trip the dance floor with her!

A zing of urgency flashed through Julien's veins. Yes, do the introductions quickly—but all the same, eloquently, so as to ensure all thought Josephine infatuated with him—and then ... "We must find your sister and say hello."


A large fern offered Matthieu partial cover, but also only partial view of Josephine and Julien across the ballroom. She held a black feather mask studded in gold grommets to her face, as Delaroche introduced her to one of the cadets from the 26th Foot. As Josephine lowered her mask she beamed and allowed the man to nudge each of her cheeks with a gentlemanly kiss.

Just how many men would have the pleasure of tasting her sweet aura this evening? Matthieu prayed not many, but he sensed it would be otherwise.

He'd had no plans of coming this evening. Especially without a lady on his arm. But after hearing Josephine explain why she loved Julien—or so she thought!—Matthieu could not stay away.

If she could just get a few moments to herself, away from the zealous attentions of Delaroche. That would be all he needed. Just a moment of her time.

And then he would have forever.

"La! Monsieur Bouchet." The teeth-grinding strains of a very familiar voice caused Matthieu to stiffen, his head peering through the divided fronds of the fern most peculiarly. "What an interesting surprise that I should find you dwelling amongst the vegetation this evening."

Hyacinth. An unmistakable signature. He snapped around and inclined his head in a smart acknowledgment. Scads of lace and sapphires covered every inch of the woman, save a generous helping of shoulder and décolletage. "Mademoiselle Lalique."

Helene snapped her beaded fan to full width and fluttered it languorously before her breasts. "I may regret my asking, but do you often linger in foliage?"

"Not usually."

"Oh, I see now." Helene joined Matthieu and peered through the now permanent part in the narrow fronds. "Spying on my sister, eh? Don't tell me this is practice for the army. Is there something you *forgot* to tell Josephine when you were at our home earlier?"

"Why would you think that?"

"Why do you snap at me so?"

Snap? He did not— Oh, to know the workings of a woman's mind. They could twist an innocent phrase as quickly as a man's head. But Matthieu could plainly see the wheels and cogs grinding beneath Helene's powdered wig. She thought she knew something. Perhaps she did know something. Ah, hell! She did. And the smugness seeping from her smirking lips was unbearable!

"Oh!" She gripped his wrist and tugged him away from the

plant. "I see Josephine has been left alone by the chevalier. Now is your chance, my curious spy in the grasses."

"Um ..." Matthieu stumbled down a few marble steps, trying not to trample Helene's skirts. While she managed to glide through the crowd with nary a wrinkle of her skirts, Matthieu had to dodge and bend and downright duck to avoid gesturing hands and spinning skirts. "Wait!"

A woman never listened when set on a goal. Damned female selective healing. Too much a gentleman to wrench his hand from her gloved fingers, Matthieu had no choice but to follow Helene onto the open patio lit by dozens of tin lumières.

"Josephine, look what I have dredged up from the bushes!"

Helene pulled Matthieu around and all but pushed him into her sister's arms. He caught himself just before touching the golden satin that covered Josephine's stomacher.

"Matthieu?"

"Mademoiselle." He offered a deep bow, regretting his mud-spattered boots, breeches, and plain blue doublet, but then he hadn't planned to actually mingle with the glamorous party guests.

"I shall grant you two the privacy Monsieur Bouchet craves," Helene said on a suppressed giggle, and left to join the party inside.

A snaking row of lumieres had been set along the stone wall that bordered the Seine. It gave the night a magical sparkle, and even offset the usual rancid smells that rose from the dark waters.

"I had no idea you were coming tonight," Josephine said. "You didn't tell me ... earlier."

So she was still miffed. She had a right. But not for long.

"Nor did you tell me you had plans to attend the ball with the chevalier. It seemed you were in quite the hurry to leave."

Though Delaroche had told him as much, to know that she had come here on another man's arm, wearing the very dress he had designed for her ... And, oh, did this fabric cling to her body as if it were a second skin. The creamy curves of her shoulders just peeked out of the tight satin, luscious treasures of flesh rose and fell with every breath she took. How desperately he pined to smooth his hands over her breasts. To lean forward and taste . . . The sight of her did things to his resolve. Urgent, traitorous things.

"Am I supposed to check in with you regarding every move I make? Why, Matthieu, if I didn't know better—"

The scrutiny of her gaze unraveled his nerves. Did she know how appetizing she looked with those delicate brown curls spiraling over her cheeks, and her décolletage surrounded by the shimmery gold fabric? A rival to Sabatier's cream puffs any day.

"Yes, I believe it is true. I do believe you are jealous!"

"Jeal—" Matthieu cleared the frog from his throat. Slimy thing suddenly leapt up there from his queasy stomach. "Jealous? Of—of . . . of what?"

"Well, I don't know. Perhaps the fact that I'm here with Julien Delaroche?" She attached the most irritatingly desirous tone to the chevalier's name.

"Julien?" He gave her a wordless, stunned jerk of his head. "Delaroche?" A croaking chuckle. "Oh. Never." Another chuckle masked the difficulty he was having in forming more than a single-word sentence. "Julien Delaroche?"

"But I think you are!" She approached him with an eager spritelike grin and wide eyes. "Matthieu, I—"

"Oh no!" He threw a palm up as if to blockade the possibility. "There is no way I will ever be jealous of that man. Why, Julien Delaroche is a . . . a lout! A rake. A scoundrel of the lowest degree. He is a cad, Josephine. The man doesn't know how to appreciate a woman beyond noticing if her breasts are large or her smile promising. He is a man whose only designs on you are to lift your skirts and be done with it!"

His arm still thrust out stiffly, Matthieu noticed now that the sparkle had disappeared from Josephine's brown eyes. Her smile had also slipped away, to be replaced by a quivering lip and tear-shiny eyes.

"Oh no, Josephine." She jerked away from his hand as he touched her. Now the tears were accompanied by sobs, still soft, yet hard enough in tone to break his heart. "I did not mean—"

"How can you speak so cruelly of the man I love?" she managed between sniffles.

"Love?" No. The word was too powerful, too strong to be used by her so unawares. She had to know. "Josephine, the man you love is standing—"

"Bouchet." Julien Delaroche, wearing ribboned gray velvet and a ridiculous wig, encircled Josephine in his arms with the deft grace of a mother eagle protecting her young. Or in this case, a vulture swooping down on his prey. "What have you said to Mademoiselle Lalique to put her in such a state?"

"I—I—" Too late. His chance had been spoiled by his own thoughtlessness. "Forgive me, Josephine?"

She sniffled and nudged her cheek against Delaroche's shoulder, prompting him to embrace her tighter. All the pieces of Matthieu's heart, which had been glued back together only hours ago, crumbled anew.

"I think you'd best leave," Delaroche growled as he brushed a finger across Josephine's forehead to push away a strand of curly hair. He didn't even give Matthieu the courtesy of his regard.

If he told her now ... No, he could not in Delaroche's presence. The chevalier would sabotage any attempts. Matthieu had no choice. And in her state Josephine would never allow him to take her away from Delaroche for a few moments alone.

Clicking his boot heels *a la militaire,* Matthieu bid Josephine adieu, only to be gifted with her silence.

The crushed pieces of his heart crumbled to ash.

The brisk walk through the crowded ballroom must have been the hardest and longest walk of his life. Not even a campaign march, stretched days into weeks, could compare.

To turn and leave the woman he loved—and in her state— in the arms of that bastard, nearly broke him. The last few steps were more a jog as Matthieu finally reached the outer doors of the ballroom and passed the liveried doormen. His boot heels echoed loudly as he marched down the length of hallway until he could finally dash to the right and rest against the wall. Alone. Defeated.

Matthieu released a frustrated breath and swiped his hat from his head. He jammed his fingers through his hair and pressed hard against his temple. Delaroche gave him such a pain in the head. Why could Josephine not see? She was not a stupid woman. But for some reason he could not fathom, she'd fallen into this trap of Julien's and now was too blinded by his shallow charms to realize that she was in the arms of the wrong man.

The wrong man!

*Julien Delaroche.* "Damn it, I hate that name."

Marching purposefully, he started to wend his way through the maze of halls, but found he wasn't really sure where he was or where he had come from. He'd stumbled on a residential area, most likely bedchambers. One door was open just a crack to emit a wide line of golden light across the marble floor.

Thinking he should tiptoe past so as not to disturb the giggling inhabitants, Matthieu placed a toe over the line of light and made to slink past, when a familiar voice startled him completely.

No, it couldn't be!

# Chapter 17

It was only after Julien had suggested for the sixth time that they find her sister that Josephine began to suspect something. Did he still adore Helene?

She was beginning to develop a horrible ache in her gut. It would do no good to worry about Julien's affections toward her sister. Nor would it serve her queasy insides to keep returning to the night's earlier events. Matthieu seemed to want to tell her something, but had only been successful in hurting her. Why couldn't he accept her love for Julien Delaroche?

"You seem lost in thought."

The possessive squeeze of Julien's hand on her waist was beginning to hurt as well. Josephine managed a lackluster nod in answer to his question. "Perhaps just a little tired."

"Already? But the night has only begun. Come." He circled her waist and started towards the dance floor. "Another minuet? Maybe we'll spy your sister. I'm sure she'll be quite upset if the two of you do not lay eyes upon one another this evening."

"No, Julien." Josephine planted her feet and strained against his gentle pull. "What I really would like is a moment to sit down. Perhaps away from all the noise and bustle. I believe I'm a touch weary, that's all.''

Disappointment literally carved into the vertical frown line that creased between Julien's brows. "Of course—''

"Chevalier!"

A man Julien had introduced to her earlier—though for the life of her she could not recall his name or rank—slapped Julien on the back and handed him a goblet of wine.

"We've just been discussing the siege at Artois. Seems there's a difference of opinion regarding which regiment has the strongest pikemen."

Josephine caught Julien's smirk. He'd much rather avoid the man himself, but then again, maybe not. "Go ahead, Julien. I'll just go find a chair."

"I should accompany you."

"No." She wanted a moment to herself. And now she had the perfect excuse. "Come look for me in a few minutes. But do stay here. I'll be fine."

"As you wish." He gripped her gloved hand, looking as if he might gift her knuckles with a kiss, when he suddenly swept her into his arms and brushed a kiss along her cheek and slid over to her ear. "I shall be miserable in your absence."

Feeling a healthy blush ride up her scalp, Josephine squeezed his hand. "Just a few minutes."

She took the marble steps up past a row of potted ferns. One of the tall plants looked as though someone had taken a tumble right onto the slender green fronds. Drink did strange things to people. Sanctuary lay just ahead in a narrow hall outside the ballroom. Backless chairs with thick azure damask cushions beckoned. Slumping against the wall, Josephine fanned her face with her feather mask and blew out an exhausted breath.

The heat of Julien's kiss lingered upon her cheek. She touched her face, following the trail his lips had taken from her cheek to her ear. *I shall be miserable in your absence.*

This whole business of courting was really very tiresome work. While she desperately wanted to be in Julien's arms, this

heavy wave of weariness had come upon her so suddenly. It
had all begun with Matthieu's appearance.

*He is a scoundrel of the lowest degree. A cad . . .*

Matthieu had had only good words for the chevalier upon
his arrival in Paris. Why now could he only batter the man
with horrendous epithets? Was it really what Josephine had
suspected? That Matthieu Bouchet was jealous of the chevalier?

But if he was jealous, that could only mean . . .

"La! Well, if you don't look like a felled doe abandoned by
her hunter. What's the trouble, sister? Has the chevalier run
you through so many introductions that you've lost your gump-
tion? It's a wonder I've been able to avoid you two, the way
he drags you about."

"Helene." Josephine gripped her sister's wrist, bringing her
prattle to an abrupt end. "Tell me something."

"Something," her sister deadpanned, surprising even Josephine with her wit.

"No, no. I'm so confused. I really do need your advice."

"Matthieu?"

"Why would you say his name? What do you know? What
is going on, Helene?"

"I should ask the same of you."

"I don't know what is going on. I don't know anything
anymore, it seems. I'm so confused about my feelings for the
chevalier and . . . and Matthieu." She caught her chin in her
cupped palm. Damn the social graces, she was tired. "Helene,
why can't I seem to keep Matthieu from my thoughts when I
should be thrilled to be on the chevalier's arm?"

"If you still don't know the answer to that one, I don't think
my telling you will make any difference."

"Tell me what?" So evasive Helene was being. Just like
Matthieu. Had the twosome been plotting behind her back?
What was going on? "Do you know something about Matthieu
that I do not?"

Releasing a heavy sigh, Helene bent to scoot another chair
close to Josephine's and sat with a pouf of petticoats and

clinking rustle of paste jewels. "Now you tell me something, Josephine."

She studied her sister's solemn countenance. "If I can."

"Do you still really believe you are in love with the chevalier?"

"Well, yes . . . of course."

"Don't answer so quickly. Think about it."

But she didn't need to think about it! Maybe. Josephine's mask slipped across her skirts and fell at her slippered toes. The smooth of Helene's fingertips across the back of her hand felt so gentle after being crushed in Julien's iron grip all evening.

*The man's only designs on you are to lift your skirts and be done with it . . .*

No! Not Julien Delaroche. He was kind and warm. When she balked at his kisses, he granted her distance. He was in no hurry to lift her skirts. He wanted their love to grow as slowly and surely as necessary. He truly did care for her.

"I do . . . love him," she absently replied. Still the fierceness of Matthieu's words made her shudder. If he was jealous of Julien . . . but that would then mean . . . She would then be forced to face her own feelings regarding Matthieu Bouchet. Which were—

"Very well." Helene reached for Josephine's other hand and leaned before her. "Then what about Matthieu Bouchet? Do you love him?"

"Of course I do, Helene. But you know it is a different kind of love—"

"Is it really?"

"Yes!" Well . . . "Oh! I don't know anymore!" Plunging into her sister's arms, Josephine squeezed Helene's narrow waist and burrowed her forehead against her hyacinth-smothered tresses.

"Watch the lace," Helene admonished, as she slipped a hand along her décolletage and raised Josephine's position.

"Sorry. Helene, what shall I do? I don't know how I feel

about Matthieu anymore. He is a friend, a confidant, why, he's like a piece of my soul. But I've never really considered him as a . . ."

"A lover?"

Josephine nodded, afraid that if she voiced the word in the same sentence as his name it might empower the odd feelings she was just too afraid to confront.

"Do you think he thinks of me in such a way?"

Helene thrust her chin proudly and flashed her gaze across the wall of glittering candelabra as if to avoid Josephine's gaze.

"What is it, Helene?"

"Regretfully, I do not know." Helene began to give the utmost attention to the smoothing of her skirts. "But you should give a care for Monsieur Bouchet, Josephine."

"And the chevalier?"

Only Helene could make a face look more distasteful than a platter of raisin-garnished eel. "You know my thoughts on that man. Ah, but it's time I returned to Monsieur Michelet's arm. I've been absent from him far too long. Please, do keep the chevalier away from my sight for the remainder of the evening. *Bonsoir,* sister. May your heart finally begin to speak the truth."

The crisp sing of Helene's skirts lost resonance as she disappeared into the ballroom. Knowing she must return to Julien's arm, Josephine stood and smoothed out her own skirts. So delicious the gold satin. Why, she'd forgotten to thank him for the gift.

"How can my heart not know the truth?" she wondered as she slowly began to walk. "I know my feelings to have been true when I read the chevalier's letters. But now it seems as if the real man does not stir up such feelings of desire. How can that be? Is it possible I can only love the man on paper? No, that's just too ridiculous. And why . . ." Her voice trailed off and was replaced by her silent thoughts.

Why did Matthieu Bouchet seem to haunt her heart?

* * *

Much as his good sense told him to hightail it out of there, Matthieu could not resist peeking inside the chamber door. One problem. The door creaked loudly on its hinges, alerting the man and woman tumbling on a grand four-poster bed.

"Who's there?" the woman called

"Perhaps a noisy mouse?" a man's voice cheerfully chimed.

"Oh, darling!" she exclaimed. "You've invited another to join our little soirée this evening. Oh, such fun. A ménage!"

"I did?" the man said. "Well certainly, I must have. But wouldn't I recall such a—Bouchet!"

Oh, hell, as if he'd not suffered humiliation enough already this evening. With one foot aimed for escape, Matthieu inclined his head in a modest bow. "Professor Lalique."

The woman bustled into a robe of cheery chiffon and frothy ostrich feathers and pulled Matthieu inside before he could protest. "Oh, such a pretty young man, Pascal. And how do you know this sweet morsel? Or better yet," she said with an appraising eye up and down Matthieu's body, "how quickly can you get undressed, young man?"

Beyond embarrassment at finding Josephine's father with a woman—and most likely naked beneath the bed linens—Matthieu stuttered, "I didn't mean to interrupt. I was just on my way . . . umm . . . I was just going to find . . . Oh hell." He couldn't help noticing an elaborate silver tray of fruits and wine amid the decadent froths of lace and pillows and satins. Smelled damn good, considering he hadn't eaten since early in the day. But—"Professor Lalique, is that champagne?"

"Huh?" His gray sausage-curled wig sitting on his head sideways and his thin-rimmed spectacles still clinging to the end of his nose, Pascal Lalique narrowed his eyes on the goblet that he held in his right hand. "Why—hic—I do believe you are correct! Bravo, young man. Quite the tack, that boy!"

He was soused! But Professor Lalique never imbibed. In fact, he always preached the dangers of indulgence to Matthieu and Josephine whenever they found Cook passed out in the garden, her head lolling across a carpet of mossy soil moistened with ale.

"Ha!" Pascal studied the goblet with eyes that had trouble staying focused. "What do you know?"

"Let me help you with your pants," the woman offered as she bent before Matthieu and fingered the metal buttons at his knees.

"No!" he said with a quick step backward. His motion toppled the woman to her knees and parted her robe to reveal ample enough bosom for two men. Or more. What the hell was he doing? "No." Matthieu flung both gloved hands over his crotch, barely avoiding her roaming fingers, and backed up until his heels jammed into the door. "No, Madame, one man is most certainly all you need—"

"Oh, silly boy!"

"Perhaps you should fetch us another goblet, Cherise," Pascal muttered in a wavy voice. "Please, do take your time. I need to speak to this young man."

"Oh certainly," she said with a giggle and a skip to her step. "Organizing your plan of attack? Hee, hee, hee! Oh, I do love your eccentricities, Pascal."

She disappeared through a heavy damask portière, leaving a mist of cherry blossoms behind. Much as he should have been somewhere—anywhere—else, Matthieu couldn't resist stepping to Pascal's side of the bed. "What are you doing, Professor Lalique? You never imbibe?"

"I—*hic*—don't?"

"No!"

Josephine's father continued to stare at the crystal goblet with the intensity of one studying a tiny insect perched upon one's nose, crossed eyes and all. "Oh." He sank back into the fluff of ruffled pink pillows, his wig completely covering his eyes. "My eyes! I can't see, boy! Help!"

Peeling the hideously curled contraption from Pascal's head,

Matthieu tossed it to the floor. "I'll have you know Josephine is here this evening."

"Josephine? You don't say? I have a daughter by that—*hic*—name."

"Such a coincidence," Matthieu offered as he scanned the room for sign of the returning woman.

"Oh!" Pascal sprung up in bed, like a rock released from the catapult. "You mean Josephine! My daughter! Is she with you?"

"Unfortunately for me she is not. Quite fortunately for you."

"Oh yes," Pascal said, slumping into the feminine fluff of bedclothes behind him. "It is great fortune she is not. Considering—*hic*—considering the circumstances. Oh bother. *Hic!* Matthieu," Pascal gripped Matthieu's sleeve. "You must help me."

"I think it's a little too late for that."

"No, it's the Duchess."

"That woman is a Duchess?"

"Yes, the Duchess Champ-chump-Chem—Bother. It seems she's set her sights for me—fetching young thing, isn't she?"

"To be sure."

"Oh, I shall burn in hell! And now she's gotten me drunk—and, oh, bother it all, I hate being soused, Matthieu. My head swims as if in an ocean of piranha, and my eyes can't seem to focus—*hic*—besides the preponderance of excess—*hic*—gas. Ah, my humors are all scattered! You must help me out of here before she returns."

"But, Professor—"

"I don't want to be here, Bouchet. As embarrassed as I already am by you finding me—*hic*—here, I must request you help me further. Can you find my clothes? I seem to have misplaced them somewhere between, 'Good evening Professor Lalique', and, er . . . 'Can we do it again?' "

Matthieu shot upright from looking under the bed. "Please, Professor, I don't want to know the details."

"Rightly so," Pascal said on a sigh and another sip of champagne.

"Professor!"

"Oh?" He suddenly remembered the goblet in his hand. "Yes, yes! Enough of this poison." He tossed the half-filled glass at the foot of the bed and ripped the bedsheets back to expose—"Well, storm the Bastille, I find myself quite bare!"

Oh hell. Matthieu remained on his knees, behind the door, where he did not find any sort of clothing other than a woman's silk stocking. "If I'm going to help you," he called from behind cover, "you'll need to dress yourself, Professor Lalique. I just couldn't bring myself—"

"Done!"

With a twinge of embarrassment riding his spine, Matthieu peeked around the edge of the door. A confection of ostrich feather and satin covered Josephine's father from neck to knee. A ribald tavern tune concerning cherry-faced wenches and boisterous soldiers echoed from just down the hall. The Duchess of Ménage was returning.

"I think you need time away from court," Matthieu commented as he motioned with exaggerated briskness that Pascal walk towards the only exit.

"Just so. There is no limit to the scandal a man can find himself in here at—*hic*—where are we, anyway?"

"Never mind. Let's be gone!" Matthieu grabbed the silver serving tray, upsetting cut yellow cheese and a goblet of wine on the bed linens.

The Duchess's singing grew louder. Pascal stumbled over his bare feet as Matthieu pushed him through the doorway.

"The floor is moving!" Pascal complained as Matthieu peeled his shoulder up and tried to lift him. "I cannot secure a good hold! Abandon ship!"

"Just a few more steps and we'll be in the clear," Matthieu coached as he pushed against the man's back, finding himself bent over behind him and crawling sideways to get momentum. "It's either that or a night with the singing Duchess!"

At that remark, Pascal dove into the hallway and Matthieu followed suit, deftly tripping the door with his boot toe to close it just as the Duchess shrieked. He slid the silver tray over the iron door handles, a sufficient lock until some wandering lackey could stumble upon the amorous duchess.

# Chapter 18

Consternation and wench's warts! Why was Matthieu doing this now? Now, of all times, when she had fallen in love with another man!

And Helene was certainly no help at all. She knew something, Josephine was sure. Which was amazing, considering Helene hadn't the ability to keep a secret for more than two minutes.

For as much as she denied her own feelings for Matthieu, Josephine knew, deep within, that there was more to their friendship than hand-holding and raids on Sabatier's sweets. She did love Matthieu. He was a good and kind man. And if she thought long enough, the idea of loving him as, well . . . a lover, was not difficult.

Such thoughts had come easily during their almost-kiss. But why—if Matthieu did love her—did he not just tell her! And how could he allow Julien to pursue her? Why, Matthieu had helped Julien into her life!

No. Matthieu did not love her. Not in the way she wished. Besides, it was too late. Julien sat next to her at this very moment, his heavy wig tossed without a care to the floor and his thumb tapping an expectant beat on her leg.

The lilt of the rambling carriage pushed Josephine closer to the warmth of Julien's arm and thigh. Though she wore a satin skirt, a lace petticoat, and another cotton petticoat, and he wore just as much in ribbon, velvet, and lace, she could feel the heat of his leg as if she were naked next to him. Or perhaps it was her own rising body temperature.

It mattered not. Tonight was for the two of them. For as much as Matthieu had gotten her to thinking about their relationship, it was far too late to deny the heart she had already lost to the chevalier. The flutters in her belly set her on a delicious edge of anticipation. The gentle smoothing of Julien's thumb over her knuckles as their locked hands rested on his thigh captured her attention. Nothing else existed, save she and the man who had written himself into her heart.

Spying a farmer packing up his flowers at the edge of the Seine, Julien called the driver to halt. He leapt from the carriage, setting it to a pleasant bounce, and returned with a bouquet of slightly wilted pansies and three daisies still looking sprightly.

"It is not much," he offered with a sheepish smile as he climbed back into the carriage. "But you must smell this one. It is incredible, like perfume."

His delight made it easy to overlook the drooping petals and droplets of stale water that dripped over her hands as she sniffed the bouquet.

"Allow me." Julien slid a daisy through her curls, his finger trailing slowly behind the shell of her ear as he tucked the narrow stem in place. "Now, think how close I must get if I wish to enjoy this flower."

"You have an appreciation for flowers?"

"Mmm," he growled as he leaned into her ear. "Now I do." But it wasn't the flower his nose was intent upon; instead it blazed a path as Julien's lips traced moth-dances around the curves of her ear. The sensation worked to ignite other parts of her body to a wicked alertness. Now this sort of soft, tender touch she liked.

Pressing her hand to her breast, where even there she felt the tingle of Julien's touch, Josephine giggled and shrugged.

"You wish me to stop?"

"Oh no! But it does tickle."

"Perhaps my touch is too rough for your delicate senses." He plucked the flower from behind her ear and stroked it across her cheek. "Of course a flower such as you would prefer the touch of your own kind." Josephine sighed and tilted her head, offering him full reign in his explorations.

Matthieu? Who was he?

"You have such a way with words, Julien. It is what endears you to me."

He snapped the stem of the daisy, which sent it tumbling to Josephine's lap.

"Let me get that." He caught her fingers in a tangle of strong male digits and soft flower petals. He pressed against her lap, crushing the flower in her palm and resting upon the sensitive vee of her womanhood.

Josephine gasped at the sudden fire that stirred in her loins. And before she could speak, Julien kissed her. Too stunned by the movement of his hand, Josephine could not concentrate on the kiss, and before she could protest, his tongue had taken free entrance.

Dear, was this to be another awkward moment? Closing her eyes, she tried not to think of the tongue intruding upon her mouth. Large and thick and . . . just sort of dashing back and forth . . . "Oh!"

"Relax," he murmured.

Hmm, as long as she kept him talking, that also kept his lips busy, and that rogue tongue.

"I know you are worried that we should take things slow." Another kiss. Quick, lip to lip, nothing else. Another, and another. When they were short and sweet, not long and sloppy, his charms were irresistible. The control he held over her was intoxicating. "But there are times when a man wishes to possess a woman—"

"Oh, but—"

"To delve beyond the laces and binding satins and discover the sweet flesh that hides beneath."

His hand ventured from her hip, up over the row of tight lacing that decorated her stomacher, and to her décolletage, where he drew one finger over her panting breasts.

"I'll not steal your virtue without your permission." His husky whispers became a sweet, enticing nectar as they entered her head. "But will you allow me the pleasure of learning your body?"

He had such a perfect way of wording things. She certainly did not wish to lose her virtue to a man in the confines of a carriage! But to *learn* her body? Why, that would involve a long and slow study of exquisite sensation and increasing delight. The trace of his fingers working across her breasts was a feeling too good to resist. More than willing to show this man she wished only to be his, Josephine tugged at the first hook that secured her stomacher. Spellbound, her eyes held tight to Julien's promising gaze. Another hook. And another. His wide hand could now trace the inner curves of her breasts. Ah, the desire did not let up, nor did the intense need for more!

Josephine gripped Julien's hand. He searched her eyes.

"You may," she said as she placed his hand upon her stomacher.

Still held captive by a gaze as luminous as moonlight across a tar roof, she drew in a breath as he quickly released the remaining hooks. He slipped his hand beneath the rigid stays, infusing her body with a hot jolt of surprise. The instant his fingers paralleled her nipple, the little nub hardened to a receptive bud of pleasure. Every gentle stroke or sudden squeeze evoked a longing surge in Josephine. And this touch she could feel even in her groin.

"Julien . . ."

"I cannot stop now, Josephine."

He whispered her name as prayerfully as a thirsty man stumbling into an open well. She wanted only to hear him whisper it again and again as his hands worked their magic upon her body. "No, you mustn't stop," she managed before a tiny moan slipped unawares from her lips.

"Yes, tell me how much you need my touch. No words are necessary. We've gone beyond words. Just the sound of your desire, Josephine. Sweet whimpers and delicious moans, that is what I want from you."

He tilted his head and drew a hot trail across her chest with his tongue. Now that was the true calling of his hot, slippery kisses! Taken by the growing demand for more, Josephine spread her stomacher wide to the blissful torture of his touch. The other nipple, sadly ignored until now, was already marble-hard and ready for his mouth. Josephine moaned and pressed her hand to the back of his head. This seemed to please him for his attentions became voracious, his tasting and licking and suckling at her breasts a driving need to overtake and conquer her.

Willingly, she surrendered.

"I could not have believed the press of a man's mouth to my breast could be so exquisite."

Julien, affixing his fingers to her breast to replace his wet lips, kissed her chin and her mouth. "There is so much more I will teach you, my precious daisy. So much more."

His hand was hard and searching as he walked her skirts up with his fingers. Josephine arched her hips to meet the stunning power of his sorcery.

She did not even notice that the carriage no longer moved. It was only the sudden jerk of Julien's head to look out the curtained windows that allowed her to collect what little sense remained and cover her exposed breasts with her hands.

"What is it?"

"We've arrived at the Lalique estate, but there is a courier waiting," the coachman called.

"Cover yourself. I'll be right back." He bruised a hard kiss to the corner of her lips and exited the carriage.

Josephine scrambled to hook up her bodice. "Horrors," she whispered. "Home already. And just when I was beginning to enjoy everything!"

The last hook took a bit of strength, but finally Josephine had secured everything back in its proper place, tied up her laces, and stepped outside the carriage. Julien stood holding a letter and talking to a mounted soldier wearing the tan and blue of the 26th Foot.

"Julien? What is it?"

"I'm not yet sure." He nodded the soldier off and watched as the rider sped into a gallop.

"What does it say?" Josephine nudged the hand in which he still held the letter.

"Huh? Oh." His attention snapped to the letter, a brilliant white flag in the dark of night, which he turned and flipped, but did not open. "It is from Commander Marechal. Orders to be issued to the 26th at once."

"What does that mean? Open it, Julien, read it to me!"

"No!" He stuffed the post inside his doublet, exposing a slash of bare chest with the motion. "I cannot take the time to read it now when the orders seem most urgent."

"But if you don't know what they are—" Josephine followed him to the carriage.

"I'll read it when I am with the troops. I must go now. If I hurry, I can catch most of the men before they leave the ball." He hooked a foot on the carriage floor, then paused and turned back to her. "We have come so close."

Josephine gripped the hand he held out, her heart screaming for some explanation. Why was everything so urgent?

"I will return as soon as the orders have been posted. I promise."

"But what are the orders? You must know, that is why you've no need to read the letter. Oh, *mon dieu,* Matthieu once mentioned that your leave may not be long. Are you being called back? Am I right? But it's been a mere week!''

He stepped down and pulled her to his body. A rigid tension made his movements harsh as he stroked over her hair. ''Give me one hour, Josephine. I will return. There are things we must do. Pleasures I've not yet taught you.''

''But they can wait—''

''No.'' He branded a kiss to her lips, hard and urgent. This kiss hurt. But it was a pain she willingly endured when granted by the man she loved. ''In one hour,'' he said again as he stepped back and took the carriage steps in one leap. ''Wait for me. Out back, by your little pond.''

He commanded the driver to turn back to the Hôtel de Ville.

The urgency of Julien's tone and the fire in his eyes did not bode well. His regiment must have been called back to battle. That was the only possibility.

The love she had just begun to enjoy would be viciously swept from her arms.

But he would return. Tonight.

*There are things we must do. Pleasures I've not yet taught you.*

Oh, Josephine! What to do?

For when he did return, surely he had every intention of finishing what they had started in the carriage. He would want to make love to her before he marched to battle. One final memory in case he should never return.

Could she?

Was she ready to give her body to the man who already possessed her heart?


Everything had to be perfect. The paper was clean and unmarred, not a fold or nick fouling its smoothness. His walnut traveling chest sat on the desk, plundered of its contents. The ink was unclumped and richly dark. Red sealing wax would represent perfect true love.

He'd paced for longer than he should have after returning from the fête. Heaven's mercy, but he'd found Professor Lalique in such a compromising position! It had been the Duchess's doing. Pascal simply did not drink. The man was more than grateful that Matthieu had helped him back to his chambers. He mustn't tell Josephine or Helene.

Most certainly not.

Matthieu had decided against searching out Josephine after that incident. It would not be wise to approach her until he had the perfect form of explanation. Something she could not turn away from, something that would be impossible for Delaroche to understand.

A letter.

Nothing else would do.

As he waited for the final grains of sand to sift onto the ink-scrawled piece of paper, Matthieu's thoughts focused on how his life was like this sand. Fine grains, each representing a day or year or footstep trod upon the ground. Each so insignificant when viewed alongside the other. And so quickly they slipped through his fingers. Only when coated with the rich black ink and glinting beneath the candlelight did any single grain stand out as a twinkling beacon. Sand combined with ink. The ink, the blood from his very soul. The sand, his life.

"For you, Josephine," he said as he carefully folded the crisp paper down each side and then with a turn, again on each side.

He held the sealing wax to the candle flame until it dripped once, twice, three times, then smeared a patch upon the paper. The ragged remainder of cork from a wine bottle served as a sufficient weight to press into the seal. Carefully, before, the wax hardened, Matthieu traced a heart into the red glob with the end of the knife he used to sharpen his charcoals.

A sudden rap at his door startled him.

Matthieu slid the letter inside his doublet and raced to open the door before whoever stood behind it splintered the wood. "Delaroche!"

"No time for formalities, Bouchet." Julien strode the length of the room and back. His jaw pulsed and his eyes blazed. Battle-ready, Matthieu observed. But for what reason? Delaroche took out a sealed letter and thrust it in Matthieu's face.

Sight of another letter only further strengthened his decision to no longer consort with this man. No longer would he be Julien's messenger of love. "Oh no. No more. I had no idea I was corresponding with Josephine when you asked me to write."

"You think I did?"

"Yes, well, take this—this false drivel to the translator at Les Innocents if you need it read. I'll not be your eyes and voice anymore. I am on my way to see Josephine this very moment."

"But here!" Julien snapped his knuckles across the letter. "It is from Commander Marechal. You must read this for me. I believe the 26th may be called out. Tonight!"

Matthieu stared at the letter held in Julien's fist. There had always been the possibility that the Spaniards had not actually retreated, but merely held their ground. But he'd never dreamed the respite would be so short. Why, no more than a week?

"Give it to me." Matthieu crossed the room and stood near the guttering tallow candle as he read the letter out loud.

As he had read all of Julien's correspondence out loud, for the man could neither read nor write.

*The 26th Foot is ordered to march to Arras. Troops shall commence at midnight on this, the second day of July. Orders issued by Commander Marechal.*

"Midnight." Matthieu released the paper and stamped it beneath his boot. "I've no time to waste. I must go to Josephine now that I know the truth."

Julien's thick fist stopped Matthieu at the door. Steel knuckles dug into his chest. "What truth, little man?"

Matthieu could not help the self-satisfied smirk as he slapped away Julien's fist. "The truth about Josephine's one true love. She loves me, Delaroche. Me!"

"You know nothing!"

"She told me this very afternoon that she loved the man who wrote the letters. She loves *me,* Delaroche. It was I who wrote those letters. And you—without so much as a glance over what I had written before sealing them up and sending them off—you haven't a clue as to what they said! Admit it, the only reason you're interested in Josephine is because you need a female body to debauch from time to time. And for some damned reason, it may even be to spite me!"

"Perhaps so," Julien raged. "And how does it feel, Bouchet, to know that it is my name that clings to your lover's lips instead of yours?"

"You're insane. I'm going there now to tell her everything." Matthieu pushed past Julien and took up his sword standing near the door.

"No one will go near Mademoiselle Lalique until I have gotten what I deserve from her. I've been courting that damned wench all week, and I've not even broached her skirts!"

"Bastard, you'll not lay another hand on her."

"Oh, I'll lay a hand on her." Julien cracked a wicked smile. "And another hand. And I'll lift her skirts and take what is rightfully mine. It is only fitting payment for the deception she played. And if it angers you in the process, all the more shall it serve my revenge."

"Revenge?"

"Does my name haunt your dreams? Every time she whispers it . . . Julien . . . do you cringe and draw a fist of rage?"

"What the hell are you talking about?"

"I've a name that haunts my dreams," he said on a mad chuckle. "Do you want to know that name, Bouchet? It is Isabelle."

"Isa—" He didn't understand. What would his mother's name . . . No, it was merely coincidence.

"I'm wanted at the Lalique home." Julien turned for the

door. Rage connected Matthieu's fist to Delaroche's jaw, but the man merely snapped off the contact like an annoying insect. And returned with a counterpunch.

Yes, indeed, the man did have a masterful right punch. Darkness fell over Matthieu's eyes. His body hit the floor.

Julien Delaroche snapped up the abandoned orders and stepped over Bouchet's body.

# Chapter 19

*Every kiss a woman receives should be exquisite and price-less.*

The thought of Matthieu's lips searing onto her own made her eyelids heavy and her senses acute to every brush of her gown across her skin. Exquisite and priceless. A kiss like a fine jewel, offered to a woman as a means of winning her heart.

Not harsh. No. Soft and supple and knowing.

Not sloppy or awkward. Never. Masterful. Pure bone-melting mastery.

"I knew you would be a good girl and wait for me."

Alone with her covered lamp and the crickets' midnight serenade, Josephine jumped at Julien's voice. She hadn't heard his boots tramping through the long grasses. Her mind must have been . . . somewhere else. Beyond the ten-foot circle of luminescence that surrounded her, everything was black as pitch, for the moon was a bare sliver above.

"I've not long," he said as he plunged down beside her on the log and lifted her onto his lap. "I need your kisses, Josephine. And so much more."

Between the quick hard pecks he pressed to her lips, her chin, her neck, Josephine managed to question him, "The orders were for immediate deployment?"

"Yes. We march for Arras at midnight."

"Oh, Julien!"

"Don't cry, daisy, I've come to spend this last hour with you, the woman I love."

Already his fingers traveled down her bodice, releasing the hooks and freeing her breasts to the warm night air. His wet mouth began searching and cleaving and pulling from her like a starved infant to breast. Fantasies of softness and grace were slathered away by the tip of the chevalier's tongue.

"I must have you before I leave," he gasped. "Josephine, understand how hard it is for a man to be alone for so long. To march off to battle, not knowing whether he will march the same path home or if he will be carried in a coffin—"

"Don't speak like that, Julien. Oh, my love, I am frightened."

"Don't be. I want to make you mine, Josephine. You must relinquish your body, so I might recall this moment when I am suffering the unspeakable horrors of war. Please, Josephine, if you have any amount of compassion."

"I do, Julien. And I do love you."

Everything was happening so fast! And it was so hard to think with his tongue snaking over her nipples, stirring her insides to a confusing mixture of sudden desire, yet a tangible uncertainty. Perhaps this was what love was all about? The heady urge to couple, the passionate want. The consternation?

"Of course I cannot send you off to battle without—without . . ."

Could she? Could she give to this man the one thing he so obviously needed? Was it what *she* needed? If only Matthieu were here.

*Mon dieu!* Where did that thought come from? No, no, if Matthieu really did love her, he would be here. And he was not.

There was only one thing to do.

''Can you offer me a vow?''

''Vow?'' Julien said from the darkness. ''What sort of vow?''

''A promise that you will marry me when you return.'' She gasped as his actions increased and she felt more a lamb ready for the slaughter than a women ready to offer her body to the man she loved. ''If you demand my virtue, than surely you must have honorable intentions?''

''Of course,'' he said as his lips slid between her breasts, stirring her to a frenzy, and yet, she could not surrender to the feeling. Not until she could be assured of Julien's love.

''Say it,'' she gasped. ''Please.''

''Say what? What is it you wish? We must be quick, Josephine! I march in an hour.''

''Ask me to marry you.''

''Marriage?''

Caught in the man's arms, her virtue on the verge of extinction, Josephine waited expectantly. Julien's expression did not soften as expected; instead his face crinkled and reddened and the muscle in his jaw pulsed wickedly.

Then he let out a burst of laughter.

''Fool girl,'' he said as he pulled her to his chest. His fingers dug into her back like no tight stays could have ever done. ''I've known you but a week. Why should I marry you?''

''But—'' Drawn totally speechless, Josephine couldn't even struggle. Her fingers, clinging to Julien's velvet doublet, were numb. As was her heart. Why was he behaving so cruelly?

''A man need not say vows to wet his rod,'' he growled and plunged forward once again to bury his mouth against her breasts. The snake's tongue flicked and circled and slimed over her body. Hard kisses quickly became painful nips.

''What has happened to you?'' Josephine pushed against his head, her hands slipping through his hair, but to no avail. ''You've suddenly changed colors. You're a monster, Julien. Let me go! What has become of the kind and sensitive man who—Oh!''

* * *

When finally he arrived at Josephine's home, the elegant house was dark. The grand oak tree shushed quietly as he forced his tired legs up the walk. Matthieu dropped his supply pack at his feet and propped his musket near the door. It took what seemed forever for the maid to come yawning to the door.

"Marie Claire, where is Josephine?"

"Asleep, I'm sure, Monsieur. She arrived home an hour ago from the ball and quickly dismissed me, saying she was far too tired to bathe. She may be sleeping in her stays for all I care. It is such a late hour. Why are you huffing so?"

"Are you sure?" He looked over the maid's shoulder, but her single candle did not illuminate anything beyond the bottom stair.

"Where else would she be?" The maid stifled a yawn with her cupped palm and closed her eyes.

"Go check for me." Matthieu wanted to burst past her and rush up the stairs to be sure but—

A sudden scream—from somewhere beyond the garden gate—alerted the two of them. The maid spun around, her candle flickering and sputtering to a hiss. Matthieu ran towards the back of the house. "She is outside!"

He tore through the gardens, crossing himself as he passed the Celtic stone. In the distance, near the pond, he saw a faint flicker of light. As he neared and could make out the mirrored flash of the pond, a slender leg kicked the air, the woman's stocking pushed down to her ankle.

His heart leapt to his throat.

"Josephine!" Drawing his sword, Matthieu raced across the field of trampled grasses.

Delaroche looked up from his debauchery. At sight of Matthieu, he dropped Josephine's head against the mossy log and sprang to his feet. He unsheathed his sword and matched Matthieu's battle cry with a proud grunt of his own.

"I hadn't expected you for at least another hour," Delaroche hissed. "Not too many men can pull themselves up after my fist has set them down."

"Perhaps you've met your match." Matthieu parried a hissing thrust, but only sliced the air at Delaroche's quick dodge. Though he could only spare a glance, he saw Josephine sit up against the log, her hands clutching her opened bodice together. Loose tendrils of hair spilled over her face and shoulders, her eyes teared. Please, he must have arrived in time!

Determined to steer Julien away from where Josephine sat, Matthieu succeeded in turning the fight across the grounds and closer to the pond's edge.

"Don't hurt him, Matthieu!"

Stunned at Josephine's blind faith, Matthieu dodged to avoid another attack and swung under Delaroche's lunge.

"You see!" Julien declared with an evil chuckle. "She is enamored. You interrupted a private liaison, Bouchet. Isn't there somewhere else you should be?"

"Same place you're supposed to be," Matthieu barked. "Josephine!"

"Please, Matthieu, Julien did not mean—"

"No! There are things you need to know!"

Cutting his words off with a sharp *thwack*, Delaroche barreled into Matthieu's chest. The two men abandoned swords and fell to the ground. Another blow to the face did little but fire the anger in Matthieu. By all means he must keep moving to avoid this oxen's steel fist. He delivered a crunching knuckle shot to Julien's cheek. The man fell silent. But only for a moment. He shook his head and returned for yet another knuckle-stinging blow.

"He did not write the letters!" Matthieu yelled.

Julien gripped him by the shirt and slammed his forehead into Matthieu's chest. His breath chuffed out of him as he hit the soggy ground. Cool pond waters sloshed over his arm.

"He lies!"

"Ask him to recite the orders from Commander Marechal," Matthieu called to Josephine. "He cannot read!"

Seeing Julien wind up for a punch, Matthieu lifted his feet
and caught him against the chest. A lucky thrust sent Delaroche
flying over Matthieu's head and into the pond. Face down,
Delaroche scrambled in the shallow waters, groping for hold.
"Help!" he sputtered. "I cannot swim!"

Copper slime swirled in Matthieu's mouth. Spitting on the
ground, Matthieu allowed Delaroche's childish tirade. And his
own smile.

Pitiful.

"Matthieu, help him!"

"It is knee high, for God's sake!"

Hearing this, Delaroche stopped struggling. Indeed, he was
able to lift his head from the water and push up. With one eye
trained on the dripping chevalier, Matthieu groped the ground
and touched the blade of cold steel. He rose and drew his sword
before him. As Julien approached, he tossed back his saturated
head, sending water droplets splinking into the pond. Then,
steel aimed for Matthieu's heart, he frowned and stood firm.

Behind him Matthieu could hear Josephine's sniffles. "It is
true," he said, still holding the chevalier's stare. "Tell her,
Delaroche! Tell Josephine who wrote all those letters. Who
read them to you."

"I'll have you arrested for assaulting a superior officer," he
hissed. "Lower your weapon!"

"No!" Josephine stood. She'd given up on holding her bodice closed. In the feeble lamplight the generous swells of her
breasts shone like delicious fruits as she stepped to Matthieu's
side. "Is this true, Julien? Did Matthieu write those letters to
Helene?"

Still the chevalier held his villainous stance. His silence
caused Josephine to snap her gaze to Matthieu. He nodded
affirmatively.

"We've somewhere to be," Julien finally said. He snapped
his stony gaze to Josephine. "Our regiment has orders to march.
If you'll step aside, I'll be on my way. And I'll have this man

marching at my heels.'' He lifted a water-drenched leg and slogged onto the bank.

Matthieu stopped him with the tip of his sword. Josephine sidled closer and hooked an arm through his. The warmth of her body spread through his own like lava covering a hillside. ''A simple yes or no is all she needs, Delaroche. Did you write those letters, yes or no?''

The heavy muscle pulsed in Delaroche's jaw. One beat. He closed his eyes. Flashed them open. ''No!''

Matthieu dropped his sword to his side. Julien trampled past the two of them, without even bothering to glance upon the woman who now stood sobbing.

''All will be well,'' Matthieu said as he pulled Josephine closer. ''I will explain everything.''

''You haven't time.'' Delaroche stopped near the log and twisted the hem of his shirt, dispersing pond water to his feet. ''It draws near midnight. I can hear the drums. You'll come with me, Bouchet, or I shall prove good on my threat to press charges against you for your seditious behavior.''

Indeed, the quiet bass thump of drums could now be heard. Their regiment, and three others from the city, marched for northern France. Matthieu could not risk disobeying orders, nor could he risk charges such as Delaroche had threatened. Sedition? Ridiculous. But it was certain the chevalier would bring as much wrath upon Matthieu as he could muster. As aide-de-camp, Julien's word would be held in high regard against Matthieu's.

Josephine's entire body shivered against his. Her hair tangled in his wet fingers as Matthieu slid them up her scalp and tilted her head to look into her eyes. Feeble candlelight glimmered in her tears. ''I did not want for things to be this way. I tried to explain at the ball. But now, I must go.''

She only nodded.

''Damn.''

''Bouchet!''

''I'm coming.''

But only in body. His heart would remain here on the bank of their wishing pond, along with the broken remains of a heart belonging to the one woman he loved more than she would ever know. And he had no time to let her know the truth.

"Now!"

"You must go. He will be ruthless if you do not obey."

Touching two fingers to her forehead, Matthieu closed his eyes and released a heavy sigh. It was only when she gripped his fingers and moved them down to her mouth to draw a smile upon her sadness that he felt the magnitude of his loss. If only he had told her sooner.

Matthieu stumbled backward. "I must go. For reasons I cannot yet explain, I believe I must stay close to the chevalier. To keep an eye on him." If only to discover who the Isabelle he'd spoken of was, and how she played into the revenge Delaroche anticipated like a child with a precious sweet. "I'll send Marie Claire out for you."

"Go!" she cried and sank to her knees.

A wave of bitter regret washed over him as Matthieu numbly turned and trudged after the swooshing footsteps of Julien Delaroche.

# Chapter 20

Helene came screaming out to the pond a few minutes later. Marie Claire followed in tow, her tin lantern flashing gold streaks across the poppy-speckled grass as she ran.

"What did Matthieu tell you?" Josephine managed between sniffles and hearty flows of tears as Helene sank to the ground and cradled her in her arms.

"He told me nothing. That horrible Delaroche dragged him through the front door bodily. What has happened, Josephine?"

"I thought you were in bed!" Marie Claire cried.

Near the garden gate, Richelieu's grumbles and curses echoed into the black night.

"Bother, I've woken the entire house. I want to go inside," Josephine sniffed. "I cannot speak. I don't know myself what has happened."

She used her sister's shoulder to pull herself up and slowly the threesome trekked to the house. Her mind swam with hideous re-creations of the night. She had been so happy at the party. So in love with Julien. Until Matthieu had left her more perplexed than she could even imagine. And now, just now, the man she believed to love her had almost raped her!

Could it be true? That the chevalier did not write the letters?

All that time had it really been Matthieu? *Mon dieu,* what did this mean?

A new tremor of tears overtook Josephine with chill shudders to match. As they gained the garden, Marie Claire's lantern flashed over fiery poppies, spotting a lacework of ivy and glinted off the roof of father's shed. They passed Cook's cross, Josephine's gaze lingering, imagining Matthieu before it on his knees as he whispered and made the sign of the cross. In the name of the Father, the Son . . .

*I did not want for things to be this way. I tried to explain at the ball . . .*

"What is this?" Marie Claire bent to retrieve a white object lying near Helene's toes. "It was not here earlier—"

"It must have come from one of the men." Josephine snatched the letter. Without bothering to read who it might be addressed to, she carved her fingernail along the wodge of red sealing wax. It popped off, sliding down her grass-streaked skirts. The paper crinkled as she unfolded it.

"Marie Claire, the light!"

*My one and only Ladybug,*

"*Mon dieu,* it is from Matthieu!"

*A week ago I returned from battle to have my heart broken. Your admission of love for Julien Delaroche ripped the very muscle from my chest and splattered it against the wall. But tonight, that carnage has been repaired. You love the man who wrote the letters? That man is I.*

*You see, Julien Delaroche cannot read or write. The first letter he received from Helene, I read to him. The man had no idea or notion what to put on paper. He implored me to write, begging me to create an irresistible missive. I struggled with this deception. Eventually, it became impossibly easy.*

*You see, with each letter I wrote, I revealed myself more and more to you. No. I did not know it was you who wrote back to Julien. But it mattered not. For each letter I wrote to Helene, I needed inspiration to draw on. An easy enough choice. You, Josephine Lalique, you inspired every word that I put to paper. While you and Julien were deceiving one another, it was I writing to you all along. Every word addressed to Helene was really addressed to you from my heart. There is no other woman for whom I could possibly form words of such love.*

*It is a love forged in years of friendship. I have never desired the company of another woman. When I am away for such long periods of time, I become this thing that can only think, need, and desire Josephine. But that is not a bad thing to be.*

*Remember that dreaded summer? But of course you do. We shall never forget. I, most certainly, shall never forget how you stood by me, and held me up through one of the hardest times of my life. From that day, I always knew that I would be the one to see you through your hard times, to stand by your side. Always.*

*I love you, Josephine Lalique. I always have. And I hope someday you can come to forgive this fiasco of misdirected missives and learn to love me also. We were both victims and instigators of deception. Now, we shall suffer.*

*I cannot bear to march to Arras without putting everything out in the open. Nor can I bear to leave without a kiss from your lips. Perhaps an admission of love. I cannot bear it. But I shall, for I have a feeling you will not learn the truth until it is too late.*

*Here is my heart, ladybug. Guard it well while I am away.*

> *Consumed by my need for Josephine,*
> *Matthieu Bouchet*

As Josephine looked up from the letter, her held breath blew across her lower lip. This letter . . . he must have come here intending to give it to her. But upon seeing Julien attacking her, he forgot his original intentions. 'Twas a good thing it had fallen in her yard. Or maybe he'd left it behind, knowing she would find it.

Then she bit her lip. She had been so wrong. Why had she not known? Not suspected that the lecherous Julien Delaroche could not possibly have written such heartfelt letters.

She traced the last few sentences with her eyes. *I cannot bear to leave without a kiss from your lips, perhaps an admission of love . . . you will not learn the truth until it is too late.*

"I must go!"

She dropped the letter and fled to the house. "Richelieu! I need to ride immediately."

"Josephine!" Helene called. "Where are you going?"

"Your bodice, Mademoiselle!" Marie Claire shrieked.

She'd almost forgotten. Quickly she rushed back so Marie Claire could assist her. Then she stuffed Matthieu's letter between her breasts and the stiff satin and ran to the carriage. It took Richelieu longer than usual to harness the horses with her breathing down his neck, but it was eventually done.

"Mademoiselle, this is highly irregular," Richelieu grumbled as he mounted the driver's seat. "I dare not think what your father—"

"Father would wish it!" she called from the carriage. "Now ride before the 26th marches out of Paris!"

By the time the carriage broached the Seine and the horses clattered over the Pont Neuf and into the courtyard of the Louvre, Josephine could see the steady line of troops marching north. Torches illuminated the bobbing rows of heads and muskets. Carts were loaded with kegs of wine and powder. A lithe order of deadly pikes towered above their owners, some of the tips flying a narrow strip of blue fabric. Children danced around a small fire, kicking their poorly booted feet into the dusty ground and jumping into mock poses of military readiness, imaginary muskets held in the crooks of their fragile arms.

Smoke and dust and sweat stirred in Josephine's nostrils as she scanned the display. More than one woman stood in tears, waving to her man, a babe cushioned against her bosom. Matthieu! His head down, his shoulders dragging, he did not seem to notice the ruckus around him.

"Stop, Richelieu! I'll walk from here."

"Mademoiselle, wait for me!"

"No, I'll be fine."

No sign of the chevalier. *Good.* Josephine ran up to Matthieu, surprising him with a touch to his arm. He turned and caught her against his heart, and she wilted into his embrace. This was home.

"Josephine?"

"You dropped this." She held the crumbled billet doux.

*"Mon dieu,* I am so relieved. I thought it lost. I completely forgot to give it to you, so caught up was I in trying to wrench Delaroche from your arms. Oh, Josephine." He hugged her, burying his face against her neck. Josephine felt certain a warm tear brushed her earlobe. "I'm so sorry."

"Do not apologize. There is no time save for what we must do. I could not let you leave without bidding you *au revoir.*"

"You read the letter?"

The soldiers who were behind Matthieu marched around him, mumbling things such as "lucky fellow" and "poor guy." Everywhere muskets clanked and swords were shuffled into their sheaths. Male voices grumbled about missing home and not being given enough time.

"I read it all. Matthieu, I was so foolish. To think I actually believed that Julien—"

He brushed his thumb across her cheek, lingering on her lips. "You had no idea."

"You must keep up," a fellow soldier whispered to the twosome.

"I need to go," Matthieu said, reluctantly pulling his hand

from her face. But in the same instant he reached up and spread his fingers back through her hair. "I cannot. Ah, I do not want to leave you, but, I must!"

"First this." Josephine pulled his head to hers, and kissed him. No reluctance. This was a kiss long awaited, one that should have been completed days ago. It felt right. Hard and long and forever, steeped with the flavor of his want and her need.

His gloved hand snaked around her waist and pulled her to him as if claiming a prize. Mine, his actions said. Yes, yours, she answered by deepening the kiss. Hold me, take me, conquer my heart. I am yours. Always. She felt a surrender of soul with this kiss. A sacrifice of heart as his power enveloped her entirely. And it was good, so good. These lips she kissed where meant only for her.

"If only I had been the first to kiss you," he muttered against her lips.

"This is the first I shall remember," she reassured. "All others pale in comparison."

But they could not reconnect. "March!" Delaroche growled as he tore Matthieu from Josephine's arms.

"I love you," Matthieu murmured as he was forced to turn away and march before the watchful eye of the chevalier.

Through new streams of tears, Josephine smiled to herself as she waved him away. "Write to me!"

Matthieu's nod said *I will.*

"I love you, too," she mouthed as the wide shoulders of Julien Delaroche blocked her view of Matthieu. The tail end of the 26th marched around a turn in the road, leaving two simmering pyres and a strange symphony of sobbing women.

An hour later, Richelieu had to pry Josephine from the spot in the center of the court before the Louvre. "They are gone," he whispered.

Gone. The word reverberated in Josephine's head, crashing from side to side of her skull with every movement of the carriage. When finally they gained her home, Marie Claire and Helene stood waiting outside the gate.

"What madness has gotten into you this night?"

Josephine did not turn to acknowledge her sister. Instead her body moved like a ghostly wraith commanded forward by the underworld.

"Josephine? Speak to me! What is going on?"

She turned to her sister. And smiled. For to now know that all along her heart had belonged to Matthieu was a splendid discovery indeed. And then her happiness turned to a bittersweet sorrow. He was gone. "All this time it is Matthieu Bouchet I have loved."

# Chapter 21

One week had passed. No word from Matthieu.

Helene reported that the 26th had been hit hard by the Spanish just off Artois. She obviously still received correspondence from someone in that regiment. Josephine could only sigh, roll away from her sister, punch her pillow with a weak fist, and close her eyes. Marie Claire reported that Madame Lamarck had stopped by. Twice. Josephine did not feel like talking. Nor eating. Richelieu had gone so far as to threaten to call their father from the king's side. So be it, Josephine thought listlessly. Her heart would not lift from this wretched state of melancholy.

Not until she received word from Matthieu.

"You've become a permanent fixture," Helene scoffed as she glanced over the untouched tray of leek and onion soup and red wine Marie Claire had left earlier beside Josephine's bed. "Will we move you out to the garden shed and cover you with cloth when the winter comes? Speaking of which, there seems to be a great flutter of activity in the aquariums. Josephine? Are you listening? Oh! I cannot endure your silence."

"Then leave," Josephine muttered, her lips muffled against the bed sheet. "Set the ladybugs free, for all I care."

"I shall," Helene snapped with a haughty air. "Leave, that is. I wouldn't touch those nasty little beetles if my life depended on it. I've an appointment with Monsieur Michelet this very afternoon. I won't even think to share my thoughts on the day's promising events, for I'm sure you'll just sigh and roll your eyes like a nasty old bat winged up and hibernating from the world."

At the slam of her chamber door, Josephine released the tears that had been dammed up behind her lids.


Week two. Neither the dark circles beneath her eyes, nor Marie Claire's clucking over her emaciated state, but incessant stomach cramps finally forced Josephine to eat. But while she grudgingly agreed to nourish herself, her soul continued to starve of the sustenance it sought.

So weak had she become, Helene had to spoon soup across Josephine's lips. After two days of that humiliation, Josephine lifted a crust of rye bread to her mouth and chewed slowly. Food had no taste. Her ability to sense the pleasures of life had literally run out of her body. Knowing she had been so close to the one man who loved her so completely . . . so unconditionally.

"I have been so cruel to you, Matthieu." She tossed the bread onto the silver serving tray. "It is fitting that I suffer now."

But one could not wallow in the dregs of desolation forever. For sooner or later either sickness or death would come. Death was not an option. Josephine had far too much pride to allow herself that slip. And as weak as she had become, she didn't wish to endure sickness also.

Survive she must. As well as she could. For Matthieu would eventually return. And she must be here for him when he did. Whether he wished to see her or not. For she felt sure that the

absence of correspondence from him was his way of saying
he'd been deeply hurt by her betrayal.

"Josephine!"

Startled by the maid's cry, Josephine jerked her hand and
spilled cold mint tea across the striped linen sheets. "Bother."
She pushed the sheets aside and leaned over to set the tray on
the table. "What is it, Marie Claire?"

The maid scurried across the room, a strange vibrancy light-
ing her face.

"Well?" Josephine said on a lackluster sigh.

Proudly, the maid displayed a small rectangle of folded paper,
its red seal centered perfectly. It was addressed, *Josephine
Lalique, Paris, Fauberg Saint Jacques,* in dark insect-track
scrawls.

*Forgive the long interval since we last communicated . . .*

Plopping on her bed with little regard for the toppled teacup,
Josephine eagerly devoured the sustenance she had been craving. In the top left corner of the letter was a pen and ink sketch
of a mouse with wings, one tiny paw raised as if to beg a
morsel of cheese. Around the words a cartouche of spring
flowers danced, given life by their creator.

"Yes, this is Matthieu," she said on a breathy sigh.

*It has been too damned long since I have spoken to you,
and now I must suffer the indignity of doing it via paper
and pen. I miss you, ladybug. My nights are a hell of
memories of our parting. Over and over that horrendous
departure plays in my mind. (Not entirely horrendous,
though I shall get to that soon enough.)*

*I wanted more time! Time to explain. Time to sit with
you, to hold your hand, to press it against my heart so
you could feel the beat of love that resides within me. It
seems that as soon as I was given a chance at winning
you, the devil himself, with a hearty brimstone laugh,*

*ripped you from my arms. Not yet, the demon said with yet another deathlike chuckle, my little game is not finished.*

*Ah, but I may have had the last laugh. For your kiss—rushed to me at the final moment before I left Paris—ah, that kiss . . .*

*That is the good part of it all. The memory of your lips pressed urgently to mine. Josephine, my delightfully curious ladybug, my one true love, the gift of that single kiss burns hot and eternal in my breast. You did not have to race across Paris to find me. But you did. Thank the Lord, you did! I cannot begin to imagine what my days might be like had I not the imprint of your kiss upon my lips, the summons of your touch at my grasp, the one moment when we joined and the world slipped away. You were mine.*

*I wish to be yours.*

*And now that you have had time to think about it, I desperately need your reply. Will you accept my heart, Josephine?*

*Perhaps another kiss to refresh your memory and encourage your answer.*

*Here, love, press your lips to this paper. Right here where my own mouth lingered as if the fibers of this flat opaque object were full and warm and red as your lips. I can feel your touch now, ladybug. You have closed your mouth against my own, the entrance to my soul. A portal no other shall enter. A haven designed only for you.*

*Tell me you will have my heart, Josephine. Send me countless kisses, even if it means an excess of pages. I will taste them all. Over and over again.*

> *My heart is yours for the taking,*
> *Matthieu Bouchet*

Along the bottom of the letter he'd drawn a ladybug, scampering through short spikes of grass, a poufy bow perched upon its head.

She was his! His ladybug!

An hour later Josephine was startled from her perusal of Matthieu's words, the touch of his kiss laid upon the paper, the unique scribble of his letters . . .

"Josephine, I swear I see a hole wearing right through the center of that paper." Helene strolled across the room and flounced upon the bed beside her sister. "Eww, there's tea soaked through to the bed ropes!"

"Is there a problem," Josephine muttered, not looking up from Matthieu's letter.

"So is this the magic elixir we have been awaiting these two horrendous weeks? Will my sister finally begin to eat and move about so we do not mistake her for a statue and plant her in the garden?"

"Oh!" Filled with the pure joy of finally receiving word from Matthieu, Josephine threw her arms around Helene's neck and squeezed. "I have never been happier. Forgive me for my pouting—"

"Pouting? You call starving yourself mere pouting? La! You were near death, Josephine! I was a moment away from retrieving Father. Promise me you will never do that to us again."

"I swear it upon my soul," she said with another hug. "Oh, I love you, Helene. I love Matthieu. He loves me. I love everyone!"

"Ah, the joys of love," Helene tra-laaed with a bored expression as she plucked at the Venetian lace bordering her elbows. Her satin skirts hissed deliciously as she leant back on her palms, awkwardly bending to the right to avoid the tea stains. "But how can you be so sure this is true, when only weeks ago it was another man who lit your fire?"

"That was a deception."

"On more than his part," Helene added with a sly note to her voice.

"Yes, yes, don't remind me. But who would have thought!

All this time it has really been Matthieu and me writing to one another. It's really so amazing.''

"You mean Matthieu was writing what Julien dictated.''

"Oh no.'' A broad smile burst upon Josephine's face as she explained.

"You mean *Matthieu* was really writing to you?''

"And Julien didn't even read what was supposed to have been written by himself,'' Josephine finished.

"The bastard! Serves him well that I dropped him when I did.''

"Yes, but just think, I might never have come to know Matthieu's true feelings for me had I not corresponded with Julien.''

"Oh, what a twisted web,'' Helene said on a sigh. She slapped Josephine's thigh and stood. "But I am very happy for you, sister. Now, will you do me the extreme pleasure of joining me at the table this evening?''

"Of course. But I must be quick, I need to write Matthieu so it will be in tomorrow's post.''

"You never did tell me how you were able to sneak Julien's letters from my own correspondence before I saw them,'' Helene said as she draped an arm around her sister's waist and the two walked downstairs.

"It is a long story,'' she said. "Suffice it to say that there is a fancily ribboned young girl strolling the cobbles of Paris, courtesy of my own creations.''


"I am saddened that your Monsieur Bouchet is once again far from you,'' Madame Lamarck said as she pinned the skirt hem on the cream brocade at the Duchess Sardou's feet. "I have so many orders from his drawings, it is incredible. I have made quite a profit on what I paid him.''

"Oh, and you, Josephine,'' the duchess chimed in, her hands clasped to her breast, "you must be absolutely stricken!''

Josephine had just blurted out everything that had happened

with Matthieu on that fateful night two weeks ago: her discovery that he had been writing to her, and that he really did love her, and that she really did love him, and that Julien Delaroche was a lout.

"I was . . ."

"I'll say," Madame Lamarck said. "I have not seen this girl for three weeks. I've been going mad without her assistance."

"I'm so sorry, Madame Lamarck. It was so selfish of me—"

"Nonsense. Love is not worth the effort unless suffering is involved. But why now have you suddenly come around?"

Plucking a heavy spool of ecru thread from the basket she held, Josephine handed it to Madame. "I received a letter from him yesterday."

"Ahh . . ." Madame muttered between tight lips that pinched down on the thread as she pulled it to length and snapped it clean from the spool.

"I remember the Duke used to write me once a week," the duchess said, her lashes fluttering as she clutched her hands to her powdered bosom in memory. "I fainted almost as much. His words were so passionate. So . . . brazen," she ground out in a husky voice. "Are your young man's letters sweet and chaste or spicy and seductive, my dear?"

Josephine felt a blush ride up her neck. "I believe a little of both. Still quite sweet, for we've only just begun our true correspondence. But . . ." Memories of their kiss could only serve her for so long! "Maybe a hint of spice."

"Perhaps you need to season the pot," Madame said. "Inspire Monsieur Bouchet to open his inner desires to you by spicing the letters yourself."

"You really think I should?"

The two ladies both nodded. The duchess giggled, setting her three chins to a gelatinous wobble.

"Oh, I do so wish to open my heart to Matthieu, but I'm not sure what to write . . . exactly."

"What is it that made you fall in love with Monsieur Bouchet in the first place?"

"His words, of course! Though I thought they were Julien Delaroche's . . . Oh, Madame Lamarck, do you think it fair of me that I hold Matthieu's affections when my own were so miserably off-target to begin with?"

"How were you to know?"

"This is true. I had fallen in love with the man who wrote the words. It mattered not to me what he might look like. And to really think on it—as I haven't been able to stop doing for weeks—I believe I have always loved Matthieu. Since perhaps childhood."

"Haven't I been telling you all along?" Madame Lamarck snipped a length of thread.

"Yes, you have! And so has everyone else. Oh, I cannot believe I have been so blind. Such a fool!"

"Don't think another moment on it, child. Finally you have come to your senses. Now you go in there and write of your desires. Tell Monsieur Bouchet what it is that you miss about him. What it is you need from him. What it is he does to you when you are lying about, dreaming that he is near."

"Really?"

"Yes!" both women cheered.

# Part Two

I have told my passion,
my eyes have spoke it,
my tongue pronounced it,
and my pen declared it;
Now my heart is full of you,
my head raves of you,
and my hand writes to you.
        —*George Farquhar,*
    *English writer of comedies*

Part Two

# Chapter 22

*My dearest Matthieu,*

*You, my love, cannot begin to imagine the hell I have been through since your hasty departure. There was a time when Helene thought to call the priest and have Extreme Unction said over my bed. But I shouldn't have you think I was near death. Still, with your letter, I was renewed. Pain, loss, hunger, and bitterness were swept away with the folded missive written by your hand.*

*You must be suffering so for it to have taken you so long to write me. I kneel before Cook's cross and say a prayer morning and night. I pray for you every day. I pray that this war will end soon. I pray that you will walk through the fields invisible to the enemy. I pray that you will survive, for we must be reunited.*

*It is imperative. For I have been robbed of you.*

*The kiss you sent me, I'm sorry to admit, has all but vanished for the many times I've held it to my lips. You wish a thousand kisses from me? You hold them in your hands now, dear Matthieu. This paper is bound with*

kisses, so fine their weaving that you cannot tell where
one might begin and another ends. So if you kiss one,
then you shall have another, and another, and another.

Just knowing you are reading this, holding my kisses
in your hands, works a mystical enchantment on my heart.
(And, it makes me wonder if it has much the same effect
on yourself.) Does your heart flutter when you hold this
letter? Mine does when I hold yours. Does your throat
dry and your tongue glance out to wet your lips as you
anticipate my kiss? Mine does. Can you feel my presence
in every word on this page with a palpable longing that
burns . . . deep . . . and lingering? I do.

I hold my left hand to my breast now as I write. My
breaths rise and fall, not quickly, but in heavy anticipation
of your touch. I wish it were your hand resting on my
bosom, just dipping over the lace of my chemise. I can
feel your caress if I close my eyes . . . You trace the
contours of my body with your fingers, as if they were
brushes stroking across a blank canvas. Matthieu . . .
Matthieu.

I need your touch. Please send it to me. Quickly!

> In breathless anticipation,
> Josephine Lalique

"So, you going to read it to everyone?"

Fanning Josephine's letter before his face, Matthieu tore
himself from the dizzying images of flesh and heavy breathing
to look Jean-Jacques in the eye—the only hint of white on his
face. No one had come close to a pond, a stream, or even a
bowl of rainwater in the last two weeks. Everyone was filthy,
stinking, and in a foul mood.

But not him! He was feeling rather randy at the moment, if
truth be told. Though it was not an entirely desirable feeling
to have when in the company of three hundred men, with not
a single woman in sight.

"I don't think I can," Matthieu said as he folded the letter.

He slipped the pewter miniature out from his leather sword belt and studied it. Josephine. Just her face and curls of hair kissing her cheeks. He wasn't sure she even knew of this portrait. He'd sketched it on the sly during one of their Sabatier raids years ago. There was a metal clasp on the back of the frame, and now Matthieu slid the missive under it and quickly slipped it inside his shirt. "It ... reveals ... some personal things. About ... her family. I'm sure Josephine would not want them known by the entire regiment."

Jean-Jacques's expression fell to the usual grimace that all wore of late.

"Sorry, man." Matthieu laid a firm hand on his shoulder. "Perhaps the next one."

He nodded, a dog deprived of a bone on a cold winter's night, and wilted into a ball next to Matthieu's feet where he would try to sleep a few hours before the whistle of cannon balls brought the entire second shift to their feet.

They'd had little if any time to rest lately. The Spanish were relentless. Yesterday Julien had led them all to Arras. They'd gained enough ground to consider the day a success.

But successes were no longer measured by enemy ground or advancement. No, the only thing that could ring a hearty cheer from this regiment's voice was a bit of belly timber, perhaps a cask of good wine. Hell, it need not even be good. It could be rancid and vinegary, for all they cared. They'd stolen a farmer's goat last week and milked her dry. Last night, they'd roasted her skinny carcass. But putting a little food in an empty stomach only serves to increase the hunger pangs, when the body knows there might be more where that came from.

Unfortunately, there was no more. Julien had sent word to Commander Marechal to send rations. If all went well, they would receive more supplies in a few days.

Matthieu glanced around the circle of men. No fire blazed, for they did not want to alert the enemy. Clothing hung in tatters on slumped shoulders and weary legs. Surely it was the dirt itself that held the shreds of fabric together in some places. Matthieu's own shirt was dirtied to a dull color and his breeches were torn at the knee, exposing his leg as he slashed through thickets of cockleburs and burning grass. Morale had already begun to wane. Without food, it would only get worse.

He patted the letter inside his shirt. Reading it had worked like a feast of roasted meat, wine, and steaming bread on Matthieu's soul. Josephine had been so . . . brazen. And he liked it. He needed just such words right now. She did love him. Bless the heavens, she loved him.

He flipped the flap of his leather satchel open and dug around for his walnut case. He had but a half jar of ink and his quill had broken in two. Fours sheets of paper were already crumpled, one sheet torn on the corner.

Jean-Jacques eyed him. "You've time. Do it now before Delaroche returns with orders to march."

Matthieu nodded. Much as he'd rather suck powder from the horn, he had to talk to the man. Soon.

After he wrote to Josephine.

If she wanted his touch, well then, he would touch her.

A winsome ladybug, perched on a wide pond leaf, batted her long lashes at a dragonfly skimming overhead. Along the margins of the missive, flowers spun in gossamer skirts and even a comical musket with eyes and arms granted Josephine a giddy smile. Everywhere, hearts bobbed and dashed and flew with the assistance of tiny wings.

*My tempestuous ladybug!*
   *Yes, tempestuous you are with your bold words and blatant desires. Do they offend me? Oh no! Rather they stirred me into such a state that for the long moments I held your letter in my hand you will be surprised to know the world slipped away. No more war, no lack of food*

*or morale. Only silence, you and I, standing together. Touching.*

*Yes, my heart does flutter, and yes, my throat is dry. And as for that burning, well, how can I explain? It is more a throbbing in a man, my lovely Josephine. And you have made me throb.*

*So I take your thousand kisses and spread them over my face, my neck, my hands, and body, until the men stare at me so oddly that I must fold them up and secret them away for another time. Can you imagine what it is like to know a thousand perfect kisses reside inside my shirt, pressed against my chest, just waiting? Waiting for release? Think about it, Josephine. I do. All the time. I have fallen into your kiss and I do not desire rescue.*

*In fact, I think of what it will be like when finally I can kiss your lips in person. It will not be a simple brush of flesh, or even a firm smack. I shall eat your lips, Josephine, devour them like a plump and juicy fruit. Sucking the passion from your mouth like the sweet flesh of a summer peach until it makes me sticky.*

*Think about that.*

*And while you are thinking, I must reach out and touch that messenger of a thousand kisses. Your lips are a perfect pair of cupid bows. Ah, but wait! You wanted my touch somewhere else I believe. Where was it? Oh, love. A little lower?*

*You are wearing the cream satin gown that I designed especially for you. (You never knew that, did you? It was I who had that dress sent to your house after soiling your own.) While I had initially designed it with a higher bodice, Madame Lamarck used some discretion. And I thank her now. With every breath you take, I am knocked over by pure delight. I reach tentatively at first, and then settle both hands upon your breasts. You draw in a breath. They rise to fill the tense cups of my hands. And I relax and begin to enjoy and . . . indulge. Warm and welcoming, each rise beckons my study of your body.*

*But how can one truly touch with only his hands?*

*Can you imagine the lazy slide of my tongue across your body? You can? Oh, ladybug, you are a brazen little wench! My wench. And my bosom, held in my hands and tasted with my tongue. They are of a flavor only you can possess, a flavor designed only for my tongue. Only heaven's mead could offer such sweetness.*

*I love Josephine relentlessly, passionately, romantically, madly, longingly, divinely . . . exclusively.*

*Might I unlace your stays?*
*Eagerly waiting for your reply, with tongue held in check,*
*Matthieu Bouchet*


*Rogue Matthieu of the Eternal Tongue,*

*Unlace my stays? But, Monsieur, they are already undone at my own hands in anticipation of your journey! Go forth, brave soldier. Explore new territories and claim them as your own.*

*Do not mind my tender whimpers and pouts, for they cannot be controlled. What your touch does to my insides! If this be a sin, then let hellfire rain down upon me, for though you are not here in the flesh, your soul seeps from the fibers of the page to plunder me as if you were. I lie on my bed now; you stand over me. What is it you wish? To suckle at my breast? Monsieur, how can I resist your hungry eyes and voluptuous heart?*

*Oh, the fire blazes hot. Your hair tangles in my fingers. I've always adored your hair, Matthieu, do you know that? The long carefree waves, whose arrangement you never give a second thought. They are free and wild. As free and wild as you make me feel with the power of your kiss, your long, wet kisses that drag and slip and suck at my breast.*

*I am being quite the brazen this time! Perhaps I should restrain my desires? Would I go so far as to promise a thing to you that I might later relinquish?*

*No. Never.*

*On with brazenness!*

*Now it is my turn to touch you.*

*Your shirt is already on the floor in a puddle. (Don't you remember? You removed it earlier.) I must push you away so I can look over your fine form. My breasts ache for your attentions, and I can see your fingers twitch to touch them. But wait! I need to slip my fingers through the fine scatter of dark hairs on your chest. I think they must be very soft, having been caressed by a shirt all their life, though perhaps a little carefree, like the hair on your head. Oh, it is great joy to smooth across them. They tickle my palm. I touch the tiny bud of your nipple. How does it feel, Matthieu? Am I being too bold? Must I forego my explorations? Please say good, and no, and no.*

*Sigh ... Another kiss? Yes please! Right ...*

*... here.*

*Josephine, explorer of new territory, and your willing canvas,*

*I love you, Matthieu!*

This letter's cartouche featured a half-clad woman brazenly sprawled in the lower corner of the paper, her pert breasts barely camouflaged by her long, streaming hair. Butterflies soared up the left margin to swirl above the head of a lovesick soldier who bore a remarkable resemblance to Matthieu.

*Mademoiselle Josephine, Brazen Wench and Tormentor of my Soul,*

*Two days have passed with little sound of cannon fire or stallion charge. I fear a plot is brewing in the Spanish ranks. Pray for us all.*

*But I can no more than begin to worry, when the*

sudden touch of your fingers pinching around my nipple shocks me to rigid alertness. And I do mean rigid, my dear. Do you know what that does to me? No, of course not, you asked how it feels. I shall tell you, it feels as if the Almighty has stroked a wave of pleasure across my entire form and the aftershocks are still shuddering through my system.

Mon dieu, we have crossed a line. You realize this, ladybug? There is no going back. Nor do I desire that either of us even consider the thought. Full charge ahead, I say! Storm the keep!

So here, another kiss for you, and yes, I'll take that one for myself, thank you very much. Do you know what I am doing right now, Josephine? I am drawing a long blade of emerald grass across my lips. Why? Because a long slender blade of grass never ceases to remind me of the time I watched just such a stalk of meadow grass lazily trace across your ankle. We were sitting by the pond. Your skirts were high enough to reveal your ankles. You were unaware of my stare. I think.

The treasures I would have given at that moment to be that blade of grass, lolling unawares across your ankle. Gliding briskly over the gentle rise of your ankle bone and smoothing the contours just above and below the graceful slope. I dare say this very moment my fingers quake at the thought. My fingers? Ho! My mouth does protest, what of me?

Hike up your skirts, ladybug. I'm waiting . . .

The days are long without you by my side. My pocketful of kisses grows paltry. Please, send more.

> Soused with desire,
> Matthieu Bouchet

*Matthieu Bouchet, Entomologist of the Highest Regard;*
*Specialty: Ladybugs*

*Dear sir, what I begin to think now each time as I draw my stockings upon my feet and reach that spot, that infamous spot, my ankles! Can you imagine, Matthieu love, I just received a new pair of white silk stockings with green clocks on them. A gift from Madame Lamarck, though I did not mention your letter, it was as if she could read your words in my eyes. She handed me a box, with a wink, and the request that I send along a kiss for you from her next time I write. So there you are. I won't spend any more time than that bestowing another woman's kiss upon you.*

*Where was I? Ah yes, hiking up my skirt. I am bent over on my chair, carefully slipping my stocking over my heel, when I pause at my ankle. The heat of your kiss runs liquid fire up through my veins. It is as if you are a slave at my feet, and I in control. But really it is you who possesses the power to bring me quaking to my knees. I cannot resist. And so I draw the stocking higher up my leg. Slowly, giving way to the silk as it becomes a sheer sheath around my flesh, I pull it higher. Up over my knee. And higher. I must push my skirts aside, Matthieu dear. Are you peeking? (Pray, you are.)*

*And now I stop right . . . here. Yes, that is perfect. You lean in. I spread my fingers through your hair. I let out an anticipatory moan. And you kiss me.*

*Right . . .*

*. . . there.*

# Chapter 23

Another letter. Another riot of passion-laden provocations and promises and kisses here and there and most everywhere.

Josephine clutched Matthieu's latest letter, which described in intimate detail his kiss to her thighs, her stomach, her lips . . .

"Oh!" Her fingers crumpled the paper against her breast where the fine holland nightshift lay untied. Stiff lace tickled her nipples. She snapped the ties together and pulled a tight bow. Still the material set her insides to a fidgety roil such as only the touch of a man's tongue could do.

"Damnation and frustration!" She sprang from her bed to pace the floor. Her desk candle had guttered to an ivory puddle, the flame fighting for fortifying air. "I cannot endure this torture much longer. How is it he expects me to read what he dreams and imagines doing to me when I am but a pining virgin! I cannot read his words without my entire body awakening and pleading for . . . something. His touch! I need his touch or I shall die!"

Slipping her damask robe over her shoulders, Josephine took off for the garden, if only for respite from her ravaged thoughts

of Matthieu and the passionate promises he'd sealed up inside
his letters. Promises released in a whirlwind with every opened
letter, set free to swarm around her body and mind, to occupy
her every waking thought . . .

"Enough!" Josephine screamed at her wandering conscience
as she knelt before Cook's cross. The grass was cool on her
bare ankles, fallen oak leaves crushing beneath her weight.
Tracing the elaborate knot-work design of the cross, Josephine
forced all thoughts of passion away, opening her heart to prayer.

"Watch over him," she whispered to the stone cross. "I
pray you, keep him safe to return to me."

And then she had a most distressing thought. "Or is this to
be the penance I must serve for the deception I wrought? Oh,
forgive me!" She threw her body forward and clutched the
cross as tears began to stream down her cheeks.

Of course she must suffer for her sins. But Matthieu had
committed no crime other than that of loving her and being
unable to admit it because of her cruel deeds.

It was a long time before she finally sniffled away the last
tear and pulled herself up from the ground.

"I will make things right," she vowed. "I will not think of
another man, ever! I will love Matthieu always, even if he
should—" Oh no, she couldn't speak that word. If he should
not return from battle, than she would bear that cross with head
held high and a heavy heart.

The creak of rusting hinges alerted Josephine. The door to
her father's shed was not secured. Cook must have forgotten
after digging around in the herb garden for this morning's
rosemary tea.

Despite Helene's reminder, Josephine had not checked up
on the activity in the aquarium since she'd fallen into a fit of
depressed longing. And now with Matthieu's letters, she had
no time to worry or even think about her father's project.
Perhaps new ladybugs had emerged from their pupas! Father
should be returning home soon to deliver the beetles to the
Queen's gardens.

She entered the cool shade of the shed. Here she could busy herself with tending to the beetles. Activity would prove a valiant sword against her relentless desires. Sliding up on the high stool that her father would often sit hunched upon for hours as he concocted yet another great invention, Josephine scanned the table.

A fine coating of dust frosted every item. It had been two months since Father had left for court. And he had sent only the one letter, the day after the ball, saying how he'd missed seeing her. Ah, but perhaps it was for the good. If Father were privy to her recent shenanigans he might become very upset indeed. But a few words, just to let his daughter know he was well? Josephine decided she must teach her father the value of correspondence. For though she had become used to his long absences, still she worried. And wondered.

What a time he must be having at court, prancing about as a beribboned fop and sharing the king's ear with the grandest people. Pascal Lalique was an enigma to Josephine, and yet, she knew her father better than anyone. He was enjoying the rewards of an inquisitive mind. A mind much like her own. She felt should *she* be invited to court some day, she might very well revel in the luxury herself. But luxury was not something she aspired to or needed to be happy.

The aquarium's chittering caused her to bend forward and rest her chin in the crook of her arm as she studied the inhabitants of the makeshift nature reserve. Indeed, it appeared the population had nearly doubled. Tiny orange and black beetles scampered across munched ivy leaves, along branches, and even up and down the yellow-streaked sides of the glass.

"Oh, dear, your living conditions are becoming far too shabby. I'm sorry, I had no right to ignore you. We must deliver you to the Tuileries soon."

It seemed more than a few of the skittering insects paused at that last remark and gave her a moment of their regard. The Tuileries would offer endless freedom and abundant aphids for these little creatures.

As for herself, she needed only one thing to be happy.

Make that one *person*.

Matthieu had sat in this very shed with her on many occasions as they'd watch her father fidget with his latest invention or concoct some new way of viewing the ordinary. A broad smile curled her lips as she recalled the one time Helene had walked in on the inquisitive trio during a frog dissection. Helene had hit the floor like a sack of market flour. Poor Father, he just wasn't comfortable with Helene and "her ways," as he described it. Marie Claire had come to the rescue that day with smelling salts and the reassurance that Helene had just been dreaming.

A sudden chill clutched Josephine's heart with a surprising tightness. For to remember that particular day always brought memories of the following morning . . .


Pulling herself up from a groggy sleep, Josephine stepped down the stairs in search of one of those nice plump peaches Cook had picked from the tree out behind Father's shed. Helene did not rise until well after the rooster had been prancing the fence for hours. It was the peace of the mornings Josephine enjoyed most. Her father would sometimes sleep in, though on other days she would find him sitting on the tiled patio sipping a cup of tea beneath the ivy-laced pergola, his legs crossed at the knee and his slipper dangling from one toe.

"Josephine."

As she stepped off the bottom step, Josephine collided with her father. This was a surprise. He stood fully dressed in work clothes and held a shovel. A large shovel designed for digging big holes.

"Father, have you plans for another great invention this morning?" Before he even spoke she knew it wasn't so, there were drawn lines around his mouth which always surfaced when he was either tired or irritable. Or perhaps it was his evasive glance that would not focus directly on her face.

"There is something I must tell you, Josephine."

She allowed him to lead her onto the patio and sat her in the iron chair, cushioned over with plumply stuffed damask.

"What is it, Father?"

He knelt before her, the seriousness in his eyes staying further questions. "Something terrible happened last night. I'm not quite sure how to tell you this, so I suppose I shall simply tell it, and then it will be done. It's Matthieu's father . . . he's been murdered."

Opening her mouth to speak did little but draw more air into the sudden gulp that formed in her breast.

"Much as I'd rather not have to tell you, I know you will have questions."

Her heart seemed to have stopped beating. Had it risen to her throat? Or sunk into her belly?

"It seems a man who fancied himself Isabelle Bouchet's suitor murdered Alphonse in hopes of eliminating him from the picture. Isabelle is stricken."

Matthieu's mother had given up her title as baroness to marry the titleless farmer Bouchet. Pure love, it had been, true and simple. A love that Matthieu constantly spoke of, and one that Josephine felt sure shaped the son into the fine man he had become.

How horrible, this news! And still she could not catch her breath.

"Relax, dear. Breathe. There, that's it. This is very hard for you, I know. It is at times like this I wish desperately for some insight into human behavior." Pascal Lalique hooked his hand up higher on the wooden shovel handle and laid the other hand on Josephine's knee. "I'm on my way to the Bouchet farm now. I've offered to dig a grave. Madame Bouchet wishes her husband buried in their gardens. She cannot afford a burial at Les Innocents. I believe I'll stay a spell, make sure Isabelle has all she needs. Will you be all right until I return?"

Josephine gripped her father's shirt with trembling fingers. "Let me come?"

"No, I—" He rose and smoothed a hand over her loose hair. How she loved it when he touched her hair and met her eyes with the wise and kind light of his own gaze. " Well . . . perhaps."

"I want to see Matthieu. He needs me, Father!"

"Yes . . . it might be a good thing if you did come along. I'm sure the boy is at tremendous odds with the entire situation."

"He didn't—" Josephine could not bring herself to say the rest, but her father understood.

"I do not know for sure. A neighbor brought me out of bed and over there in my nightshirt and boots. Isabelle was hysterical. I have a feeling Matthieu might have seen the man who did this."

"Let me change quickly," she whispered.

The trek across the meadow to the Bouchet farm might have been the longest walk in Josephine's memory. She walked alongside her father through unplowed clods of dried mud, pumping her fists to keep stride with his long steps, her breaths panting in rhythm with his. Neither spoke. Words were not needed.

They both knew the Bouchet family had been irrevocably shattered with this single selfish act. Matthieu had told her that there was a man pursuing his mother. Isabelle had implored him not to bother his father with it. She had no interest whatsoever in this man, and Alphonse would only get upset. He was simply a man from her past who did not know how to let go. She would handle things as well as she could. But never, never, must Matthieu tell his father.

Isabelle Bouchet had been terribly wrong. For now her husband was dead, and Matthieu would forever regret not telling his father.

The Bouchet cottage rose into view along the horizon, cirrus clouds floating overhead like a blanket and a swirl of squawking swallows circling the house. On the neighboring plot a great white windmill stirred the air. They walked carefully through the corn, ready to tassel and smelling deliciously rich as Josephine trailed her fingers along the stalks, each taller than she by a head. When they stepped out of the cornfield and came upon the house, they found Matthieu standing in the open doorway, his gaze fixed to the sky, his hands stuffed in his pockets.

Josephine followed her father's example as he quietly approached the young man. Pascal stopped, jammed the tip of his shovel into the grassy lawn, and scanned the horizon along with the silent sentry of the house.

"Out back," Matthieu finally said as he drew one hand up along his suspenders and gave them a lackluster pull. "I've already laid his body out, covered it with Mother's homemade shawl. I'll get a shovel—"

"No," Pascal stayed Matthieu with a careful hand, though he did not touch him. "I will do it."

The two held each other's gaze for a moment as Josephine hung back in the cool shade of the house. Gentle consolation lingered in her father's soft blue eyes. He spoke to young Matthieu with the understanding of one man to another. Finally Matthieu conceded, stepping back into the house.

"Check on Madame Bouchet," Father said to her as he stepped around the side of the house. "I'll come for the three of you when I've finished, and Matthieu and his mother may say their farewells to Monsieur Bouchet."

On only a few occasions had Josephine entered the cool emptiness of the Bouchet cottage. A simple oak table and straight-backed chairs, crockery and a bare supply of cooking utensils hanging over the washtub. The fragrance of dried meadow flowers misted down from overhead.

Yet with all the spartanness of their surroundings, Matthieu's father always made sure his son had the necessary supplies for his sketches and painting. A fine frame of oak had been fashioned by his proud father and placed around Matthieu's sketch of his parents—sitting with their backs to the viewer, their arms wrapped round each other's shoulders, their bench, the graceful arc of a quarter moon.

Trailing a finger along the pale scrubbed pine that lined the kitchen wall, Josephine slowly approached Matthieu. Having never experienced a family loss herself—she hadn't known her mother who had died giving birth to her—she was a bit confused as to what she should do. Matthieu stood in the corner beneath a dried spray of fuchsia heather, his arms snapped tight around his chest, his head bowed. The faint scent of candle wax directed Josephine's gaze to the burning flame sitting on the center of the table. It might have burned through the entire night, forgotten during the commotion.

"How is your mama?"

"She is dressing," he mumbled. "I feel she may be far braver than I."

"Oh, Matthieu." Josephine rushed to him, but paused, not sure if she should touch him, offer to hold him. "I'm not sure what to do." She stumbled over her thoughts, throwing out words here and there. "I've never known . . . Are you all right, Matthieu? Oh, of course you're not. Oh . . . Matthieu?"

He raised his head and the two held watery gazes for a moment. His look spoke to her like a chorus of angels moaning a funeral dirge. He felt lost, alone, confused, hateful. The rage of feelings battling within left him at a loss, ultimately and utterly emotionless.

"Come to me," she finally said.

He fell into her arms, hooking his fingers behind her shoulders. And there in the cold silence of the morning, Matthieu's sobs spilled over Josephine's body and echoed inside the house for what seemed to be hours.

But at that moment, Josephine knew she belonged nowhere else. In Matthieu's arms.

That evening Matthieu did not appear at the Lalique supper table. Unusual for a Wednesday night. The following evening he was absent also. Four days passed, until finally he arrived, dressed in his Sunday best—the new shirt Isabelle had sewn him that summer, and a pair of Alphonse's patched breeches—looking bewildered and lost.

"We've shepherd's pie," Josephine offered as she slid her hand inside his. The conversation was stupid, but she felt that maybe just the sound of a caring voice was better than nothing at all.

"That sounds exquisite," he managed in a soft murmur. "Mama . . ."

Helene rounded the corner, munching a crunchy garden-fresh scallion and paused. "Are you all right, Matthieu? How is your mother?"

"Mama has decided to join the Carmelites," he announced. "Immediately."


With a sigh, Josephine laid her head on her bent arm and watched with dull interest as a slash of sunlight played across the dirty aquarium glass. It had been so soon after Matthieu's life had been ripped to shreds by the cruel murder of his father, that Isabelle had fled to the convent at Sainte Geneviève's. She reasoned it would be best for both of them. Matthieu must move on, as she must close herself away from the world for her sins.

Her sins. Josephine had always wondered about that phrase, repeated to her one quiet evening by her father after they'd seen Isabelle to the convent.

The farm belonged to Matthieu, but he hadn't been able to work the crops by himself. At Isabelle's suggestion, he rented the land out to two families and took an apartment in Paris in the Latin quarter. Eventually, he signed on with a regiment. Two years he had practiced and drilled and maneuvered, until finally he was called to war.

But as much as that dreaded summer had twisted itself deep beneath their flesh and forever emblazoned its wicked memory in their hearts, Josephine was quite relieved to see that it had not outwardly affected him beyond the occasional mood swings and sudden bouts of silence. He was a proud man, and, as taught by his father, took life in stride, learned from his past, and surged forward with an independent spirit.

It was his love for art and the ability to see the whimsical in even the worst of life that kept Matthieu Bouchet afloat.

"Matthieu," she said on another sigh. "We have been through so much together. Now, we cannot be apart. I must find a way to see you. How cruel that as soon as I discovered your love, you were ripped from my grasp. If only we had been given one evening . . . One night to fulfill our desires and bond our souls forever."

Another sigh. She lifted one corner of the steel-meshed aquarium cover. A ladybug slipped out and began to crawl down the outer side of the glass.

"No. Perhaps this is for the best. Had we acted on our hidden desires immediately, we might never have come to learn what true love really means. I have loved you since our first summer together, Matthieu. And now I know that our love is the true and pure love that is the basis of a lifelong relationship. A passionate relationship . . . Oh!"

Frustration reaching its peak, she beat the table with her fist, startling the escapee beetle into a flutter of newly born wings. It wavered and then suddenly dropped to the floor.

"Dear. You are just a newborn. Your wings are much too fragile for extended flight." She knelt on the floor and scanned the recesses under the drawer-lined wall where the beetle had fallen. The heavy dust on the floor stirred up a sneeze. "Achoo! Oww!"

She squeezed the top of her head, which had hit the cabinet. There was no way to see under the cabinets unless she lay down and pressed her cheek to the floor. When she did, Josephine discovered a row of long narrow drawers. "Secret drawers! Father, you sneaky man!"

Too curious to bother with the ladybug that now scampered through her finger trails of dust-smeared flooring, Josephine pulled the small metal ball attached to the first drawer. Inside lay a stock of charcoal pencils and a book on mammal anatomy.

The next drawer revealed a neat stack of drawings. She pulled out the top one. "Matthieu's drawings." She drew her finger along the white margins that surrounded the frog study Matthieu had sketched years ago. Its stomach had been carefully slit and pulled back with pins to reveal the inner organs. "All this time Father has preserved them. Oh, Matthieu."

He had needed her then, and she, without really knowing what she was doing at the time, had offered him the support and closeness his soul demanded.

"We have always been meant for one another," she said as she carefully replaced the drawing. Now there was just the last drawer.

This one stuck so that she had to tug roughly to get it to crack open. A whisper of ribbon slid over Josephine's fingers as she reached inside and pulled out a thin stack of letters. "What is this? Has Father been holding out on me all these years?"

She turned the stack over, the ribbon a barrier that she at once respected . . . and in the same instant she could not resist tugging the loosely tied knot free. Judging from the partial yellowing around the edges of the paper, these letters had been sitting in the drawer for quite some time. Though . . . not more than a few years, for the ribbon still retained a smooth texture; the violet satin had not begun to decay.

"And just who is my father's secret love?" All the blue wax seals were broken from the paper.

"Isabelle Bouchet? But . . ." She quickly checked all the letters and found the addresses the same. "Why would father have Madame Bouchet's correspondence? Something so . . . intimate."

Perhaps they were not as intimate as the letters Josephine and Matthieu had been exchanging. Surely that was it. These were business correspondence, which perhaps Madame Bouchet had asked Father to look after before she left for the convent years ago.

"But I'll never know until I read them." Nibbling her lower

lip, Josephine pondered her rights to intrude on Madame Bouchet's private correspondence. She had no rights. But rights be damned!

"Ever curious."

Pulling herself up and ignoring the dust that painted her night robe and gown, Josephine stepped to the window. Using the dust mote-filled streak of sun as her lamp, she silently read through all five of the letters.

When she finished she fell to her knees.

*"Mon dieu!* Matthieu must never know!"

# Chapter 24

"How much longer will this war continue?"

The wind pushed through the trees, but offered no answer to her question.

"Josephine?" Helene pushed her chamber door open and stuck in her newly coifed head. A mass of curls dangled over her ear on either side of her head; she was simply mad about the new rage in ear wires.

"I must see him."

Josephine stormed past Helene, gripping her sister's arm as they made their way down the stairs, en route for the dinner that Marie Claire had just announced.

"I must see Matthieu," she said. "Will you help me?"

"But what can I do?"

"Think of a plan; there must be some way to get to him."

"Josephine, I will not have you riding into battlegrounds. I simply won't hear of it. And if Papa—"

"But I need Matthieu." They stopped just outside the dining room. Garlic and rosemary scented the air. Josephine gripped her sister's arm and found her eyes. "What if he never returns? I must take a chance now, Helene, before it is too late."

"Matthieu is a fine soldier—"

"It matters not! Fine or unskilled, a man on the battlefield is a target. There is no justice out there. Matthieu could be felled as easily as Julien may."

"We can only hope," Helene muttered.

"Please." Josephine hugged her sister, releasing her built-up tension in a hearty squeeze. "I would die for him, Helene. And if it means I shall be granted just one moment with him, to kiss him, and touch him, than that is a risk I will take. Helene, I love Matthieu. I cannot bear this!"

"My, my, what a month's worth of correspondence has done for your frame of mind." Her sister studied her with an apprehensive pout. "Let me think on it. I won't promise anything."

"*Merci!*" Josephine kissed her sister quickly and pulled her into the dining room.


A few hours later, Josephine stood before her cheval mirror, transformed. Constance made adjustments to the felt hat they'd borrowed from Richelieu unawares, tucking Josephine's long strands of hair up and under, though a flip of her hair hung out in back. To give the illusion of hair, but not that of a woman's, Constance cooed conspiratorially.

Josephine cooperated, though she stood in a sort of daze. She was still trying to comprehend all she had read in the love letters sent to Madame Bouchet. They had not been sent by Matthieu's father. Or, thank God, by Josephine's.

All were signed by Nazaire de Lisle, Baron de Challes. The man who had hung for the murder of Alphonse Bouchet.

She dared not mention her find to Helene. She dared not even speak, for fear of blubbering into a ridiculous wail. What would this information do to Matthieu? He must never know. Never. And she must speak to her father regarding his part in the whole sordid affair. As soon as she returned from Matthieu's side, she would pay a visit to court and summon her father.

Olympe stood back, finger to lips, summing up Josephine's

attire. Helene, snacking on vanilla and strawberry petit fours with dainty fingers, offered a stream of advice.

"You mustn't speak any more than to say yea or nay gruffly, or someone shall discover you," she said on a delicate nibble of sugared frosting. "I must admit this scheme is a rather clever one."

"I do hope it works," Olympe said as she worried her lower lip. Her frantic gaze made Josephine feel as though she were being prepared to hang not hitch a ride with the post carrier.

"As long as Father does not find out, I believe it should work," she said tentatively.

"Most certainly," Helene agreed. "Cook will hold her tongue as well as Marie Claire. Richelieu will be our only problem."

"Not if we gift him with the 1590 Pinot Noir he checks every day to ensure the bottle is not dusty or broken."

"La!"

Constance stood beside Olympe. Her vanilla scent lingered around Josephine. "A fine young lad you are indeed, Mademoiselle Jos—Oh dear! Whatever shall we call you? You must have a code name of sorts. Hmm, like the Masked Rascal, or the Violet Rogue."

"But I thought she wasn't going to speak," Olympe cried.

"The Masked Rascal?" Josephine wondered. "Is that a former beau of yours, Constance? A dandy who slipped his hands up your skirts at a party?"

"Joseph," Helene offered from the lace-covered settee. "Monsieur Joseph Lalique, en route for the 26th Foot with urgent orders from—Oh bother, what are her orders?"

"Is that necessary?" Constance said as she drew a lazy finger along her generous décolletage, caught in a wondering daze. "Can't she just be a traveling rogue?"

"I shall worry about such details if and when the time comes," Josephine said. Besides, she had too many other things to worry about. As long as her disguise worked with the post carrier, she foresaw no trouble gaining access to Matthieu's regiment.

She checked her baldric, borrowed from Constance's brother, Stephan. It held her own sword—a weapon she would not be afraid to use if provoked. "This is an excellent plan. The disguise is only for the road travel. Once I arrive, I'll not keep my identity a secret."

"And just what will you keep secret?" Constance drawled, her crimson smile growing wicked beneath sparkling eyes. "You don't plan to gift your lover with your virtue, do you?"

"Well, I . . ." Josephine had been thinking to do as much. That is, after all, what had prompted this whole masquerade. She wanted Matthieu! She missed him and needed his touch. She didn't know if she could be content with anything less than making love.

But now there was a new twist to the skein. She had to go to Matthieu to see what he knew of his father's death. The letters from Nazaire de Lisle had revealed why it had happened. A why Josephine felt sure Matthieu was unaware of. A why he must *remain* unaware of. "Of course not. I'm simply going to see that he is well and not starving." Josephine caught Constance's suspicious lift of chin. The woman tossed a sly glance to Helene.

"Oh, I don't know!" Josephine plopped onto the bed beside Helene. Her sister coaxed Josephine's head down onto her shoulder. "If he is not starving and if he is well, then I don't know if I can resist throwing myself into his arms. I miss him, Helene. I need him. How will I know what is right to do?"

"You will know when you look into his eyes," she said. "He will ask without having to utter a word, and you will reply in kind."

"But not in the middle of a war!" Constance complained. "The two of you must steal away."

"Oh, yes, to a cozy little inn." Olympe mused dreamily.

"With candles and wine," Constance chimed in.

"Of course, you mustn't forget the wine." Helene stood and

gestured the trio to follow her towards the door. "Let us select an exquisite vintage to send along with Josephine for her rendezvous with Monsieur Bouchet. And while we're at it, we'll bring up the Pinot Noir for Richelieu!"

Amidst a collection of conspiratorial and excited giggles, the girls joined Helene as she opened the chamber door.

"Father!"

At Helene's scream, Constance shuffled in front of Josephine. Father? Now what would she do? Here she stood in breeches and baldric, sporting bucket-topped boots and a brightly plumed felt hat.

"A soiree of giggling girls," Pascal Lalique pronounced with a grand bow. Mauve ribbons splattered him everywhere the eye could see. In his long curled wig, twined in the lovelocks at his neck and on his wrists, on his silver damask toes. "I am home from court, with many a tale of intrigue and spectacle and a few gifts beneath my coat flaps. Helene, a kiss for your father. And Josephine?"

"Yes, Father," Josephine said from behind Constance. "You look a regular rogue. And what a surprise, we did not expect you home for . . . well . . ."

"Weeks!" Helene tossed out. "Come, Father, let's go downstairs and we'll have Cook fix you something to eat. I understand the entire court has been at Fountainbleu? The ride must have been tedious and long."

"Yes, and we really should be on our way," Olympe said as she bypassed Helene, squeezing her generous girth through the little space Helene offered. "It was so good to see you again, Professor Lalique. Coming, Constance?"

"Right on your heels, dear heart. Professor Lalique."

The two girls quickly took the stairs, their skirts hissing angrily as they dashed for the front doors.

This left Josephine completely exposed to her father.

"Come, Josephine." He turned and with a swish of ribbon and lace started down the stairs. "I want to tell you and Helene all about my newest invention, one that will surely be all the rage this winter. Coal-heated shoes!''

Catching Helene's nervous shrug as she led their father into the salon, Josephine figured he was just too excited over his return to have noticed her dress. She stepped back into her chambers.

"Josephine!" Pascal called up.

"Coming, Father!"

Wench's warts, no time to change into a gown, or a shift and robe. Well, as long as Father did not feel the need for his spectacles, she would be safe.

"Oh, and Josephine?''

She stepped out into the hallway. Father peeked around the corner, the ridiculous pink ostrich feather in his hat dusting the wall.

"Why ever are you dressed like that? Is there a costume ball this evening? Come down here. Tell me all about this man with whom you will be attending. Sakes, I've been gone far too long to come home and find my youngest daughter so grown-up and going to costume balls."

Josephine took the steps one by one, dreading the emergence of the truth, but knowing she could not deceive her father. She could not go through with her plan.

"It is not a costume ball I am planning for," she said, linking an arm with her father's and walking with him into the salon.

"Oh? Then what? Has the acting bug bit you? Perhaps an afternoon at the theatre?''

"Not exactly.''

"Don't tell me you *prefer* this manner of dress?''

"I had planned to hitch a ride with the mail carrier this afternoon en route for Arras.''

"Hitch a ride!" Pascal spun her around to look her in the eye. If he hadn't looked a beribboned fop, Josephine might have found the strength to cry, but as it was, she wasn't sure whether to laugh or flip the preposterously poufy feather from her father's face. "Did I hear you correctly? My youngest daughter is dressing as a man to go gallivanting about the countryside? And to what end? La! Josephine, this is not like you.'' He paused, thumbing his chin. ''Well, perhaps it is. But I won't have it! I simply will not allow you, no matter how impulsive and carefree you care to be.''

''I need to see Matthieu Bouchet.''

''Matthieu—''

''Father, you are never home and so you do not know what has happened these past few weeks. I am in love with Matthieu.''

A smile crept onto Pascal's face, just beneath the tip of the pink plume. ''Matthieu Bouchet? Yes, yes, a fine young man.'' He blew at the intrusive feather. ''Most discreet if I recall correctly. Hmm, I was wondering just how long it would take you to see what was right in front of your eyes. But, Josephine, the man is at war. War is not a woman's place. You must remain at home. He will return.''

''No, Father, you don't understand. We were torn apart the moment after confessing our love for one another. I am so worried I shall never again see his face. His regiment was called months ago. I receive letters from him . . . but . . . Oh, Father, what if he is killed? I just could not bear it. You know Matthieu is not the sort that belongs in the trenches.''

''Right enough.'' He pondered the situation with his usual contemplative brow.

''I love him. I want to be with him forever. You see, I must go.''

He pulled her to him and hugged her. ''When did this all happen?''

The smoothing trace of his hand over her back lulled some of the tension from Josephine's frazzled mind. ''I have loved him for a very long time, Father. Unfortunately, I just realized it when he was last in Paris. My heart belongs to Matthieu Bouchet. It always has.''

''I could have told you that years ago.'' He kissed her forehead and smoothed the felt hat from her head, which released the coil of hair Olympe had unsuccessfully pinned. "But I didn't. You were still much too young, had a lot of learning and growing yet to do. I'm not sure if you're even old enough now—"

"Father! I am nearly two and twenty. I shall be an old maid soon."

His chuckle was welcome even though her heart was breaking. "I know that. It is just there are times I wish you could have stayed my little girl forever. That impetuous little pond-splasher who liked to study frog's intestines and dig holes in Cook's garden in search of earthworms."

"So it was the truth," Helene cried as she seated herself at the table Cook had set. "Marie Claire led me to believe I had just been dreaming. Horrors!"

Josephine and Pascal exchanged winks.

"Intestines and frogs! I cannot endure such conversation at mealtime," Helene moaned. "Sit, Father. You and Josephine can discuss vulgarities after we eat."

"But the post leaves soon!"

"I'll not have my daughter rampaging the countryside dressed as a man," Pascal said as he paced to the door of his study. "I simply will not have it! And that"—He ended with a punched fist through the air—"is my final word!"—and left the room, slamming the door behind him. A tuft of pink feather sifted to the floor in his wake.

Josephine looked at Helene, fighting her quivering lower lip, the imminent tears, the urge to let loose a loud wail. She could not lose Matthieu. She had to see him!

The study door swung wide. Pascal Lalique entered the room with a grand flourish and a new air of confidence. "So it's decided then. I shall escort you myself!"

"Yes!" Josephine plunged into her father's arms, upsetting the dainty cup of chocolate Cook had placed before Helene, and splattering the cold brown liquid all over her skirts.

* * *

Night had fallen, and with that a new rain of enemy fire. Matthieu had just finished his watch, and by rights was granted a four-hour rest. But he could not bear sitting in the barracks by himself while he knew his fellow soldiers were out there battling for their lives.

Some men fought for their country, some because they felt it was the right thing to do. Others hadn't a choice, having been released from prison and the prospect of the gallows to serve.

As for himself, being a soldier did give Matthieu a sense of purpose. He was standing in defense of the defenseless. The farmers, the children, the women, and poor. He would fight for France to the death. But at the moment his heart was not in it. So much had happened in the one week he had been on leave.

He finished tying twine about the stack of letters he'd received from his ladybug. He'd slipped the pewter-framed miniature in between the dozen letters for safekeeping. Next to his heart belonged the words and picture of the woman he loved. He was able to secure them against his chest by slipping them inside the seam of his sword belt and pulling the thread tight and tying a knot in it.

He placed his hand over his chest and the letters. "I wish that we had been granted more time, that things had been different, Josephine. Could you have been my wife, waiting at home for her husband?" A heavy sigh slipped over his lip. "No. I imagine not."

For he hadn't a title to offer her. Or holdings in land or any other riches. He was a simple artist, a man of quiet reflection, one who only knew how to express his emotions on paper. Perhaps she would have been better off with Julien Delaroche? At least he held a high position in the army. He was a chevalier, an honor bestowed for courage, or . . . purchased by titled relations.

Fool!

"Don't think like that," he admonished as he picked up his musket and hooked the barrel in the crook of his elbow. "She loves you. Josephine does not judge a man by title or rank or even wealth."

And neither did Pascal Lalique. Though the man did wish the best for his daughters, there was something about Josephine's father that endeared him to Matthieu all these years. He cared for Matthieu. Had encouraged his drawing and studies. The man would have him as a son-in-law, Matthieu knew this.

Now, if he could just stay alive long enough to know if Josephine would have the same.

# Chapter 25

They'd been on horseback for hours. Josephine felt the sore-ness building in her thighs with every sure step of her horse. Though Matthieu had taught her to ride years ago, it had been months since she'd been on a saddle. Her back ached, her fingers were stiff, and she smelled quite ripe. But as long as her father seemed to be holding up—and he held up the conversation, too—she would not grumble. Now was the time. She must reveal what she knew.

Calling her father to a slower pace, Josephine sidled up to his bay and explained her discovery of the secret drawers in the shed. As she detailed opening each one, she saw her father's face draw into solemn acceptance.

"So you found Isabelle's letters."

He used her Christian name so casually! "Yes."

"And of course you read them. You would not be my daughter had the curiosity of a cat not strangled your discretion long ago."

Much as he was absent from her life, he did know her well.

"I did. Oh Father, whatever possessed Madame Bouchet to

leave such things in your care? Do you know what this would
do to Matthieu if he were to discover the truth?''

Reining his horse to a halt beneath the narrow column of a
silver poplar, Pascal gestured for Josephine to dismount and
join him at the base of the trunk. Afternoon was giving way
to evening. A half disk of brilliant gold blazed on the horizon.
Still, they had a few hours to darkness. Rest would prove most
beneficial for them as well as for the horses. Josephine stretched
her legs and bent her knees. Removing her hat to swipe a hand
across her brow released her hair in a tumble over her shoulders.

"Come." Her father held out his hand. "I will tell you all
I know, and when I am finished I believe you will agree with
what I have come to think over the years. Matthieu is a fine
man. He has endured much. And Madame Bouchet is of the
same ilk. They are survivors, both of them.''

Raking her fingers through her loose tresses, Josephine
approached her father, who was unpacking a bottle of wine
from their supplies. He took a healthy slug from the brown
bottle and handed it to Josephine. It felt good to wet her mouth
and rinse away the dust.

"You remember I spent some time at the Bouchet farm after
Alphonse's death." Her father pressed a hand against the trunk
of the poplar and raked his other fingers through his hair.
Without his spectacles perched at the tip of his nose, he cut a
rather fine figure, Josephine observed. "I wanted to ensure that
Matthieu received all the help he needed with the crops. That
simple chores were done and preparation for winter begun.''

"Yes, I remember you were there off and on for a few weeks.
That was very kind of you, Father.'' Josephine kicked the base
of the tree with her boot toe. Her mare nickered and joined the
stallion in the shade ten feet away.

"Yes, well . . . Isabelle Bouchet took me aside the day we
buried Monsieur Bouchet. You see, I knew before Matthieu
that she had plans to leave for the convent. She took me into
her confidence and asked that I not tell him; that it was her
place. Which I respected.

"But what you don't know is that I slipped out and went to Isabelle that same night. I thought . . . well . . ." He seemed to struggle for the right words. "I felt that maybe I could encourage her to stay for her son. But Matthieu was old enough to be on his own, we both knew that. And so, after listening to Isabelle's reasons for going to the convent, I knew it was best for both of them. At least, for a while."

"You don't think it should have been forever?"

"Josephine." He smoothed his finger under her chin. "Isabelle has only been at Saint Geneviève for six years. She has no intention of taking vows."

"Six years can be forever to a son or daughter." The sudden intrusion of tears weakened Josephine's resolve. Turning from her father, she sniffed and brushed the back of her sleeve across her eyes. Six years. Or six years broken up into short little visits between long stays at court; they were virtually the same thing.

"Isabelle was heartbroken, Josephine. She needed to distance herself from . . . well, from the world. You must know it was the hardest decision of her life, leaving Matthieu. But you must also know, after reading those letters, it was the right decision. If any of the truth in those letters were to come out, Isabelle and Matthieu would both be devastated."

"You are on such intimate terms." Josephine sucked in a breath of bravery and turned to face him. "Is there something more you wish to tell me?"

"More? Oh, no, Josephine! There is nothing between Matthieu's mother and me." He bent to catch her evasive gaze. "No more than a deep and caring friendship that has developed over the years. Much like your and Matthieu's relationship, I imagine."

"Father, my relationship with Matthieu is not exactly what I would expect of you and Madame Bouchet."

"Really? Er, oh yes, dear me. I had almost forgotten." Was that a blush on his face? Or merely exhaustion. "We are simply friends, Josephine, do not worry. I love Isabelle, but it is her strength and courage I admire most." He paused. "Though she is rather lovely."

Father did have a wandering eye when it came to court lovelies. Josephine was thankful they remained at court instead of following her father home. Not that she begrudged him the right to a relationship, but the thought of having a court *preciuse* as her stepmother . . . Horrors! Oh, why even think of this now?

"I understand. But why did Isabelle leave these letters with you? Why not burn them?"

"I've not read them myself."

The idea had never occurred to Josephine. But of course her father, out of honor and respect would not intrude. "I've been so unthinking. But you must know—"

"Isabelle told me everything the letters contained. She, too, felt they must be burned. But a deeper part of her soul commanded she save these letters in case some day Matthieu should need to know."

"I can't imagine Matthieu asking such a thing of his mother. He has known only love and kindness from Isabelle and Alphonse Bouchet all his life. To reveal such information to him now would only . . . oh Father, it would crush him!"

"I agree. And that is exactly why I plan to go to Sainte Geneviève immediately after we return. After six years, she must have had time to think on this very thing. I feel sure, that is, I hope she wishes these letters burned."

"I pray that, too."

A pale blue butterfly danced by and disappeared into the brilliance of the sun. Blue mixed with gold, like the brilliance of Matthieu's eyes. How she missed him. That her father had agreed to escort her to Arras was the kindest gesture of all.

"You have always given me the best that you can," she whispered. "I love you, Father. I think it has been far too long since I've said that to you."

She heard him sniff back a tear as he pulled her into his embrace and whispered, "I love you, Josephine."

* * *

A heavy silence blanketed the encampment. Peace had reigned for a blessed hour. After sharing in the dried meat and molding cheese heisted from the Spaniards' unattended camp last night, Matthieu took this opportunity to slip away from the men. On the hillock behind their camp, he found that Julien Delaroche had had the same escape in mind.

Thinking to turn back, Matthieu paused, but Julien looked up and waved him over. A mass of stars shone in place of the lacking quarter moon. Matthieu could just make out the shapes of trees jutting like black columns into the grayness, and fallen branches spiking up from the ground. It was impossible to discern any more than the smoldering of Julien's gaze when he turned and looked at Matthieu.

They hadn't looked one another in the eye since that fateful night they'd marched out of Paris. And that last look had brewed with rage, malicious vengeance, and an unrepentable anger.

Matthieu's feeling towards Delaroche had simmered to a gentle boil over the weeks they'd fought. Knowing Josephine loved him, meant all the world to him. Nothing else mattered.

But he suspected Delaroche's anger still bubbled. Every once in a while the angry stew would even spit, with a snap of the tongue or ridiculous order issued with dead-calm resonance. Revenge? Isabelle? He'd yet to discover what Delaroche had meant. But he would.

Now, the stillness of their surroundings cast a preternatural horror over the entire landscape, and chilled through Matthieu's bones like a ghost stalking an attic.

"It actually sparkles."

Matthieu was startled out of his own thoughts at Julien's words. "It?"

"The sky," he said.

Between the lacework of a towering elm, the dark sky did appear to sparkle as if a dazzling mesh of intricately cut crystals. He had no interest in discussing the designs of the landscape or the sky. He studied the shadows, noting that Delaroche's hand rested on his musket. Always ready. A soldier's credo.

"You know . . ." Matthieu started, sensing the man's sudden tension in the straightening of his shoulders. "She was never yours to begin with."

Julien snorted. "You've been thinking about it every moment of every hour since we marched from Paris, haven't you?"

"That fact seems to please you."

The chevalier spat into the brush before them. "Immensely."

Holding a firm jaw, Matthieu watched as the slender reed of grass Delaroche held between his teeth flicked up and down. Matthieu moved his hand to his hip. The handle of his dagger pressed deep into his palm. "You know that I would protect her with my life," he said.

Julien stood, crooking his musket in his right arm, and kicked the log, setting Matthieu off balance. The anger of his conviction rode down Matthieu's spine with sharp prickles. "It is a foolish man who worships any woman. You say you would die to protect her?"

"Whatever it takes."

"Yes, yes. A hero's words. What if it takes murder?"

"Murder? What are you—"

"We are all capable. As proven by my own father."

His father? *Murder?* A heavy gouge of evil premonition dug into Matthieu's gut.

"But be warned, Cadet Bouchet, I will not abide this liaison after Mademoiselle Lalique has so thoroughly entwined me in her web."

"You've no right!" Matthieu stood up against Delaroche. Together the two men held less than a square yard of space, their stern regard for one another easily visible in the darkness. "She does not love you. She never has."

"Are you willing to die to find out?"

Memories slammed Matthieu's conscience. His father had died for love. The man who murdered him had killed out of

twisted love. *We are all capable. As proven by my own father.*
This was beginning to feel eerie, and yet, so oddly familiar.

"You would follow in your father's footsteps, Delaroche?"

"Would you follow in *your* father's footsteps?"

Narrowing his gaze on the man, Matthieu could not find a
hint of expression in his shadowed face. "What do you know
about my father?"

Delaroche tugged the brim of his hat over his brows and
turned to leave. Matthieu stopped him with a dagger to his
neck. "Tell."

"Once again you threaten the life of a superior officer."

"You know something, Delaroche." Matthieu fought for
control, for restraint. He could not taint his mother's name or
Josephine by killing Julien Delaroche—though at this very
moment, he sensed he had reason. Delaroche's hard swallow
pressed against Matthieu's dagger. He eased up, moving the
blade slightly, so as not to cut flesh.

"I know what most of Paris knows. That Alphonse Bouchet
was murdered out of jealousy. And that act saw the guilty
hang in the gallows, his breeches stained while the woman he
worshipped—so foolishly!—spat upon his love."

Yes, but most of Paris was not aware of the jealousy. A fact
Matthieu knew because he had kept his mother's secret. Could
it possibly be? This sounded too damn familiar to be true!

"What was your father's name?" Matthieu urged with a
turn of his wrist, setting the blade into fleshy resistance.

"The same as mine."

Delaroche. Not de Challes. Nazaire de Lisle, Baron de Challes; murderer. Matthieu would never forget that name for the
rest of his life. It was late, he was tired, he was, no doubt,
getting worked up over a mere coincidence. He relaxed his
jaw, though it ached with tension. "Why did you bring this
up? Your father has murdered, what has that to do with you?"

"We all suffer, Bouchet. It seems there are times you forget
you are not the only one."

Releasing his hold on Delaroche, Matthieu stepped back and

expelled his breath. For a moment he thought he stood in the presence of the very blood that had taken his father's life.

"I know not the life you have led, Delaroche, but it appears you use your father's crime as an excuse for your own behavior."

The click of a steel musket barrel against the metal buttons on Julien's doublet resounded in the stillness. Sweat streamed from Matthieu's head. He hadn't realized just how worked up he had become.

"From your tone, I wonder if you are accusing *me* of something."

"No! But perhaps that is what makes it so easy for you to even think of defiling an innocent woman."

"Perhaps so!"

Matthieu hit the tree behind him with a jaw-crunching thud. Delaroche held him pinned to the rough bark, the violence in his eyes catching the starshine like a demon harvesting fire.

"And perhaps it is for that very reason," Delaroche hissed, each word pronounced clear and succinct. His palms pounded against Matthieu's shoulders. "That reason of association to crime, that I chose to change my sur name from de Lisle to Delaroche."

"Nazaire de Lisle," Matthieu gasped.

"Oh yes. Nazaire de Lisle, Baron de Challes." Releasing his grip on Matthieu's shoulder, Delaroche stepped back. "You know, I was going to steer clear of you. Thought it best just to leave well enough alone. But you came to me, if you remember. And I couldn't resist."

Noticing Delaroche's perplexity over reading a simple letter, Matthieu had offered to help. He'd not even suspected . . . had no reason to even consider . . .

"All this time you've been plotting, pursuing Josephine . . . only to hurt me? Is that what you meant by your name haunting me?"

"And doesn't it?"

Such triumphant satisfaction in his sneering words. Yes,

Matthieu had come to abhor the name Delaroche whispering from Josephine's lips. How well this man had played him for a fool!

"It is a wise man who chooses his fights well," Julien continued. "But I see now it was inevitable. I had always wished for a chance at revenge. That chance was granted the day you transferred to the 26th Foot. I bided my time cautiously, befriending you while a plot brewed in my head. And such success! Forever my name will haunt you. You know it, Bouchet. Your Josephine will never forget Julien Delaroche."

"Bastard!"

"You wish to bash my face into the very ground in which our fathers now lie?"

Levering himself away from the tree, Matthieu slammed into Delaroche. The ground caught the two of them with a hard *thunk*. All the anger over his father's unnecessary death submerged and fashioned itself into violent rage. Matthieu repeatedly slammed his fists into Delaroche's face. It felt good to release the pent-up emotions that had been buried for years. Damn good.

This is what should have happened that night. It should have been his fists pounding into the Baron's face, beating down the tainted love he proclaimed for Matthieu's poor mother. He might have been able to save his father. If only his mother had not pleaded he remain with her . . .

Delaroche had ceased to fight. Blood coated Matthieu's knuckles. His breaths heaved from his gut. One last time, Matthieu raised his fist, lingered in the air . . . Her face appeared . . . "No." Josephine's sweet smile. His mother's tear-filled eyes . . . Violence would serve nothing but a revenge his heart had never desired. He'd forgiven his father's murderer years ago. The dead cannot come back. A man's best revenge was to forge ahead, make a new and better life for the family he yet had.

Matthieu rolled off Julien's inert figure. "I cannot punish you for a crime your father committed. You are not your father."

Delaroche slipped his hand across his face, wiping the blood from his nose across his cheek, but did not answer.

"Justice will never come. We have both lost our fathers to one unspeakable act. Life goes on. It is what we make of it! Not what our fathers tried to design."

"You may feel vindicated wetting your fists with my blood," Julien spat. "But I will not be appeased by a few words about forgetting the past. You have not yet begun to suffer, Bouchet. You'd best guard that woman of yours with both eyes peeled and a fortress of weapons."

Matthieu gripped Delaroche by the shoulders and wrenched him up from the ground. "For as long as I am alive, you will not go near Josephine. I swear this. You'll have no opportunity to torment her."

A sudden burn speared Matthieu in the side. W-what? Had Delaroche stabbed him? Dropping the chevalier, he clutched his chest. In the distance the smoke of enemy fire fizzled and dispersed.

He'd been shot!

He fell to his knees, gripping the ooze of hot blood and torn flesh at his breast. A sparkle of starshine shivered into a blur. He closed his eyes.

Julien de Lisle lingered in the grass until he felt sure the stray shooter had left. Smearing the tip of his tongue over his lips, he tasted his own blood. After what seemed forever he pushed up and looked at Bouchet. He heaved the man over onto his back. A crimson flower spread across his chest. Dead? He couldn't be sure. But—

"It looks like my opportunity to torment your Josephine has just presented itself."

He spat bloody saliva near Matthieu's leg. "Remember my name, Julien de Lisle." He picked up his musket and marched slowly and with determined satisfaction back to camp.

# Chapter 26

With speed and care. As written on the outside of every single letter Matthieu Bouchet had sent her, Josephine navigated the back roads and traversed the forests of France to gain the French encampment situated behind an abandoned flour mill just south of Arras.

Rumors scattered through the taverns where she and her father had stopped for drink and directions. The Spaniards and the French were talking of putting an end to the fighting. True or not, she could not wait another day to see Matthieu. To be in his arms, to look into his eyes and to know that he still lived.

For if anything were to happen to him—

"I hope the rumors are true," came her father's words.

"There is an odd quiet about," she said, observing the surroundings. A raven flew overhead and butterflies filled the air. Even as they passed a line of lime trees, she noticed a squirrel scamper along a lower branch. Odd that these creatures should be around during battle.

Gaining the 26th's encampment was easy enough. Much to Josephine's relief the men greeted her and her father with the

hopeful news that the troops were meeting on the field at noon
to discuss the Spanish surrender.

"We could not have arrived to better news," Pascal said as
he hooked a protective arm around his daughter's shoulders.

"Josephine!" From the circle of dark-eyed, tired soldiers
stepped Julien Delaroche. He stood tall, shoulders thrust back,
his eyes a mask.

Instinctively, Josephine cringed. "Who is this?" her father
asked.

"Chevalier Julien Delaroche," he offered as he stepped forward to bow before Pascal.

There was something odd about his manner, Josephine
thought, noting his darting almost suspicious gaze as he looked
her father over from head to toe and sucked on a split lower
lip. His left eye appeared swollen and purple.

"Chevalier Delaroche," Pascal offered curtly.

"My father," she said. "Professor Pascal Lalique."

"Ah, professor!" exclaimed one of the soldiers behind
Julien. "I have seen your musical chaise *percee*. It is a
wonder!"

A few chuckles bubbled up and with the tension blessedly
broken, Josephine's father offered a thankful bow.

"Musical commodes?" Julien wondered on a sneer.

There wasn't time for a discussion of melodic commodes!
Much as she despised even looking at Delaroche, Josephine
gripped his leather doublet and pleaded, "Where is he? I've
come to see Matthieu."

"Of course." Julien placed a heavy hand on hers. Touched
by a beast's tentacles. She tried to pull away, but when Josephine looked up into Julien's eyes she saw the wicked lust
dancing there. He had been so close to raping her after the ball.
If not for Matthieu . . .

"Unhand my daughter, you."

A snap and scrape of steel. Pascal held his dagger before
Delaroche. Julien stepped back and spread his arms wide. "You
threaten an officer of the king's army, Monsieur."

Pascal stood firm. "And you soil my daughter with your eyes, Chevalier."

*"Touché."* Delaroche took a step back from Josephine, raising his palms in surrender. "I've not seen your Monsieur Bouchet."

"But you were the last to check his post," was hollered up from the ranks.

"Er . . . yes." Delaroche cocked his head and sucked in his bottom lip. Blood trickled down his chin. A fresh wound, Josephine observed. "Oh, you mean *have* I seen him? Well, I did a few hours back. It was still dark. At his post—"

"He should have returned by now," a scarred soldier barged in. The gaunt lines of his face and the tattered hem of his breeches ruffling over his boot tops made a sick lump form in Josephine's gut. All the men were in the same condition. Oh, where was Matthieu?

"Weren't you supposed to relieve him, Delaroche?"

"All was well. He sent me on my way," Julien offered flatly. When he turned to Josephine, pure wickedness flashed in his eyes. He was not telling the truth. As he'd not gifted her with one truthful word since his return to Paris months ago.

"How did you get that cut on your lip?"

He narrowed his gaze and chucked out a burst of derisive laughter. "You ask a soldier how he comes by his wounds?"

Frustration! He was being too damned evasive. Now she felt sure something was wrong. And it involved Matthieu. "Which way?" Josephine pleaded. "Where is his post? I must find him!" She started for the shattered windmill blades that had been dug into the ground to circle the encampment. Just a quick jog away lay the forest. "Somebody show me the way!"

The soldier with the scar cutting through his cheek joined her. "I will, Mademoiselle."

She followed her guide, Jean-Jacques, until they fell upon a faint path stomped through tall grasses that edged a farmer's trampled wheat field. A bushy-tailed squirrel jumped from an overhead branch, stripping Josephine's nerves clean.

"Are you all right, Mademoiselle?"

"Yes. Just give me a moment to catch my breath." She swiped a hand over her sweating brow and braced both hands on her knees to draw in a few deep breaths. Still in breeches and doublet, she'd garnered more than a few surprised looks from the soldiers. Dread over what she might find lying out in these woods threatened to bring tears to her eyes, but the desire to find her lover overcame that emotion and replaced it with a strange sense of need and determination.

"Shouldn't Monsieur Bouchet see us by now?"

The man scanned the field and surrounding bush. "Indeed . . . he should."

Josephine read the unspoken meaning in his words. Something had happened to Matthieu!

"The lookout post is just ahead," Jean-Jacques said, though now his pace slowed to a walk.

Her father caught up and gripped Josephine's shoulders. "We'll find him," he reassured. "Have faith."

At the sight of Matthieu's prone figure, Josephine let out a shriek and plunged to the dew-wet grass beside him. A wide red stain flowered his shirt. Right over his heart.

"No!" Josephine fought against her father's struggles to embrace her in his arms.

"Have faith, Josephine." While he cooed gently and tried to pull her away from Matthieu's inert figure, her entire body began to tremble. She wanted to touch him! To hold him! He could not be dead.

Jean-Jacques pressed a hand to Matthieu's neck. Josephine gasped as the evil smell of blood set her tears free. It seemed like forever as she and her father awaited the man's signal for either life or death. At the lift of the soldier's smile, Josephine broke free from her father.

"Alive?" She made her own check against Matthieu's neck. He felt cool, though not deathly cold. But there—"His heart beats! Father, he is alive."

Pascal gently prodded the stain of crimson on Matthieu's chest. "But for how long? He's been shot in the heart."

She didn't want to hear such words. Josephine pressed her forehead to Matthieu's. Cold and salty was his flesh, as she kissed his dirty face, his lips, his eyelids, his cheeks, in an attempt to revive him. His jaw remained slack, his eyes closed, a smudge of dirt dashed across his left cheek. "Open your eyes for me, Matthieu. Please! It is Josephine, your ladybug. Oh please!"

"Return to camp and bring medical supplies," Pascal commanded the soldier. "Josephine, I must take a look at the wound."

The firm press of her father's hand on her shoulder begged cooperation. No. She would not let go. For if she did, would that tiny part of Matthieu that must sense her presence cry out? Would he die if she let go of him?

"Just step to the other side," her father directed. "You needn't move away. Keep talking to him. If he is anywhere near consciousness your voice may call him out."

The professor peeled away the bloodstained shirt while Josephine pressed her cheek against Matthieu's. "You cannot die now," she whispered in his ear. "We've not yet had our tomorrows." She touched his wrist, where Isabelle's lace was spotted crimson.

"Interesting."

"Please be gentle, Father." She reached down to clutch Matthieu's hand. It was warm and moved easily to form against hers. What she wouldn't give to have him return her squeeze.

"Most interesting."

"What?"

Her father's voice took on a curiously analytical tone. "It seems the rib bone stopped the musket ball—"

"What!" Josephine turned. Her father held a thick stack of letters, a delicious grin planted on his face.

"This packet of letters must have slowed the bullet's progress." He spread the letters to fish out an object embedded between the handwritten layers. "Thanks to this pewter frame. Why, it's a picture of—"

"Jos . . . Josephine . . ."

The sound of her love's voice frissoned through Josephine's system like wine bubbles rising to the surface of a goblet. "Matthieu!"

Star-sparkled eyes observed her with drowsy longing. "Ah . . ." He managed a sloppy smile. "I knew that all the angels in heaven had to look like my sweet ladybug."

Professor Lalique chuckled and stepped away from the two, tucking the bloody mess of letters under one arm. He turned and busied himself with the observance of the local foliage.

Forgetting her worries, Josephine hugged Matthieu tightly. He moaned and she readjusted her arm so that it was not directly across the wound. "You are not in heaven, Matthieu. You are alive."

"Good," he said on an exhausted breath. "But I still think you're an angel."

"Er . . ." Pascal leaned in and said his hello to Matthieu. "I do think we need to get you back to camp. Patch you up. It appears the bleeding has stopped, but you do need medical care. Were you struck by enemy fire?"

"I believe . . . so. Last night."

"That would make sense," Pascal deduced, "since they are talking surrender this morning."

"Last night? But Julien said he had seen you a few hours ago."

"Yes." Matthieu blindly groped about and Josephine rewarded his efforts by gripping his searching hand in hers. "I have something important to tell you. I—" He stopped to draw in a labored breath. "I discovered something about the man who murdered my father. He had a son."

Josephine and her father exchanged nervous glances.

"A son by the name of Julien. Delaroche changed his surname to avoid the stigma of his father's crime," Matthieu went on, his breath weakening. "He knew all along, Josephine. In

Julien's twisted mind, he felt he deserved revenge upon me for his own father's death. Can you believe that? When it was *his* father who killed *mine.*''

"Oh." Pascal smoothed a hand over his sweaty brow. "Dear. His . . . the baron's son?"

Josephine looked to her father. He hadn't any idea that Julien was the baron's son? *Mon dieu,* but this made things all the more complicated. Pressing a frantic kiss to Matthieu's lips, she whispered, "Is that all you learned?"

"Is that not enough?"

"Yes," her father broke in before Josephine could even consider how to reply. "That is enough. Let's get you back to camp, Matthieu. If not, your troops may march in triumph without you."

After being bandaged by the lovely nurse Josephine and putting some bread in his stomach, Matthieu had revived sufficiently to meet the Spaniards on the field of surrender at noon. By nightfall the regiment had reached Compiègne, where they planned to stay the night and make Paris by the next evening.

As much as Matthieu encouraged Josephine to ride ahead to Paris with her father, she would not leave his side. And that suited him perfectly.

Before Pascal left, he laid a hand on Matthieu's shoulder and said, "You're a good man, Bouchet. I know Josephine will not ride with me, and I leave with no worry. You'll take care of her, just as she has taken care of you. But do remember . . . though you have my blessing, son, I much prefer my daughter wed as a virgin."

Matthieu was taken aback. But with the professor's smile and wink, the tension had immediately lessened. He preferred the same. But he wasn't sure if he could stave off his desires that long. Perhaps Compiègne would have a priest?

As the soldiers staked out their claims in the stables behind the sign of the *Petit Chat Noir,* Matthieu smiled to himself to find his ladybug had already curled up on a clean toss of straw, her dark hair strewn like spilled ink across the golden hay. Every man in the regiment whispered around her. All treated her as a sleeping princess not to be disturbed.

"I thought her a fool for what she did coming to see you," Jean-Jacques said. "But now I can only wish to have such a fine and honorable woman myself. You're a lucky man, Bouchet. Heed her father's words and make her an honest woman before you seek her favors."

"I will. Besides," he said with a sweeping gaze around the stables and the three dozen soldiers sprawled on any available patch of floor, "I'm sure I'll have the eyes of every man on me tonight."

"Keeping you honest," Jean-Jacques said with a hearty slap to Matthieu's back. "Sorry, man, forgot your wound. You'd best rest yourself. We've a long march home tomorrow."

Settling into the straw next to Josephine, Matthieu concentrated for a moment on the sparks from the bonfire that snapped just outside the tavern. The crisp aroma of burning ash combined with the fresh straw to mask the unpleasant odor the regiment had developed during the campaign. A handful of men were availing themselves of the serving wenches, with dibs for second call being offered by those already in their cups.

Here in the stables a wave of solitude whispered through the air. Glancing about, Matthieu exchanged looks with some of his fellow soldiers. Jean-Jacques returned home to a wife and six children. Matthieu could sense the relief in the man's face as he granted him a smile and then closed his eyes. Gaspard had a fiancée waiting for him in Paris. He, too, had a stack of love letters clutched in his dirty hands.

Delaroche—or rather, de Lisle—was not to be seen. Must be inside wenching, Matthieu thought. The bastard. Julien had known all along that his father had murdered Alphonse Bouchet.

Matthieu pressed a palm over his bandaged chest. Delaroche had left him for dead. His intentions?

*Isabelle. That name haunts me . . .*

And now Julien's name truly would haunt him—just as the man had planned.

Matthieu would not rest until he returned to Paris and saw his mother. As far as he knew, Delaroche had not approached Isabelle. Yet. Perhaps he didn't know where to find her? Perhaps it was as he had said, the notion for revenge did not surface until Matthieu introduced himself into Julien's life.

Ah, but tomorrow promised another long march. Without peace of mind, Matthieu would be far too weary. He turned and placed a hand upon Josephine's hair, so soft and smooth beneath his callused flesh. Even through layers of dust and dirt, her soul shone brightly. Such pluck she had shown riding to Arras just to be with him.

Adjusting his weight in the straw, Matthieu pulled up his knees and laid his head against Josephine's shoulder. Like a walk through a summer meadow of flowers, her sweet essence breezed through his troubled thoughts, cleansing them into sleep.

Morning found him lying on a rope bed, naked to the world. Someone had spoken. Was it the same person who had stolen his bed sheets and clothes?

"What is it?"

The swish of skirts dusted his leg. "Chevalier Delaroche, I was told to leave this with you."

Julien flipped over to his stomach and scanned the room. Not even a damned shirt to cover his ass! Ohh . . . misery! Even to think gave him the most splitting ache in the head. He'd drowned his miseries last night, that was sure. It was much too early to move, let alone speak.

"What the hell is it? And be quick about it. It's damn early."

"It's past noon, Chevalier. Your regiment marched hours ago."

"Hell." Well, it wasn't like he was needed anymore. The

Spaniards had surrendered. The French were victorious. It was finished.

With one exception; Bouchet still lived.

The tavern maid dropped a flat object on the bed near his nose.

"I did not read it. I cannot. The soldier who left it with me said it was found during a final sweep of the encampment. He told me you would see to it that Monsieur . . . oh . . . what was the name? Ah, yes, Bouchet! Will you see he gets it?"

Julien growled in what he hoped the woman would take for a yes, and slapped his hand over the letter.

"Good enough, Chevalier. There's biscuits and ale below."

The slam of the door did hideous things to the glob of brains that sloshed around inside his skull. Julien curled his fingers around the post. "Damn Bouchet, when will I rid you from my life?"

# Chapter 27

The 26th Foot entered Paris beneath a shower of rose petals and a mist of sweet summer rain. A bride and groom were dancing beneath the flowers outside a small chapel as the soldiers marched by. Wedding guests swept some of the soldiers into the dance, which they giddily joined.

Josephine slipped down from her mount and just as easily slipped into Matthieu's embrace. They must look a sight, she thought as they embraced beneath the storm of crimson petals, she in dusty breeches and boots, her lover bandaged and bloody.

But the entire regiment was welcomed to the party and within minutes two more casks of wine were opened to flow as freely as the laughter. It was the finest heroes' parade the soldiers could have asked for, considering King Louis was away at Versailles hunting, quite neglectful of his duties to the returning army.

"Dance with me," Matthieu said in a drowsy voice. They'd marched for hours, Matthieu walking alongside her mount, his hand drifting from his musket to the horse's hindquarters, to her leg, which he would squeeze.

"You're exhausted," Josephine said as he pulled her close and buried his face in her tumbling curls. "What you need is to come home with me. I'll have Cook and Marie Claire make you up a fine meal and a warm bed."

"The only meal I want is standing in my arms," he whispered so that only she could hear amidst the cheers of the wedding party and the hoots of the grateful soldiers. "Quench my thirst with your kisses, ladybug. Feed my soul with your body. Press close to me, love, and dance me to heaven."

On the outskirts of the wedding party, they danced beneath the soft summer rain spilling from the clouds, their hair spotted with rose petals, their hearts bursting with joy far beyond the newlyweds'. In Josephine's arms stood *her* man. The only man she would ever love. Though tired and wounded and barely able to keep his eyes open, Matthieu's hold on her waist was firm, his hold on her heart incomparable.

He swept his nose along her jaw, and found her lips. Reality lost its strength and desire overwhelmed her. In Matthieu's arms, a surrender to passion came easily.

"Finally, you are mine," he said. "Finally."

He claimed her as his own with a kiss that spoke from the heart. The fleeting kiss she'd given him before he'd marched for Arras could not begin to compete with the dazzling intensity of this one. Down to her very soles she felt the heat of his desire as he brushed her lips slowly, experimentally, lingering over a delight long awaited. As his breath hushed across her lower lip, he held her gaze steadily. The world was lost in the sing of violins and hearty cheers of soldiers.

They kissed lazily, drunkenly, drawing out the divination of pleasure. Gentle presses. Lingering tastes. And never did their eyes stray from one another. Josephine spoke to Matthieu silently until she knew she had touched him with her eyes.

"Be my wife," he whispered in a languid tone that matched the pace of their kisses.

She did not move, could not break contact with him. Instead, Josephine closed her eyes. In satisfaction. In joy. "I will."

Their circle of salvation within the world become wider and vividly bright. As Matthieu slid his hand up through her hair, she relinquished her heart to him. Take it, she said with her kiss. Hold it forever, it is yours. Kiss me deeply and with the passion that we have only dreamed of.

"I am yours, Matthieu," she said on a bliss-tainted gasp. "I am yours."

The joy in his smile worked as an erotic elixir that streamed down her throat and ignited the want in her loins. She wanted him now, marriage be damned. Not a soul on this earth could part their bodies until they had joined this night. She would not allow it.

"I no longer have a room."

He had been thinking the same thing as she.

"There is an apartment above Madame Lamarck's home in the Tuileries. Her boarder passed on weeks ago and she's not yet rented it out. It will be perfect, Matthieu. We can speak to Madame tomorrow and make arrangements. You can stay there until—"

He stopped her with a bruising kiss that promised to be relentless in its pleasure. "Until after the wedding?" he said with a secret smile. A splat of water bounced from his eyelash and splattered her nose. A shared raindrop.

"If we post the banns tomorrow, we can be wed in three weeks," she said, suddenly realizing that it was really to be. Joy! She was to be Madame Bouchet! "But I cannot wait that long. Come, Matthieu, I know desire burns inside you, too. Those letters you wrote me, the things you said!"

She gripped his hand and started down the cobbled street. If they ran, they could be there in half an hour. But he did not move. Instead he jerked her hand and she stumbled back into his embrace.

"Oouf! Gentle, love, remember I'm a wounded man."

"Sorry." She kissed his shirt right above the bandages. "But why do you tarry?"

Was he having second thoughts? After all this time did he not want her?

"Your father gave me his blessing before he left last night."

Sweet father! But Josephine knew that Pascal would. "Then what is the problem?"

"He also said he preferred his daughter to be wed before she is bed."

"My father said that? I cannot believe he would speak so of me."

"He is your father." He easily wrangled her back into a lazy embrace. "He loves you. He only wishes the best for his daughter."

"So we must wait?"

"I didn't tell your father that I would . . ."

She stared at him until he brought his gaze back to hers. "I made it very clear how much I love you. He trusts that I will take care of you, Josephine, and Pascal knows I would never do anything to hurt you. So . . ." He touched her forehead with two fingers, then traced a smile across her lips.

"So! Let's go! Quickly, I cannot wait!" Gripping his hand she dodged a dancer with a goblet held high above his head. Exhaustion be damned!

"Slow down, woman! Ladybug! You're leading a wounded man by the tether of your desires. Gently, please!"

The rains began to pour, washing away the dust and dirt with crystal strokes. Giggling all the way to the apartments, Josephine found the key Madame Lamarck kept behind the counter, slipped a candle and pewter stand under her arm, and quickly brought them to the bare room.

Matthieu leaned against the wall, panting and shaking the water from his hair. "Not even a bed," he observed from behind her as he shook his tousled head, dispersing cool rain across the floor.

No firewood, not even an abandoned chair or scrap of clothing. The room was completely empty save for a single fire dog holding dusty court in the hearth. The windowpane was pulled high upon its pulley allowing a fine sifting of rain across the sash. Weariness nagged up and down Josephine's back, but she could not fight the zinging energy that circled her insides and danced her every nerve ending to a fine point.

"Would you prefer we wait? Until we have a proper bed?"

He quirked a dark brow and pushed a strand of hair from his eyes. Josephine could not judge his expression. Was he really considering they wait? After they had both waited so long?

"Matthieu?"

Still he remained by the door, sweeping the room and her with a curious stare. Then finally, "Mademoiselle."

"Monsieur?"

"Those clothes you wear . . . Doublet and breeches? Why, they are scandalous! Not to mention soaked, which makes them highly immodest. I'll have you remove them. Right now."

# Chapter 28

Finally she would be in the arms of the man she loved. His touches would be tangible, not just black lines shaped into letters. His kisses would sear her desires like no paper kiss had ever done, while his eyes, those beautiful star-sparkled eyes, spoke far louder than any *billet doux* he had ever written.

Josephine hooked her finger on the first button of her doublet, delighted with the idea of stripping away her soggy men's clothes and diving headfirst into the adventure of sexual lust. Then . . . she changed her mind.

He stood there by the wall, not making a single movement. Just waiting, looking ever so delicious even wounded and weary and soaked to the bone. She should be feeling tender nursing instincts towards him, instead, want rippled through her body. Slowly she drew as close as she possibly could without touching him beyond the brush of their clothes. His sharp gasp pleased her. No, she'd not bumped his wound. She'd touched his want. Looking up into his eyes, she softly demanded, "You first."

Matthieu didn't even blink. "Very well. But you may have

to help with my breeches. I wouldn't want to bend too far and risk opening the wound.''

She smirked at his straight face. Such a cad. "You needn't bend to reach your waist, Bouchet." Hooking her finger along his waistband, she sashayed her shoulders shyly. "Are you trying to employ me in lascivious actions upon your person?"

He shrugged and offered a hopeful, "Yes."

She didn't need such coaxing. Josephine studied the candle-flame reflection dancing in Matthieu's eyes. Though he did not smile, she could tell it was only because he was trying desperately to appear serious. This game of dare she could win.

As she laced her fingers through his slick waves of earth-brown hair, dispersing a few rain-moistened flower petals to the floor, he began to unbutton his doublet, which soon slipped to the floor at their feet. The shirt ties at his neck sprung free at her touch and Josephine slid her hands between fabric and flesh. In reaction, Matthieu expelled the breath he had been holding since she'd closed the distance between them. He offered a slight groan as he lifted his arms to assist her in removing his shirt.

Curiously she drew her fingers along the line of white linen that circled his chest; bandaged properly at Compiègne by a tavern wife, Josephine took slow inventory of his every flinch. Nerves or desire? Or still a bit of pain? Hard, smooth curves slipped under her palm. His nipple was like a hard tiny pebble under her fingertip, and she was reminded of their correspondence.

"Yes," he said, placing a hand over hers. "So, now you know." He kissed her forehead, luring her higher.

Rough stubble coated his jaw. She liked the contrast in texture from his smooth hot chest, sprinkled lightly with dark hairs, to this patch of facial hair that made him uniquely male. His upper lip sported a burgeoning mustache. He'd always been clean-shaven, but she rather liked this new style.

"Josephine," he said as he clutched her wrist, though did

not move her away from his mouth. "I must warn you the dangers of your leisure."

"You do not like my touch?"

"Oh, yes," he drew out the words and kissed the tips of her fingers, each one receiving such attention that they would have no cause for jealousy of the others. "But for every moment we luxuriate in the discovery of one another, my desires increase a thousandfold."

"Not so terrible by my thinking," she offered with a playful pout.

"Nor by mine. But heed my warning, you play with fire, ladybug. And I will not be responsible should the flame blaze out of control."

His voice had taken on a husky, wanting tone, oozing with a sweet honey that drew her nearer and nearer.

"Scorch me," she said, leaning up to whisper into his mouth. "Burn me with your kisses, Matthieu."

The pressure of his hand to the lower center of her back levered her forward and into his kiss. The heat the two created by touching their lips together could melt the icebergs of the Artic. Sweet, delicious flames singed down her throat, branding her as his own.

Pressing tightly to her lover's body, Josephine wasn't aware of anything but the teasing sweep of Matthieu's tongue behind her upper lip, until he moaned and pulled her hips even closer to his. It was then she felt the hard rod pressing against her. This weapon he would use to claim her. Fighting her curiosity had never been easy. She wanted to touch him, hold him . . .

"You were undressing me?"

"Mmm," she said distractedly.

He gripped her hand and pressed it flat against his belly. "You stare at me as though I were a beast."

"Oh no!"

"Then feel, lovely one. Touch me. Know that I am only a man."

"Only?" Warming to her curiosity, Josephine brushed her

palm downward, delighting in the fine spray of dark hairs that began just above his navel. "You are a man," she said in a voice surprisingly similar to Matthieu's wanting groan. But she enjoyed it.

Snuggling her side against his so that she could continue her exploration of the golden curves and firm lines of his body, Josephine bristled and let out a giggle as he nudged his nose through her hair and nibbled her earlobe. "So you are hungry, too?"

"Famished," he said. "And I intend to sate my hunger right now. Your turn. Release those buttons and lift your arms."

When she stood before him, her vest and shirt puddled on the floor next to his, Josephine cupped her hands to her mouth to catch her giggles.

"What is this?"

"It was Helene's idea." She lifted the holland chemise and pulled the hem from her breeches so the long gown fell to the bottom of her buttoned breeches. "She said it would be far too scandalous for a lady to dress without chemise and stays."

Matthieu touched the whaleboned red damask. "Your devoted sister has got you trussed up like a holiday chicken. You mean you rode all the way to Arras and two days back wearing this damned contraption?"

She nodded and offered a giggling shrug. "I couldn't imagine riding horseback without, well, some kind of support. You men have it entirely too easy. No extra flesh up top to jiggle and bounce as you ride."

"I guess so." He drew his fingers thoughtfully across his chin. "Turn around and let me free you, ladybug. Lift your hair."

Threading her fingers up through her hair, Josephine smiled as he fussed for long minutes with the knot Helene had tied in the laces of her stays. A sailor's knot, she explained, and Matthieu grumbled that he wasn't a sailor, he was a soldier. When finally he succeeded, the gradual loosening of her stays gently drew down her ribs until finally she relaxed with a deep breath.

From behind, the husky intake of air from her lover's mouth hissed near her ear. He reached around and slid his hands along her sides, gently massaging her. "I imagine that damn thing must work hell on a woman's flesh."

She tilted her head back and rested her cheek aside his. Stubble brushed her chin, tickling her into a giggle. "It leaves impressions that stay for a good part of an hour sometimes. Oh, that feels wonderful, Matthieu." Her spine tingled and the muscles in her back screamed with joy as he worked his fingers along the center, kneading gently, smoothing and tracing the deep indentations.

As he lifted the chemise from her shoulders, Josephine crossed her hands over her breasts. Instantly her nipples hardened against her wrists. Matthieu remained behind her, intent upon his endeavors.

"Are you frightened?" he whispered in her ear.

"Perhaps a little. Only because this is so new to me." The attentive rhythm of his kneading felt so wonderful. "Don't stop, Matthieu. I love you."

"You've marks on the front, too," came his gentle whisper. He slowly worked his way around her sides, where she always noticed the irritation the most. Madame Lamarck sewed the seams along the sides because that was the least noticeable part. "Why do you women torture yourselves so?"

"We want to look splendid for our men."

"I rather liked you in breeches and shirt."

"I rather liked the dress you designed for me."

His hands paused at her waist. The weight of his head sat on her shoulder, his chin nudging her flesh as he spoke. "You really did not guess it was from me?"

"Not at first. Actually, not until you wrote it in your letter. How foolish of me to even think that—"

"Oh no." He slipped a finger up over her mouth. "No mention of that man's name tonight. Promise?"

She nodded. He pulled his hand away.

"Now, where were we? Oh yes. Here. Press your back

against my chest. Mmm, you are so hot, Josephine. Ah, what that does to me. Now close your eyes and let your head fall back against my shoulder.''

He stood against the wall and, as Josephine allowed her body to relax into his, she noticed again the hard presence of his desire melding into her derriere. But there was more than that to concentrate on as his magical fingers danced over her ribs. With his touch it was as though each rib, once a prisoner, were being granted release. An exhilarating sensation zinged in every part of her body. Her toes danced within the cramped boots. Her knees locked and bent and locked once again, unable to decide what to do. A hum of new sensation stirred in her loins. And in her heart, her soul sang. Call it desire, or need, or desperation, she cared not.

All that mattered was that she liked the feeling.

When he slid his hands along her arms and gently coaxed, she allowed him to place her hands at her sides. Now she did not want to open her eyes. It was too pleasurable to blindly enjoy the touch of his palms cupping her breasts. ''Yes, touch me, please.''

At another deep intake of his breath, Josephine realized that it pleased him just as much to touch her in such a way. His entire hand fit across each of her breasts, though they did not contain her generous swells by any means. It was almost unbearable to think . . . And so she stopped thinking, and gave way to pleasure.

Turning in his arms, Josephine followed that inner part of her soul that knew exactly what it wanted, exactly what it needed. Kissing him hard and driving her hands back through his hair, she stirred him to a new pace. Every squeeze of her breast, gentle touch, the soft thumbing of her nipple, fanned the fire until she felt quite sure that she had been burned. Over and over.

''*Mon amour,* you excite me like nothing I have ever known.'' He lowered his mouth to her nipple.

Josephine could not control the pleading moans that slipped

unbidden from her mouth. Tangling her fingers within his hair she pressed him closer, feeling that should he stop she might go insane for the lost contact. "Never stop," she gasped. "Please."

"Always," he murmured.

She wasn't even aware of his moving to the other breast, for his thumb remained to ensure one was not untended. A deep roil stirred in her gut. The sudden press of his hard shaft against her groin sparked a new fire. Josephine clenched her legs together, but she felt the moistness grow hot and urgent within.

"It has been days," he said, lifting his head to catch her gaze, though his hands still massaged her marbled nipples, "yet still you carry the fragrance of the gardens behind your house. Josephine, you cannot know what the smell of your flesh—all flowers and woman and rain—does to me."

"If you are feeling anything like I feel now, Matthieu, I fear we shall both burst into flames very soon."

"Oh no," he said with a growl, "not yet, ladybug. We've much more to do. We both still stand here in breeches and boot. Have you forgotten your mission to strip me bare?"

"You are a rather demanding one, aren't you?" But even as she spoke, Josephine released the buttons down the left side of Matthieu's breeches, and then the right. He lifted his knees for her to unbutton the cuff and heeled his boots off while she did the same with hers. Lost in a frenzy of flying boots and tossed breeches, she paused only long enough for him to unbutton and remove her pants.

"Now," he said as he caught her in his arms from behind. She dropped her breeches at her feet. "Do you wish to turn around, or might I torment you as before?"

Much as she wanted to spin around and feast her eyes upon his body—she had never looked upon a naked man save for the statues at the Tuilieries—Josephine sank into his embrace as once again he played her body to a tumultuous chord. By the time he reached her hips, she felt as though she were a

violin with tightened strings. One touch in just the right place
would snap the string into a delicious curl.

"Relax."

"I am," she whispered.

"I was talking to myself," he said with a snicker. "Sorry.
Mm . . ."

"When we were younger, did you ever think this day would
come? You and I. Naked?"

"Yes."

"Really?"

She wasn't sure how to take this information. "How long
have you loved me, Matthieu?"

His firmly sculpted chest muscles melded against her bare
back. "Always. Much as I tried to convince myself otherwise.
I've been afraid to surrender to love, Josephine."

Completely understandable, knowing his history. "But now
you are not?"

"I always felt that we would be together. But I would not
stand in your way when your feelings for another man were
so strong."

"No, my feelings were always for you, Matthieu."

His fingers made their way through the soft curls at her loins.
Josephine reached back to spread her hands over his hips and
smooth them across his buttocks. Their firmness tempted her
to squeeze, to devour handfuls of him as she wished. Each
squeeze made him groan and pump his hips against hers, which
worked to wedge the still unseen rod between her buttocks.

"You know there is a place within women where all desire
resides?" he said from over her shoulder.

"I didn't know that. But how do you, Monsieur Bouchet?"
Another squeeze of his flesh; he reacted in kind.

"Would you have me totally ignorant of this magical place
I speak of?"

Sly. But she could not protest. Not when his finger parted
her nether lips and began a steady rhythm against her mons.
Each stroke dove inside her, just barely, but enough to wet his

trail and make it slick. Indeed, he spoke the truth. "Ignorance is such a crime," she managed. Her thighs became weaker with every thrust of his finger.

"Mm, ladybug." He pressed hard into her hips, imprinting the power of his own need in steady pumps. "I need you. Now."

Too frenzied to answer—she felt so close to *something*—she nodded furiously.

"Lie down," he commanded. "On our clothes, that should serve our needs."

To break contact and lower herself to the floor was both unbearable and incredibly easy, for her legs were as weak as noodles in broth. The candle flame flickered angrily as she settled to the floor on her back.

Looking up at Matthieu, erect and proud as the flame danced across his body, made her gasp. What she had seen in the Tuilieries had not prepared her for the glorious reality.

"Come," she said, holding her hand to guide him over her. "Make me yours, Matthieu. Fill me." She reached and found the hard shaft that bobbed above her aching loins.

He drew in a hissing breath through clenched teeth and guided her hand lower. She knew he wanted her to grant him entrance. As he waited, he danced his tongue over her breasts, then up her throat, and kissed her. Savagely. Nips and bites might have sparked at her mouth, but they burned all the way down to her womanhood.

Hugging Matthieu's hips with her legs, Josephine released the heavy, pulsing member. Drawing her hands over his back, she clung with desperation and the anticipation of finally coming close to that earlier *something*. His entrance was hot and brutal. The first thrust pulled a painful gasp from her lips as she felt his length fill her completely.

"I've not harmed you?"

"I don't know," she dumbly replied. "But you mustn't stop."

"Only once," he said as he drew his length out of her. "Never such pain again. I promise you."

"It is already gone." She clutched his hips and guided him deep within her. "Oh, Matthieu, I do not know what to think, what to say, what to do. I only know I wish this never to end. I want you inside me forever, moving like this . . ."

Words escaped her. Within, she felt a blazing burst of flame envelop her entirely. It was too much to bear. Her muscles gave way and a climax of exquisite joy washed through her body, pulling her hips up to meet Matthieu. He held her tight as she bucked, releasing his pleasure in an animalistic moan.

Josephine knew they had become one. Nothing could ever part them now.

The floor left much to be desired as far as comfort demanded. But he had no intention of moving away or startling Josephine out of her peaceful sleep. It was as though an angel had fallen from heaven and landed in his arms. The sun had just peeked over the horizon and cast a lazy sheen of pre-light across the room.

Pale cream flesh, her face; and soft rosebud eyelids trimmed in thick dark lashes that could have served as trimmings on a fancy hat or gloves. Her lips were slightly parted to allow her soft breath to escape. Matthieu touched the perfect indent just above her upper lip, smoothing his finger down the sweet little curve and over the lips that had kissed and sucked and bitten at his flesh with such verve last night. She'd drawn out the animal in him, and just as easily tamed it to a lulling beast at her side.

His ladybug. Really his.

The lips beneath his fingers suddenly curled into a smile. "It is morning already, lover?" So beautiful her smile in the early morning light. A tousle of hair framed her face and drifted over alabaster shoulders and onto the wrinkled scatter of their clothing.

"The smell of baker's yeast rises from the streets below, but I shouldn't consider it morning until the sun has risen above the trees."

"Then we've time still."

"Time?" He shifted on his hip, adjusting his weight by hooking a foot between her legs.

"To break our fast," she said, opening her eyes. "I'm dreadfully hungry."

"I'll run below and purchase us some fruit—"

Her fingers closed his mouth abruptly. "Not for food, silly. I need more of this." She gripped his member, bringing it to instantaneous alert. "I've a bone to pick with this fellow." Giving it a squeeze, she bent to study it curiously. "Do you know he was bothering me all night? Everytime I moved, he'd tap against my leg or my hip, begging for more."

"He did, eh? Ohhh." Her sure grip rendered him speechless. A fine feeling, indeed.

"Do you call yours Jacques?"

"Do I—What? Jacques?" He propped himself upon his elbows. So sweet she looked with that curious flash to her eyes. Ah, his ever-curious ladybug. "Why would I?"

"Constance says some men name theirs."

"Oh, did she? And what else did she tell you about men's cocks?"

"That they are often what men listen to before their own minds."

"A woman would say that."

"What was that?" She tilted an ear to listen to his member. "You don't say?"

"Josephine!"

"He said he's sorry about last night. And look at him now, so eager." She tossed Matthieu a sweet glance and a wink, then leaned in for a yet closer inspection.

"My brazenly curious ladybug!" Matthieu twined his fingers through her hair, drawing out one long strand, wanting to pull her close so that her lips would touch his shaft, but not daring to be quite so forward. The stroke of her cheek along his member, cool and smooth, shocked him stiffer than a musket barrel.

"You haven't much control over it, do you?" she wondered as her explorations prompted her to kiss the engorged tip.

"Er . . . not always. No. Oh, Josephine, that—that—"

"You like this?" A wet tongue glided down his length.

Like it? "Did you care for the way I touched and suckled you last eve?"

"Oh yes." She understood exactly what her touch did to him. And she wielded that newfound power well. "So in payment for your constant interruptions last night, Monsieur," she spoke to his pulsing member, "I shall now show you exactly who is in control this morning."

The trace of her tongue drawing slowly up the length of him shattered any desire to protest. Matthieu rested his hand on Josephine's head, without bothering to direct her action. He let his hand fall to the back of her neck. She wanted control? She could have it!

Her fingers curled into the nest of hair that grew at the base of his member. The sudden scrape of a fingernail across his inner thigh shot through him like the fire that had burned both of them last night. It was when she grazed a nail across his baubles that he was quite pleased Pascal Lalique had raised an inquisitive daughter.

"I think we know who is in charge now," she said, gripping him firmly. "No comments?"

"Mmhmm," he managed as her mouth opened wide to sheath him in a tight cove of wet heat and suction. "Ah . . . Josephine . . ." She wasn't aware of what would happen if she continued! Or maybe she was. Hell, who was he to protest?

Up and down she worked until every inch of the thick vein pumped more and more tension into his gut. He could not hold back, would not, for the pleasure this sweet vixen granted him. As his seed burst forth, she drew back to receive it across her lips and chin in a startled gasp. Riding the climax for another moment, Matthieu finally collected himself and sat up to embrace her. ''I'm sorry.''

''Your seed,'' she said in astonishment as she traced her lips curiously with her fingers. Her giggle relieved his worries. ''Indeed you have broken my fast!''

Amidst his own chuckles, Matthieu wiped her face clean with his shirt and kissed her and stroked her breasts into hard buttons to nurse upon.

''I guess I was not in such control after all,'' she remarked as he traveled kisses past her waist and over the slight mound of her abdomen.

Her giggles contracted her stomach muscles and jerked her knees against his hip. She tasted salty and sweet and of wines yet to be discovered. And now it was his turn to feast.

''Have you learned a lesson then, little vixen?'' he asked from the vee between her legs.

''You wish me never to tease that splendid instrument again?''

Wench! Planting a kiss to her mons, he slapped her thigh and declared, ''Wife, you may do as you see fit with my body. As I shall yours.''

''Wife?''

''Soon enough,'' he offered. ''I'm sure your father will demand the banns be posted immediately after I see you home.'' She was ready, he found, as he slipped his finger inside her and traced the rim of her secret cove. Soft and slippery and pulsing with expectation. ''After all I have done to your body, will you still have me as your husband?''

''Only if you promise a repeat performance each and every night.''

''That I will, ladybug. That I will.''

# Chapter 29

Though he'd thought his seven o'clock arrival rather early, Pascal quickly discovered that the nuns passing by had to have risen with the dawn. Everywhere a scurry of activity filled the walls, floors being scrubbed, windows being cleaned, and, somewhere in the distance, choirs singing to heaven.

As he followed Mother Angelica down the corridor past a vivid riot of stained glass, he realized he was a bit overdressed in his periwinkle satin and mauve ribbons in this solemn, studious place.

"She takes her morning tea in the garden," Mother Angelica informed him as they left the stone walls of the institution and stepped immediately onto a finely trimmed lawn of the most emerald grass Pascal had ever laid eyes on. Not even the Tuileries sported such greenery. He was duly impressed.

"How has Madame Bouchet been?"

"You may ask her yourself," the nun said as she stepped aside to reveal a woman sitting on the grass beneath a huge weeping willow. "I'll leave you to privacy."

Pascal bowed to the nun, feeling rather like a peacock, as

his plumes dipped near the sister's habit so she had to brush them away. He should have worn the more subdued cream velvet.

The willow was nearly as wide as the entire garden behind his house. It stood like an umbrella, with a generous opening beneath it for picnics and even walking. Pascal had only to bend to go under and then was able to stand tall. "Isabelle. I, er . . . it is Pascal Lalique."

"Ah, Professor!" Wide blue eyes smiled more than her fragile lips could. Pascal's cheeks heated at the sight of Isabelle's simple beauty.

"Forgive my sudden call, but I do have some pressing business to discuss with you." He stabbed at the ostrich feather dangling over his right eye and then finally removed his hat, tucking it under his arm. "Might I inquire as to your health? You look well."

She patted the bench beside her, inviting him to sit. Though she wore widow's weeds, the muddy violet only served to set off her features in stunning design. Delicate as porcelain and possibly as frail, Pascal observed, but still so young and vibrant in her expression and her actions. Pascal did a quick visit to his memory. She must have just entered her fifth decade, the same as he. Alphonse Bouchet had been a lucky man to have been loved by this woman.

"I am very well. I thank you for your concern, Pascal." She pressed a delicate hand over his. "Tell me, I've heard my son's regiment received the Spanish surrender a few days ago. Is Matthieu well? Has he returned to Paris?"

"Oh yes, he is well. Other than the gunshot wound—"

"He's wounded!" She gripped Pascal's wrist, an altogether intimate act that took him by surprise. "Does he suffer? Tell me please, Pascal. That must be the reason he hasn't yet come to see me. He's hurt?"

"No, he's really quite fine." Though where Matthieu was— and with his daughter—Pascal also wanted to know. "The bullet just nicked a rib. He's some hard bones, that boy, to stop a bullet. But he is quite well indeed. I expect he should even be in Paris today.''

With Josephine. Pascal did not want to consider what he knew might have happened to waylay the two from returning home last evening. Oh hell, he knew they were happy and together. Strangely, the idea did not bother him as much as it should a father of a maiden. Matthieu was a good man. He could ask for none better for his daughter.

''What is it that brings you here, Pascal? Matthieu is well. What can it be?''

The time had come to face the past. He'd dreaded this visit since Josephine first mentioned the idea. He had forgotten the stack of letters Isabelle had entrusted to him years ago. Now they had resurfaced to haunt them both.

Carefully he withdrew the letters from the leather purse tied at his hip and laid the packet on the bench between the two of them.

The flicker in Isabelle's golden orbs was that of instant recognition.

''Josephine found them, I'm afraid.''

''She read them?''

''Yes. Though you mustn't condemn her for her curiosity. Because of their location, she suspected them to be letters of mine.''

Now her head lost its buoyancy and she caught her forehead in her palm. ''Not a day has gone by that I don't think of that horrendous summer.''

''Please, Isabelle, I did not come to cause you further grief.''

''It is a grief of my own making.'' Tears had already begun to trickle across her cheeks.

Pascal swallowed. Bother, that he should bring such a delicate woman to this state. Why hadn't he just stayed home and minded his own business? But he knew why. He cared about Matthieu far too much to let this information fall into his hands.

''I've kept these . . .'' he began, slowly measuring his words, ''only because you requested such of me. I know that you

thought to show them to Matthieu some day. But with the
events that have come to pass . . . my dear, I just don't think
it right. Matthieu loved Alphonse. He is the only father the boy
has ever known. There is no need to reveal the truth to him.
He is happy now."

How much she had already suffered was obvious. To inflict
the same hell upon Matthieu just wasn't right.

"Pascal." With a gesture she requested he help her stand,
and walked over to the thick trunk of the willow. The lower
branches had obviously been pruned to allow one to stand
without mussing one's hair or hooking a wimple. "To keep
this information from Matthieu"—she turned and her face was
clear of tears or sorrow—"would be a far worse betrayal than
the truth." Steely determination clenched her fist and drew the
corners of her delicate mouth like a tightly closed purse.

"Don't you see, Pascal? Because I chose not to speak the
truth to Alphonse, he was murdered!" Isabelle looked away
through the willow fronds and clutched one fist to her breast.
*"Mon dieu,* how I regret that I did not tell Matthieu immediately. This wound has been left to fester far too long. I am glad
you came to me today, for I know that I must go to my son
and tell him everything. It is his birthright."

"You cannot!" Pascal found his voice rising to agitation.
He checked himself; no one in the garden to hear him. Ex-
cept . . . he glanced up to the ceiling of leaves . . . *Him.* He
lowered his voice. "Matthieu is just now beginning to heal
over his . . . father's . . . death."

"No!" She passed him by, pacing to the edge where the
narrow willow leaves laced them inside a netting of silver. "I
can never forgive myself for the evils I have brought upon my
family."

He rushed to her and gripped her by the shoulders. Long
tendrils of her loose sandy brown hair brushed over his knuckles. Ah, she smelled clean and sweet. "But you were the victim,
Isabelle." She looked away so that he had to shake her to
return her gaze to his. "Look at me. None of it was your fault.

You were . . . you were violated both in body and mind. The baron used you in a sick game of revenge. The death of your husband lies only at the feet of his murderer. Never yours!''

"I have come to accept that. But Matthieu—"

"Yes, Matthieu! Think of what this would do to your only child. To know such a thing. You say it is his birthright. What birthright? The baronage? He can never claim it. You know that, Isabelle.''

A trail of diamond tears slipped noiselessly down her cheek. When she spoke it was tentatively. "I should have confided in Alphonse. My silence only gave the baron more power against the both of us. And now it has come back to haunt me. Why now, Pascal? Why come to me now?''

Pascal drew his hand over his face and clenched his jaw. "There is another man. A Chevalier Julien Delaroche. He has worked some foul deeds against Matthieu and Josephine. He claims he is the baron's son.''

Isabelle's hand flew to her mouth, her eyes growing wide.

"Fortunately I believe we have seen the last of him. But I thought you needed to be aware of that fact before you decided whether or not to tell Matthieu what is contained in these letters. Delaroche is an evil man. He involved my daughters in a vicious scheme of senseless revenge against your son.''

"The baron's son, how old is he?''

"I am not sure. I'd judge near to Matthieu's age. He is aide-de-camp of the 26th Foot. He tried to seduce both my daughters and then use them against Matthieu.''

She nodded over and over, taking in the facts, sorting through them. Calculating, thinking.

"Isabelle, are you listening to me?''

"I have been so cruel to Matthieu.''

"You mustn't say things like that.''

"As soon as his father was taken from him, I, too, walked away. I abandoned him, Pascal! I have been so terribly, terribly cruel! How my dear boy ever survived is beyond all rational thought. Oh—'' She suddenly reached and touched Pascal's cheek. ''But he did have you.''

Guilt cleaved its ugly claws into Pascal's gut. Now the heavy silk and ribbons weighed heavily upon his shoulders. He had grown so comfortable at court. The unspoken rules, the society within society. Easy enough to forget one's own responsibilities when surrounded by royalty and wealth and luxury beyond all imagination. ''Yes, well . . . I'm afraid I have not been around all that much for my daughters lately. Nor your son.''

''But he loves you, Pascal. Matthieu comes to visit me regularly when he's not on campaign, and he always speaks highly of you. It is not the time you give him, but the quality of the moment shared. I don't think he would have done as well as he has without your concern.''

''Nonsense.'' He paced past her, not willing to accept the least bit of credit for the raising of such a fine young man as Matthieu Bouchet. ''The boy had Alphonse as mentor and guide. I see your husband in him everytime he is near; you must know that, Isabelle. Pride, honor, and integrity. Matthieu would sooner take his own life than harm any man, innocent or evil. And such respect for my daughter . . . I trust him completely with Josephine. Matthieu was molded by what he always speaks of as the greatest love in the world, the love between you and Alphonse.''

''Yes, we did have a love beyond all others,'' she reflected. ''Perfect and unconditional.''

''It warms my heart to know that Alphonse's son is in love with my daughter.''

''Josephine?''

''Yes.'' It was a relief to allow a smile to replace his guilty visage. ''I feel sure the banns will be posted soon.'' They had better be if what he suspected had happened last night!

''Oh, Pascal, that is a treasured bit of news. Sweet Josephine. Matthieu's ladybug. I do love her so. I've often wondered if the two would ever discover they were born for one another.''

''I believe they finally have,'' he said with an inward grin.

But if Matthieu did not see Josephine home soon, the boy would have hell to pay. Well, he must at least up the appearance of a concerned father.

"Then can you not see, Pascal?" A soft breeze sifted through their silvery umbrella. "Matthieu is happy, and if he has Josephine beside him, he can surely handle the truth. He must know."

Releasing a heavy sigh, Pascal toyed with a long silvered vine that hung nearly to the ground. Much as he hated harming Matthieu, he hadn't any right to interfere. Perhaps Isabelle was right. With Josephine by his side, Matthieu could weather any storm.

Blood does not always run thicker than water. It simply did not!

He turned to Isabelle, forced a quick smile, and bowed his head. "I leave this in your hands. You have heard my opinion. As Matthieu's mother you know what is best for him."

She bent to retrieve the letters and fingered through them carefully. "I won't let him read them. I'll just tell him. It would be best to hear it in my own voice, from my heart. Don't you think? Oh!"

"What is it?"

"Weren't there more? It's been so long I can hardly recall."

"There were five letters that Josephine gave to me. Just as there were originally."

"You sort through them. I count only four. My fingers are trembling so."

Once, twice, Pascal counted only four letters in the ribboned stack. "Bother. I believe I've misplaced one."


The plump copper-haired wench with ample enough bosom to serve two men had the ability to balance three tankards on one hip and two pitchers of ale on the other. She was the only one of the three wenches serving this evening that Julien had yet to lure upstairs to his bed. She couldn't keep her blue eyes off him as she wove through the men, doling out piss-warm ale and lackluster reprimands to keep their hands to themselves.

She most likely wouldn't have a free moment until well after midnight, he figured. Fine by him. He could wait. He had the whole night. Hell, he had the rest of his life to bed each and every woman residing in Paris, and those beyond the city walls as well. And then forget their names as quickly as he left their parted legs.

A swig of warm ale sloshed down his throat. Julien reached inside his doublet, down to his waistband, and pulled out the missive. He smoothed the folded letter across his lips as he pictured the scribbles inside that he could not read.

Oh, he recognized the addressee—Madame Isabelle Bouchet. Unfortunately, he did know that name. And the sender's name, Nazaire de Lisle, Baron de Challes. Sending a letter to that bastard's mother. And judging from the wear on the folds, it had been written years ago. Possibly around the time of the murder. Damn! He had to find out what the indecipherable words meant.

"Coming, Chevalier?"

He landed his sights on the delicious bosom that rose and fell before his eyes. Glancing up, he saw she held a promise in her eyes. Coming? If only.

"Not yet. Can you tell me if there is a notaire about? I've urgent business."

"I believe Monsieur Cellier down at Les Innocents might be called out. If you mention my name, he may not even be angry."

Sweet girl. "I shall return and have you for a midnight snack."

# Chapter 30

Josephine was dearly pleased to find that her father was not in when she and Matthieu arrived home just after noon. Finally she was able to release the death grip she'd held on Matthieu's hand all the way there.

"La! Look who the cat dragged in." Helene skirted down the stairs and slipped an arm through Matthieu's, drawing her I-know-all look up to Josephine. "So the impetuous heroine who dashes off to war returns with her hero in arms."

Josephine noticed the color ride up Matthieu's neck. How sweet that he should be embarrassed now, when just last night . . .

"Father expected you some time ago," Helene cooed as she trailed a teasing finger along Matthieu's arm.

Strangely riled by her sister's blatant flirtations, Josephine pushed between the two and pulled Matthieu out back towards the garden. "Will he be home soon?" she called back to her chagrined sister.

"I believe so. He's gone to Sainte Geneviève. He said to tell Matthieu not to worry, he just wanted to assure Madame Bouchet that her son had returned unharmed."

Josephine froze under the door frame as Matthieu turned to thank Helene. There was another reason her father would suddenly decide to visit Madame Bouchet. A reason they'd discussed all the way to Arras. He had gone in hopes of convincing her not to reveal the contents of the letters to Matthieu.

"That was exceedingly kind of your father," Matthieu said as he nudged Josephine out onto the sun-splashed patio where they were greeted with the distinctive shrill of a lark. "Why do you suppose he felt it his duty, though? I do intend to visit my mother today."

Oh dear. Josephine prayed her father had succeeded in swaying Madame Bouchet to their side. Matthieu must never know. The truth would destroy the many wonderful memories he had of his family. She did not want to start her new life as his wife with a cloud as black as hell hanging over their heads.

"Perhaps," she drawled teasingly as she led him to the wooden bench canopied by ivy and roses and pulled him beside her, "he wishes to discuss the possibility of our nuptials with your mother."

"Do you think he presumes?"

As if he would expect anything else after their absence last night. Father must know the entire 26th returned to Paris at nightfall.

"Matthieu." Forgetting her worries she slipped her hands into his. "The entire city of Paris thinks we belong together. I don't know why I never realized it before. Madame Lamarck and Helene hounded me about you."

Matthieu smiled and said, "Which reminds me, I've a visit to pay my employer. I wonder how well my designs have done at court."

"You really care?"

"Compared to supporting a wife on a soldier's wages, yes, I do care. I rather like the idea of supporting myself doing what I enjoy. It would not be so much a job as an adventure."

"Madame Lamarck adores you."

"And I adore her for the kindness she has granted us both."

''Are we the only two in Paris who have just now come to realize that our love was decided long ago?''

The brush of his stubbled chin across her knuckles sent a shiver and a vivid memory of their lovemaking through Josephine's mind. She could still taste his salty flavor on her tongue. Sense the heat of his flesh in her very muscles, as they reacted to his touch.

''You forget that it was you I wrote those letters to all along, ladybug. I have loved you always.''

And she him. How could she have been fool enough to allow an infatuation for Julien Delaroche to interfere in something so right?

''How could I never once have suspected those letters might have come from someone else?''

''What about me? Delaroche couldn't believe that I didn't know the difference between your writing and Helene's. I guess I've never read anything that you've written. Or if I did, I just didn't notice the handwriting well enough to recall it later.''

''And you've never once written to me, Matthieu. So how was I to know? Your talents are with paper and pen, but in drawing and painting. I've never known you to embrace the written word so heartily as you did when writing those letters.''

''When one takes the time to contemplate a loved one with blank paper and pen in hand, it is not hard to find the words. You might say my drawings, my images of you, were translated into words. It was very easy, really.''

So why had she made it so difficult for the both of them by blindly believing in another man's deceptions?

''I am so sorry for the mistakes I have made. I hurt you.''

At his direction, she sank back into his embrace. A rogue leaf fluttered to her knees from above. ''While I'll admit that your confession of love for . . . that man . . . ripped my heart in pieces, I also knew, deep in my heart, that it could not endure. You have a tendency to see only the surface of things, ladybug. At least until your curiosity finally forces you to inquire into the inner nature of things.

"Ever curious."

"Yes, and don't certain parts of my body adore that curiosity?"

She snuggled close and slid a hand over his lap. "Indeed."

"Ah, but ladybug, I should have told you as soon as I knew myself that this friendship we have had over the years had become so much more to me."

"Why didn't you say something when you knew the chevalier was also vying for my affections?"

"I wanted only your happiness. And if you had been genuinely in love with the chevalier, that is a sacrifice of heart I was prepared to make."

"I love only you, Matthieu."

"Will you promise me that we will always be truthful with one another? Never keep anything from one another?"

Did he have to word it quite that way? *Anything* from one another?

"Josephine?"

"Hm." She gave a shrug and a nod of her head. "Never."

Her evasive answer seemed to satisfy him. Josephine felt like shrinking to the ground and crawling under a rock. But she simply couldn't tell him what she had discovered in the letters. Not yet. Not now. Not in any way she could possibly fathom. Of course she would always be truthful with him.

But this one secret she must keep. She was allowed one secret, wasn't she?

She embraced him around the waist, pressing her cheek against his shoulder. He still smelled of their union, musky, male, and right. Which suddenly reminded her. She still wore the breeches and boots she had donned days ago. "How can you hold me?"

"Well, I put one arm here, and the other—"

She sat back and fanned the openings of her doublet as she realized she must smell less than desirable after her trek across country and back. "I do need a bath and a change of clothes."

He nuzzled her hair, an action that sent nipple-hardening shivers through Josephine's body. "Can I help?"

"Only if you wish Father to witness just how much you really care for me."

"Perhaps I'll wait out here."

She stood and slipped the doublet from her shoulders and shrugged her fingers through her hair. Badly tangled and in need of a thorough combing from Marie Claire. The whorls of her fingers held traces of dirt along with a fresh callus from her adventures. How could he bear even to look upon her? "Give me an hour, love. And in reward for your patience, you won't even recognize the stunning beauty who returns to your arm."

"I've already got myself one beauty," he said with a cocky wink. "If you've got another one around here somewhere you'd best send her on her way. Nothing can tear my eyes from my ladybug."

*"Mon Dieu,* I love you." Plunging into his embrace, Josephine kissed him hard.

"On second thought," he said as he stood to escort her into the house, "perhaps I should see to getting myself some new clothes. I shouldn't wish to face your father looking as I do."

"But, Matthieu, Father will understand—"

"Father will understand what?"

The twosome froze. Pascal Lalique stood in the doorway, looking rather a fop in periwinkle satin and a multitude of ribbons, and not altogether pleased.

"Monsieur Lalique?" Matthieu couldn't read the solemn expression on Pascal's face. He decided silence would best serve until he knew if the man despised him for keeping his daughter last night, or if he even suspected. Well, of course he must! But the last time he'd seen Pascal, *he* was in a very compromising position. Was it too much to hope that he would be lenient in hopes of retaining Matthieu's silence?

Josephine slipped from his embrace and rushed to her father's side to plant a kiss on his cheek. Yes, by all means placate the man.

"One thing I do understand," Pascal started as he hooked a possessive arm in his daughter's and stepped towards Matthieu, "is that the entire 26th Foot returned to Paris last evening. I left my daughter in your trust, Monsieur Bouchet. And yet, she did not return to my home as I expected last night. Can you explain that to me?"

A lump formed in Matthieu's throat. Explain? Even the part about her breaking her fast this morning?

"Father, Matthieu has asked me to marry him," Josephine rushed in.

Still maintaining the stern composure of a rock—quite a feat when festooned with mauve ribbons—Pascal said, "I should hope so." His gaze stayed Matthieu in his position but two feet away. Close enough to reach out and strangle a man, but far enough to give a bit of escape if necessary.

"Father, don't be so hard on Matthieu. It was me," Josephine pleaded. "He wanted to see me home last night, but I wouldn't allow it."

Settled to silence with a raise of her father's hand, Josephine offered Matthieu a miserable I-tried look.

The solid contact of Pascal's hand to Matthieu's shoulder felt like a boulder balancing precariously, ready to roll to the side and crush his face. "You are like a son to me. And while I cannot condone your keeping my daughter away from my home last night, at least you've offered to do the right thing by her."

The man was making this as difficult as possible. Much as he had wanted Josephine last night, Matthieu now regretted the act for the mistrust he had stirred in her father. Pascal Lalique was the father he no longer had. He needed this man's trust as well as his respect and love.

But . . .

"Forgive me, Monsieur," Matthieu looked directly into Pascal's pale brown eyes, "but it is not a question of doing the right thing. I freely offered Josephine my heart, my undying love, and the honor and protection she deserves for as long as I live. I wish her hand not out of necessity, only out of love.''

Pascal smiled so widely the vibrancy glistened even in his eyes. ''I know,'' he said with a tickle to his voice, ''You have my blessing, son. Let us go post the banns and announce to all this perfect match.''

A group hug, a few sniffles from Josephine, and all was well.

If only his own father were here to share in his joy, Matthieu thought. And his mother.

''Helene mentioned you were going to see my mother?''

Pascal pulled out of the embrace and adjusted the lace at his wrists, glancing briefly toward Josephine, and then cleared his throat. ''Yes. Er . . . I went to tell her that her son was well and returned from war.''

''But I plan to do that myself today.''

''Yes, well . . . I . . .''

''It has been a long time since Father visited Madame Bouchet,'' Josephine jumped in. ''Hasn't it, Father?''

She nudged Pascal in the side, and he spit out, ''Yes, that's exactly right. I fear my attentions towards your mother have been quite lax of late. I used to visit her more often. So you see, I went for myself also. I hope you do not mind, Matthieu. I did mention I thought you and Josephine might be making an announcement soon.''

''It was very kind of you, Monsieur.''

''Please, Matthieu, you must call me Pascal. Or better yet, Father.''

Deep emotion glistened in Matthieu's breast. ''Father?'' he whispered.

''I shouldn't wish to replace Alphonse in your heart, but I would like it very much if you would call me Father.''

''Oh, I will. Father,'' he tried the title again, finding it felt as if a long-lost friend had suddenly been found. Family and love. Oh, he was truly blessed! "You've been so kind to me over the years. I can never begin to repay you."

"Only treat my daughter with all the care and kindness I've come to expect from you myself," Pascal said with a hearty slap to Matthieu's arm. "Come now. We should leave posthaste for Sainte Chapelle. Or perhaps Sainte Geneviève?"

"Sainte Chapelle," Matthieu offered, as he knew that was the church the Laliques attended. He'd attended mass there a few times himself with the family.

Josephine slipped to Matthieu's side and dropped a kiss to his ear. "I love you."

He squeezed her hand, never wishing her to leave his side. Every touch from her shot desire through his bones. Every whispered word sounded like liquid passion. But he had nearly forgotten his own plans. "Perhaps we can delay our mission for an hour or so?" He heeled a muddy boot against the stone step. "Allow me to clean myself up and become more presentable for the priest?"

The professor drew a gaze over Matthieu. "Two hours?"

"Thank you, Monsieur—er, Father."


As the front door swung shut, Pascal raced to catch it before it closed completely. He watched until Matthieu's confident strides took him down the front path and out of view.

"What is it, Father?"

Pascal swung round and gripped his daughter's arms. "I've just come from speaking to Isabelle Bouchet."

"Yes, I know that. Were you able to convince her?"

"I'm not sure. But whether or not she chooses to tell Matthieu is really entirely her decision—"

"But Father!"

"No, listen." He pressed a finger to her lips, then corralled her into his arms. ''There is something more. I returned the letters to Isabelle and she counted them . . .''

''Yes?''

''Josephine,'' he gripped her shoulder, more for support than anything else as he felt his courage leave him in one breath. ''There was a letter missing.''

# Chapter 31

Matthieu headed straight for the Boulevard St. Germaine and quickly outfitted himself in new attire. It had taken less than an hour to gather new breeches and a smartly embroidered doublet (which he would wear for his wedding, but it was also fitting for today's visit to the priest). When the tailor had suggested buckled shoes, Matthieu could not bring himself quite that close to fashion. "These will do fine," he'd said with a tap to his boots, that motion knocking a chunk of dried Paris mud from the heel. With a grimace the old man conceded, but would not let Matthieu leave his shop until he'd sewn lace around the folds of his boots. "For the lovely lady," he said. "It is easily removed after your nuptials with a few snips here and there."

Thinking himself quite the dandy, Matthieu clapped the felt hat on his head. Then, blowing the billowing red ostrich feather away from his nose, he walked onward.

Whimsy loosened his stride to a bouncing pace. He was going to marry his ladybug! How many times had he thought of that very idea over the years? Many, and many more. It was almost as if it were something he knew would come to him eventually. Good things come to those who wait. Right?

Though his dreams had shattered that ill day that Josephine had announced her love for Julien Delaroche. To imagine such a thing!

"Fancy meeting you," a voice called from a side street connecting to the Rue de Seine. Matthieu slowed his pace, unable to locate the position of the speaker. Long midday shadows traced from overhanging roof tiles to darken the walls and alleyways. "And looking a cavalier in ribbons and lace."

Matthieu self-consciously touched the wide Venetian lace that rimmed his doublet collar, the same the tailor had sewn to his boots. Still he could not see where the voice came from, or determine who it belonged to.

"Who's there?" He then noticed the muddy boots crossed casually at the ankle and followed them up to look into the grinning face of Julien Delaroche. Make that Julien de Lisle. "You." Matthieu resumed walking. "I wish to never concern myself with you again, Chevalier. If you really *are* a chevalier."

"Fair enough," Julien said as he followed.

Matthieu picked up his pace and laid his hand over the sword at his hip. No ribbons there, he would not have it.

"Oh no, you needn't worry, Monsieur," Julien said. "Just a moment to bend your ear?"

Coming to a halt, Matthieu spun in the dry Paris dirt. "Be quick about it."

An odd glimmer flashed in Delaroche's pale green eyes as he reached Matthieu and then walked past him, circling him slowly as one would a bonfire on a cold autumn night. He still wore his fighting clothes. A spatter of dried blood decorated his thigh. *My blood,* Matthieu thought as he remembered the night he was shot.

"You must be disappointed to see me alive."

A dismissive shrug. A shake of the head. "No longer."

"But you left me there to die."

"You were barely wounded," Delaroche countered with a

casual chuckle. "Besides, your precious Josephine was by your side to cure your ills. Did you ease your pain in her soft—"

*Smack.* Julien caught Matthieu's soaring fist in his open palm. "Hear me out before you choose to silence me with your fists," he said.

Much as he desired to dash his mark again across Delaroche's blackened right eye, Matthieu decided to let the man speak, and then be gone. "Speak. Quickly. Josephine and her father wait my arrival. We go to Sainte Chapelle today to post the banns."

"Ah, well, then, congratulations are in order."

Matthieu believed Delaroche's sincerity as much as he believed the earth was flat. Damned if he wouldn't like to push the ramscuttle over the edge.

"Very well, I'll not dally any longer. I've something for you, or rather, your mother." He produced a folded post, the red seal visibly broken. "This was found in the area where you were shot. Addressed to Madame Isabelle Bouchet. There's that damned name again. You see, I shall never be free of it."

"Let me have that," Matthieu said as he swiped the air, but Delaroche quickly snatched it to his lips.

"I wonder why you would be carrying this post to your mother. It is not from you."

"How would you know? Have you suddenly been gifted with the ability to read?"

"I've just come from Les Innocents."

What was so important that Delaroche actually paid someone to read the missive to him? "I had no such thing on my person. I don't know where it came from."

"Then perhaps it was Mademoiselle Lalique or her father. Of course, that is it. One of them had it. And since it is obvious that you have no knowledge of it, then it seems possible they wished to keep this from you. Such a pity. And so underhanded, really."

"Enough!" Matthieu snatched the letter from the man's hand.

"I shall leave you to read in peace," Julien offered with a grand bow, sweeping his hat across the ground. "You may find me in the Rue de Dragon, above the tannery."

"I've no concern for your address." Matthieu clenched the letter in his hand. Curiosity urged him to rip it wide and read the words, but anger would not allow him to look away from Delaroche's steely smirk.

"You say that now," Delaroche dripped cool syllables. He eyed Matthieu as he smashed one gloved fist into the cup of his other palm. "But I reckon you'll have a change of heart soon enough. Good day to you, my er . . . brother of the blade."

With a cocked hat and a stamp of his heels, Delaroche marched towards the heart of Paris. A small crowd of curious onlookers, disappointed at the lack of violence, dispersed as well.

The parchment was badly crumpled. The wax seal, pushed to the limits of its adhesive duties, detached and hit Matthieu's boot toe before bouncing to rest on a scrap of torn burlap abandoned in the street. Stepping carefully over the mud-glutted center gutter, he took refuge against the shaded wall of a closed apothecary shop.

Reading the large scrawls to himself, Matthieu saw that indeed it was addressed to his mother. But at their old address outside the walls of Paris, not the convent. The paper looked old, though not stained or torn; the creases were set, the edges dusted with time.

Why would Josephine *or* her father be carrying such a letter? It didn't make sense. Had they been carrying it to him? Josephine hadn't mentioned as much. Surely she would have after what she had just promised him. To always be truthful. Or had it been as Delaroche has said, that they had plans to keep it from him? But for what reason? How did a letter addressed to Isabelle Bouchet come to be in the hands of the Laliques anyway?

Though he knew Josephine waited for him, and that what he held in his hand was addressed to his mother and was most likely for no one's eyes but her own ... Matthieu could not fight the curiosity that tore at him.

"Ever curious," he whispered Josephine's self-proclaimed motto as he slowly turned the missive over and folded it open.

The large, liquid scrawls made it hard to decipher, much less read. Perhaps it was merely a long-lost love letter from his father to his mother? In which case, he should not read it. On the other hand, it would only renew his faith in the man he'd come to venerate as the master of strength, pride, and honor. Yes, he must. To read his father's words would only burnish his love for the man, and wouldn't it also be a wonderful start to his own marriage?

Turning away from the tree, Matthieu read the words slowly to himself.

*My dear Baroness,*

*You see, I consider you mine even though you choose to board with that worthless farmer. When will you tell him, Isabelle? When will you forsake your rigid pride and reveal the truth to Alphonse Bouchet? Only then can we be together. You claim to love the man, but you will have more than empty emotion from me. I can give you the world, Isabelle. Riches and fine dresses and jewelry that will dull in comparison to the sparkle of your smile.*

Matthieu paused. This was not from his father. But whom? He glanced over the salutation. Baroness?

*Did you ever tell him, Isabelle, of that precious night we shared? Though you fought me with nails and fists, I know, deep inside, you enjoyed every sweet moment of our coupling but one week before your wedding vows. Even when blood dripped from the corner of your mouth, still your screaming kisses begged for more.*

Matthieu's knees buckled.

*I still recall the taste of your panting screams on my lips.
Bittersweet. Like a golden persimmon, not yet ripe, that
puckers one's mouth after the first bite.*

Her panting screams? Had this man . . . violated his mother?
No. The thought was too insane . . . *one week before your
wedding vows . . .* Why write a letter? And why—against all
that is good in the world—had it been preserved?

*Now tell me, Isabelle. (Because I know you will not tell
Alphonse.) Do you not think the child of our union is
growing to resemble me? That dark, wavy hair. So much
like mine. And the defined chin and cheekbones.*

"No . . ." Matthieu felt his breath escape and his lungs
deflate. Of its own volition, his hand went to his head, touching
his hair. Alphonse's hair had been straight as a stick and the
color of straw. The contours of his face slipped beneath Matthieu's fingers. His father had been heavy of face and body . . .

*Leave Alphonse Bouchet and return to me with my son,
Isabelle. Or I shall kill the man you call husband.*
                    Lord Nazaire de Lisle, Baron de Challes

A wave of dizzy nausea felled Matthieu to his knees. He
caught himself with his palms against the ground, pinning the
hideous missive beneath one hand. He felt sick, like he could
retch right here in public.
*. . . return to me with my son . . .*
"No," he moaned.
*Or I shall kill the man you call . . .*
"No, it cannot be. This man . . . killed my—Oh, *mon dieu!*
All this time . . . The Baron de Challes was my father!"

# Chapter 32

A flurry of activity set a mood of festivity. Marie Claire finished lacing Josephine's stays, while Helene pinned the loose strands of her hair up with pearl-dotted hairpins. She wanted to look perfect for Matthieu upon his return. Together they would announce to the world their intentions of loving and living as man and wife.

A squeal of delight escaped Josephine's lips. She couldn't help it!

"Oh, sister, you are really too much for me today." Helene finished and paced before Josephine to admire her handiwork.

"Are you not happy for me, Helene?"

"Oh yes!" She hugged Josephine and pressed a kiss to her cheek. "You mustn't think anything but. It is just that, well . . ." Her shoulders sank and she plopped on the bed with a sigh. "I wonder when it shall be *my* turn. I am the oldest. By rights—"

"Perhaps Father will take you to court with him on his next visit," Josephine offered, knowing it would be just the thing to brighten Helene's mood.

"You think?" She did indeed straighten on the bed. Why, her cheeks even pinkened and that *Helene* sparkle returned to her eyes.

"He did mention as much to me when we were riding to Arras." This little white lie could be easily remedied after a firm talk with her father regarding Helene's welfare. With her marrying, Helene would go absolutely stir-crazy sitting home alone. "You mustn't fault Father for his lack of attention over the years. He is a man raising two girls by himself. Of course he doesn't always know what is best for us, or what is expected. But you'll see, Helene, Father loves you and he now realizes that he'd best see to your betrothal."

"Oh, happiness!" Helene kicked up her satin heels and giggled, prompting Josephine to do the same, over Marie Claire's protests to be still. "I shall find myself a titled rogue, perhaps a viscount or a marquis."

"Why not a duke?" Marie Claire mumbled huffily.

"Why not, indeed?" Helene cheered as she rose to dance about Josephine, her skirts skimming the air with a joyous hiss. "A duke it shall be!"

"Your grace," Josephine offered with a curtsey.

"Silly girls," Marie Claire muttered as she gathered her sewing basket and opened the bedroom door. "Oh!"

Josephine and Helene stopped spinning at the maid's sudden cry. There in the doorway stood Matthieu Bouchet, dressed in new finery—lace even!—and looking the cavalier. Yet it was the anger in his eyes that struck Josephine like a poison arrow to the heart.

"Leave," came his bellow, as violent as a flame of dragon's breath.

Helene hustled at Matthieu's curt command—though perhaps not quite realizing the gravity of Matthieu's dark mood. With light dancing steps, she linked her arm in Marie Claire's and paused by the door to blow a furtive kiss to Josephine. "Do you wish me to stay?"

"No," Josephine said at the same time as Matthieu.

The door closed with a *click*. The man who had just last night caressed her in his gentle arms and driven her body mad with lust, now held such violence captive in his eyes that Josephine dared not speak. He frightened her. And that fact horrified her beyond speech.

"When," he began sharply, "were you planning to show me *this!*" He whipped a folded missive from his doublet and held it before her. At that distance Josephine could not read it, but the paper was crumpled and dirty; certainly not any letter from her.

"Matthieu, I don't understand," she managed. Clutching her throat tentatively she approached him and bent to study the letter. She recognized Madame Bouchet's name. "Oh, *mon dieu,* the missing letter."

"The missing letter!" he raged. "So you *did* know!"

"Yes, but—"

"Damn you, woman. Was your promise to me just hours ago only a farce?"

Josephine swallowed a meek no, before she could speak it.

"Do you know what it says in this letter?"

Shrinking from his fiery voice, Josephine couldn't force a single word from her quivering lips.

"How could you do such a thing to me?"

Josephine was sick with regret. She hadn't done anything to him. Not physically. But what hurt had she caused by plotting to keep such information a secret?

"Can you deny that you and your father had no intention of showing me this letter?"

Damn, damn, and damn! How the hell had that letter fallen into Matthieu's hands? He should never have discovered the truth in such a manner. Though . . . how *did* he come upon it? "Where did you get it?"

Slamming his arms across his chest, he took another step towards her, closing their distance to an arm's length. "Julien Delaroche."

"How did *he* get it! It was in my father's care—" She

slapped her hand to her mouth, but Matthieu followed in kind, pressing his hand over hers and backing her up to the wall.

"You guard your words like a whoreson fears discovery," he hissed. "I trusted you not to keep secrets from me, Josephine."

Yes, he did. And now she had rewarded him with betrayal.

"You knew the contents of this letter when you promised to hold no secrets from my ears. Correct?"

She could only nod. The urge to pull him close into her embrace and silently console him as she had always done in times of dire circumstance was only that—an urge. For she knew without a doubt that if she were to lay hands on him now he would pull away.

"I thought I was doing right," she managed to mutter. "I did it only because of my love for you, Matthieu."

"Love?" He pushed away from the wall, leaving her to grasp for the bedpost so as not to tumble onto her weak knees. "Ha! You call this love?" The paper ripped as he slashed the letter viciously through the air, back and forth until it was nearly cleaved in two pieces. It was as if he were forcing the horrid words to pay the price for the damage they had caused.

"My father is a murderer!" he shouted. "The man I once believed to be my own flesh and blood was *not*. I am nothing!" He spun and caught Josephine with an iron glare that worked to pin her against the wall more firmly than any hand could do. "You tried to keep this information from me?"

Where was Father? She desperately needed his calm head to reason with Matthieu when she was too frightened even to think!

"Did you?"

"Y-yes. But only to protect—"

"That is all I need to know."

He stepped back, his boots cracking across a stray hairpin Marie Claire had dropped on the pine floorboards. He'd every intention of returning to her arms and then on to the church to post the banns. Until but moments ago, he was hers.

And now . . .

"I take my leave of you, Mademoiselle Lalique. Give your father my regrets concerning the planned nuptials. I cannot love a woman who would keep secrets from me. Nor"—he stopped her with a wall of his hand—"can I allow you to marry a man such as I. The son of a murderer and defiler of women. Half brother to that bastard Delaroche." He snorted out a breath of laughter, looking up to the ceiling. "Bastard? But it is I who holds that title, not Delaroche. Surely the devil himself is having a hearty laugh at my expense this day. My God has betrayed me, as have all the people I have ever cared about."

"No, Matthieu, let me explain!"

He left her chambers in a clang of sword and spurs and seconds later the front door slammed.

Tears tore across Josephine's cheeks. Falling to her knees, she fisted her hands against her eyes and screamed.


She meant the world to him. The sun did not rise without her permission, and flowers looked to her for an example of beauty. In all the time he had known Josephine Lalique, Matthieu had never once felt that he would ever have a reason to mistrust her.

Now, not only had he discovered the hideous secret of his paternity, but that also it was a secret Josephine had every intention of keeping from him. God's blood, such betrayal!

Cursing himself a fool, a ramscuttle, a no-good lackwit, Matthieu pushed his way through the evening shuffle on the Boulevard Saint Michel. The clatter of carts and shouts and bells filled Matthieu's head with a dizzying array of noise. A man yowled as a barber yanked a rotten tooth from his jaw. Blood spattered stone walls. Ladies clapped and cheered. It gave him an ache in the head. He wanted to be away from the crush of Paris, away from people, away from this damned letter still clutched in his hands.

Shoving aside a young man more occupied with scratching

his jaw than getting out of traffic's way, Matthieu raced to the Pont Michel and squeezed to the railing. The view of the Seine offered little respite from the crush around him, and the smell that rose from the darkened waters did nothing but sicken. Holding the letter over the stone railing, he tore it into strips until they were so narrow he could not tear another length, then let them fall to the broth-colored waters below.

Gone was the written proof. But the knowledge of his lineage was forever burned into his mind and heart.

He was of criminal blood. The Baron de Challes murdered Alphonse Bouchet in cold blood. A crime that could only have happened because someone had kept a secret.

What must he do now?

Catching his forehead in his gloved hand, Matthieu strained against the cacophony of city noise and the noise in his mind. Delaroche's evil laughter as he'd handed him the missive. *My name will haunt you . . .* Helene's silly giggles. *You really do love her . . .* Josephine's wordless admission of guilt, a sentence pronounced only by the pity and misery in her eyes.

He'd had no choice but to renounce his engagement. He did not know whether he could allow himself to yield to the voice that urged forgiveness. Even if he could, it would not change anything. For though a deep inner part of him pined for her touch, for her love, this new knowledge would not allow that man to perpetrate such an act against her. For that man, Matthieu Bouchet, was evil, dark, and unfit to touch one such as she.

''I thought sure he would be here.'' Isabelle's heart sank as Pascal led her inside the clean stone walls of his foyer and gently caressed her shoulders. ''Now what shall I do? Oh! What is that sound? Is someone weeping?''

''He was here,'' Pascal said with his usual softness and dignity. ''He accused Josephine of lying to him and renounced their engagement. She has been sobbing for over an hour. Matthieu has the missing letter, Isabelle.''

"How?"

"It seems . . . oh dear. Do come sit down. This is going to take some explaining."

"I cannot." She stayed her position. If she sat to rest, she'd never find her son. And to talk to him now was imperative. "It matters not how he got the letter. Only now, I must find him and explain. Imagine his state."

"I need only to look upon my daughter to know his state, Madame."

"Poor Josephine." She laid a hand on Pascal's, trying to convey as much compassion as she could muster, considering her own stripped emotions. "The brunt of my son's anger should never have fallen on her. She is too kind, and innocent of my betrayals. Do you have any idea where he may be, Pascal?"

"None whatsoever. He's yet to let an apartment since returning to Paris, for Madame Lamarck is away at court. He frequents no taverns."

"Delaroche," Josephine sobbed as she entered the foyer.

Her eyes were puffy and red, her hair tangled about her face. The cream satin finery she had donned for church was now wrinkled from tears and emotions. Isabelle took her in her embrace. "My dear, I pray you can forgive me."

"I realize now how wrong it was to even think this information should be kept from Matthieu. He should have been told . . ." Josephine managed, between her rhythmic sniffles.

"Why do you say Delaroche?" Pascal asked. "You think Matthieu has gone to him?"

"The letter was given to Matthieu by Julien. He is Matthieu's half brother. The man has been a thorn in Matthieu's side for months now. There is no doubt he made sure Matthieu read that letter as some sort of revenge on his part. Or else," Josephine looked into Isabelle's face, "he seeks you at the convent."

"Yes, he will come for me, I pray," Isabelle said. *"Mon*

*Dieu!* Once again my silence works to destroy the heart of a man I care for more than my very life.''

''Ask at the Louvre for the location of Delaroche's apartments,'' Pascal offered, and then, ''Would you like me to accompany you, Isabelle? I really should—''

''No.'' She stayed both father and daughter, who had opened her mouth to second her father's suggestion. ''I must face my son alone. I thank you for your support, Pascal. And Josephine.'' She smoothed her hand along the girl's tear-soaked cheek. ''I promise to set things straight between you and Matthieu. You are the only woman for my son. I should suffer endlessly after to know it was I who pulled the two of you apart.''

''I insist,'' Pascal said as he hastened into a coat and pulled a felt hat from the hook by the door. ''I am also at fault. This situation demands my attention as well.''

''And mine!'' Josephine declared and gathered her gloves and mask.

# Chapter 33

"I wondered how long it would take you to find me."

Matthieu remained by the door. Julien *de Lisle* sat at a trestle table near the one window in his minuscule apartment. The chevalier filled his glass with a dark wine that reeked of vinegar, and sipped. Sipped. So casual an action. But all the while the man's eyes studied him with the precision of a predator sizing up his prey.

"You gave me directions, it wasn't difficult at all. Where else to find a beast like you but in the Rue du Dragon?"

Delaroche gave an acknowledging tilt of his glass. Perhaps he was well into his cups. "You've read the letter?"

Grinding his teeth to prevent spewing curses, Matthieu merely nodded. His clenched fists pressed against his thighs. He must remain calm. Violence would solve nothing—though the anger churned relentlessly as if a beast had been set free with the reading of that hideous letter.

"Well then, come sit down, brother. Have a drink." A splash of murky crimson spilled over the man's finger as he filled his glass to the brim and took a hearty swig.

''I'll not call you brother.'' Matthieu remained near the door. ''Nor will I ever call that . . . murderer . . . father.''

''Call us what you will, but the fact remains that blood surpasses all. Pity I did not know of our blood ties earlier, I shouldn't have tried so desperately to part you and your wench.''

''I believe that like I believe you are a chevalier,'' Matthieu snarled. Cool metal brushed across his hand as his fist grazed his sword hilt. ''The title is as phony as your name, isn't it?''

A shrug and a dismissive wave of his glass. ''It was necessary to change my name after father's unfortunate deed. Most impossible for a murderer's son to procure employment. Delaroche sounded so much better when preceded by chevalier.''

''I should have expected as much from the likes of you.''

Julien only laughed. ''Yes, well, my *likes* are the same as yours, eh?''

Fighting his anger was becoming much harder when faced with Delaroche's cool demeanor. No, the man was not soused. He played this conversation too well to be in his cups.

''So what is the occasion for this cavalier attire?'' he said with a glance over Matthieu's new clothing. Matthieu had forgotten the lace and new doublet. Now, he almost felt silly. ''Ah yes, your nuptials. The posting of the banns,'' Julien proclaimed grandly with glass raised high and pinkie finger extended.

''No more,'' Matthieu huffed. At the man's raised brow, he continued, ''I would not allow Josephine to associate with a cad such as you. Now that I know I've the same blood in my veins, I cannot allow her to do the same with a man such as myself.''

Seeming pleased at this announcement, Delarouche jumped up and gained the floor until he stood nose to nose with Matthieu. He stank of fermented wine and weeks of sweat. His hair hung in greasy tendrils over his shoulders. Not even a tavern whore would have his nasty hide, purse jangling or not.

''Speak for yourself, Bouchet. You may claim to be as twisted

as our father, but do not presume to lay that label on myself.''
He drew a slow gaze over Matthieu's features.

His gut tightening into knots, Matthieu felt an unavoidable
conflict coming. In fact, he wished it. Physical, brutal, and
mindless enough to slake his own sudden need for revenge. ''I
do. A man is no better than the blood from whence he was
born. And if that brands a black mark upon your head, it is
only because it is true.''

The blow of Julien's fist to Matthieu's jaw knocked his head
back with a snap. The doorjamb caught his body and dug into
his shoulder blade. Another blow to his gut expelled his breath
in a gasp.

Unsheathing his sword, Matthieu backed toward the window
where he had seen Delaroche's weapon. He tossed the thin
blade to Julien.

Catching the sword and quickly spinning the half-shell hilt
to fit his grip, Delaroche laughed as he took stance. ''You're
too damned honorable to be a criminal's son! I think the blood
of that tramp you call a mother poisoned your system.''

''The baron raped my mother!''

The kiss of steel shivered in the air. The room was small,
but the men didn't need much space to lunge and riposte.

''How do you know it was rape?'' Delaroche growled as he
bent at the waist to avoid a high lunge to the shoulder. ''I bet
the whore came crawling to Nazaire after she was married
because it was *he* she truly desired!''

''It was not! That letter written by the baron's hand said as
much. He forced himself on my mother one week before she
was to wed! The baron tormented her for years because he was
too insane to accept that she did not love him!''

The hiss of Delaroche's blade wisped by Matthieu's ear;
how had he allowed him to get so close? The return of his
opponent's blade took advantage of his surprise and sliced
through the shoulder of his doublet.

''I am beginning to understand now, Delaroche. I had almost
thought to condemn myself. But maybe I'm not the man my

real father was. Though I see his blood has rot *you* to the core. So you changed your surname. Cunning, I'll give you that. So you have been planning your revenge for how long? Since I joined the ranks? Or earlier?''

Delaroche drew up straight and squared his shoulders. With a snap of his head, he imposed a deadly gaze upon Matthieu. ''I tried to turn the other cheek for many years after my father's death. Call it fortune or fate that you joined the same regiment as I, but it was then I realized you'd not suffered enough for the crime of my father's death. You cannot know the torments I suffered after I was left penniless, parentless, and without a name.''

''Suffering is in the eye of the beholder.''

''You had a mother and a home!''

''You stood to inherit your father's title!''

''It was stripped from him as he was stripped before the gallows. Corruption of blood by means of an unspeakable crime. Besides, it is the eldest son who inherits a title!''

The eldest son? Stunned by Delaroche's announcement, Matthieu almost lost an ear, but the slash of air swung towards his head prompted him to duck. Holding his sword to ward off further attacks, Matthieu carefully stepped two paces back. *The eldest son.* He knew that Delaroche was a few months younger—they'd once compared their ages during campaign.

By all that was sacred, *he* was the eldest son. He would have held the title of baron. What a morbidly astonishing revelation. To think. A titled man. What he could have given Josephine . . .

No. A title would have meant nothing to Josephine. And it would have meant so much less to Matthieu to have received it from evil blood.

''You are thinking what you could have done with such a title?'' Julien mocked. ''Perhaps taken a finer lady than that bourgeois tease.''

''A title tarnished by innocent blood! I am glad that honor did not befall me.''

The fight abandoned for the moment, Delaroche let his sword

swing from an extended finger, back and forth. "And to think I endured those idiotic love letters just to get to you."

"I always knew they were a lie. You never did love Helene."

"As soon as I learned the woman I had debauched was a sister to the Josephine you so frequently spoke of, I saw my opportunity."

"Helene was never debauched by you! She remains as virtuous—"

"So you think?" Julien snapped his sword back into grip and slid the blade teasingly across the blade of Matthieu's sword. "And do you know this sister on intimate terms as well? My, my, perhaps your criminal blood does run deeper than I suspected."

"That is enough!" Determined to end this ludicrous exchange, Matthieu lunged, catching his blade on target— Delaroche's heart.

The man froze, his sword arm raised in defeat, his eyes narrowing with defiance.

"You wouldn't. Not your blood brother."

"Try me." Matthieu pushed the sword tip deeper. It cut through Delaroche's thin gauze shirt, and crimson pearled down the steel blood groove.

"You sonofabitch! I'll not rest until my name echoes like a madman's bellows inside your head. Do you know what it is like to have that woman's name constantly groaning in my mind?"

"What woman?"

"Isabelle!" Delaroche roared. "Day and night I listened as my father roamed the halls in a drunken stupor, moaning that hideous name. Isabelle, Isabelle! I tell you the name is like a dagger in my heart. My own mother died, ignored and unloved; she too, a victim of my father's misdirected lust. Isabelle! That the baron would commit such a crime all in the name of that whore!"

"I can stop the pain," Matthieu ground out. He pressed the sword deeper, setting a fast stream of blood down the blade.

''No, Matthieu!''

Seized from behind by an embrace that could only be his mother's, Matthieu had the forethought to stand firm against Delaroche. He reached back with his free hand, trying to dislodge his mother's grip on his waist. ''Step outside or you will get hurt! This is between him and me!''

''No, it is between you and me.'' she said, her grip clinging to his waist. ''My silence has brought you to an act of desperation. Do not harm this man, Matthieu. Walk away from him. If it is revenge you seek, than it can only be satisfied upon me.''

To hear such words from his mother tore at his already tattered heart. For all the pain she had caused him today, he wished only to think of her walking hand in hand with Alphonse Bouchet. *No two people loved each other more.* She had been violated. It was not her fault. She had been too scared to reveal the truth. He could not blame her. He mustn't!

Pulling back his sword, Matthieu delivered a punch to Delaroche's jaw that knocked him flat. The sizable chevalier fell, unconscious, one leg tucked under the other, the wine bottle upset and dribbling over the table.

Still Matthieu studied his opponent. For to turn around and face his mother . . .

''Come,'' were her gentle words as she tugged his right arm. ''Let me tell you everything.''


Josephine stood silently in the doorway to Julien's chambers. Though she desired only to thread her arms around Matthieu's shoulders and kiss him until he forgot all the horrors of the day, she knew he must hear from his mother first. Only then might she be granted the opportunity to be redeemed in his eyes by explaining her wish to keep such a horrid truth a secret.

Matthieu followed as his mother pulled him from Delaroche's room, until they stood under an open skylight cut square into the stone apartment building. White afternoon sun fell upon his mother's tear-streaked face, illuminating her alabaster skin with the radiance of a heavenly being.

But she cried.

And her tears cut into Matthieu's heart. Not even Delaroche's sword could hurt so deeply.

"I never . . . wanted you . . . to find out in such a way," she stuttered.

Her thick, wavy hair, bundled into a circle upon her head, gave way to long wisps that caressed her cheeks. Matthieu pushed the strands behind her ear and tilted her chin up. "It's over."

"No, it's not!" she said, clutching his hand. "Not until you've heard the story from me. From my lips."

"Don't do this to yourself, Mama," he cooed, raising her gloved fingers to his cheek. She smelled of vivid summer grass and softly tanned leather. "I've read the letter. Is it not enough that I know?"

"I was too frightened to tell Alphonse . . ."

A heavy lump formed in Matthieu's throat. She seemed determined to tell all. And the truth was he did want to hear everything. To know once and for all the story of his birth. "I remember you once telling me you had given up the title of baroness to marry Father—er, Alphonse."

She nodded, drew in a deep breath, and slumped against the wall, an understuffed rag doll abandoned by a child on the street. Still she held his hand. A link to sanity—for both of them. "I was betrothed to the Baron de Challes, you know that much. I had every intention of honoring that betrothal until I met Alphonse Bouchet at the farmer's market on the Quai Saint Bernard. Oh, Matthieu, the first time our gazes met, I knew that man had been made exclusively for my eyes. And he felt the same."

Matthieu leaned forward to touch a glistening jewel at the corner of her eye. Her pain dispersed in the whorls of his fingertips.

"From that day forward I vowed I would marry Alphonse

Bouchet, titles and riches be damned. I wanted love, Matthieu. Was that so selfish of me?''

He could not fight the strain of tears in his eyes. ''You and Alphonse had the greatest love in all the world, Mama. You should never regret your decision.''

''I didn't! But the Baron tormented me for years. He had formed this sick sort of attachment to me, Matthieu. Oh, it's horrible to think of—''

''Then don't.'' He pulled Isabelle into his embrace and pressed his lips to her forehead. ''From this day forward, we shall never, either of us, think or speak that man's name.''

''He defiled me, Matthieu.''

''Mama—''

''I must tell you this! All the time I daren't tell Alphonse because the baron threatened to kill him. He was so evil, Matthieu. He would send lackeys to our farm once a week, just so I could not forget his presence. When I discovered I was with child, I knew not whether it was my husband's or Nazaire's.'' She sniffed back the tears. ''But it mattered not. I planned to bring a child into this world and surround it with all the love I could afford. I loved you even when you were but a babe inside my womb. It wasn't until you were four that I began to see the resemblance to Nazaire. You've my hair and my eyes, Matthieu, but you've Nazaire's grace and form. And your face . . .'' She smoothed her gloves over his cheekbones and his jaw. ''Alphonse was never the wiser. And for many years the Baron left me alone to raise his son.''

''He knew?''

''I suspect he wasn't positive you were his son until that afternoon you and I went to town to purchase the fabric for your shirt.'' She gripped the lace on his shirt, but didn't seem to notice it was new. ''Do you remember?''

A flash of childhood, warm summer day, dancing around his mother's skirts in the marketplace. He must have been seven or eight. A horse and rider barreled towards them, intent on plowing right through them. Matthieu had dashed in front of his mother, spreading his arms wide to cover her skirts. The horse's nostrils flared. Matthieu had closed his eyes . . .

The rider swerved, stopped, and dismounted all in less time than it took for Matthieu to finally pry his eyelids open.

"He just stared at me," he said now, remembering the look on the man's face. Cold evil in dark eyes, a commanding manner that said he wielded power.

"He followed us through Paris that day," Isabelle said.

"I never noticed."

"He knew then," she said in despair. "It was not long after that he began to write me sick, twisted letters. But he never approached myself or Alphonse until the night he came to our home, years later."

"That's enough." They both knew what came next. Isabelle had clutched Matthieu's sleeves, begging him not to go outside. Stay with me, she cried. It is between the two men. And so he had remained in the house, sensing his mother's fear, and wanting to protect her.

The arguing voices had come to a sudden halt. The first thing Matthieu saw after he dared pry his mother's arms from his neck and peek out the door was the cloud of dust stirred up in the wake of the baron's retreat.

Alphonse was dead of stab wounds to his throat and heart.

"My father is a murderer," he muttered, lost in a vicious memory of blood and pain and a mother's cries for mercy. "That bastard . . . my father . . ."

"No!"

The determination in Isabelle's voice snapped Matthieu from his horrific reverie. She bracketed his head between her palms and her voice grew heavy. "Not your father, Matthieu. Alphonse Bouchet is the only man who can ever lay claim to that title."

"But—"

"The Baron may have been the one to lay the seed, but it was Alphonse who was there for your birth. It was he who watched you rise from your knees to wobble along in infant skirts. He was there to nurture and guide you. He is the one who encouraged your studies in art. He loved you, Matthieu. And that is what is required to hold the title of father. You are not like Nazaire. Blood means nothing. Nothing!''

*You are not like Nazaire.*

''I want to believe that, Mama.''

''Believe it. Believe it in my pride, son. Can't you see in my eyes how proud I am of the man you have become? And what of Josephine? Is there a woman more in love with my kind and gentle son? Do not waste another thought on the baron. Fight his evil legacy with the good memories of your real father. Alphonse Bouchet.''

Catching his mother's hand in his, Matthieu pressed her palm against his cheek and kissed her wrist. She was a strong and wise woman. He realized now why she'd fled to the convent. For it was months after the murder before Nazaire could be found and brought to justice. She had to be safe. But she'd left him behind . . .

No, he mustn't even think to ask such a thing. She'd been distraught, confused, her one true love had just been brutally murdered. She did the only thing she knew to do at the time. After all, it was only her that the baron had wanted, not his bastard son.

Matthieu touched his mother's forehead with two fingers, then traced a smile across her lips. Not like Nazaire. Never. How could he have, for even one moment, allowed himself to think such a thing? He was surrounded by love and goodness, and need never fear succumbing to the evil in his father's blood. His mother was right. Alphonse Bouchet had raised him to honor all men, and to treat them as justly as he should demand in return. Fairness, pride, integrity. The threads of his very soul had been woven by the only man he must ever call father.

And then there was his other family. Always, he had Josephine. He'd left her with such hateful words. Words she had not deserved. Words for which he must now somehow make amends.

"Josephine!"

Remembering he'd left her alone in Delaroche's room, Matthieu sprang upright.

"Where is she?" Isabelle pulled herself up beside Matthieu.

The two ran down the hallway. Delaroche's door stood wide open, the room empty. The window slats had been pulled open and hung still upon their hinges. Matthieu dashed to the window just in time to see Julien Delaroche mount his horse and flip a cocky wink up towards the window.

Josephine lay across the horse's shoulders, unconscious.

# Chapter 34

She surfaced from a groggy, gut-crunching darkness. Rhythmic chops bit into her stomach. Her chin banged against the side of a smelly, sweaty . . . horse!

Like the sudden snap of a twig under foot, Josephine realized Julien had knocked her out while she had stood in his doorway, respectfully offering Matthieu and his mother the privacy they required. Somehow, Delaroche had gotten her unconscious body past the twosome and tossed her over a horse's back, and now they were barreling down a street that moved by Josephine's eyes so fast she couldn't begin to guess where they were.

"St-stop!" she managed. Any more than one word and she might bite off her tongue for the frantic pumping motion of the horse.

Julien reached for her arm and jerked her up to sit astride just behind the horse's withers. Thinking to slip out of his grasp, Josephine did a double take on the quick skim of cobbles below. If she were to jump, she'd risk her life.

"Where are we going? Where is Matthieu?"

"Silence!" he barked in her ear. His grip slid around her

waist and clenched like a wooden torture shoe intent on breaking bones. "Your fiancé is far behind in that ill-begotten carriage of your crazy father."

"My father is not crazy! Whoa!" The horse veered sharply to the right, setting Josephine off balance. Much as she daren't move any closer to Delaroche, she had to slide her leg over the horse's neck to secure a hold. Her fine satin skirts were dirty and already torn. The only possible way Julien could have gotten her out of his apartment without Matthieu spying them, or alerting her father . . . Had he taken her through a second-story window?

"Don't move."

"I'm losing hold. I'll fall!"

"You've cursed me since the day we met, wench." He wrenched her backward, allowing her to slip her right leg to the other side of the horse. Her skirts were barely wide enough to accommodate the movement, stretched tight they could only allow her to bend her legs and grab hold with a tight knee-grip near the base of the horse's neck.

"Matthieu will find me," she said aloud, though it was more reassurance to herself than a threat to her captor.

"Of course he will." Delaroche's thighs squeezed tight against Josephine's legs as he kicked the steed in the hind-quarters, setting their speed to a dangerous gallop. "But by that time it will be too late."

"Watch out!" Josephine shrieked. A wide-eyed street urchin dashed to the wall of a tavern just as the twosome galloped by. "You could have killed that child!"

"Enough of your mouth!"

"Tell me where you're taking me."

"We're going where no one can save you, wench. We're riding straight to hell."


Fortunately the Boulevard Saint Michel was one of the few wide streets in Paris. Delaroche put more than a few in danger of being trampled beneath his horse's hooves, but for the most part people were able to dash to the protection of a wall or pull a loved one out of the devil's path before it was too late.

Wishing he could unharness one of the two horses that pulled this wreck of a carriage, Matthieu tried to stifle his worries by focusing on keeping Delaroche in his sight. Unless the chevalier took a sudden turn, all would be well. But where was the man headed? And with his poor Josephine slung over the horse like a sack of river eels!

The Ile de la Cite was soon ahead. Nôtre Dame's spire speared the blue sky to the right. Delaroche swerved left down the road that bordered the Seine, avoiding the Pont Michel. Did he plan to cross the river on the Pont Neuf? The Conciergerie posted guards routinely about the island and would surely sight Delaroche. Even if he did make it across, the Louvre and the King's army waited not far away. He was acting a fool!

Though no more the fool than Matthieu felt. He'd left Josephine alone in Delaroche's room. Without protection! He should have anticipated Julien's next move. He should have—

Ah! There were just too many should-haves. Now was not the time to reprimand himself for things that could never be changed. He must focus all his energy on seeing his ladybug safe and secure in his arms.

"He's heading for the bridge!" Pascal called from the carriage. Isabelle had volunteered to stay behind for fear of putting too much weight in the carriage and slowing their pursuit, but Josephine's father would hear nothing of abandoning his daughter to that bastard's arms.

Delaroche's stallion mounted the wide wooden planks of the Pont Neuf and jerked to a halt.

Yes! He was changing his mind. Turning back or pausing to think. Enough time for Matthieu to catch up and—

"No!"

Delaroche dismounted. But it wasn't surrender Matthieu saw

in the soldier's eyes as he pulled Josephine down from the
horse and raced to the bridge's rail . . .


His steed abandoned, Delaroche dragged Josephine towards
the bridge railing. Much as she tried to kick him in the leg,
she only succeeded in pounding her slippered toes against the
hard-boiled leather of his boot. He held both her wrists behind
her back and pushed her towards the wide stone railing. Hard.

Equilibrium took sudden flight as her head plunged over the
railing and the dark muddy waters of the Seine came into view.
The stench twisted up her nostrils and stirred the bile in her
shaken gut. Two narrow fishing skiffs disappeared beneath the
bridge like silent sea monsters forging the cool waters. Did he
have plans to dump her over the edge? Please no. She could
swim, of course, but in these skirts?

Gripping a wooden pole set into one of many curves in the
railing, used by hawkers to display their wares, Delaroche
mounted the railing, taking Josephine with him.

''No!'' Unable to secure footing, Josephine's leg slipped
over the rail. Her foot hooked the narrow decorative ledge that
jutted out at an angle and skirted the bridge. With the agility
of one of the caged monkeys in les Jardins de Plantes, Julien
pinned her to his body, his elbow around her neck, while his
other hand held the vendor's post. Balancing on the foot-wide
ledge, Josephine could not look down and had to feel with her
slippers so she would not fall. The flash of a plan occurred—
she could easily pull Julien over her head and into the waters—
but that would dislodge her hold as well.

''You're insane!''

''Your hero has arrived.''

Indeed, her father's carriage rolled up the Pont Neuf and
Matthieu jumped to the ground, sword in hand, and a stern
look of determination stretching his usual smile into an angry
growl.

Delaroche's grip snapped her head back against his thigh. "And we are ready to depart."

"No. Do not do this, Julien. Matthieu has done you no wrong!"

"He was born."

"Release her!"

At Matthieu's cry, Josephine felt Julien's leg slip down the side of her arm and touch the ledge. "No, Julien, you cannot swim!"

"He who is born to be hanged shall never be drowned."

"This is suicide!"

"Perhaps."

Her left foot slipped and toed the air as the heavy bulk of her captor's body set her asail. Her scream pealed like a falcon winging in for the kill. Julien shouted something about taking her to hell . . .

With but two horse-lengths between them, Matthieu watched Josephine suddenly take flight. But this ladybug had no wings with which to fly. His lungs strained with a fierce battle cry. Without the luxury of a moment to think, Matthieu leapt, and in one great stride mounted the stone railing.

With a second stride, he too, took to the air.

Cool, polluted water filled Josephine's mouth as she struggled to surface. Delaroche's grip on her neck had been broken midair. Now she fought against the pull of her saturated skirts. She swallowed foul water. Choked and spewed. It was impossible to see anything, save the feeble illumination of the surface light. A great thrashing kicked at her skirts—Julien's pawing and groping hands—but she was able to propel herself up and forward.

As the blessed light of day filled her eyes, she gasped in lungfuls of air, and jerked to avoid the splash of another body plunging into the river. Matthieu surfaced next to her and spewed a murky fountain of the Seine into the sky.

"Grab hold of me," he sputtered.

"No! Save yourself," she managed as she treaded water, her chin dipping beneath the surface with every word she spoke. "I can swim, but not for long in these skirts. I can make it to the bank!"

Her lover suddenly disappeared beneath the surface. Josephine groped for his hand, but she was too water-heavy to do him much good. Three . . . four . . . five seconds passed as if an hour each. Then, with a splash and a gasp, Matthieu's head surfaced.

"Kick off your boots if you can," she sputtered. "They will drag you down."

"I just did. Where is Delaroche?"

The bank, walled by stone, was but an arm's reach away. Iron rings planted to aid boatmen—and unfortunate divers— waited her touch. She would make it. But Matthieu would not unless he followed close behind. "Leave him to save himself!"

"But he cannot swim!"

Indeed, Josephine had not seen Julien surface, nor were there any telltale bubbles rising to the surface.

"I must find him." Matthieu thrust his doublet over his head and tossed it away from him. "He is my brother!"

Before she could protest, Matthieu's seal-capped head plunged downward and the waters became still.

She grabbed the iron ring. Her father waited on shore, lying prone, his arm stretched out to her. Their grip was slippery, but with the unspoken knowledge that he would never let go. Never. Her foot found another ring underwater, and the feeling of safety fell heavily upon her. Giving in to the weight of the water, Josephine let her shoulders relax and her head loll back.

"Josephine! Your grip is slipping!"

But she did not react, other than to be thankful that someone gripped her hand just as it slipped from the upper rung of iron. As Pascal levered her ashore and she felt the heavy suction of her skirts drag her to the ground, Josephine kept her eyes pinned to the spot where she had last seen Matthieu. The brown water sloshed and waved, but no bubbles. Where was he!

Frantic, Josephine plunged forward. Pascal caught her around her shoulders and yanked her back into his embrace. "You cannot go back in there."

"Matthieu!"

"He will not sacrifice his life with you watching."

Drawing a heavy breath of air into her soggy lungs, Josephine sank into her father's firm embrace. As he smoothed away heavy clumps of hair from her face, she choked up stale water. She began to shake, her lips quivered, and her stomach lurched.

*Please let him surface. Please let him surface!*

The waters broke to spew forth a man. "Matthieu!"

In that same moment, he gasped in a swallow of air and submerged again.

"No!"

The devil be damned, she could not watch the man she loved with all her heart die for a man who would have killed him had he had the chance. "Let me help him, Father. Please!"

But he pulled her close, pressed his cheek to her's, and whispered a firm reassurance. "Have faith, Josephine. Matthieu is a good man."

*But the Lord takes the good ones, too.*

"There!" Her father released her and scrambled to the river's edge. "He's got him!"

Barely able to keep his eyes above water, Matthieu slowly made his way to the bank until Pascal was able to grab Delaroche's inert body and heave him ashore like a dead sea otter.

"My love," Matthieu gasped as his hand slapped into Josephine's. Though he was not yet out of the water, she knew all would be well. And just as her father's grip had spoken his silent love for her, her grip was sure and true. It could only have been the hand of God Himself that lifted her lover from the waters and deposited him on the shore alongside Julien's body.

A small crowd of fishmongers and children had gathered around the foursome, which Pascal now tried to hold off as Josephine bent over Matthieu.

"Step away, folks. Give them room."

His eyes closed from exhaustion, a slimy gob of river grass streaming down his forehead, Matthieu gasped and heaved and drew in generous swallows of air. All the time his grip never faltered. Josephine still held him tight.

She swiped away the green ribbon of grass from his face. Now tears mixed with the water that dripped from her hair, and—overwhelmed by the moment—Josephine collapsed upon Matthieu's heaving chest. "I thought you might never come up."

"Nonsense," he said in a breathy huff. "There was a moment I had so much water in my mouth I thought it just as easy to give in and sink to the bottom—"

"Don't say that."

He slid a shaky hand along her hip, down over her thigh and finally, from sheer exhaustion, it dropped to his side in the grass. "I knew my ladybug waited on shore, her bright eyes studying the waters as patiently as she might observe an aquarium of beetles ... waiting ... I could not give up, Josephine. You make me know that I can survive anything with you by my side. You hold my heart in your hands."

"I do," she said with a sniffling smile. "And I'll have you know, Matthieu Bouchet, it is a prize I'll not relinquish anytime soon."

"Delaroche. Where? How is he?"

Reluctant to tear her attention from Matthieu, Josephine glanced quickly at the still body of Julien Delaroche. Prodded by a curious observer, the chevalier's knee bent, then fell slack, the heavy white lace dancing around his boot rumpled and dirty. "I think he is dead."

"It cannot be." Matthieu rolled to his side and pushed himself up. A soggy clasp smacked flesh against flesh as he pressed

Julien's hand into his own. "We need help! Someone! Call the surgeon!"

It was difficult to understand Matthieu's drive to save this man who had so recklessly betrayed them both. Or perhaps not. Matthieu was kind and proud. It was exactly like him to care about his half brother.

Julien had been under the water for a very long time. Josephine wasn't sure but she feared that no man could survive such torture. Could he? Drawing in a breath to stave off her burgeoning tears, she laid a hand on Matthieu's shoulder. "It is too late."

Matthieu jammed a heel into the wet ground and levered Delaroche's body onto its side. A stream of brown water slithered from Julien's bluing lips. "Slap him on the back!" Matthieu directed Josephine.

She looked up into her father's eyes. He said not a word, but a simple hopeful nod spoke volumes. Josephine began to slap Julien on the back.

"Hang him upside down," came a sarcastic voice from the crowd that encircled them like three fenced chickens. "That'll help the water drain out."

"Unlikely," Pascal noted dryly.

"I don't think it's going to work," Josephine said with another firm whack to the soldier's soggy back.

"Enough." Matthieu dismissed her with a decisive gesture and then lifted Delaroche's head upon his knee, hugging him to his belly. A gesture of forgiveness and hope. "We never had a chance to be brothers."

After pushing the long strands of dirty blond hair from Julien's closed eyelids, Josephine let her fingers trail up and smooth across Matthieu's cheek, compelled once again to offer him silent reassurance. Always, she would stand by his side.

"We might have been good brothers, mightn't we?" Matthieu said.

"Perhaps."

"He just needed someone to love him. He never had a loving

family like you and your father and Helene . . . and Richelieu and Cook.''

''No.'' Josephine felt the light touch of her father's hand to her shoulder. Still, she could not leave Matthieu's side. He needed her now, as much as he had needed her that dreadful summer. ''Like you, he was . . . not like his father. Julien was a fine soldier.''

''Indeed.''

A heavy sigh slipped from Matthieu's mouth. Two fingers touched softly to Delaroche's forehead, and then he traced a smile across his lips. ''I will remember your name, Julien, my brother. I promise.''

Suddenly a gurgling cough of water sprayed the air. Julien's body jerked and his arm flayed out.

''He's alive!''

Julien gagged and snapped his knees to his gut, rolling to his side. A small river flowed from his mouth until finally his chokes and gasps drew in more air and began to settle to raspy breathing.

Much as she should have dreaded seeing this man breathe another breath of air, Josephine couldn't help but be as joyous as Matthieu. A thunder of clapping and cheers erupted around them as Julien scanned the wondering faces until he stopped at Matthieu.

''You . . . saved me?''

''He did,'' Josephine quickly said what she knew Matthieu would not.

The brothers held each other's gaze for what seemed to Josephine like hours. But it was mere seconds before Julien's hand, shaking and blue, rose to touch Matthieu's. Ten fingers touched, then curled into a tight clasp.

''Brothers,'' Matthieu said.

''For good or for ill?'' Julien asked.

''Indeed.''

Unable to resist contact with Matthieu for another second, Josephine thrust her arms around his shoulders and hugged him tightly. Pascal leaned in and offered to make a preliminary examination of Julien.

And while the world continued to breathe and cheer and smile and exhale and skitter on around them, Josephine and Matthieu lost themselves in an embrace of the soul.

# Epilogue

*Six months later . . .*

Enchanted Winter was the theme of Louis XIII's costume ball. All around Pascal whirled a glittering array of white and sparkling costumes. Louis himself was the Snow King in a diamond-encrusted snowflake crown, and a long ermine robe sparkling with more diamond snowflakes. His queen was a snow lily, exquisite in white satin and canary jewels.

Matthieu's designs had become an overnight sensation at court. And while Madame Lamarck had recently been swept away by an Italian actor and moved to Venice, she'd been more than thrilled to pass her royal clients on to Josephine and Matthieu. Now a gown by Bouchet was a much sought-after prize. Josephine had hired three additional seamstresses, and Matthieu oversaw all the design and financial aspects of the Boutique Bouchet.

Feeling an itch ride up his back, Pascal stretched his furry paw behind and managed to shift his fur doublet up and down just enough to relieve the tickle. A polar bear, indeed. Josephine had a wicked sense of humor.

But she'd certainly been right regarding Isabelle's gown of soft pinks and blues and silvers. When she spread her arms wide, a gauzy cape of multicolored butterfly wings whispered beneath the sparkle of candlelight.

"It was good of you to attend the fête with me tonight." Pascal refused Isabelle's offer of wine with a furry paw.

She gave a delicious sigh and lowered her ruby-encrusted mask to expose a dancing smile. "It has been so long since I've been outside the convent, I've forgotten how much I enjoy the bustle of life in Paris. I've actually been considering taking an apartment close to Matthieu and Josephine in the Marais."

"Isabelle, that's fabulous news!" In his excitement, Pascal pulled her into a literal bear hug. "If there is anything I can do to help you, you mustn't fear to ask."

"Actually, there is something."

"Anything." Pascal checked himself. He sounded too eager. But, well . . . he was!

"With Matthieu so busy at Josephine's side, I don't wish to bother him. I need someone to escort me when I choose a house. I've no idea how to appraise real estate. And I do have a sizable inheritance from my parents that Alphonse and I had always intended for Matthieu's grand tour. Could you spare me a day or two to come house hunting with me?"

"Madame, I am at your disposal. If perhaps . . ."

"Yes?"

"You'll return the favor?"

"Certainly, Pascal. What do you wish of me?"

Beyond her touch? Pascal shook his lascivious thoughts away. "I wonder if you might attend Helene's nuptials by my side? She and the Viscount Castelot are exchanging vows in February. I believe . . . the fourteenth."

"I would be honored, Pascal."

Then she did touch him, on the cheek—about the only bit

of flesh exposed by the fur that encompassed his entire body. And Pascal actually blushed.

Much as he abhorred parties, Matthieu could never refuse Josephine's wishes. And while he felt rather silly dressed all in white, he was at least less whimsically dressed than the other guests. And the look on Josephine's face when she'd seen his "knight errant" costume had been more than enough to make his heart sing.

Delaroche had made fun of him for being a white knight, and Matthieu had returned with a crack about Julien's unicorn costume. "Making an ass of a unicorn, eh?" he'd said with a smile. The two had come to an easy friendship over the past few months. After he had wed Josephine, Matthieu decided to hire Julien on as a deliveryman. Part-time, of course, until the man could secure a more profitable job. Which he had—in a manner of speaking. Funny how quickly Julien had taken to the milling of flour after the lovely young Emmanuelle had caught his eye. The life of the country gentry was not far from his reach. And Matthieu was glad for his brother. Very glad.

Ah, but where was his ladybug? He'd decided an hour ago that enough was enough. One could only trade pleasantries with the foppish royals and bow and accept the King's praises so many times, without coming away with a fierce pain in the head.

"Lover."

Her voice slid up his neck and slipped inside his ear like a fluttering moth teasing a candle flame. Matthieu slipped an arm around the white satin that covered his wife's slender waist and pulled her to his body. Instant want flamed through his being. The soft red ladybug wings billowing from her sleeves slithered in enticing whispers across his leg. A crown of rubies circled her forehead and from that flowered two diamond-tipped antennae.

''I want to leave,'' he said, crushing one hand over her breast and squeezing.

She moaned. Oh, how he loved to hear her whimpers of desire. ''Perhaps.''

''Perhaps?''

She slipped out of his grasp, leaving behind a small folded paper in his white gloved hand. Matthieu watched as she glided noiselessly across the marble floor and disappeared through the two-story portières of white and silver brocade.

''Perhaps?'' He studied the paper. It was no larger than his palm, and bearing her exclusive seal, a ladybug pressed into red wax. Ah, he thought, just like the intimate letters they had once shared, now carefully preserved at home in a chest of cedar lined in purple velvet. How he had come to know his ladybug from those written words! It had been months since they'd written one another, for they were never apart for more than a few hours at a time. But he realized now how much he missed their correspondence, their pouring out of emotions in ink, forever preserved on paper to be reread, savored, and remembered.

Eager to read the *billet doux*, Matthieu cracked the seal and unfolded the paper. Immediately his heart sank. There were but three lines written in Josephine's delicious scrawls. Three measly lines? What of that lingering emotion and lust and passion and—

*Oh, hell, read it then!*

> *Beneath the willow tree in center court.*
>    *Midnight.*
>
>                              *Ladybug*

An irrepressible smile burst upon Matthieu's face.
Of course, there was much to be said for brevity.